The
COLLECTOR
of BURNED
BOOKS

Center Point
Large Print

Also by Roseanna M. White and available from Center Point Large Print:

Shadowed Loyalty
Giver of Wonders

The COLLECTOR of BURNED BOOKS

Roseanna M. White

CENTER POINT LARGE PRINT
THORNDIKE, MAINE

This Center Point Large Print edition
is published in the year 2025 by arrangement with
Tyndale House Publishers, Inc.

Copyright © 2025 by Roseanna M. White.

All rights reserved.

The Collector of Burned Books is a work of fiction.
Where real people, events, establishments, organizations,
or locales appear, they are used fictitiously.
All other elements of the novel are drawn
from the author's imagination.

The text of this Large Print edition is unabridged.
In other aspects, this book may vary
from the original edition.
Printed in the United States of America
on permanent paper sourced using
environmentally responsible foresting methods.
Set in 16-point Times New Roman type.

ISBN: 979-8-89164-624-7

The Library of Congress has cataloged this record
under Library of Congress Control Number: 2025936627

To Ashlynn McFarland

For every time you said,
"When are you going to write
one set in World War II, Miss Roseanna?"
When I got the idea for this one,
you were the first person I thought of.

So to you, sweet friend—
lover of books . . . overcomer . . .
depth-seeker . . . and woman of God.
I hope my characters can have just a
fraction of your spirit and grace.

PROLOGUE

10 May 1933
The Opernplatz, Berlin, Germany

They meant the fire to blaze, to consume, to crackle its way into the night with a ferocity to match their beliefs. They meant it to roar, louder than the so-called fire incantations of the thousands of gathered students, louder than the words Goebbels shouted into his microphone about how this new Reich would be a phoenix rising from the ashes of these defeatist books.

God had other ideas. God and the very nature of the kindling.

Books didn't like to burn. Ilse laughed when he attributed likes and dislikes to books, but it was true. Part of their nature. Their paper wasn't dry kindling, it was pressed with ink and made from pulp not devised for flammability, covered with cloth. And the older books, like the ones on the cart behind him? The ones with leather bindings and gold lettering? The ones on *parchment?*

Those resisted burning like the pyres of martyrs receiving salvation from on high. They would only smolder, more likely to go out than to catch.

These students had it all wrong—backward. Books didn't burn. Books *ignited.* They lit the burning in others. Not with paper and match. With ideas.

But then, that was their very argument.

A misting rain continued to obscure his view out the window, and he watched the scene blur. Black umbrellas crowded the square, but closer to the struggling pyre they vanished. The students closest to the fire burned brighter than the books, ignoring the elements. They were making a statement, and nothing could stop them.

His deepest fear. His deepest dread. *Nothing could stop them.*

He'd thought it impossible. Ludicrous. Germany, his beloved fatherland, had so much beauty and culture and brilliance in its history, in its potential. He knew it because he'd read all these books those students were burning. He knew the minds his ancestors had possessed, the collective knowledge passed down. It was beautiful. It was good. It was fair.

But it hadn't stopped resentments from smoldering ever since the war when he was a child. It hadn't stopped the impossible from happening last year, after Hitler was elected. It hadn't stopped the Nazis from dismissing everyone of Jewish heritage from their positions. It hadn't stopped the nightmare from smoldering on from there.

The ache in his chest hadn't let up since. Wouldn't. Couldn't. It could only grow worse with each book added to the "banned" list.

An arm slipped around his waist, and he didn't need to look down to recognize Ilse. Her sigh was sweet and small and as aching as the hole gaping ever larger inside him. She rested her head against his shoulder. "You saved many of them."

"Books? Yes." He nodded toward the misted panes of glass. "But what of them? What of all those people?"

Her arm held him tight. "We could leave. Like the others. Go to France or England or America."

If it were only about the words, the paper, the ink, the bindings, maybe he would. If the books were his only concern, he could preserve them elsewhere—that was the beauty of books. One could never destroy them all. One could only make a weak-flamed statement with a few.

But it wasn't only the books. It was the generation so quick to denounce them. "I can't, Ilse. I can't abandon them."

She knew it, but still she sighed again. "What then? Will you stay and fight? Be a voice of reason in the madness? It'll get you sacked, at best. Arrested, quite possibly. And what of me then? What of *us*?" She moved her other arm, and even in the darkness he knew what she would be doing. A new move, but one that had already become familiar. She pressed a hand to her stomach, protective and awed, over the little life growing within.

It was his turn to sigh. "When I was eight, when we first moved onto Sonntagstraße, there were a few bullies that liked to torment Rolf. They would make fun of his lisp. Have I told you this story before?"

His wife shook her head against his shoulder, and he could feel her smiling. "No, but I can imagine where it's going, knowing how protective you were of your brother. You confronted them?"

She knew him well. He smiled a grim smile, no brighter than the half-hearted bonfire outside. "I tried. But I was eight, small for my age. They were . . . I don't know. Ten? Twelve? I got a bloodied nose, two black eyes, and a cracked rib for my gallantry."

"Aw," she crooned at him, running a hand up his rib cage. "My poor knight! What did you do? Or your parents?"

The flames in the square struggled, leapt when more kerosine was splashed onto them, painting oranges and yellows on the rain-blurred windowpane. His students shouted, arms pumping the air. As if they could bully away the ideas they found so offensive.

"My father sat me down, after Mutti had patched me up. He praised my bravery, my courage. My desire to protect the innocent, no matter the cost to myself."

Ilse breathed a laugh. "That sounds like him."

"Mm. And then he looked me in the eye and told

me what I lacked was discernment. I had failed to consider that I was outnumbered five to one, and that I was fighting well above my weight-class. I had failed to take into consideration that the fight was doomed. Lost causes are all well and good, he said. But sometimes we must bide our time. Grow. Let them grow softer, kinder, wiser themselves. Or at least wait for help to arrive. Otherwise we find ourselves unable to fight at all, because we've been defeated too thoroughly."

"Choose your battles," she said on a low exhale.

"And bide your time. Not for revenge—but for the chance to build friends instead of enemies. That's what he told me that day. That the only way to defeat a bully was to win him over. The only way to truly defend what you believe is to make your enemy believe it too. Make him your friend."

"And did it work? With those bullies?"

At the thought of Erik, he wanted to smile. At the sight of the brighter-now fire, he couldn't. "One of them. The ringleader. The others drifted away when he changed. It's ideas that win, Ilse. Ideas that always win. We just need to bide our time, until they're ready to listen again."

"But from here? Darling, they're mad, it's *all* mad."

It was. But that only reminded him of something his godfather had said a few years ago, before his opinions had forced *him* from Germany. "It's as Josef said. Madness can never be cured from the outside. It can only be healed from within."

"Josef *left,* my love."

"Josef gave up. Consigned them to their madness." He shook his head, almost wishing he could do the same. But deep down, he was still that eight-year-old boy, ready to take on five neighborhood bullies just to keep them from taunting his brother. "I can't do that."

As if to mock him, the flames reached higher through the night.

ONE

14 June 1940
Champs-Élysées, Paris, France

It was a parade for no one. Or, no. It was a parade staged only for the cameras set up along the street, one of which ticked and whirred outside the door she'd ducked into five minutes before, when she heard the tanks coming. Corinne Bastien had no good reason to be standing now in Cartier, watches that cost a year of her professor's salary displayed in their glass cases behind her. No good reason at all.

But several very bad ones. She watched the panzers roll slowly down the street, soldiers waving from the hatches as if to adoring crowds, smiles wreathing their faces.

The streets were empty, but for those cameramen.

Corinne pressed the book she held to her stomach. An older man stood beside her, another erstwhile pedestrian caught outside when the Germans approached. He'd been in front of her. He'd begun trying all the doors that weren't boarded over—shut, locked. That was when the proprietor—or perhaps only a clerk?—from Cartier swung open his door and motioned them inside.

He hadn't needed to tell them to hurry. The rumble of tanks that shook the ground beneath their feet had done a fine job of that.

She shouldn't have been outside. She'd known the risk, even before the announcements appeared this morning cautioning all citizens to remain indoors. But she'd run out of time yesterday, and she'd still had two loads of books to drop off. If she hurried, she'd told herself, she'd be fine. She knew Paris far better than the invading German army. She could avoid them. Be invisible. Make her deliveries in two different batches and then scurry back into her burrow like the scared little mouse they'd expect her to be.

The streets were *empty*. Never, in the fifteen years she'd called Paris her home, had she seen them like this, not even during the bombardment earlier that month, and it was every bit as haunting as the German words shouted from loudspeakers. *"Welcome your liberators, citizens of Paris!"*

"Liberators," the man beside her muttered, looking as though he'd like to punctuate the curse by spitting on the floor. If so, then the expense of that floor stopped him. Or perhaps his manners. He, at least, looked like he belonged on the Champs-Élysées. Trousers and shirt and jacket, all tailored. Shoes of leather so fine her fingers itched to touch them, to see if they were really as smooth and buttery as they looked. A gold watch gleaming from his wrist that could have come from this very store.

Clearly *he* hadn't just been making a delivery to someone whose flat was above the Arcades.

On the other side of her, the merciful clerk touched two fingers to his forehead, his heart, his left shoulder, his right. "*Sancts Michael Archangele, defende nos in proelio, contra nequitiam et insidias diaboli esto praesidium.*" His voice was soft and low, barely a whisper.

She translated the familiar words in her mind without thought, praying them along with him, making a mirroring motion with her right hand. *St. Michael the Archangel, defend us in battle, be our defense against the wickedness and snares of the devil.*

Monsieur Fine Shoes snorted. "We have already lost the battle, my friend. Or haven't you noticed? Cross yourself all you want. God has abandoned us. The evil is *here*."

Corinne lifted her chin even as she gripped the book more tightly. "The cross isn't meant only to ward off evil, *monsieur*. It's meant to strengthen us against it."

Another snort as fine as his shoes. "France has no strength left. Your cross is about as effective as the Maginot Line proved to be."

Swallowing past the sudden tightness of her throat, Corinne turned to the shopkeeper. "Is there a back door I could use?" She had work still to do today, even if every business in Paris was boarded up and closed. Even if nearly everyone she knew had fled the city days ago in a march as silent as a procession of ghosts. Even if her university had barred its doors and hunkered down.

The clerk nodded, and the dull gleam in his eye seemed to say he understood her need to keep moving. He held out a hand toward the glass cases, the space behind them, and the door that opened up into the back rooms.

The cases were as empty as the streets. No gold and diamond and platinum winked out at her. She hadn't even noticed that when she'd hurried inside, and she could hear Oncle Georges in her head, chiding her for her inattention. *If you want to remain unseen,* he had said uncountable times, *then you must see everything.*

Her fingers twitched over the fabric casing of the book she clutched, fighting even now against the retort that she had voiced nearly as many times. *I see words, Oncle. Ideas. Not things.*

She had to learn—that was the lesson he'd been drilling into her for the last year. If she wanted to help, if she wanted to do something other than run away like everyone else she knew, if she wanted her efforts to *matter,* whether the Sorbonne let her teach or not, then she had to *learn.*

The clerk paused once off the showroom floor to look back at her. She found herself suddenly aware of her hastily selected skirt and blouse, the lack of care she'd given her hair, the slapdash application of red lipstick. *She* certainly didn't look like she belonged in Cartier, and this man would recognize that in a glance. He had eyes strangely like Oncle Georges's—aware, alert. He saw her.

But he smiled, sad as it looked on his aging face. "I am Hugo."

"Corinne." She dug up a smile of her own, though it surely looked no gladder than his. "Thank you. For . . ." She motioned to the front door, locked again behind them, and then to the back door she could glimpse at the end of the hallway.

"If we do not help each other, who will? These are times to be *more* willing to reach out to our neighbors, not less."

Most of the men who made their living on the Champs-Élysées wouldn't consider her a neighbor. She had spent her childhood in a town so small it rarely appeared on maps, the countryside laboring to recover still from the last war to maul it. It had been only fifteen years ago that Papa had moved Maman and her to Paris to chase their dreams. Education, for both of them. Careers. Futures.

Papa had given them those dreams. Sometimes she still looked back on those few years she had with her stepfather and marveled at how, short as his time with them had been, he'd changed every single aspect of their lives.

They arrived at the door, but Hugo didn't reach for the knob. He peered through the glass, this way and that. "You will be too young to remember the last time Germans were in France."

"I remember." Most of the memories were vague, writhing things. Impressions more than images. She remembered the hungry days and the haunted nights. She remembered the fear that had so permeated every day of her life, she hadn't even recognized it as such until it faded away. She remembered the lack of color, the yawning emptiness, the sucking mud left in the wake of raging armies.

She remembered stubbing her toe on something, realizing it was a boot. Seeing the boot had a leg still inside it. She remembered thinking it a corpse she could scavenge food from—then watching in horror as mud-caked eyes blinked wearily, deliriously open.

It was the boldest memory she had from those days, despite the whole scene being mud-brown. *Papa.* She hadn't known it then. But she knew it now. Trapped in that quagmire was the only father she would remember, struggling for one more breath.

Hugo's lips offered another echo of a smile. "Then you remember that when the Germans arrive, the food vanishes."

The hungry days. She nodded, once. Briskly.

Hugo settled gentle fingers on her wrist. "The Germans will want to shop. The owners will return eventually, the stores will reopen. This street will be alive again soon enough. Money will flow—food, perhaps, with it. Come here when you are hungry, Corinne. I will always put something back."

It was the sort of kindness she would expect of family, perhaps from friends. But from a stranger? She knew her confusion was written across her face, likely underscored by every ounce of suspicion her uncle had trained her to have. "Why? You don't even know me."

His answer was to reach up and pull from the neck of his shirt a necklace, tugging until the pendant slipped free. She recognized in a glance the Miraculous Medal—bright blue, like cerulean hope. A nearly exact match to the one she wore around her own neck. The one that rested on the outside of her blouse, where he'd clearly seen it. "This is how he gives us the strength to withstand evil—through each other." He offered another smile, brighter by a degree. "We are here, you and I. While so many are not. We stand. We stay."

"We stand." He *was* like Oncle Georges, he *did* see. Perhaps his eyes had been trained for commerce, for the next sale, for identifying from whom he could earn his commission. But it served him well now too. She gave him a nod that she hoped said that she saw as well. Or was learning to. "Thank you, Hugo."

He slid the bolt on the door, swung it open, and nodded her outside. "Go with God, *mon amie*."

She slid out into the daylight, nostrils flaring at the odd smell of the tanks' exhaust that filled the streets, mixing with the acrid sting of the oil reserves the French army had set ablaze to keep the Germans from seizing it. Wrong, all wrong. Paris was supposed to smell of baguettes and pastries, flowers and creperies. There should have been laughter from the café across the street, the clinking of wine glasses, music from the concertinas the Gypsies played for the tourists.

The only sound was the clatter of panzer treads over the pavement a street over.

Though the book weighed heavy in her hands, she wasn't about to cross in front of that parade in search of Amalie to give it to her. Instead, she wound her way back to the Boulevard Arago. None of the Métro trains were running, which meant that the half-hour trip took over an hour. Sweat clung to every crevice by the time she turned onto her street, the June sun mocking the metal storm that had rolled in under its swastika banners.

She nearly shouted when she saw the figure locking the door of the library next to her flat. What was Monsieur Kantorowicz still doing in the city? Shrugging off her exhaustion, she ran toward him, arriving just in time to watch as he wrenched the small sign off the building.

Why did it feel like he'd yanked the very heart from her chest? "*Monsieur*? I thought you long gone."

Kantorowicz spun, eyes wide in his long face, though they relaxed again the moment he spotted her, and he huffed out a breath. "Corinne. Where have you been? I've been waiting for you."

She ignored the chide, turned it back on him. "Shouldn't you be on your way to England?"

He waved a hand. "I am leaving the city now—though I do not know if I will make it to England or just hide away in some pretty little French chalet." He tried a smile that fell flat. Concern darkened his eyes. "You have heard, I trust? That we have been officially shut down and handed to the Germans to be destroyed?"

She swallowed, her feet stepping involuntarily toward the library. It looked bereft without its sign. She'd grown accustomed to seeing the German words "Deutsche Freiheitsbibliothek" there on the front. "The Library of the Burned Books." It had become a beacon. A hand always beckoning her. *There are secrets in here,* that sign had always promised. *There are ideas so powerful the Reich tried to destroy them.*

"I heard." Her gaze moved back to Kantorowicz as he dropped the keys into his pocket. She'd heard, but she'd railed against it, hadn't really believed it was true. That it was just going to be abandoned, turned over like a gift to the Nazis.

Her heart thudded as he held out a hand. "You'd better give me your key. You don't want to be caught with it."

"What? No!" She still had a load of books to smuggle out before the Nazis arrived, books with carefully encoded markings in their margins. Books she still had to somehow get into the hands of the students scattering all over France, back to their provinces. This was the only purpose she had now, with the university abandoning ship just like the rest of Paris's citizens. To let them observe, to gather the information they sent back to her, to send it on to the true French government, already in England, via Oncle Georges's contacts.

Kantorowicz shook his head adamantly. "It is too dangerous. You can be assured that the Nazis will waste no time in confiscating every book in there. You do not want to be seen as an associate of the place, or they'll lock you up too."

She wanted to scoff, to insist that no Nazi would look at her and think her dangerous. *No one* thought her dangerous, with Maman's honeyed curls, the petite frame she'd inherited from her father's side, and the ridiculous lips that made everyone think she was still a teenager long after she'd left those days behind her.

It was her greatest weapon, Oncle Georges had pronounced with a grin. Well, her second greatest. Her mind ranked first, of course. But her deceptively innocent appearance was a strong second.

She hadn't bothered arguing—she'd been using it to her advantage too long, much as Maman chided her for it when she was growing up. An angel with a forked tail, she had called her. Corinne's lips twitched at the memory.

Juste ciel, but she missed her mother. It made her feel far younger than she was, this constant, soul-deep longing for the sole companion she'd had every day of her life, up until a few weeks ago.

Kantorowicz raised his brows and inched his palm closer to her nose. "Now. For your own good."

She was well enough acquainted with his stubbornness to know he'd stand here until she relinquished it, or follow her up to her flat if she claimed not to have it on her.

"Fine." She dug the precious bit of metal from her pocket and slapped it onto his palm.

He leaned over and kissed her cheeks. "Watch yourself, *ma petite*. Be safe."

"You too." Tempted as she was to beg for the key back, she pressed her lips against it. It would look odd, would tip her hand. She would just have to content herself with finding a way in once he'd gone. Maybe she could pick the lock. How hard could it be? Women managed it with a bobby pin in the movies. Then it would be a simple matter of digging out the spare key from the circulation desk's drawer and pocketing it for future use. She gave him a quick embrace, careful to keep the book's title out of view. He'd recognize it.

He was distracted enough that he didn't do more than squeeze her and then step away, toward the auto waiting at the curb. She said a quick prayer that he would make it safely and quickly to wherever he was going.

Holding her ground, she watched until he had the engine roaring to life and was pulling away, so that she could lift a hand in farewell.

Another friend, gone. Chased away by the Nazis swarming her city. The hot sun pounded down, magnified by the injustice of it all, until it lit the coals smoldering inside her. The fuel-tainted breeze fanned the flames higher, brighter.

She looked down at the book in her hands, almost expecting it to burst into flames along with her soul. But this tome had already been condemned to flames, and it had survived. It always would.

She would too. She would burn and she would fight and she would win. No locked door would stop her, no empty flat, no German army, no looming days of hunger. She strode to the door of her own building and then jogged up the stairs to her flat.

Oncle Georges was wrong. Her best weapon was neither her mind nor her looks.

Her best weapons were the books—and she was going to use them well.

TWO

Christian Bauer had always wanted to see Paris. But as the car, one of many in the cavalcade, drove down the abandoned streets of the city, he had the distinct impression that this was not how Paris wanted to be seen.

There were no artists set up on the streets. No romantic music from a concertina. No scents of bread wafting from bakeries. No couples strolling arm in arm down the avenues, their gazes locked on the Eiffel Tower in the distance. No locals darting in exasperation around tourists.

There was only a scorching sun beating down, making the interior of the car so hot he found himself wishing he could peel off the suffocating jacket he couldn't quite think of as *his*. There were empty, mocking streets. Litter danced in the wind kicked up from the line of autos, and from some distant street he could hear German words squawking from a loudspeaker.

Call him a romantic, but that was all wrong. He loved his mother tongue with a depth that surely surpassed the average German, but even he knew it shouldn't have such a prominent place here. Spoken, of course. By tourists and expatriates and the educated. But it shouldn't be shouted in these streets with the help of amplification.

If he dared to voice that out loud, he'd likely be court-martialed.

"Is this it, Professor?" Gunter Kraus said from the front as he broke formation and halted the car in front of a stately building. "The university?"

Christian peered out the open window, reading the French inscription on the building with ease. One hall, at least, of the Sorbonne, without question. He'd never seen it in person, but it matched the photographs he'd perused. "It is. Though I don't see a soul moving about." He reached for the door handle, and Kraus all but squealed his objection. Christian sighed. "I can open my own door, *soldat*."

"Can, yes—but shouldn't. That is why you have me, *ja*?"

He set his jaw, but it wasn't enough to keep the words from grinding out. "I am a professor. I don't need a . . . servant."

Instead of being offended, Kraus flashed him a white-toothed grin. He couldn't be more than twenty—the very age Christian was accustomed to seeing in desks in his lecture hall or scouring the shelves in his library, not in pristine army uniforms. "You're also a *sonderführer*. Given considerable power in Paris, I might add, as the *bibliotheksschutz*. And that comes with appearances you must keep up."

He tried not to wince at the rank—but who could blame him? It wasn't even a *real* rank, honestly. Or at least, it hadn't been before they'd created it three years ago for men like him. Men utterly untrained in anything tactical or military, but who had some specialized skill the Reich decided they needed. A rank for veterinarians and translators and construction engineers, who were rounded up and forced to serve, the threat quite clear. Saying no was not an option. They would serve, or they would be sent to one of the dreaded concentration camps.

Who ever would have thought they'd need *him?* Even the title of *bibliotheksschutz*, library protector, was a mockery. He sighed and waved a hand at Kraus. "All right then. Open my door already, you lazy boy."

Kraus laughed in a way Christian suspected he'd never do in the presence of a *real* commanding officer. He shut off the car first, then let himself out, jogged around, and opened Christian's door with a flourish.

He was a good boy. Bright, full of life, puffed up on the figment of victory and the chance to make something of himself, lured in by the romantic, empty promises of glory.

Christian had never been to war, but he knew those promises were empty. He read—and not just the rubbish propaganda being published these days, either.

Stepping out into the full sun was a trade-off from suffocating in the stifling interior of the car.

At least out here he could move around, take it all in. He patted Kraus on the arm. "Give me a moment. Don't leave without me."

Kraus's brows flew up. "Of course I won't. I'm to be at your disposal every moment, sir." He snapped into a salute.

Christian fought back a grin. "Such pageantry—it's sure to turn my head. When I return to my lecture hall, perhaps I'll demand all my students greet me so."

Seemingly against his will, Kraus gave another grin. "I'd like to see that, sir—perhaps I'll join my cousin someday at university and sit in on one of your classes. I mean, assuming you ever lecture on something other than literature."

His own brows lifted now. "It *is* my specialty. Hence . . ." He motioned to the brilliant white facade of the Sorbonne, admiring the sculptures carved into the space between its columns and its peak. His aim wasn't just any part of the massive university—he was looking specifically for the library. "What is your cousin studying?"

Kraus breathed a laugh. "Haven't a clue. Something with books. He'd be right at home here." The boy's wince, however, said *he* wasn't.

Opposite how Christian felt as they started along the path. This world he understood. The sprawl of a university, even one he'd never seen before, was as familiar as his own skin. That's why he'd wanted to come here first, rather than the National Library. He missed traveling the walkways between buildings like he missed—

He cut the thought short, pushing it all aside. He couldn't afford to miss anything. And why should he? He'd only been gone two weeks from his faculty position, since he'd received the unequivocal summons from Goebbels himself.

You didn't argue with the Minister of Propaganda when he said you'd been carefully selected to head up a special team in Paris, to be sent in the very minute they took the city, not unless you wanted to die in one of the filthy prison camps. You packed your bag and wondered how you would look in a beret.

Answer: laughable.

Kraus craned his head this way and that as they walked. "Not a soul—you're right about that, sir."

"And I suspect that means the buildings are all locked up tight." He could have tested the theory on any number of doors they'd strode past, but he wasn't interested in if just any building was open. He only wanted one.

Another boyish grin. "We can take care of that. Don't worry." Kraus patted his sidearm as if it were a chatelaine.

Christian scowled, but alarm nipped at him. Kraus seemed a friend when they were bantering in a car. But none of Christian's friends brandished guns like keys. "We will do no damage."

"But—"

"I have many libraries' collections to catalogue and . . . relocate." He nearly winced at the word. "If this one is closed, we will simply try another, and another, until we find one we can enter without vandalism. We are gentlemen, Kraus. Not thugs."

His companion looked none too convinced, nor as if "gentleman" was something he particularly aspired to. He had, Christian had already learned, grown up on a farm about an hour out of Berlin. He'd spent the last several years striving to excel in the Hitler Youth, not to learn table manners or niceties.

He was *not* Christian's typical student—or at least, not what his students *used* to be. He had to remember that. He mustn't forget that this amiable young man was trained to conquer and kill, not to converse and catalogue.

Christian had to watch himself. Every moment. Every day.

They found the library a few minutes later, evidenced by the towering shelves of books visible through the equally towering windows. The sight made his heart thump in exactly the same way it had whenever he saw Adele Werner when he was fifteen—the chest-filling race of first love.

Adele had long since drifted into the realm of memory. The books . . . never.

He tried the door, unsurprised to find it locked tight. Kraus's mouth twisted. "Are you certain you don't want me to force it?"

If they broke this massive, story-and-a-half high double door, there would be no fixing it. He shook his head. "If the university personnel do not return in a week or two and I cannot find my way in otherwise, we'll examine what can be done." He had a job to do, after all. And failure would come with consequences.

Kraus grunted. "Should we try the other libraries then? Or would you prefer to find your quarters and get settled?"

He already knew his assigned quarters would be in some hotel or another, conscripted by the army. He hated hotels.

But there was one other library he'd been instructed to find and take possession of quickly. One whose collection was of primal interest to the Reich. One that was to be guarded with singular purpose. One whose door would be normal enough that even if Kraus did some damage, they could simply replace it.

He pivoted, facing back toward the car again. "To the Boulevard Arago. We will find the Library of the Burned Books and set up our headquarters there."

Kraus's brow furrowed. He trotted along beside Christian's long strides. "Set up there? But shouldn't that place just be burned? It's in the very name, isn't it? Aren't those all the titles by our enemies, filled with un-German ideas?"

Ideas opposed to the Reich, anyway. He sent Kraus the same look he gave his students when he'd asked a deep question and they'd tried to get away with a pat answer. Even so, his realization of minutes before rang like a gong in his mind. *Watch yourself, Christian.* "When the army takes possession of enemy headquarters and finds their intelligence files, do they burn them?"

Kraus's expression shifted. "Of course not. They read them. Learn whatever they can from them."

"So why would we do any differently? This little library is not a French institution, Kraus—it's German, populated entirely by those who fled the Reich, filled exclusively with the writing that got them exiled, as well as what they've written since. Do you not think we should know what that is? Their new writings? Should we not be aware of what work they've done from that library? Should we not examine how many Frenchmen have been borrowing its titles?"

Enlightenment flashed in Kraus's eyes. "Ah. Yes. Very wise."

Wise. It didn't feel wise—it felt wretched. Wisdom was all a man like him ever hoped to achieve, but something he'd had infinite cause to question over the last decade. Were any of his life's decisions what one would call wise? If so, how had he ended up *here?* Wearing a uniform he despised? Working for the very thing he hated—the suppression and destruction of knowledge? Alone, but for a young man assigned to be his helper who could never, *never* know who Christian really was? He'd always fancied himself what Voltaire had styled a "man of letters." Now, though? What man of letters hid behind one with a gun?

Soon enough they were back in the car, and Kraus was using a Parisian map to navigate them to Boulevard Arago. He had no trouble doing so, clearly skilled at orienteering.

At least the Hitler Youth taught *something* worthwhile.

Christian made an effort to regulate his breathing as they finally pulled to a halt on the empty street, in front of the building with a metal 65 on the wrought-iron gate separating it from the pavement.

Sweat trickled from temple to jaw. He swiped it away, then curled his fingers into his palm to keep from reaching for the door handle.

The men who ran the library wouldn't be here. He was supposed to locate and question them, but it wouldn't be as easy as strolling inside and finding them all huddled together.

Kraus opened his door, and then the gate, which was latched but not locked. Christian stood on the pavement surveying the building for a long moment, but Kraus slid past him and moved to one of the windows, cupping a hand to peer through the glass into the darkened interior. "I see books—but it doesn't look like any library I've ever known. It's a mess."

Interesting. Had the directors tried to remove anything incriminating? Christian stepped up beside Kraus and peered in too. He nearly laughed at his own question. This didn't look like a room that had been emptied of anything. Rather, it looked like one trying to hold three times the number of books it could rightly fit. They were jammed everywhere, stacked three deep on sagging shelves, horizontal as well as vertical, with boxes upon boxes besides. If there were any system of organization, it certainly wasn't visible from out here. This was clearly not a building meant to be a library—just a rather small house poorly converted and not nearly large enough for its collection. " 'Mess' is an understatement, I think."

Kraus sent him a concerned frown. "Are you sure about this?"

In answer, Christian took a step back and motioned to the door. "Let's see if we can get inside without going to headquarters for the keys the French government promised. I don't suppose you know how to pick locks?"

The young man shrugged and moved to the door. "I've had to open a few on the farm when we couldn't find the keys. Although those weren't very sophisticated." He tested the knob, and his eyebrows leapt upward. Sending his startled gaze to Christian, he demonstrated its cause by pushing the door open.

Christian frowned. "How very odd. I wonder . . ." Was it possible? *Were* some of the men who ran this library still here? Blast, but he hoped not. Detaining and questioning the authors was *not* what he wanted to do on his first afternoon in Paris.

He rushed through the door, ignoring Kraus's objection. "Wait! Sir, you're supposed to let me go first so I can make sure there's no threat."

Christian snorted and reached for a light switch. As the golden glow came up, it showcased the true understatement of Kraus's choice of words outside.

This was no mere *mess*. This was complete chaos. He couldn't decide if it made him want to weep or rub his hands together in glee.

Chaos meant days, weeks, *months* of bringing order—a process that sounded like absolute heaven just now. Because it was something he knew how to do. "I think," he said, "the only threat here is of those shelves giving way and toppling."

Even so, the unlocked door *was* curious. "*Bonjour?*" he called out, careful to keep any German accent from his French. "*Il y a quelqu'un?*"

He didn't honestly expect an answer to his question of whether anyone was there, and he was relieved not to get one. All was silent in the building. Kraus relaxed behind him, and Christian blew out a breath as he looked around. "They must have simply forgotten to lock up in their haste to evacuate."

"You . . . just need me to guard the door while you're working, right? You don't expect me to . . ." Kraus waved an illustrative hand at the stacks and piles.

A chuckle warmed Christian's throat. "Books not your favorite things?"

Rather than answer directly, Kraus moved to the circulation desk piled high with them and picked one up, grimacing. "We used to have a copy of this. I remember my father trying to defend it, to say it was a good book, full of wonderful ideas—or harmless ones, anyway. Completely overlooking that it was written by a Jew."

The chuckle turned to a knot. It sounded very much like one of the children's stories that had been produced in a magazine for schools—"*Gift im Bücherschrank*" or something of the sort. In which the Reich-minded youth helped his father see the error of his ways and purge their home library of the "poison on the shelves."

Kraus tossed the book toward the rubbish bin. Christian snatched it from midair, knowing his frown was back in place. "Did I not make myself clear, *soldat*? We are not getting rid of these books yet. We—or I, at least—will be studying them."

The look on Kraus's face of pure, disgusted torture made a shiver run down his spine. In another setting, another decade, it would have been amusing or pitiable. Here, now, it was a warning. Because this young man may only be enlisted, but Christian had read several news articles already of "heroic" young soldiers informing on superiors who weren't Nazi enough. "You can't mean to read all these books."

Carefully, he chanted to himself silently. *Carefully.* He must not only convince Kraus now to trust his future actions, he had to somehow instill confidence in his qualifications. Make Kraus believe Christian was exactly who the Ministry wanted him to be.

Sadly, he had years of practice at that. His eyes scanned what titles he could see. "I daresay I already have—or most of them, anyway." At the alarmed look the young man sent him, he arched his brows. Just a professor instructing his pupils. That was all. "How do you think the Ministry knew which books to put on the banned list, Kraus? Why do you think they sent me to deal with them?"

His assistant relaxed. "Of course." He moved farther into the room, flipping open covers here and there. "Did you know any of the professors who refused to help? Who condemned the book burnings? Spoke against the Reich and defended the Jews?"

"Several." Their faces haunted him at odd moments—friends, once. Old men who had been his mentors. Young men who had been his confidants. Men with wives and families depending on them. "Many were forced out of the public universities and found positions at small, private institutes. A few were arrested." Their families had been reduced to near poverty, forced to leave their city homes and seek refuge in obscurity.

He knew of only one who continued to speak out—and he managed it only because he had friends in high places who covered his tracks for him. And because his speaking was too far over the heads of most of the party officials supposed to keep an eye on such things for them to realize he was a dissident. A thought that always tried to make Christian's lips twitch into a smile. When society deliberately cultivated ignorance, they paid the price.

Refuse to read anything that might be distasteful, and one soon lacked the ability to understand it.

Christian wondered not for the first time if it was his own friend in high places who had gotten him this position. Why else would he have been chosen, given everything?

Kraus swiped another slender book from the

stacks. This time a wistful look crossed his face. "Mama used to read this one to us children—before it was banned, I mean. Before we understood the dangers of its ideas."

Christian bit back all his thoughts on those supposed dangers. "How many siblings do you have?"

"Three. A brother and two sisters. I'm the second eldest, behind Erna."

"Do you miss them?" He must. One didn't just leave a house so full of family without a few pangs along the way.

But Kraus shrugged. "I intend to make them proud." He arched a brow Christian's way. "What of you, Professor? Did you leave a family behind in Berlin?"

"Only my books." He reached for a copy of *The Time Machine*, translated into French. He'd read a German version when he was a boy, and then in its original English as he was learning the language. It wasn't anything in the book that had landed it on the Reich's forbidden list, it was simply that H. G. Wells was vocally anti-Hitler.

So many children who had missed the wonder of imagination in these pages, just because the author had been condemned for his opinions.

Kraus snorted another laugh. "Not *these* books, I daresay."

"Certainly not." He'd removed all the banned titles from his home library, just as he'd been ordered. But he hadn't offered them up on the pyres seven years ago. He'd relocated them all into the university's archives, claiming they were among the valuable collectibles that needed to be preserved. He visited them at least once a week, to whisper an assurance that someday, they'd be on his shelves again instead of trapped in suffocating boxes. Someday, they'd be free.

Silly? Probably. But they were all he had left to remind him that once, Germany had embraced ideas. Once, free thought had been valued.

He drifted his way through this first room, into a second, sweeping his gaze over the motley collection of books that were mostly in German, but also in French and English. He knew and had read nearly all of them, had met many of the authors before they left Germany, when he was just a young member of the intelligentsia eager to be accepted by his literary heroes. He understood why they'd gathered them all under one roof—a statement, just as surely as the fires had been.

But why had they neglected the library so? Why had they let their statement fade into chaos?

He turned into another room and went utterly still, every sense snapping into alert. Something was different in this one. It didn't feel like a room filled only with books—it felt . . . occupied. His nose picked up a hint of fragrance not present elsewhere—lilac?—and it made his spine stiffen. He flipped the light switch. "*Bonjour*?" He kept his voice low, calm, and continued in French, "You can come out. You won't be harmed."

The light caught on something shining like gold, but it wasn't text stamped onto leather or cloth. It was hair, and it turned into a headful of curls as the young woman who'd been crouching behind an overflowing table stood.

Definitely *not* one of the exiled German writers he'd been told to locate and question.

She didn't look abashed at having been caught. She didn't even look frightened, really. As her gaze landed on him—no, on his uniform—she looked absolutely furious.

Christian leaned into the doorway, mostly to assure her that he was coming no closer—she *must* be frightened under the anger, mustn't she? She'd been hiding, after all. And he studied her for two seconds, three.

She was pretty—the sort of pretty that would no doubt have Kraus's eyes going wide when he heard their voices and came to investigate. The sort of pretty boasted by the students he was accustomed to seeing at desks in his lecture hall or browsing the stacks in his library, young and fresh and untried by life. The sort of pretty that made his thirty-five years feel ancient.

Her chin ticked up, the red-painted cupid's bow of a mouth setting in a firm line. "This is private property," she said, her tone even and sure.

His brows lifted. "Yours?"

A puff of breath. He could all but see her debate a lie, like countless students had when he pressed them as to *why* their essay was late. Like them, she must have decided he'd know it for what it was. "It's run by friends of mine. I promised to care for the place in their absence. I . . . clean for them."

He lifted a brow and glanced at the teetering stacks, the mess of papers on the table in the center of this room, the poorly folded newspapers in a bin, their German headlines declaring very un-Party thoughts. One of the German-language "freedom" papers run from Paris, no doubt.

She acknowledged his silent question with an almost-smile. "By 'clean,' I mean dusting—not tidying. They never let me do that."

"Ah." The shelves were in fact free of dust, so he decided to let her think he believed her. He straightened, moving one step into the room and out of the doorway. "I am certain the gentlemen of the board appreciated your help, but I'm afraid those services will no longer be required—and in fact, I've been ordered to keep all French citizens from this library. So, if you would?" He held out a hand toward her, palm up.

She frowned at it. "What?"

"Clearly you have a key, given that the door was unlocked. If you would give it to me, please? And then I will escort you out."

She seemed to be debating something, which

spoke either to stupidity or bravery or perhaps a combination of the two. After a moment, her shoulders sagged. "Fine." She edged forward and dropped the bronze into his hand, scurrying back as if standing so close might scorch her. She glanced to the wall, and his gaze followed hers.

A poster hung there, one he'd seen before, though they didn't last long in Germany before they were ripped down and thrown away. Goebbels standing in front of a pile of burning books, the flames leaping up the side of the paper and igniting the Reichstag.

A clever piece of propaganda that had convinced most of Germany that the Nazi Party was willing to burn more than books it disagreed with—that it had in fact been responsible for the destruction of the old government building, the bastion of Hitler's opponents. They'd blamed the destruction on the communists, using it as an excuse to force them all from power and seize complete, uncontested control of every agency and bureaucracy.

Was it true? No one knew. But most, at this point, believed it.

This young Frenchwoman wouldn't be mourning the loss of the old regime, though. She would simply see that he was wearing the same uniform as Goebbels, and that he'd come to take possession of the very books depicted in the poster.

"Professor?" Kraus moved up behind him,

and Christian heard him unholster his weapon.

He held up a hand. "Easy, *soldat*," he said in his most calming tone, in German. "It's only a local girl who had a key. Which she has turned over."

He expected, when he glanced over at the young man, to see his eyes flash with appreciation when he spotted the pretty girl. Instead, Kraus glowered. No, he *snarled*. "This place is for Jews and communists. Which one is she, do you think?"

It was dangerous logic. Popular logic. Logic Christian didn't dare to refute. All he could do was order Kraus back into the hallway and step out himself, holding an arm out in invitation that the girl would know was a command.

She wasted no time in rushing by. And yet, as she hurried along, she kept looking at particular spots on particular shelves, as if hunting for particular titles. He glanced where she did but didn't spot any that usually appealed to young women of her age.

Upon reaching the front door, he expected her to dash out and disappear. Instead, she paused and turned, features set in an expression so neutral it could be nothing but a mask. "You said you'd been ordered to keep all Parisians from the library." At his lifted-brow acknowledgment, she went on. "What then? You will simply . . . lock this place up? Or haul all the books out and burn them as you did in Germany?"

She was too brash. Too mocking. With too many of his fellow officers, it would land her in a heap of trouble. Christian drew in a long breath. "Most of Paris's libraries will be dismantled."

"What?" The bluster vanished, and her face washed pale. "No!"

He could understand her reaction, but it made Kraus reach for his holster again. Again, Christian had to hold up a hand before the young man and switch to German. "She is only upset about the loss of Paris's books. It's understandable."

Kraus looked dubious. "It's just *books*."

He'd liked Kraus well enough during the drive from Germany, but he suddenly doubted whether he could handle months or even years in such company. *Just books* indeed. "If it were so simple, Goebbels wouldn't have ordered me here, would he have? If books had no power, they never would have been banned."

Kraus granted it with a snort.

The girl gripped the doorknob and turned, slipping out onto the street in the next moment. But not before he saw the sheen of tears in her eyes.

Christian sighed and did nothing to stop her. He merely held out the key she'd given him to Kraus.

The young man took it, but his expression remained hard. "I think, Professor," he said, "we had better just change the locks."

THREE

8 July 1940

Corinne had always been an ace at note-taking. It had served her well in school, at university, and in her postgraduate studies. She could read a paragraph and distill it to its key points without even needing to pause to think about it. If only life were a well-ordered paragraph—or even a disordered one—she could make sense of it. Learning to apply her skills to observations of people, however . . .

She wiped another trickle of sweat from her brow and dragged her eyes away from the disturbing scene at the National Library. Watching "the professor" direct Nazis hither and yon hadn't been her goal for the day—she'd merely been walking past when she spotted the unfortunately familiar form, and her steps had slowed of their own accord.

Three weeks had passed since the army had rolled into the city. When it became clear that they weren't bombing buildings or shooting citizens, Paris had begun to wince its way to life again. The Métro trains were running. Cafés had reopened. Grocers had unbarred the doors to their shops. More people hurried along the avenues, heads tucked down, than had been left in the city at the start of the occupation, which meant they were sneaking back in from wherever they'd hidden in the countryside.

Even so, it was an empty shell compared to what it had once been. No streets crammed with autos and pedestrians, only the occasional Nazi car, the occasional Nazi inform, and Parisians doing their best to ignore the existence of both, like they were nothing but stray cats.

She granted herself one more moment of watching swastika-banded soldiers carry boxes of books to waiting lorries and then forced her feet onward.

Too late. She felt eyes on her, and it itched like another trickle of sweat. A glance showed her that it wasn't the professor who had spotted her—it was that low-ranking henchman of his, the one called Kraus. Any time their paths had crossed on Boulevard Arago, he'd given her a look so dark it seemed as though he'd have preferred to greet her with a blade or a bullet.

She turned her face forward again and told herself not to increase her pace. Running would get too much attention.

The cardinal rule of most Parisians had become "avoid notice whenever possible." She'd already made a mess of that on day one when she'd had to repeat the key-turning-over bit twice in the course of an hour, but she'd promised herself—as she would her uncle—that she'd do better.

She made a mental note of how many soldiers she'd counted coming in and out of the library, just for practice, and set her sights on the bright red awning at the end of the street. The café had been her choice, but she was regretting it now. When she'd chosen the location, she hadn't realized walking by the library would gut her so.

Oncle Georges already sat at one of the little tables, a cup of *café au lait* beside him, half empty, and a book open before him. He closed the book and stood as she approached, of course, offering her a grin. They exchanged the customary cheek kisses, and he pulled out the other chair for her. She sat and prepared a smile for the waiter who appeared, placing an order to match her uncle's.

"You look troubled," Oncle Georges said in a tone that sounded like he was giving her a compliment. It matched the warm smile, the twinkle in his eye.

How did he do it? Look so blastedly easy, when he was anything but? Another lesson she needed to learn if she wanted to succeed at this new career. And she did—she *did*. She wanted to do something that would make a difference, help her students do the same. She wanted it all to *mean* something—otherwise, Maman was trapped across the Channel for nothing.

Her palms were damp, and she wiped them on

her linen skirt, keeping her own smile in place. "Did you see the library?"

He lifted his cup and took a sip. "Difficult to miss. How many soldiers did you count?"

A test, not an actual request for information. She didn't answer while the waiter came with a cup and saucer, then poured coffee and milk into her cup simultaneously. First she thanked him, and then she took her own little sip, just as she always did. "Twelve?"

Her uncle chuckled and tapped a calloused finger to his cup. "Question or statement, *mon chouchou*?"

Her breath blew out, vibrating her lips. "Would you like to know how many boxes of books I saw them move?"

Another chuckle, this one genuine. She knew him well enough to hear the slight difference in tone, but she doubted anyone else would. "You know your own priorities, I suppose. There were only ten soldiers, counting the officer and his aide."

"Kraus."

His fingers stilled. His eyes blinked—once, slowly. His gaze settled on her face instead of looking out at the street.

Corinne shifted on the metal of her chair. She probably knew Georges better than anyone else in France did, but it never helped in these moments. The ones where his gaze shifted from that of a doting uncle to that of a man who didn't just *have* secrets, but who collected them like books on a shelf. "He and the officer have made their headquarters at the Library of Burned Books. I've seen them about. Heard them calling to each other." *Met them rather stupidly.*

Had he been a less disciplined man, a hiss of breath might have eased out between his teeth. Georges, of course, only took another sip of coffee. And his eyes relaxed again. "What is the officer's name?"

She shrugged and circled a finger around the rim of her cup. "The men simply call him 'professor.' I didn't recognize his insignia from the ones you'd given me to study."

"My fault—I apologize. The documents I had are out of date. The Party created the *sonderführer* rank three years ago for cases like this one—when they need a civilian expert to assist with specific parts of a military campaign." Georges gave a shrug so very expressive, she marveled yet again at how French he was, despite having not a drop of Gallic blood in his veins. "He no doubt is simply a librarian or expert in literature. They have art experts here too—I saw them at the Louvre, stealing away whatever hadn't been hidden by the curators last year."

Her fingers tightened around the cup—which she didn't realize until Oncle Georges sighed and tapped a finger to her knuckles. "Your temper continues to give you away, *mon chouchou*."

She relaxed her hand. "Sorry. But is it not enough that they've overrun our city? Must they steal everything of value too?"

"They seem to think so." He leaned back again, his face shifting into lines that mixed concern with confidence. Lines he'd earned when younger than she was now, serving as an Allied soldier and scout during the World War. She had no memory of Oncle Georges without those lines. They said he saw the dangers, the evils. Recognized them for what they were. And dealt with them. "I don't like that they're quartering so close to you."

"Not *quartering,* per se. They must have rooms elsewhere—the professor fellow is just using the library as his office."

The twist of Georges's lips showed the same amused confusion she'd felt when the officer had told her his intentions. Georges had been in the library many times. He knew its . . . quirks, she'd call them, as surely as she did. "An odd choice."

"I thought so too."

"Well." He managed a shrug this time with only his eyebrows. "Keep an eye on it—from a distance. The fewer interactions you can manage, the better."

"I've been avoiding them." She left off the *mostly,* but he must have heard it somehow anyway. His brows lifted now, that same insistence for honesty that he'd been using to get her secrets from her since she was small enough to sit on his knee and nestle into his arms and confess that, yes, she'd stolen a *bonbon* from the jar after her mother told her she wasn't to have any sweets because she'd lied about a fight in school. She focused on the summer-weight wool of his jacket instead of his face. "I bumped into them their first day there."

"Bumped into them." His words would have sounded flat to anyone else. They sounded like accusations to her. "On the street, I suppose?"

She blew out another breath. It was no use trying to lie to him. "I was in the library when they arrived. I said I dusted for the owners—that was it. The professor fellow took my key, saw me out, and told me not to come back."

The fact that Georges actually squeezed his eyes shut in frustration told her more than shouting would have done that she'd made a misstep that had him doubting she could be trusted with anything. That he was considering taking from her this one chance to do something that mattered in the war. "Let's ignore the fact that I know very well Kantorowicz reclaimed your key. Let's focus on the fact that they now know you're familiar with the place—no, *associated* with the place. You've put suspicion on yourself."

She already knew it, but hearing him say it

made her shoulders pull up. "It is only a library."

"Filled entirely with what they consider dangerous, deceptive, and treasonous works, and run by men who are quite literally on their enemies list." He still spoke quietly, but intensity filled the words. She watched him catch himself, draw in a careful breath, and return to that easy demeanor. "Do you know the meaning of the word 'cautious,' Rinny?"

She forced a grin. "Of course not. That's why I was always your favorite."

He snorted a laugh. But then his face went sober. "I promised your mother no harm would come to you through this. Why are you trying to make a liar of me?"

She drew in a long breath of her own, praying some of his calm would come with it. "I'm sorry, Oncle. I know . . . I know I shouldn't have done what I did. But that doesn't mean I've ruined everything."

Does it? As a child, she would have tacked on the question, her brows drawn and begging for reassurance. But she couldn't be that child anymore. She had to prove, to all of them, that she could handle this.

Oncle Georges considered for a moment and then gave her a small smile. "If mistakes couldn't be turned into opportunities, I'd have been dead decades ago. Just . . . tread carefully from now on. Please."

Her shoulders relaxed, and she nodded. She had been—that's why she hadn't picked the lock again and claimed that half-dozen books still marked with her encoded instructions, the ones that gave her nightmares every night. The ones she'd meant to get into the hands of her students, so that they could make their observations, add their own markings, and send them back to her.

None had yet, of course, even of the ones she'd managed to deliver. The only things she had to report thus far were things Georges had seen for himself—which made her wonder if all the work she was doing would ever even matter. But he must still believe she could help. Fifteen minutes later, as he gathered up his things and leaned down to give her cheeks the obligatory kisses, he whispered, "Your new code is in the book I left on the table. Learn it—burn it. I'll find you when next I'm in Paris. Probably three weeks or a month."

She wanted to ask him where else he was going. She didn't. She merely hugged him back, kissed his cheek, and gave him a doting-niece smile. Then she picked up the book as if it were hers, added her own coin to the ones Georges had tossed to the table, and left.

For the sake of her own blighted curiosity, she went next to the Sorbonne, where she verified that few people were about and most buildings still locked. No doubt if she needed the comfort, she could have gotten into the one with the offices—she could have let herself into her mother's familiar room with her copy of that key, settled into the chair she'd spent so many happy hours in, curled up with a book while Maman graded essays. She could have breathed in the scent of old books and new paper and fresh ink and lilac that equaled her mother in her heart.

But it only would have hurt. Reminded her that Maman wasn't here. That, for the first time in her life, she was alone. Completely, mockingly alone.

No. She instead tried every grocer between the university and her flat until she found ones with food enough to exchange for her money, and then she returned to Boulevard Arago.

The little library stood dark and locked, tempting her to try forcing her way in again like the Germans had done. All the more tempting, really, because of her uncle's insistence of caution.

Because she knew the danger wasn't just in getting caught breaking in. The danger was in *not* getting in. In leaving those books in there. No matter how she told herself that they couldn't link them to her, that the markings would mean nothing to them, their presence still haunted her.

She should have resisted the urge to use them as her means of sending codes with her students. She should have used her own books, or theirs.

That's what she got for putting poetic justice above practicality.

The sound of a German engine turning onto the boulevard convinced her to jog up the steps to her own building. Through the door, up two more flights of stairs, and to the flat that had been home longer than any other place in the world.

Maman was still everywhere here too, offering the comfort she'd denied herself at the university. Corinne put the groceries away, trying not to focus on the increasingly barren shelves. It would only get worse. She knew that. Right now, it was manageable—Paris had, after all, been rationing wine and meat and sugar for a year already . . . supposedly. Mostly, they'd ignored it. But now?

A problem she would address another day. For now, she double-checked the lock on the door and opened up the book Oncle Georges had left for her. Proust. She'd read *Swann's Way* three times already, but still the words tried to pull her in, keep her from her task. She had to make herself flip page after page, searching not for the author's words, but for what her uncle meant her to learn.

In some places, he'd written in the margins. In others, words were underlined, sometimes in black, sometimes in red. She wrote it all down, word by word, filling them into the structure of code he'd already made her memorize.

The instructions were simple in theory. Complicated in execution. *Need more eyes in the Pas-de-Calais region. Activate pigeons there.* There were a few other similar instructions, making her mind's eye fly over the map she'd pull out later, the one she hadn't dared to actually write on. Even so, it didn't require circles or pins for her to remember where each student had gone. To know who was in the regions her uncle had noted, who would be their eyes. Their winged messengers. She'd have to send a postcard with that phrase she'd taught them all. *Have you read any good books lately?* Innocuous to any censoring German eyes. But her students would know it meant to report on any German activity they'd observed, to write the information in their own code, penciled into the margins of the books she'd sent them with. They'd send those books back to her, and she'd pass the intelligence along to Georges.

Footsteps, heavy and rhythmic, brought her head up, and her pulse with it. None of her upstairs or next-door neighbors had returned to Paris yet. There shouldn't be any footsteps so near her door. Not welcome ones, anyway.

Without a moment's hesitation, she shoved her papers into the book and hurried into the small kitchen, shoving the whole lot, her pencil included, into the icebox.

Seconds later, a knock landed on her door.

She tried to remember all her uncle had taught her. Tried to project an air of calm and coolness, to borrow his ease, to be the detached professional she was supposed to be. Her hands shook.

Fine then. Forget professional. She would simply be a child determined to steal a chocolate without getting caught. Pretend it was a relative at the door.

"Coming," she called, as if it were only a neighbor in the hallway. And it could be—perhaps someone had just returned and wanted to see if she was all right.

She knew better. Still, she jolted a bit when she pulled open the door and reality assaulted her.

She would never, *never* get used to Nazi uniforms in her city, on her streets, in her hallway. And the officer they called the professor shouldn't expect anything else.

Besides, he looked even more surprised to see her than she was to see him. His brows crashed down, and he glanced at a paper in his hand. "Pardon me," he said, his French as flowing and perfectly accented as it had been three weeks ago. Deceptive, that. Treacherous. His words said *I am a friend,* but it couldn't be more a lie. "I am looking for Madame Yvonne Bastien. Or more particularly, I am looking for books checked out in her name from the library next door."

She clutched the door, keeping herself in the space to make it clear he was welcome no farther.

"My mother. She is not here, though, I'm afraid."

The professor looked up again, his gaze softening. He was probably trying to sort out if she was young enough to *need* to live with her mother. To determine how forcefully he should speak. "When will she be home?"

Her chin came up. Part of her wanted to lie, wanted to make him think Maman would be home any minute—and so not realize she lived here alone. But he was next door too much. He would know who came and went. He would catch her in that lie within days, if not the moment she spoke it. "Hard to say, given that she's not in Paris."

He sighed and lowered the paper to his side. "Forgive me, then. But you must let me in."

"I most certainly must not."

He looked, as he held up his hands, palms out, like a nice man, with gold-wired spectacles and boring sandy hair. A respectable one. A trustworthy one, if one were stupid enough to ignore his uniform. And of all the things Corinne had been accused of being over the years, *stupid* wasn't one of them. "I am only after the books checked out from the library, *mademoiselle*. Return those, and I promise you I will leave and never disturb you again."

For the space of several heartbeats, she didn't move. How could she? How could she just let a Nazi into her home, even one whose face was all gentleness and respect? It was a show, nothing more. Though she wasn't ignorant enough to assume all Nazis were the same, the fact remained that this one had come to Paris specifically to rob the city of its literary heritage. By her definition, that made him more monster than man.

Which meant that if she didn't let him in, he'd just call his too-eager-for-violence henchman. *Caution, mon chouchou*, she could hear Oncle Georges saying in her head.

She drew in a long breath, let it slowly out. And then swung open the door. "Fine then, come in. But make it quick."

He wouldn't, though. She knew he wouldn't.

Because the books he wanted weren't here.

FOUR

Christian had heard it said—in his circles at least—that Paris was a city of readers. A city of books. Without doubt, a city of libraries, too many of which he had already seen, at least from the outside.

A thought he'd never expected to think. There was no such thing, in a good world, as *too many* libraries. And in ages past, he had dreamed of visiting Paris for the sole purpose of touring as many of them as he could squeeze into a week or two.

Not like this. Not knowing that he would be greeted at each institution not as a fellow booklover, but as an invader. Not when he knew that he wasn't there to run his fingers over the spines in appreciation and select a few with which to pass his afternoon, but to determine which could stay, which would burn, which would be sent back to Germany.

He caught himself just before he sighed but couldn't quite bring himself to tear his gaze from the bookcases that took up every spare inch of wall space in the small flat. Whoever the Bastien women were, they clearly loved books. He indulged in a quick clearing of his throat. "These are all your mother's?"

The young woman—who hadn't deigned to tell him her name—blinked at him. He could all but see the calculation ticking through her eyes as it so frequently did in his students'. What truth to give, what to withhold. But after a moment, she shrugged. "We consider most of them to belong to both of us."

"You have eclectic taste." He granted her the reprieve of looking away from her, back to her shelves. The one he stood in front of now was fiction, alphabetized by author's last name; but the one on the opposite wall was nonfiction, organized first by subject, then by author's name, so far as he'd been able to tell in his quick glance.

She didn't want him here. He didn't blame her. He knew very well that Parisian women had been warned by their well-meaning neighbors who remembered past wars to avoid being caught alone with any soldier, lest they be assaulted. He didn't know how to assure her she was safe with him. And knew she wouldn't believe him anyway.

So instead of trying words, he would prove his innocent thoughts with actions and respect the space she'd put between them.

He scanned the titles on the topmost shelf of fiction, then had to scan them again when he realized he hadn't paid a bit of attention to whether any were from the list he'd held out to his hostess, which she hadn't taken.

None were from the library next door, not that he could tell. Still he pulled out one of the books, smiling at the gold-leaf printed title. "*Grand Hotel*. I haven't read it in French, but the original German *Menschen im Hotel* was brilliant."

Mademoiselle Bastien folded her arms across her chest. "Are you baiting me? Vicki Baum is a Jew—that book, along with all her others, has been banned by your people, hasn't it?" Her chin came up, eyes spitting fire that she really needed to learn to bank in the company of anyone in a Nazi uniform. "Are you going to take it from me? Burn it?"

The sigh he'd held back a minute ago leaked out. He slid the book back into its place. "I regret to say that we'll be calling on quite a few prominent writers residing in Paris and confiscating their private collections, when their lineage or works label themselves enemies of the Nazi Party." He paused, but her eyes only narrowed at his use of the word *regret*. "But private citizens such as yourself will not have your libraries searched through. Generally speaking."

Her golden brows arched. "Generally speaking?"

He held up the list again. "I search only for these. Although . . ." He hesitated, not wanting to say the next words, but having little choice. "I'm afraid we'll have to interview your mother when she returns. Her interest in these titles has gotten the attention of the Party."

The girl straightened, eyes flashing. "The Party will be waiting a good long time for that *interview*." She said it like she meant *interrogation*.

He frowned. She'd said that Yvonne Bastien was "not in Paris." Did she mean . . . was her mother *dead*? Was he causing her distress by even mentioning her?

A million thoughts whirled through his head. She could have been killed during that single bombardment of Paris in June. There had only been two hundred some civilian casualties, but what if this woman's mother had been one of them? It would explain the hostility in her eyes. The defiance.

Then again, those could be explained by youth. He oughtn't to jump to conclusions. "You say she's not in the city? If she fled before our arrival, why did she not take you with her?"

Another quick calculation spun through her eyes. Then a jerk of a shrug. "Her work took her out of the country. Mine kept me here."

Out of the country, not just Paris? Then who knew when or if she would be allowed to return. If she'd fled to England or America or another Allied nation, there was no way she'd be let back into occupied France.

So then. No interview. Just the books. He turned back to the shelves. "Very well. If you can simply help me gather the books she'd checked out, I'll be on my way." He stepped back, letting his brows draw together again, clasping his hands behind his back to keep from reaching for any other beloved titles that his fingers would thumb through of their own volition, if he let them. "I don't imagine library books would be shelved, would they?"

Mademoiselle Bastien breathed what could have been a laugh, in different circumstances. "Honestly, it's hard to say. Maman is not known for her order. I find her things in the strangest of places. It's even possible that she forgot they were library books and packed them in her trunk." Strange light filled her eyes. "Quite possible indeed. She would have thought only that she hadn't finished reading them yet and wanted to do so."

His eyes scanned the room. Though the bookcases took up all the wall space not occupied by the windows, a sofa and two chairs, two end tables and lamps were still crammed into the space, leaving just enough room to walk the shelves and sit without banging one's knees into one's neighbor's. "She would have taken library books with her out of the country?" His horror must have colored his tone.

Her spine snapped straight. "No one was thinking quite clearly, what with bombs falling around us."

"Of course." He held out the list again. "Even so, she surely did not pack eighteen books in her trunk, all of them borrowed. If you help me, I'll be out of here more quickly."

After a bracing inhale, she snatched the list from his fingers and then retreated a step again, putting a chair between them. Why did it feel as though she were putting on a show as she read the list?

Answer: Because she was clever. Clearly.

She would know that she ought to guard her every action and reaction around him, so of course she exaggerated her study of the list, no doubt to prove to him that she was doing what he asked.

He'd already memorized the list, so while she mumbled something about checking her mother's room, he continued his perusal of their shelves.

Was it his fault that he kept getting lost in the collection? The Reich should have known the pitfalls of sending a booklover to hunt down books. It was a quest full of delightful rabbit trails and tangents. When the *mademoiselle* emerged again, hands empty, she caught him with his nose in *Les Misérables*.

She huffed.

He offered a smile by way of apology. "I've only read the German, but I've heard it is best in its native French." The first pages bore out that theory. Why had he never sought out Hugo in his original language? He ought to be slapped for the oversight.

She looked as though she'd be happy to do the slapping. But instead of a rebuke, she said, "Your French is very good."

He slid *Les Mis* back into its spot, though not without a wistful sigh. He'd have to find a copy at whatever booksellers were open again. Jean Valjean would be a better companion for his evenings than the other officers who kept badgering him to join them on the town. "I was taught French by my godfather, who had spent decades here in Paris." He pressed his lips together before anything more could slip out.

It seemed even that was enough to make her brows pucker. "Godfather? I didn't think Germans had such things."

"We are not all atheists." His lips quirked up. "Or even Lutherans, believe it or not." He nodded toward her, tapping his chest where her necklace rested on hers. "I am Catholic too."

If he'd hoped it would spark camaraderie, that she'd realize that the Catholic sectors of Germany were the least receptive to Naziism and the most quickly persecuted, he was sorely disappointed. Anger flared in those blue eyes instead. "Clearly you need to read the section of Aquinas that addresses just wars. This does not qualify."

Did anything? Nothing offensive, anyway. The only just war, it seemed, was a defensive one. But there would never need to be a defensive one if everyone abided by those rules of righteousness.

He narrowed his eyes at the end table and skirted the couch—the long way, to avoid entering her personal space—to approach it. "I am not the one who declared war on France, *mademoiselle*. I am not even a soldier who marched on your land with a gun pointed at your neighbors and friends. I am merely a professor, drafted for service because of my work at the library of the University of Berlin." He crouched down, as much to avoid her dagger of a gaze as to investigate the book under one of the mismatched legs of the end table.

"You are stripping Paris of its literary heritage!" Her words weren't a shout. They were a low thrum, a hiss of steam, a venting of the same anger that burned in her eyes.

"Nonsense. Paris's literary heritage runs far deeper than a few rare first editions or cultural collections. Man cannot steal it away." He trailed a finger over the spine of the slender tome that made the mismatched fourth leg the same height as the other three. "I will try not to be offended on behalf of books everywhere that you or your mother chose to use one for such an ignominious task . . . but a library book? Have you no respect for other people's property?"

"Pardon?" Even as she spoke the word, bafflement in her tone, she moved over to where he crouched. Another breath of what could have been laughter slipped from her lips.

What would a real laugh sound like from her?

She didn't crouch down, but she did shove a hand through her curls, pushing them back from her face. "Maman. She is the queen of improvisation, and she will use whatever is handy . . . which is always a book. Just a moment."

She vanished from the room for a minute, returning with a folded-up piece of cardboard. "Here."

He took the proffered substitute, braced the table up with one hand, and slid the book out with the other, replacing it with the cardboard. "Not thick enough." He eased the table back down but then held it in place so the lamp didn't take a tumble. "Do you have another piece?"

Another minute while she went to find more, and this time it did the trick. Christian stood with a nod, Francis Bacon's *New Atlantis* in his hand. He flipped it open to the back to be certain it was the library's copy and not one of their own—and indeed, the lending card and pocket were there on the inside back cover.

He frowned, though, at the date. "She checked this out over a year ago."

The young woman shifted from one foot to the other. "Did she?"

No shock. No bafflement in her tone, not this time. If anything, amusement. He lifted his brows. "I realize not all libraries have the same loan periods, and that perhaps she renewed it, but . . . a year?"

A smile twitched in the corners of the girl's lips, quickly tamped down. "Order isn't exactly the forte of the directors of the Library of Burned Books, either, I'm afraid. It is no wonder Maman got along so well with them. They stamped dates, yes, but in recent years they seldom if ever checked to see where books went after they were checked out."

Amusing. And horrifying. It was no wonder the place was in such disarray, if that was how they handled their loans. "I see. Well . . . one down. Seventeen to go." His own lips twitched. "Should we check cupboards? Under beds? Perhaps a step stool has been built of them?"

Instead of granting him a real laugh, she stiffened. "Do I have the right to say you will *not* be pawing through our personal things, or will any objections be overruled anyway?"

He knew the look in her eyes—St. George, prepared to slay the dragon. A look he'd seen on many faces he admired, in people ready to face down injustice, whatever the odds.

He'd just never expected to be the dragon. He drew in a deep breath and skirted the room again, aiming for the door. "How about this? You have the list. Return the books to me when you find them. You may have a week. If you haven't returned them by then . . . well, I'm afraid I'll have to visit again and assist you with the search."

He glanced her way, not expecting any softening this time. Certainly not gratitude. He expected exactly what he saw—a stony facade barely covering the magma glowing underneath.

What surprised him was that she spoke as he reached for the latch. "Why? You have every library in Paris to sort through, haven't you? Why are you so obsessed with a few books borrowed from this one?"

He paused, considered. Turned. "Because, *mademoiselle*, in every other library in Paris, the shelves are filled with collections—some books that are approved by the Reich, some that are rare and valuable, some that they are indifferent to, some that are on the *verboten* list. They require, as you say, sorting. Their patrons can be left mostly in the hands of the directors, who will eventually be given . . . guidelines for who can still enter." He didn't wince as he said it. He'd had years to master his reactions, after all. "But *this* library—it is unique. It is *all verboten*. Every author is banned. Every director is labeled an enemy of the Reich. Every subscriber and patron is immediately suspected of communism, Jewish heritage, or anti-Hitlerism."

She folded her arms over her chest. "Some of us read those books because they represent ideals of freedom and imagination."

He bit back a smile. "As I said. Anti-Hitlerism." He pulled open the door before she could think that through. "I have superiors, *mademoiselle*. If I do not recall every one of those titles and question each and every patron still in Paris, I will be punished. And surely you won't doubt that I am a selfish creature who wishes to avoid punishment?" He stepped into the corridor and positioned his military-issue cap on his head, wishing for his fedora instead. "One week, *mademoiselle*, or I will be knocking on your door again."

He didn't turn back to see her reaction. He merely flattened himself to the wall when quick footsteps sounded in the stairwell.

The feet, which belonged to a middle-aged couple hauling suitcases in each hand, came to a halt the moment they caught sight of him. The woman's eyes went wide, wild. "Corinne? *Ça va?*"

Corinne, was it? Apparently so—the young lady assured her neighbors that she was fine, that he was only there to fetch books her mother had borrowed from the library next door, that he was *leaving*.

He would have, without more than a nod, had a slower set of steps not been drawing near too, along with a thud-thud-thud that sounded very much like a suitcase being dragged up the steps. He jogged down a few and caught sight of a child—a girl, perhaps eight years old—struggling with her luggage as she turned onto the landing.

Ignoring the squeaks from her parents, Christian moved to meet her, took the suitcase from her with a smile, and said, "Allow me. Young princesses such as you shouldn't have to haul their own luggage."

The girl giggled. Her parents didn't. But that was all right. He jogged back up the stairs, sending them a raised brow. "This floor? Which door? I'll just set it outside for you."

"You needn't, sir," the father said. *I don't want you to know where we live,* he might as well have shouted.

"Very well." He held the suitcase out to Corinne. "*Mademoiselle* will help you, I have no doubt. *Au revoir*, Corinne."

She not only hadn't given him permission to use her given name, she hadn't even revealed it to him. Was it petty of him to use it then? Yes. But it was the only real victory he could claim from the visit, aside from the abused Bacon, so he took it. He gave her a smile and left the case in her hands, tipped his hat to her neighbors, gave a wink to the little girl who was now tucked behind her mother, who perhaps hadn't been taught to hate him yet, and moved down the stairs.

Sunlight and a warm breeze met him on the street. As did Kraus, stepping out of the library and tapping a cigarette from a box of them. He'd done that exactly once inside, and Christian had burst into full librarian mode, lecturing him for a solid ten minutes on the dangers of smoking in a room full of books and papers and magazines.

The *soldat* nodded a hello and lit up. Then frowned at the single slender book in his hands. "Thought you said the Bastien woman had a dozen and a half checked out."

"Mm." Hence why it had warranted a house call from him and not one of the men assigned to help him in his tasks. No other single patron had so many titles listed beside her name in the disorganized records of this library. "It seems the lady has left the country, and this is the only one her daughter could readily find."

He didn't mention that the daughter was the same girl they'd first caught inside the library. Not given the way Kraus had scowled at Corinne each time they caught sight of her on the street.

Kraus frowned. "So where are the rest?"

"There, probably. Her daughter claims she's very disorganized. I've given her a few days to locate them before I help with the effort."

Kraus nodded again and pulled the key from his pocket. "Back to the National Library, then?"

"Let me fetch my bag from inside first." They'd returned here for lunch, solely because he'd needed the privacy his chosen headquarters provided him. He'd thought to tick an easy item off his to-do list with the visit to the Bastien residence next door . . . but it seemed there were no easy tasks on this list, not really.

A few minutes later, briefcase in hand, Christian walked with Kraus to their car and then rode in silence back to the Biblioteque Nationale. Crates upon crates of books had already been sorted through, their fates assigned . . . but they hadn't yet put a dent in the collection. As Paris's premiere library, this one had been assigned as his top priority, after securing the Library of Burned Books.

As Kraus opened his door for him outside the graceful columned structure, Christian stood immobile for a long minute while his assistant parked the car elsewhere, staring up at the facade. He knew many librarians, many professors of literature, both German and foreign. There were men aplenty who had been the ones to recommend books for the banned list to Goebbels. Why was *he* the one sent to Paris? Why had it fallen onto *his* shoulders to dismantle the libraries?

Other men, men who had been quick to join the Nazi Party, who had joyously thrown their own books onto the pyres, would have been better suited to this task. Other men would have no qualms as they marched into each Parisian library and declared it to be the property of the Reich.

And maybe that's why you're here, something whispered inside him. *Not because your hard-*

headed friend pulled strings he shouldn't have for reasons of his own. But because you don't thrill at it. Because you understand the cost. Because you understand what these people are losing.

He let his eyes fall shut for a long moment. He did, yes. But understanding didn't stop the French from labeling him an enemy. How could it, when he strode inside even now in his pristine uniform, giving orders that would attempt exactly what he claimed to Corinne no one could accomplish?

He'd spoken truth, when he said that a people's heritage—literary or otherwise—was something more, something deeper than the physical items that could be stolen. He believed it. He *had* to.

Didn't he?

He strode past the emptied shelves, toward where he'd left off before they stopped for lunch. And he drew up short when his commanding officer, Oberstleutnant Ackermann, stepped out of the stacks.

Christian remembered—barely—to snap a salute. "Good afternoon, Oberstleutnant."

"Bauer." The man was perhaps a decade his senior, but unlike Christian, he'd seen war before. Had fought the French before, and the English. Had been injured in the trenches and had spent his recovery in hospital learning to hate . . . well, everyone, from what Christian could tell. The enemy. The Jews. The men who had chosen pursuits other than the military.

Christian had been too young to fight in the World War, but that didn't stop Ackermann from hating him too—or at least disdaining him for his pursuit of academia instead of the military.

"The going is slow," Ackermann said, nodding toward the empty shelves closest to the door and then looking over his shoulder at the vast number still to be sorted through.

Christian inclined his head. "I was ordered to be meticulous with this one, sir. To show all of Paris what to expect from us."

Though Ackermann couldn't argue with the orders that had come straight from Goebbels, his face twisted as though he wanted to. "I suppose the next ones on the list should be quicker—the foreign libraries, filled with only the scribblings of communists and enemies."

He did indeed already have orders to simply close several of the libraries—the Czech one, the Russian one—and do whatever he pleased with the books inside, with a recommendation of destroying all the "rubbish."

The last thing he wanted to do was sentence an entire collection to the burn pile. But with Ackermann watching over his shoulder and the list of people to find and interview growing by the day, he didn't know what else to do.

Paris was indeed a city of libraries. A city of readers. And the Reich wanted all of them controlled, labeled, and any so-called threats neutralized.

At this rate, Christian was going to be here for years. Stuck in a city that held far too many secrets, under the watchful eye of a man who had no respect for him or his work, needing to guard his every word. His every move. His every thought.

Well. *That* wasn't so different from Berlin.

Ackermann's gaze flicked past Christian as new steps came up behind him, and he gave a quick dismissive salute to whoever it was. "Afternoon, Kraus."

"Oberstleutnant." Kraus's voice all but dripped admiration . . . and Ackermann lapped it up like a cat with a saucer of cream.

Christian could understand Kraus's attitude—much like a student who discovered that the dean actually knew his name. What made his shoulders go stiff was the fact that Ackermann greeted Christian's attendant with familiarity and warmth.

Did they know each other outside of this billing? Unlikely. Kraus had grown up on a farm outside of Berlin, after all, whereas Ackermann hailed from Hamberg. No, so far as Christian could tell, their only connection was this job—was *him*. The one above, the other below, both with their eyes fastened to him far more often than he would like.

Ackermann even now sent the younger man a knowing smile and gave him a playful punch in the shoulder. "Holding up all right beside *der bücherwurm?*"

If he meant the epithet as an insult, he'd have to try harder. *Bookworm* was a badge of honor in Christian's mind.

Kraus laughed and snuck a sideways glance at Christian. "Of course, sir. My mother will be pleased to know that I'm getting an education as I serve my country, thanks to the professor."

Christian offered a shrug. "A teacher cannot help but teach." Unfortunately, all too often students chose not to learn. He wasn't yet sure what category Kraus would fall under. Sometimes their conversations were free and easy, and Christian could even lead him into a discourse on ideas, not just facts.

Other times, it was like a steel trap had slammed shut on the boy's mind, and nothing could pass through it in either direction.

Just now, Kraus was clearly in his soldier mindset, not his student one. Eager to impress the *oberstleutnant*.

Ackermann chuckled, clasped his hands behind him again, and pointed his toes toward the door. "Just see that you spend more time cataloguing than teaching, Professor. And if you need more assistance, say the word. We want this business concluded as quickly as possible."

"Of course, sir. I'll let you know."

He was still trying to decide if it was a good thing or a bad that his superior called him *professor* just like his men did, when the man paused a few steps away, spun, and leveled an uncompromising glare at him. "And Bauer—join us officers at dinner on Saturday. It isn't healthy to stay barricaded in your rooms all the time."

What could Christian do but smile and agree?

FIVE

13 July 1940

Two days. Corinne had two days left before the professor came knocking on her door again, and she was going to have to get crafty. Her knuckles fell from Trinette's door, behind which there wasn't the slightest stir.

She hadn't really expected her friend's family to be back in Paris. They had a family estate in Provence that they'd retreated to for the duration of the war. That was why she'd recruited Trinette to her work. Still, a part of her had hoped. Prayed. Passing her the banned book would be so much simpler than sending it to her.

Just as she'd prayed each day as she gathered in the post that there would be a book-shaped parcel with her name on it in the letter box on the ground floor of their building, something with information on German movements penciled into the margins in code. Surely someone had learned something useful by now.

Her uncle had warned her that intelligence was a game of patience, of long periods of inaction interrupted periodically by harrowing close calls that could get them all killed. She'd assured him she could handle it.

She might have been wrong, she had to

admit as she opened her box yesterday evening.

Nothing. And not even a postcard to soften the blow. All the girls were still away from Paris, and none had yet sent her any word. Nothing for her to pass along to Oncle Georges, nothing to send on to de Gaulle and the Allies, nothing to make her staying here worthwhile.

Still, she darted through the familiar alleyways since she was so near to Amalie's flat, in the Arcade above the shops on the Champs-Élysées. Evening was falling, though with the slow, sultry sun of July that took forever to give way to night. Laughter floated down the avenue.

If she closed her eyes, she could pretend it was the right sort of laughter—Parisians out enjoying their Saturday night. She could pretend that those weren't Nazi uniforms on the men striding down the sidewalk, that the gaily clad women on their arms weren't betraying their country.

Don't judge what you don't know. A whole chorus of voices clanged that wisdom in her ear. Papa's voice. Maman's. Oncle Georges's. She didn't know those women's stories. She didn't know why they'd responded to the flirtations that the German men would lavish on anything in a skirt.

Perhaps they took Pétain's advice and embraced their occupiers as friends . . . but just as likely, they were desperate. Desperate for security, desperate to escape the uncertainty of empty shops, desperate for information on what had become of brothers and lovers who had been captured on the front when Pétain had surrendered.

Still, she didn't particularly *want* to know their stories right now. She wanted to find her own friends, her own family. So she darted into the rose-scented courtyard that would lead her to Amalie's flat. A ring, a knock.

Silence.

Corinne sighed, even though she'd expected nothing less. Moving slowly now, giving the quartet of laughing people ample time to pass by, she regained the street—and nearly jumped when a figure stepped into her path.

"Sorry! I didn't mean to startle you." Hugo of Cartier backed up a step, hands up in apology. "I thought that was you I saw enter the courtyard. I only thought to say *bon soir* and see how you're doing."

Letting fall the hand that had flown to cover her racing heart, Corinne smiled. "No need to apologize. I think I must have expected you to be . . ."

He gave a solemn nod, sparing a glance over his shoulder at where the two couples were entering a restaurant. "You are wise to be cautious. Are you in a rush?" He motioned toward the street. "I was just on my way home. My wife will have dinner on, and our daughter is home. She is close to your age, I imagine. Twenty." An indulgent smile overtook his mouth.

She didn't correct him on the assumption—he must have forgotten that she'd already told him she'd lived through the last war so was clearly older than twenty. She was too busy being torn between the thought of an evening's company with someone other than herself and the thought that she shouldn't impose on anyone else's stores of food.

Hugo leaned a little closer, eyes gleaming. "One of my customers insisted upon tipping me with a very nice bottle of red this week. And another passed along a cut of meat he said he had no need of. Eh?"

Meat he had no need of? Clearly a Nazi officer, then—no Parisian had a surplus of meat, no matter how wealthy, not for the last year. And while part of her would rather spit on anything offered by a German, she was no fool. Who knew when next she'd get more than a soup bone or a single chicken leg?

Besides—one more night of only her own thoughts for company and she might go mad. Corinne smiled. "That sounds delightful. If you're certain your family won't mind the intrusion?"

"Of course not! They have both been complaining about the lack of friends. And Liana!" He chuckled, shaking his head as he led her along the avenue. "She is having trouble with her beau, I think, though she keeps insisting Michel is nothing but a friend."

He offered his elbow, and she tucked her hand into its crook.

Such a simple action, but it made years fall away. She was strolling down this street with Papa, on her very first trip to Paris. He had Maman on one arm, Corinne on the other, and he had this way of holding himself . . . no one ever looked at Pierre Bastien and thought he didn't belong on the poshest streets in Paris. He'd made her feel like she could belong here too. Like she could have any dream she wished for. He'd made her believe that miracles could happen, that anything could become reality if you believed.

He'd lived, after all. When he should have died. He had ten good years with them, when the physicians had insisted he wouldn't last six months.

And he'd made her feel, with that simple offered elbow, like . . . *someone.* Someone who mattered. Someone who could make a difference. Someone who could dare to dream.

Strange how this near-stranger could make her feel the same way just by inviting her home to meet his family.

She cleared her throat as they strolled along, after Hugo indicated that they'd catch the nearest

Métro. "Tell me about your daughter. Is she your only child?"

"No, no," Hugo said with a laugh. "Just the only one still in Paris. We have five children, but the older four have all moved away. Liana fled before the bombardment, upon her mother's insistence—stayed with Gigi, our oldest, for a few weeks. But she couldn't handle the quiet of the countryside, she said. So back she came. I shouldn't have been relieved." He sent her another twinkling smile. "But I confess I was. The flat was so quiet without her. We'd been dreading her admitting she was in love with Michel, that they would marry, that she too would leave us."

She couldn't exactly assure him that his youngest wouldn't soon spread her wings and fly the nest—it was what children did, after all. So she grinned. "My mother constantly teases that I'll be home forever, that there's no boy in Paris good enough to catch my eye."

That much might be true. Her bar was set rather high, after all. Papa's fault. When she'd seen what true, selfless love looked like, how a gentleman should treat his wife, she couldn't settle for anything less.

Hugo chuckled and patted her hand. "Too bad our boys are married already. Although I have a nephew..."

She cut him off with a laugh. "I did not accept

your invitation so you could play matchmaker, *monsieur*." Even if it felt so deliciously *normal* to talk of such things.

Eligible nephews, married sons, picky daughters—conversations of years gone by. Things they spoke of before all talk turned to refugees, invaders, and surrender. *War.* What a wretched thing.

They paused at the corner to wait for a break in traffic, lights from the restaurant beside them drawing her eye. When night fell, the lights would all vanish behind thick blackout curtains she could see on the side of each windowpane, and the streetlights would be barely glowing behind their stifling blue paper. For now, though, with summer night still hours away, the glass sparkled clear and bright, giving a full view inside . . . to tables filled with Nazis.

Officers, mostly. Groups of men crowded around petite tables that seemed too small for them. Other tables where half the seats were taken by Parisiennes with red lips and blank eyes and expensive dresses from last season. Waiters bustling about with tight lips and chilled champagne and half-full plates.

Her throat went tight. She wasn't *hungry,* not yet. Not like she remembered being as a child. Not like she'd probably be come winter—the ignored rationing of last year was already being reworked by their occupiers. Everywhere she went, Corinne heard whispers about how it wouldn't just be meat, sugar, and alcohol that were restricted soon. It would be everything. Bread. Pasta. Rice. There was talk of ration tickets and assigned grocers.

Talk. Perhaps it was just talk. They could pray so. But even if the rumors were unfounded, *waste* was unthinkable already. There simply weren't shipments of food coming in from the country like there used to be—it was all being used by the Germans, sent back to *their* families.

She hoped the kitchen staff boxed up all that uneaten food and took it home with them.

Hugo must have noted the same thing, given the *tsk*ing sound he made. "Some people have no manners." Manners? "Though I suppose you're accustomed to being stared at—even so, it's rude."

Stared at? Her eyes left the waiter and his tray and needed no search to fly straight to the man who was looking at her.

Looking—but not staring, not like Hugo meant. No, the professor was studying her from behind his glasses as if trying to sort out what a girl like her, who lived in a flat on Boulevard Arago, was doing on the Champs-Élysées, on the arm of a man old enough to be her father who was dressed far more sharply than she was, when she *ought* to be at home searching for her mother's missing books.

She was debating whether to lift her chin and

send him a challenging look or turn away as if she hadn't recognized him. Before she could decide, the man seated next to him—this one was an *oberstleutnant* if she was seeing his insignia clearly through the glass—leaned over, his eyes on her too. He said something that no doubt matched his leer.

The professor blushed—*blushed!*—and made some reply, moving his gaze back to his plate.

Hugo tugged her forward, across the street. Maman had taught her how to sashay to catch anyone's eye—a lesson of laughter and playful scolding and many wobbles on the heeled pumps she'd never worn until that day. A lesson she did *not* put to use now. No, she kept her spine stiff and straight, her stride brisk and efficient, hips as still as possible.

She wasn't above using her looks when it suited her, but she wanted to *avoid* the Nazis' attention, not capture it.

"Several of those men have been into the shop," Hugo said after a few minutes of silence, as they took the stairs down to the Métro. "One or two seem like good enough men. Others?" He gave an exaggerated shudder. "Stay clear of that one who leaned over when he noticed the other staring, I'd say. He struck me as a grasper."

Her brows lifted, even as she breathed a sigh of relief at the cooler air of the underground. "Grasper?"

"The kind who is eager to become more than he once was. Eager for the symbols to prove his status. The kind who thinks a fancy watch—or a pretty mistress—will convince the world that he is somebody worth knowing."

"Ah. I know that kind." She glanced over her shoulder, even though she could see the older officer only in memory. He certainly hadn't abandoned his dinner to find her. "I've no use for them."

Hugo chuckled. "Clever girl, as I suspected."

They bought their tickets and gained the platform just in time to catch the train. Running again, yes, but far from full these days. They had their pick of seats and settled in without any bumps or *pardonnez-moi*s.

Hugo settled into his with the ease of a man who took this exact train every night and knew it as well as he did the pavement outside his shop. And he studied her in that way she'd noted on their first introduction—like Oncle Georges did. Like he saw far more than the tailored blouse, the simple skirt, the hat positioned with care over the curls that didn't want to stay contained in their chignon in the day's humidity.

She tucked an escapee back into place beneath a pin and lifted her brows. "What is it you see, *monsieur*?"

"Moreau, by the way. Hugo Moreau." He repositioned his fedora a bit so he could lean back. "My wife and I have been praying for you every day, you know. She has dedicated a decade of her rosary to you each morning."

Corinne's lips parted, but it took her a long moment to find words. Even then, all she could manage was "Why?" She'd met this man only once, briefly. She was surprised he'd even *told* his wife of her, much less that they'd remembered her in their daily prayers.

Hugo chuckled. "My *grand-mère* always said that like-souls know each other. Perhaps it is strange for you to think of being a like-soul to an old man like me . . . but it is not odd for me. When I heard you chide that other man in the shop that day, I knew. I knew you were a like-soul. I told Babette that I had a feeling our paths had crossed for a purpose. So we have prayed. That they would cross again when it was the Lord's timing. That he would show us the purpose."

A tickle moved up her spine. Like a chill but . . . not. Pleasant instead of startling. Like the first touch of snow, glazing the world in crystal and diamond.

She hadn't given much thought to Hugo since that first meeting—she'd been too busy thinking about her own problems, her goals, her *job* now that Hitler had his swastika flying from the top of the Eiffel Tower.

What a fool she was. How arrogant. How selfish. Her hand moved up to the Miraculous

Medal, its cerulean-blue promise too forgotten despite the fact that she put it on anew every day, took it off every evening.

It was supposed to remind her to pray. To seek knowledge beyond her own. It was supposed to be a call for grace, given to those who called upon the Lord and his sacred heart, poured out in love for them.

Clever, Hugo had called her. But she wasn't. Not when she'd forgotten the most important thing. "You shame me, *monsieur*—in the best possible way. I ought to have been praying for you too."

He didn't look offended at realizing she hadn't been. He just chuckled and let his eyes slide shut after what had probably been a long and hectic week. "The young have the luxury of forgetting such things."

"Not now, we don't." And she was no doe-eyed ingenue, no matter what the curls made people think. She knew better. Maman had taught her better. "Thank you for reminding me of that."

The ride was short—only two stops—and then they were disembarking and reemerging into the long golden light. Corinne followed Hugo down the street, around the corner, and to a row of tidy townhouses that promised an interior a good deal bigger than the cramped flat she and Maman shared.

Their windows were still blacked out, much

like her own. No longer in fear of a Nazi bombardment—but perhaps in hope of a British one. A strange sort of hope, that.

"Babette!" Hugo called the moment he had the door open. The smell of roasting meat wafted out, making Corinne's stomach go tight. "You'll never guess who I've brought home for dinner!"

"Who?" The voice sounded too young to be Babette's, and the young woman that appeared from a hallway was most assuredly Hugo's daughter, not his wife.

She looked familiar. The sort of vague familiarity that usually meant Corinne had seen her about the university without ever having been introduced—her name certainly wasn't familiar.

Liana must have been thinking the same thing, given the thoughtful narrowing of her eyes and purse of her lips. "Have we met? At university, perhaps?"

"Not officially, but you do look familiar." Corinne held out a hand. "Corinne Bastien."

"Bastien!" Liana took her hand and leaned in to kiss her cheek. Her eyes had lit up. "Are you related to Professor Yvonne Bastien?"

She couldn't have stopped the smile had she wanted to, any more than she could stop the pang of missing her. "My mother."

Liana squealed. "She's my favorite professor! Or *was* before she abandoned us for her sabbatical." Laughing, Liana pulled her inside, motioning to the tree for her hat and purse. "Papa, however did you meet my literature professor's daughter?"

"Providence, clearly." Hugo put his fedora in its place on the tree and waylaid his daughter for a kiss on the cheek. "She is the girl I valiantly rescued from the panzers a few weeks ago."

Liana's eyes widened. "No."

"*Oui.*" Corinne shrugged, her lips settling into a comfortable smile that she'd had no reason to wear this last month. "I'd have been flattened if he hadn't intervened."

"Hardly. But you may have been forced to act for their cameras or risk their wrath, and we can't have that." He stepped around them, toward what must be the kitchen, since it's where the smells were coming from. "Babette?"

"Coming!" An older version of Liana emerged a moment later, an apron tied into place over her neat blue dress, a tea towel in her hands. Given her expression, she'd heard the exchange—at least the last part—and she held out a welcoming hand. "Corinne! How good to meet you. A true answer to our petitions."

A knot of humility lodged in her throat. She'd hoped to make a difference in this war, yes. To do good things—things she was equipped to do. She'd hoped to use her connections to keep information flowing to the true France in exile in England. But she'd never imagined being the answer to anyone's prayers like this, when they had no reason to pray for her. She had to swallow before she could manage to say, "It's so good to meet you, Madame Moreau."

She waved that away. "Oh, call me Babette, please. And welcome. I've just got everything on the table—let me set another place, and we'll be ready to eat."

The meal was delicious, but even more nourishing was the companionship. Corinne hadn't really *conversed* with anyone but Oncle Georges since the invasion, when all her friends and students fled Paris. She'd exchanged words and pleasantries here and there, but always there was a wall in place, it seemed. On her part, if not everyone else's.

She had no idea who among the Parisians had resigned themselves to the decisions being made in Vichy, and who had this constant burning coal in their chest as she did. Who so wanted life to go back to "normal" that they would welcome their occupiers, and who would work to undermine them.

A note had come round today from an acquaintance at a magazine, asking if she'd write an article about flourishing under the new regime, and she could only stare at it, fury and sorrow and an endless sense of helplessness churning out as hot tears. *Flourish?* Were they to *flourish* under the Nazis? She had opinions on how to do so, opinions that would talk about flowers blooming in desolate cracks, about faith growing under persecution, about light finding ways to break through the darkness.

But that wasn't the kind of article the editor was asking for. The kind that his new Nazi supervisors would approve.

She couldn't write the article they wanted, the one that would encourage French people to embrace the new regime, to bow to it. Someone would though. Someone would think "Well, it's a paycheck" and scribble some nonsense onto paper. And the magazine would run it, and her neighbors would read it, and while some would huff, others would think, *Maybe this is the only way. The way we survive.*

If she'd wondered how far she could trust the Moreaux, though, the question was answered after dinner when Hugo led them all into the sitting room, where a radio held the position of honor on a marble-topped table. He switched it on—and shot a look at his wife when the words of Radio Paris greeted them.

Babette laughed. "Someone came to the door earlier—what was I to do, leave it on the BBC when I didn't know who was calling?"

Given that the Nazis were attempting to make it a capital offense to listen to anything but their own new propaganda station, Corinne had taken to leaving her own wireless set tuned to Radio Paris too, though she listened to it only enough to scoff and stay up-to-date on what the enemy wanted her to think. To hear what Pétain, whom she'd once respected as the great victor of Verdun, was peddling now on behalf of his Nazi overlords.

Liana motioned for Corinne to sit beside her on one of the twin settees. They listened in silence for a while, concentration on the three faces of the Moreaux as the English program finished up.

"Do you speak English?" Liana asked after a few minutes—perhaps she'd noticed the lack of pucker to Corinne's brow. "I can translate for you, if not. A bit, anyway. Sometimes they speak too quickly for me to follow."

Corinne smiled. "I do. My father was English—he was injured and left for dead in the last war. My *maman* nursed him back to health, and he decided to stay here."

She hadn't told anyone that story in years. Not since Papa had died. She didn't know why, exactly, other than that it felt like a part of him she could hold tight to. Protect. But she wanted to share it with these new friends who had welcomed her so fully into their own secrets.

They trusted her. With no reason to. They *chose* to trust her, because God had crossed their paths.

She would choose the same.

Liana's lovely brown eyes went wide. "How romantic!"

"So you are half British?" Babette frowned at

that. "You'll want to keep that quiet, I think—I know several English ladies who have been arrested already and sent who knows where, just because of that."

Stepfather. She should have said *stepfather,* but she never thought of Papa that way. He was just . . . *Papa.* She ought to correct them now, but the more important part seemed to be Babette's concern. "Not necessary. He . . . Papa was ill for so long, unable to even speak his name, if he could even remember it. My mother started calling him Pierre, just to have something to call him. He eventually managed to whisper 'Bastien' as his name. One night when he seemed near death, she called the priest in to give him last rights, and that's what Father entered into his records—Pierre Bastien." She shrugged. "It became his name, after he got well. He kept it. With all the confusion of the war, all the records lost in our town, no one questioned it. He was simply issued new papers and given a French passport."

Babette looked relieved. "Good then, that no one knows."

"But he taught you English?" Hugo put in.

Corinne nodded. "He did. He said that knowing several languages would serve me well. He taught me English, German, Greek, and Latin."

"Gracious." Liana winced. "Cruel man."

"Learned man," her father corrected. The

gaze he settled on Corinne was different now, somehow. "A *very* learned man, I should think. Though perhaps that shouldn't surprise me, if your mother is also a professor."

"It was Papa who encouraged her to go to university and eventually become a professor, though she was older than most students." Until him, Maman said she'd thought no further than the border of their village in the Somme region. About nothing bigger than finding food enough for her and Corinne.

But when he'd seen the yearning for knowledge in her mother, he'd done something he'd sworn he'd never do. He reached out to the family he'd let think him dead for nearly a decade. Reclaimed just a bit of the world he'd abandoned to stay with them. So that he could give them an education.

"So very romantic," Liana said on a sigh. But then she snapped back to attention when the broadcast switched to a more familiar voice—one of the French broadcasters who had traveled to England to remain on the air, speaking directly to those still in France, sharing the news the Nazis wanted to keep from them.

Corinne fell silent too, taking in every word.

She said her farewells after the broadcast so she could get home before the curfew the Germans had instituted, assuring the trio of concerned Moreaux that she would be perfectly fine venturing through the city on her own, that she did it all the time. And with summer's long days, there was still daylight in the sky even now. More, she promised to join them again for dinner next Saturday, *every* Saturday, and she and Liana had set up a time to meet for lunch at a café near the Sorbonne on Tuesday too.

The Métro ride did nothing to disturb the sense of peace from her unexpected new friends, and the streets between the stop and her flat were blessedly clear of Nazis. When a wisp of music made its way to her from some open window, she let the notes carry her feet into a few swing steps as she opened the door and headed straight for the letter boxes.

A twist of her key, and there—another answer to prayer, this time to one she'd actually prayed. A book-shaped parcel, wrapped in brown paper, addressed in a familiar hand. "Praise God." She kissed her medallion and then the book from Maelie.

Her elation lasted exactly twenty-two more seconds—the time it took her to dart up the stairs to her floor.

Then it came crashing down in a million shards of broken crystal. Because the professor—the *Nazi* professor—sat in front of her door.

For a fraction of a heartbeat, she considered spinning around and running for it. But before she could act on that impulse, much less think it through, he stood.

With his hands out. And his shoulders drooping. And an expression on his face of . . . what? Apology?

It rooted her to her place, one step from the landing. Her fingers clutched the book. The book that would have markings in the margins. The book that, if he looked at it now, before she'd had a chance to erase the pencil marks, could land her in prison. Executed. Could bring their fledgling intelligence network crashing down before they'd had a chance to do anything worthwhile at all.

He didn't reach for the book. Didn't come any nearer. "Forgive me for intruding. I only . . ." He winced, letting his arms drift back down to his side. "I wanted to warn you, and I couldn't risk doing it when Kraus was nearby."

"Warn me?"

"This was stupid," he muttered in German, reaching up to pinch the bridge of his nose, dislodging his spectacles to do so. No doubt he assumed she couldn't understand him.

She did. And his clear second-guessing of whatever he'd come here to warn her about made something relax. One degree. No more. "Warn me of what, Professor?"

He drew in a breath, puffed it back out. And looked up. "First—introductions. I'm Christian Bauer, professor and head librarian at the University of Berlin, and it was rude of me to use your name the other day without permission. I apologize."

He didn't stretch out a hand to shake, but it felt like he did. Verbally, he did.

So . . . to shake, or to slap it away? She crossed her arms over her stomach, holding the book tight against her. Because he surely wouldn't think such a thing odd, given that he'd cornered her outside her flat. "Corinne Bastien." It wasn't forgiveness, exactly. But it wasn't exactly *not*.

He nodded, taking it as the truce it was. Not peace—but a momentary ceasefire. "And again, I am sorry for . . ." He waved at her closed door. "I don't mean to intrude. And certainly didn't intend to startle you. I only . . ."

Color rose in his cheeks, which was what made it click into place. Her lips almost, nearly curled up. "Are you here to warn me about your friend with the lecherous eyes?"

"He isn't my *friend*." Another wince. "He's my commanding officer. And yes."

"All right . . . noted." She took the final step. "Though given that the one time our paths have almost crossed was in a section of the city where I only go rarely, your warning is a bit unnecessary, *non*?"

His look was long, even. Waiting. "My commanding officer, *mademoiselle*. That means he could well decide to drop in any moment next door to check on my progress. Or he could mention the lovely young woman with blonde curls he saw in the hearing of Kraus, who could say we have a neighbor matching that description."

She rolled her eyes. "An argument that makes sense only because *you* know the connection. I am hardly the only woman with blonde curls in Paris, and Kraus would have no reason to assume I'd have been on the Champs-Élysées tonight with my friend's father."

Moreover, what good would the warning really do if the man did come here? She couldn't exactly hide in her flat all day every day. Classes would be starting back up soon, which would keep her away from home most of the day, yes, but she'd have to come and go.

Bauer granted the point with a curt nod. "As you say. An overreaction on my part. I only felt guilty, being the one to inadvertently draw his attention to you. I apologize for that too. I was only surprised to see you there."

Because she belonged *here,* in the 13th *arrondissement*, peopled more by professionals and academics, writers and the stray artist here and there, rather than *that* part of the city, where only the wealthy and elite dined and shopped.

She granted it with a tilt of her head. "I appreciate the concern."

He nodded once more and then moved toward the stairs, circling in a way that kept three feet between them at all times. Which shouldn't have made her soften another degree but did.

He went down two steps, then stopped with an "Oh" and pivoted to face her again. He reached into his pocket and pulled out a slender wooden disc, about an inch thick, and held it up to her.

She just stared at it. "A . . . coaster?"

He motioned with it toward her door. "For the leg of the table. It's a better solution than the cardboard, which will compress over time. And the same thickness as the book. I checked it to be sure."

He'd checked a coaster's thickness against the book he confiscated? And, what, had been carrying the thing around in his pocket? Corinne reached for the wood slowly, waiting for any trap, any ultimatum, anything to make sense of the Nazi officer in charge of ruining one of the most precious things in her world being unnecessarily kind to her, when she'd shown him nothing but disdain.

The moment her fingers closed around the side nearest her, he released it. Touched the brim of his cap in farewell. And spun away.

Corinne waited until his footsteps faded, until she heard the door open to the street and close again. And then she drew out her key, let herself inside, and sagged against the door. The book, with whatever secrets were penciled into its pages, she set on the nearest flat surface. And she closed her eyes and tried to make sense of the world.

SIX

15 July 1940

"Professor Bastien," Christian said for the third time, following the frazzled secretary as she opened yet another filing cupboard. He was beginning to wonder if perhaps he'd lost his capacity for French—but even if so, the name ought to have been recognizable.

"Doctor Bastien?" the woman asked, thumbing through files.

"I . . . don't know her degree. I only know that I'm looking for Yvonne Bastien."

"Oh, she's on sabbatical." The woman pulled out a file and marched back to the desk with it.

Christian barely reined in an exasperated huff. He'd been relieved to see life at the university again, had thought to ask a few quick questions so that he could have an excuse for marking the woman off his list, but getting answers from anyone here was proving as effective as trying to herd kittens. "I am aware of that. Do you know where she went? Or when she's expected back?"

"Went?" The woman blinked at him. "I only know she has no classes on the schedule for the next year. But if you want to speak to Doctor—"

"No. Thank you. Never mind." He was already

running late for his next appointment—he shouldn't have detoured here.

Frankly, though, he dreaded his next appointment and had ever since the note had arrived that morning from one of the dozens of checkpoints around the city. *Abraham Cohen has reentered Paris. He has been detained and is awaiting you.*

Dread coiled in his stomach. He'd hoped that the Jewish writers, exiled to Paris seven years ago from Germany, wouldn't return to the city when they'd had the good sense to flee. Hadn't Abraham Cohen a shred of common sense? He *knew* that the very people who had run him from his homeland had now taken over Paris. Why would he return?

Christian strode along the pathways, dotted now with the students and faculty who had been absent upon his arrival in the city, toward the car Kraus had kept idling at the curb. The young man leapt to open his door for him, dragging his gaze off a few pretty students who were pointedly *not* looking his way.

Christian slid into his seat in the back.

"Any luck?" Kraus asked as he checked for traffic and pulled into the street.

"No. Just confirming what I knew from Mademoiselle Bastien. I think I ought to assume she's not in territory we hold and leave it at that."

"Once you get the books back, you mean."

Kraus shot him a raised-brow look in the rear-view mirror. They'd spotted Corinne entering her building the other day, and Kraus had drawn the connection between their intruder and the Bastiens. "Today's the deadline you gave her for that, isn't it?"

And he'd been expecting her knock on the library door every day. Well, not yesterday. She'd be at Mass, observing the Lord's Day, not searching for missing books or expecting him to be at the library. And he wasn't about to tell Kraus that he'd seen her Saturday evening . . . twice. "It is."

"What will you do if she fails to deliver? Arrest her?"

"For a few missing books checked out to someone else?" He met Kraus's reflected gaze in the mirror, striving for the same disdain he'd give a student angling for an extension on a paper because he wanted to take the week off for a holiday. "You are too eager to see that young woman punished for her associations, *soldat*. You told me the story of convincing your father to get rid of books on the banned list—would you want to be punished for him ever having had them to begin with? Or what if you'd gone searching for those children's books and found them gone, and your parents were not there to question? Would you want to be arrested for that? Or would you assume the books had been got rid of already?"

Kraus's eyes had returned to the road, but his fingers tightened on the wheel. "It's entirely different. Madame Bastien couldn't have just *got rid* of library books."

Christian snorted. "She could have returned them ages ago, though. You've seen their abysmal recordkeeping. Perhaps they aren't in the *fraulein*'s flat because they're back in the collection already and simply not marked off. Perhaps they'd misplaced her card."

The library used no record system like any he'd ever encountered. Instead of a master register, they had cards for each patron, on which they listed the titles checked out and, in theory, the dates of both borrow and return. But they were a mess, dates missing all over the place and occasionally with question marks in their place—likely because the cards had been misplaced when the books were returned. Some people had multiple cards, though the previous ones weren't full—again, evidence of bad filing.

Frankly, he was surprised to even find a date stamp at what passed for a circulation desk. They might as well have scratched "whenever you feel like returning it" on the due date line.

There clearly wasn't a librarian among the directors. Nor, it seemed, anyone who cared to learn a quick system of organization. No, there were only writers and philosophers who deemed their time better spent on thinking and recording their thoughts than on worrying over how anyone could find a blasted thing in their library.

From the front seat came a grunt that wasn't a granting of his point so much as a recognition of the futility of arguing with his superior.

A month in this city, in this boy's company every day, and Christian was exhausted with watching his every step, his every word, his every *thought*. He hadn't dared let crowd his mind the things that mattered most—the memories, the prayers, the soul-deep ache for all he was missing. If he dared, outside of the dark of his hotel room barracks, someone would find out. Someone would know. Someone would find those precious things and destroy them, just as they'd done with everything else that mattered.

He was exhausted already—what would he be like in a year? Two? He would be forced to watch the Parisians shrink and fade, and he'd shrink and fade along with them.

His eyes slid shut for a split second. He needed a friend—just one friend in this lonely city. And though he couldn't imagine Kraus being that person . . . perhaps he could be something, anyway. Something more. Quietly, he asked, "Why do you hate that girl so?"

Though he could see only the upper sliver of the young man's head in the mirror, the tension around his eyes was enough to let Christian guess that his mouth had gone tight, his jaw clenched. Perhaps Kraus would refuse to answer.

But after a long minute of silence, he finally said, "She is the most dangerous kind of enemy, isn't she? Beautiful. Young. Compelling. She could lead people astray so easily. But she *is* an enemy, we know that. Her presence in that *place* proves it. She is a lover of contraband, raised by a woman who was one of the library's most dedicated patrons."

Christian let the words hover in the warm air of the cab, let them ring in Kraus's ears as surely as they did in his. He considered his response carefully, weighing it out gram by gram. "Those books were not contraband *here,* not until we arrived. The Bastien women were breaking no law, no rule, no guideline even by reading them. Just as you weren't when you read the poetry of Heinrich Heine as a child. You didn't *know* the ideas or the author were undesirable, my friend, until someone *taught* you."

"Always the teacher." Kraus laughed through the words. But then he went silent again for a beat. Two. "You think you can *teach* her?"

They drew to a stop at an intersection, giving Christian a chance to gesture toward one of the infinite propaganda posters tacked about the city. "Is that not what our every effort is striving to do in France? We replace their philosophy with our own. We shout it from every radio station.

We put it up on every wall, so that wherever they go, this is what they see. When their own government speaks, this is what they say—not 'Liberty, Equality, Fraternity,' but 'Work, Family, Homeland.' *Our* motto, in their words."

He hated the fervor he could put so easily into those words, from years of practice at exciting students to care, even when he'd gone numb inside. When loss stacked upon loss, and all he'd wanted to do was stop fighting. Stop caring. Stop *breathing,* because every breath hurt too much in his silent world.

Kraus eased onto the gas again, the eyes in the mirror gone thoughtful. "You really think these French people will sway to our side?"

He thought some already had, because there were always those who valued being on the winning side above sticking with whatever beliefs were convenient in times of peace. He thought others would, because resisting took energy that would fail as the food did, as the heat did in winter. Because anything could become normal, given enough time.

He thought some never would. That they would die before they gave up, because they believed just as he did that the true heart of a nation couldn't be invaded, couldn't be overthrown, couldn't be stamped out by madness, not completely. That as long as even a few held fast to that heart, there was hope for them all.

"I think," he said slowly, "that the words we hear, the words we read, the words we sing along to on the radio and study in the papers with our morning coffee, become our thoughts. I think our thoughts become our beliefs. And I think our beliefs become our actions. That is why Goebbels sent us here, Kraus. Because words form the foundation of society. *Ideas* create culture. Control them, and you can control . . . everything."

Truth, however unfortunate. And yet not, solely because it was impossible.

No one, not even Adolph Hitler, could control every word, every idea. And the more he tried, the more the world would see his madness, and the harder they would fight.

Please, God. Please, let it be so.

Those silent words, more a prayer than he'd uttered in far too long, made his throat ache with the yearning to speak them out loud. He hadn't wanted to pray, not since his world went so silent. But here, now, surrounded only by people he didn't dare to trust . . . he needed that, at least. One friend who would never betray him.

A friend he knew would forgive him for the long year of silence. Who stood always with arms stretched wide to receive him, wide as the cross on which he'd hung for the sake of that forgiveness.

Kraus let out a long stream of breath, and his arms relaxed on the wheel. "So . . . we should talk to the *mademoiselle*? Win her over?"

They should do no such thing. But he smiled, just as he would for a student who had ventured to answer in class for the first time. It didn't matter what they said, only that they were saying it. Thinking it through. Taking a risk. "Win the youth, and you win the country."

Hitler had proven that in Germany too. It was the students who had led the book burnings, the bannings. The children, like Kraus, who had shamed their families into complying with each new regulation. If it weren't for the Hitler Youth, the German army would be a much smaller force.

But he hoped and prayed that the students of France wouldn't bend so easily. They would be a force—students always were—but it was yet to be seen what *kind* of force they would be.

Resistance? Or true surrender?

Kraus pulled over in front of the Hôtel Lutetia, now the headquarters of the Abwehr—German Intelligence. This time, Christian had no trouble waiting for his aide to come and open his door for him. The trouble was in convincing his legs to hold him when he climbed out of the auto.

He'd been doing his best for the past seven years to stay *out* of buildings like this, out of the attention of the Abwehr, of the Gestapo, of the Party in general. He chose his words diplomatically . . . most of the time. He kept his true opinions to himself—with perhaps one or two exceptions.

And look where it had landed him. Not in a Gestapo holding cell, it was true—but striding into an interrogation of a man who'd once been a friend, wearing the uniform that would tell Abraham Cohen in a glance that they were enemies now.

They weren't. But Christian couldn't let him know that.

Thank God, his legs were as well accustomed to striding forward when his mind was a million miles away as his lips were at smiling when he felt a blink away from tears. He was inside the hotel in seconds, striding straight for the lift. He knew what floor he needed, what room.

He knew that Ackermann would be there, along with at least one of the intelligence officers who had dined with them on Saturday, and likely an SS officer. Christian was to be the representative of Goebbels's Ministry of Propaganda.

Such irony. Such horrible, hideous irony.

The room was, at least, not an interrogation cell. No bare bulbs swaying dramatically overhead, no blood stains on the floor. It was just a hotel room, with the beds moved out and a table moved in.

Abraham Cohen sat on one side, blessedly free of bruises and blood—his hands were in cuffs on the table, but that was all. He didn't look up, but he appeared unharmed.

Christian's muscles relaxed just a bit. Perhaps they would be civilized.

He was the last one to enter, apparently—only one chair remained unfilled on the Nazi side of the table. And for whatever reason, they'd left him the middle seat. He took it, offering no apology for his lateness.

Apologies showed weakness. And while he strangely didn't mind revealing that vulnerability to his book-loving neighbor on Boulevard Arago, he wouldn't show even a scrap of it to these colleagues. He simply sat, opened his briefcase on his lap, pulled out pen, paper, and the file he'd requested that morning on Cohen, and then reclasped the case and set it on the floor beside his chair.

Ackermann cleared his throat. "I thought we said ten-thirty."

This time, he pulled out the smile he reserved for other faculty who meant to belittle him and thereby advance their own prospects. "Does Herr Cohen have another appointment to keep?"

Ackermann's smile was stiff, but the Abwehr man on Christian's other side, Wagner, laughed. "We waited for you, Bauer, since you're most familiar with Cohen's . . . body of work."

"Indeed." He didn't look over at Abraham, but he could see the man shift and knew Abraham was looking at *him* now. Christian prayed he'd have the wherewithal to keep his recognition from his face. Rather than glance up to see, he flipped through a few pages and made a few notes in a shorthand that the others wouldn't be able to make sense of.

Largely because it was senseless scribbles. He already knew what he meant to say here, just as he already knew every article, poem, treatise, and book the man before him had written.

But there was a script to follow. One he'd written himself as he lay awake in the pre-dawn. Scribbling complete, he finally looked up, careful to keep his expression bored. He met Abraham's eyes. And he willed the man to see the truth hidden beneath the layers of role in his own. "Could you please state your name for the record?"

Abraham didn't move. Didn't draw in a breath. Didn't so much as blink for ten long seconds. And when he did, he shifted his gaze to Wagner, then to Ackermann. At last, he said, "Abraham Cohen."

"Residence?"

Another hesitation.

Christian looked up once more from his paper. "We already have it down as 39 Rue de Tolbiac, per your papers at the checkpoint and our own records. Your silence speaks only of your intentions not to cooperate, which I do not advise." *Just follow my lead, Abraham,* he silently willed his old friend.

Abraham cleared his throat. "Your records are correct. I live at 39 Rue de Tolbiac and have done so since I first arrived in Paris in October of 1933."

Ackermann shifted beside Christian but didn't speak. He was there, Christian suspected, solely to oversee him. Report on him. Tell Berlin whether or not he could do this job.

He couldn't. But he would anyway. Somewhat. "I have here a list of known associates and colleagues of yours." He slid the sheet across the table, full of names of other writers who had left Germany for Paris in the thirties . . . and who weren't currently in the city. "Do you know the whereabouts of any of them?"

Abraham took the paper with his cuffed hands, read through it slowly. Shook his head. "It was chaos. I thought to meet up with a few in the country, but I didn't. I don't know where anyone is."

It could be a lie, but it could sadly be true too. Either way, Christian was satisfied with the answer, and neither of his companions interjected.

He pulled forward another sheet of paper with three long columns on it. "We have already visited your flat and confiscated the following *verboten* literature." He passed the paper over to Cohen. "You will see there that the list includes the manuscript you'd left behind when you fled Paris—no great loss to you, as all publishers have been issued orders to refuse contracts to any

Jews—as well as the book that came out in . . ." He consulted his notes, though he didn't need to. "February of 1939." It had been April by the time a disguised copy had made its way to Berlin and into Christian's hands. "Are there any other books, articles, or other writings that you have published in the meantime?"

He looked up, met Abraham's eyes. The man slowly shook his head. "The new book took all my time and attention. I'd only just finished it."

Christian nodded. "Very good then."

Wagner leaned an arm onto the table, looking at Christian rather than Abraham. "The new manuscript—you have it?"

Another nod.

Wagner lifted his brows. "And? Have you reviewed it?"

"Not in full, but I've got through half of it." *Bored,* he told himself. *Unimpressed.*

Wagner raised his brows. "Well?"

The smallest, most disdainful shrug. "I found it to be just like his previous works, of which my opinions ought to be known." *Brilliant* had been his exact words in his last review for his favorite literary journal—in early 1933, before the burnings, before Abraham fled. He hadn't dared publish such opinions since.

Abraham knew, though.

And he was wagering that neither Wagner nor Ackermann did. Neither were avid readers, so far as he could tell. Certainly not Ackermann, with his muttered *bücherwurm* insults.

Wagner pursed his lips. "Cohen's writing itself isn't incendiary, correct?"

"Nothing but useless philosophical drivel. His crime is his heritage, not his words." To punctuate his point, Christian shuffled the pages together again. "I advise that he be entered in the Jewish registry once it's operational, of course, but otherwise released. With, naturally, the instruction that he neither write more nor attempt to refill his bookcases with *verboten* literature." He offered a sardonic smile. "I can provide a list of approved books, Herr Cohen, if you need a few recommendations for better reading material. *Mein Kampf* earns our highest praise."

He, Abraham, Josef, Father, and Earnst had torn it to literary shreds when it released in 1925. Even if Abraham didn't remember the literary review Christian had written of his 1933 book, he would remember *that*. There was no way he could forget the laughter, the hours of conversation, the foamy beer and pretzels that went stale in their basket as they pointed out the fallacies of each argument and opinion the upstart politician had written.

It was the first Christian had been accepted by his father's crowd. The first they began to view him as an equal, not just a child. He'd been only twenty, still in university. But he'd known that he never meant to leave academia. That this circle, his father's friends and colleagues, were who he wanted to be his own. That if he could find a place among the intelligentsia, he would live a happy life.

How naive he'd been.

How he wished he could return to those days.

Abraham gave a tight smile. "I've read it. Twice."

Wagner pushed back from the table. "Someone will escort you out. You may return home, but do not attempt to leave the city again. You will soon have to register as a Jew and check in weekly with your assigned office. Curfew is in effect for all Parisian citizens from nine p.m. until five a.m. Jews are allowed only on the last Métro car in a line, at designated cafés—a list will be provided to you by your registry officer—and in certain stores, which will be on the same list. By week's end, no person not born to French parents will be permitted to hold any job in the city." Wagner rattled it off in as bored and perfunctory a tone as Christian had employed. He stood. "Any questions?"

He clearly didn't mean to answer any, given the way he tugged his jacket back into place and reached for his cap.

Cohen cocked his head. "Not for you, sir. But if I could ask that one about books . . . ?" He nodded toward Christian. Pasted on a smile.

"Acceptable ones, of course. Since it seems I will have ample reading time."

When Ackermann stood too, Christian held his breath. He could just as easily refuse the request as allow it . . . but he didn't. He merely followed Wagner out, with a laugh about leaving the *bücherwurms* to their talk—and a caution to Christian not to take too long.

He didn't dare let out a breath of relief, not even when the door closed behind them. Doors still had ears. But he did let his eyes slide closed, let his shoulders sag. Then he pulled a sheet of paper from the bottom of his stack. "Book recommendations." He slid it across the table, meeting Abraham's eye. "Have you read number four?"

Three Comrades by Erich Maria Remarque. Abraham surely knew what he was asking. *Where are Josef and Earnst? Have you seen them lately?* They'd been inseparable, once. Abraham, Josef, Earnst. They'd decided to leave Berlin together, and though their departures had been staggered, Christian knew they'd met up again here, had continued traveling in the same literary circles.

Abraham shook his head. "I haven't." Regret clouded his dark eyes. Silently, he added *I'm sorry.*

As if *he* had anything to apologize for. Christian nodded. "What about number ten?" *The Passenger* by Ulrich Alexander Boschwitz.

Have they fled France? Gone to England? To America? Even Free France would suffice, though they were sure to suffer from lack of food in the coming months and years too.

An Allied country would be better. America best of all. Perhaps then they, at least, could stay away from this war. Could escape its claws. *Please, God.*

Abraham let out a quiet breath, his shoulders lifting. "I . . . don't know. It does not sound familiar, but . . . as I said. Chaos."

Christian let himself slump in his chair. Told himself for the thousandth time that in this case, no news of them was good news. As long as they weren't here in Paris, then he could believe they were safe. Out of Nazi-controlled territory. That they stood a chance.

His old friend, one of the few people left in the world who remembered Father, one of the men who'd helped usher him into the world he loved so much, regarded him with a look of pure sorrow as he fingered the corner of the book list. "Am I able to . . . get these books from a library?"

Christian winced and tossed his eyeglasses down so he could rub at his eyes. "Not the one you belong to. It was the first to be shut down. I myself am keeping it under lock and key. I have in fact set up my personal headquarters there—I find working among books far more productive than a hotel room."

Abraham's eyes were the ones to slide shut this time, in obvious thanksgiving. "I daresay that one wouldn't have these titles anyway. But there are others."

Did he really mean libraries? If so . . . "They've all been ordered not to lend books to Jews. You will have to purchase any title you want. From, of course, a vendor approved for your people." What if he was really asking about where to meet with his compatriots? Underground gatherings?

About those, Christian had no knowledge, if they existed.

They would. He had to believe that. As he'd said to Kraus in the car, the young people wouldn't sit idly by, once they made their choices. But that didn't mean they'd made any strides quite yet. It had only been a month since Pétain surrendered.

Abraham nodded and folded the list. "If you've headquartered at that small library . . . you may have run into one of its neighbors? She and her mother were dear to me. If you tell her I am well, that I send my greetings . . . ?"

Eyes going wide, Christian leaned back. Corinne? Were she and her mother really that close to the men who ran and organized—or failed to organize, as the case may be—the Library of Burned Books?

Why? *Were* they communists? Jews? Corinne didn't look as though she had any Semitic blood, but that didn't always mean anything.

He prayed she was neither though—because if she were, then she'd be forced to register too. She'd come under the scrutiny of officers all too eager to teach the people they deemed inferior a lesson.

She could well end up at the mercy of Ackermann, who had mused for fifteen solid minutes about her curves, her face, how he'd like to get a taste of her. It had been all Christian could do to force his dinner down.

It didn't matter. Regardless, he couldn't give a message from Abraham to Corinne. "I'm afraid Nazi officers aren't in the habit of passing along messages." If he dared to try, she would see straight through him. Know that he passed it along as a friend, not an enemy.

And he couldn't afford to let anyone know who his friends really were.

But . . . perhaps, if she brought any books back today . . . "I can perhaps mention that I interviewed you today. Offhandedly," he said under his breath, praying the words were too low for anyone but Abraham to hear.

Abraham nodded. "She is . . . lonely. Has been since her mother left before the invasion. Be a friend, if you can." Abraham not only spoke in the same bare murmur, he said it in English—unlikely to be understood by either of the officers who had been here with him, if they lingered outside the door.

Christian wasn't sure *he* understood either. Because surely Abraham Cohen wasn't suggesting that he trust Corinne Bastien that much? With who he was? With . . . ?

He shook his head and stood. "If you read English, then I suggest you pick up a copy of number twelve. A highly enjoyable story." *The Most Dangerous Game* by Richard Connell.

Abraham's eyes glinted. "I've read it. It is, after all, the most popular short story ever written in the English language. Very intriguing premise too, isn't it? Rainsford didn't ask to be put in the game. But he was. So then, his job was to survive it."

The challenge was clear. None of them had asked for this, none of them *wanted* to be the prey in this madman's deranged hunt. But they were. They *all* were.

Their job was to survive it. To accept that the training they'd received might amount to nothing, that sometimes they might have to swim around the long way to avoid the dogs, that there would be a struggle that could well kill them.

The character survived. Won. And ended the game so no other victims fell prey to it.

Christian was none too sure he had the stamina of Rainsford. And certainly wasn't about to trust any other fellow victims of the hunt. It was Rainsford's skill as a hunter himself that had given him an edge with the evil Zaroff—if some other panicked, shipwrecked passenger had been on the island at the same time, would he really have worked with them?

Unlikely. He'd have known that trusting someone else would get him killed.

Christian put his briefcase on the table again, slid the papers into it, and met his friend's gaze one more time. He didn't know if he'd ever see him again. Didn't want to leave now with frustration and thrown gauntlets between them.

He didn't want this man to leave thinking Christian's father would have been ashamed of him. But he couldn't make promises he had no intention of keeping.

So he did the only thing he could think of doing. He lifted his right hand and spread it wide over his heart, as he'd done the day he realized he was in love. The men had laughed at him, but it had been a good-natured laughter. They had all been in the same place. They all knew the joys, the pitfalls, the ups and downs that would come.

The heartache. The tears. The crying out to a God who seemed so far away.

Abraham spread a hand over his own heart too, in a silent covenant. And then, with a sad little smirk, he lifted his other hand and spread his pointer and middle fingers into a *V*.

For a second, Christian could only see it as the red *V* stamp he'd been forced to use in book after book as he consigned them to cupboards and boxes and closets—*Verboten*. Forbidden.

Then he realized that it wasn't that *V* at all. It was the *V* that defaced posters all over the city. The *V* of a people not ready to give up, not ready to surrender. It was the *V* of *la victoire*—victory.

He returned the salute, feeling the strangeness of Abraham's smile on his own lips. Not a smile he ever gave to his students, to his colleagues. Not a smile he ever remembered giving to anyone. Unpracticed. Unbridled.

Full of reckless hope.

It was enough to carry him back out of the hotel, back into his car, back to his work at the National Library. It lingered still as Kraus drove him once more to the Boulevard Arago, where he'd write his reports for the day before trudging to his room for the night.

It nearly stuttered when he saw Corinne Bastien lingering by the door, three books in her arms—only three.

He could feel Kraus's gaze latched to him as Christian made his way toward the door, key in hand. He wouldn't be surprised by leniency, not given the conversation they'd had earlier in the day. But he wasn't convinced of its wisdom either, Christian knew.

"You're back later than usual today," she said by way of greeting, flicking her blue gaze from him to Kraus. "I was about to slip them through the book return slot."

He had no obligation to offer her excuses, of course. But since she gave him the perfect opportunity . . . "An interview interrupted my workday—with one of the directors of this place, as it happens, upon his return to Paris." He reached for the books, made a show of reading the titles. "Abraham Cohen. Know him?"

She didn't start. Didn't widen her eyes. Showed no distress, though surely she felt some. She only fastened on a smile as crooked as the halo of a fallen angel and said, "It's impossible to live where I do and not know all the regulars. Monsieur Cohen was always kind to me. I hope he is well?"

"He is." He looked at the last book in the stack, barely holding back a frown. It felt . . . new. Had Professor Bastien been the first to borrow it? He flipped to the back inside cover, glanced at the borrow card. Hers was the sixth name on the list.

"Is there a problem, Professor? Aside from the incompleteness of my stack, I mean?"

He glanced up at Corinne. No guilt limned her expression, darkened her eyes, tugged at her posture. Just curiosity.

Perhaps. He closed the book with a snap and put on a dismissive smile. "Only, as you say, the incompleteness. But I am encouraged that you've found these three. I shall help you look for the others sometime this week, *oui*?"

That easy posture went stiff. "I will keep searching. You needn't bother—"

"No bother at all." He fit the key into the lock and opened the door, knowing Kraus would bar her from following. His aide was still far from fluent in French, but he'd probably picked up a few words here and there. Enough to get the gist of the conversation. "Let's say . . . tomorrow? Perhaps at lunch time?"

Her chin came up. "I'm afraid I already have a lunch date tomorrow. And classes are starting again on Wednesday, so I won't be at home regardless. I have to be there to prepare."

He paused, fingers curled around the door. *Classes*. His soul yearned for them. "At?" It was none of his business. He was merely curious. Did she attend the university at which her mother worked? It seemed likely. "The Sorbonne?"

Her eyes narrowed. Answer enough.

He smiled. "I could meet you there in the afternoon. Give you a ride home."

"Absolutely not."

He'd known she would refuse—to be seen getting in a car with a Nazi officer, after all . . . But he smiled. Shrugged. "Very well then. When you arrive home. Let us say . . . five o'clock?"

The moment she agreed, he knew well she'd seen the trick. Saw it in the glimmer of amusement in her eyes—at herself. Saw the single spark of respect, quickly covered by annoyance. She spun on her heel and marched away.

Christian chuckled as he moved into the library, pausing at the circulation desk as Kraus continued toward the water closet. He drew out the patron cards, flipped that bottom book open again, and made a quick comparison.

His brows drew a little tighter together with each name he checked. Granted, the records were dreadfully incomplete . . . but the list on that card and the cards with the borrows for each name didn't even begin to match up. And the few entries that did, the dates were years apart.

He flipped quickly through the other two books, the middle one with a card just as mismatched, the top one, decidedly more worn, its corners gone soft and round from much handling, the only one of the three whose records more or less matched the official record.

But even that one . . . He flipped through the pages, pausing when a black thread caught his eye.

No, not a thread. Rubber. Eraser detritus.

At the sound of a flush from down the hall, Christian closed all three books and slid them onto a shelf.

"All well?" Kraus asked as he came back down the corridor.

This smile was the absent one he gave to students who just wanted acknowledgment between classes, when he had time for nothing but that smile and a nod. "Indeed." He glanced at his watch. "Give me thirty minutes to update my files, and then we can go and find dinner."

Kraus grinned and took his usual seat behind the desk. "Perfect."

SEVEN

16 July 1940

Corinne sipped her *café au lait* and flipped another page in her book. She didn't need to glance at her watch to know that Liana wasn't due to join her quite yet, but even so, she'd been ready to leave the university and chase away the thoughts nipping at her with some coffee before she smiled for her new friend.

She shouldn't have visited Maman's office this morning. She'd known it was a bad idea, but she'd given in. She'd unlocked the familiar door. Breathed in the familiar scent of typewriter ribbon ink, old books, the rubber of bands that would no doubt dry rot before anyone used them again.

Her absence wasn't supposed to be so long. She'd only been going to England for a few months to set up their little fledgling spy network on that end, to solidify associations with the British intelligence agency at Bletchley Park, before tension could turn to war . . . they'd thought.

They'd thought, with France's army planted at the Maginot Line, that there would be time for her to take care of things there and come home. They'd never dreamed the Germans would bypass the Line and come through the Ardennes. They'd never dreamed that France would surrender so quickly, that Paris would be declared an Open City, unprotected, not fought for or over, that the government would retreat.

They'd certainly never dreamed that an enraged English fleet would threaten to sink French vessels that didn't destroy themselves, to keep them from enemy hands—and that they'd follow through with it.

The alliance they'd counted on, she and Maman and Oncle Georges, had gone up in smoke with the French fleet at Mers-el-Kébir two weeks ago, when the Brits attacked and sank them to keep them from German hands. Until then, she'd still hoped. Hoped Maman would be able to sneak back into France.

What hope did she have now?

Corinne took another sip of her coffee, willing her mind onto the pages of her novel. Instead of thoughts of Maman, trapped in England, even though Corinne was beginning to wonder if this little spy network of theirs was even worth the risk. Instead of thoughts of Christian Bauer, who would be invading her flat again that night to search for more books she didn't have—the embodiment of that risk.

She tapped a finger against the edges of *Quinzinzinzili*, but even the post-cataclysmic tale of science fiction wouldn't distract her thoughts.

She could think only of how the edges were worn smooth, soft as velvet—something she hadn't had time to fake on the two new books she'd handed to Bauer yesterday. She'd slammed them against corners, flipped the pages over and again, opened them wide so the spines creaked and groaned in protest. She'd glued new library pockets to the inside back covers, had creased the cards before she tried to remember which patrons she'd heard talking about the titles over the years.

Were Kraus the one to examine them, they would have passed inspection. At least given the disarray of the library's records. But Bauer? He'd known something was wrong, even if he hadn't called her on it then and there.

He would. She knew he would. She'd hoped and prayed he would simply glance at the titles and mark them off the list without looking any further, but no. Of course not.

And so she'd been forced to stand there while he noted whichever telltale signs she'd either left or neglected in her haste, pretending Maman had caught her at the chocolates again, determined to escape punishment.

Giving up on the novel, she tucked a slip of ribbon in the pages and closed the cover.

Abraham was back. That news had kept her up half the night too. Was that good? Bad?

Bad—it must be bad. He ought to have known better. Given that the Library of Burned Books had been the very first library to be put under Nazi control, it stood to reason that its directors, patrons, and subscribers would be of interest to them too.

She would have to pay him a visit soon. Make certain he and his wife were well. That they had food. Books.

Her eyes burned. How were they to provide for themselves? When she'd inquired at the Sorbonne that morning, the pinch-lipped secretary had told her what she'd feared would be the case. One of the provisions for reopening was that anyone not French-born of two French parents was to be expelled at once.

No Abraham teaching about poetry and philosophy. No Josef giving lectures on history. No Earnst debating theology with Catholics, Protestants, Jews, and atheists, forcing them all to think outside the boxes of their own understanding.

Juste ciel, if she didn't interrupt her thoughts soon, she'd end up crying.

"Corinne, *bonjour*!" Liana gusted into the second chair at the tiny table, the serious light in her eyes belying the bright smile. She wore a fashionable ensemble, complete with a wispy yellow scarf over her dark hair and tied in a chic knot under her chin. She leaned in for the obligatory exchange of cheek kisses.

Corinne was suddenly very aware of the circles under her own eyes from yet another night with too much worry and too little sleep. Of the way tiny little lines always showed around her eyes on such mornings. Of how tired her muscles had felt as she walked here from the Métro stop.

Oh, to be twenty again.

"Do they have *croissants* still? I'm starving." Liana made the declaration flippantly, motioning for a waiter, but she clearly heard herself. She winced, lowering her hand. "It's going to get worse, isn't it? Worse than no butter, no pastry."

Corinne's lips would offer only the tightest of smiles. "To quote your father, *You are too young to remember the last war,*" she said. "The hungry years. But if it drags on . . . I imagine so."

Liana blew out a breath, put in her order for coffee and a *croissant* when the waiter came over, and then leaned back in her chair, eyes on Corinne. "Forced to be in by nine each night, yet still you look exhausted." Her brows lifted, along with the corners of her mouth. "Or perhaps you were at an all-night cabaret?"

Corinne rolled her eyes at that suggestion. "Hardly. Who can afford those things now?"

Chuckling, Liana reached for Corinne's book and slid it around to face her, presumably so she could read the cover. Her brows knit. "What kind of title is that?"

"I have no idea yet. It's science fiction." Corinne let her mouth twist. "I'm not certain how far I'll get. The premise is that there's a world-wide war—another one—and a Japanese scientist develops a chemical reaction that causes mass extinction."

Liana pushed the book away as if *it* were the poison. "I think you ought to be reading a nice romance story instead."

"I do believe you're right." When the waiter returned to fill Liana's cup, she let him refill hers too. Then she called up a smile. "So your father mentioned a man called Michel?"

They chatted about simple things like love and how you ever knew when someone was the one you wanted to marry while they ate and sipped. And Corinne smiled because, a year ago, those were the complicated questions. Would she ever meet someone who made her heart come alive, as Maman's and Papa's had with each other? How would she know?

Now she wished those dreams were the ones she could sigh over, long for.

Liana leaned closer. "A few of us are having a . . . poetry reading. Tomorrow evening. It will be over before curfew, of course—in the basement of a building two streets over, owned by the family of one of my friends. You could come."

Corinne trailed a fingertip along the rim of her empty-again cup. "Poetry."

The tilt of Liana's head said it was definitely *not* poetry. "Rousing old French poetry. You know the kind—the verses that speak of our heroes of old."

The ones who spoke of freedom. Of revolution. Of honor. "I do love that poetry," she said slowly. Letting her fingers drop from the cup, she nudged the top of her fork a bit to the left, her knife a bit to the right on the serviette, so that their bottoms touched. A subtle *V*, like the ones people made with their Métro tickets, with their feet as they sat, with paint whenever they dared deface a Nazi poster. "I don't know if I can make a reading tomorrow night though."

On the one hand, she wanted to keep her finger on the pulse of such things, especially if it would be students at the meeting, so close to campus. But if Oncle Georges found out—and he would—that she was part of some sort of resistance that he hadn't preapproved . . . She didn't want to jeopardize the work she'd already agreed to. Not to mention she didn't fancy being the sole professor in a group of students. "Liana . . . I didn't think to correct your father's assumptions the other night, but you ought to know—I'm a decade older than you. I *teach* at the Sorbonne, I don't attend."

For a moment, Liana's eyes went wide. Then she grinned. "Even better. Having a professor among us will lend us credence."

Corinne sighed a laugh, shook her head. "I really can't tomorrow though. Will there be other meetings?"

"Probably. I hope so." Liana arched her brows.

"Why can't you make tomorrow? Do you have a date?"

Corinne rolled her eyes. "No. I haven't . . . my mother accuses me of having been too focused on my education for too long. I've not taken time for such things."

The purse of Liana's lips was playful again. "Well we can't have that. Michel has a handsome friend, older than us—he's the studious type, just received his doctorate last spring, I think."

"In what?" Not that she was interested in being set up, but she couldn't resist the question.

Liana waved it away. "I don't know. Something in science—physics? Chemistry? It's all beyond me, which is why my eyes cross when he speaks, despite the very handsome mouth doing the talking. Perhaps you could follow along, though." She tapped the novel on the table. "You picked *that* up of your own will, after all."

"A novel is hardly a scientific treatise," Corinne said with a laugh. But she could generally follow the conversations of physicists and chemists, if they didn't get too technical. She'd read Aristotle, Archimedes, and the other Greek fathers during her lessons on the language as a teen. Maxwell, Faraday, Planck, and the like during her own schooling at the Sorbonne.

She'd had a horrible time deciding what to focus on in her studies. Everything interested her. So she'd dabbled for a few years, as Maman had jokingly called it, before settling where she knew she was strongest—linguistics, philosophy. Between those two she hadn't been able to decide, so she hadn't.

A shadow fell over her—a familiar shadow, which had her spinning in her seat and leaping to her feet. "Oncle Georges!" She kissed his cheeks, even as she wondered what in the world he was doing here.

She never assumed her uncle showed up near the Sorbonne by mere coincidence. There were no such things as coincidences with him, only careful planning, evaluations, and follow-through.

If he was here, it was because he'd been looking for her. And as always, he found her without too much trouble.

He smiled with that ease that perfectly covered every single thought in his head. "*Mon chouchou.*" He motioned her back to her chair and pulled over an unoccupied one from another table. Nodded to Liana. "*Bonjour.*"

"Ah. Oncle Georges, this is my friend Liana. Her father is the one who rescued me from the parade the day the Nazis took Paris." She'd told him the story, of course, though she hadn't seen him since Saturday, to update him on her acquaintance with the rest of the man's family. "Liana, my uncle, Georges Piers."

Oncle Georges held out a hand, clasped Liana's.

"*Enchanté*. I didn't realize Rinny had met her savior's family."

Liana laughed. "He waylaid her on Saturday and forced her home to meet me and Maman. I've declared her my new best friend."

No doubt because all her others had left Paris, but Corinne wasn't about to argue. All of her friends had too.

Liana frowned though and looked between Georges and Corinne. "Your . . . mother's brother?"

"Father's," Georges answered, obviously having no reason to know it would contradict too much of the story she'd told. Or failed to tell.

Liana's frown deepened.

"Stepbrother," Georges clarified, eyeing Corinne with veiled questions. "Hence the different surnames."

"But . . ." the brunette dropped her voice low, leaned in. "Wouldn't that make you English too?"

Georges blinked. Then sent a second blink to Corinne, so heavy with accusation that she nearly winced away from it.

Shouldn't the waiter have refilled their coffee again? She could have used the distraction of sipping it. "They're on the up-and-up," she murmured in English, hoping Liana wouldn't know the idiom. Papa's English, smooth as butter, posh as first class.

Her uncle let out half a breath, then cut it off.

"You could let me be the judge of who learns *my* secrets," he said. In his own English, Cockney and harsh. All the proof anyone would ever need that he was no blood relation of the man called Pierre Bastien.

"She didn't tell me your secrets." Liana had clearly understood his accusation, though she answered in quiet French. "She didn't even mention you. I'm sorry if I . . . I'm sorry. I should go." She reached for the purse she'd set on the table.

Oncle Georges reached out, his hand hovering over hers, his smile easy again. "No, no. Please. I'm sorry if I startled you. It is only that . . . yes. I am. Or was." His words were in French again, colored with the accent of the Pas-de-Calais department he'd learned it in, his shrug so Gallic that Liana frowned again.

"You don't *seem* . . ."

Georges laughed, and to Corinne's ears, it was sincere. His eyes had joined his lips in their smile, twinkling. "I have been here since I was sixteen. I lied about my age to join up for the last war—or rather, I assume I did. I didn't honestly know my exact age." He shrugged again, his face mimicking the motion in that way Papa had never learned to do. "I've lived far longer here than I did there."

Interest sparkled in Liana's eyes. "But then you . . . found a brother? Half—or, no, step?"

Something in her gaze must have convinced Georges of what Corinne had decided so quickly upon meeting the Moreaux. He smiled. "I'd never met Corinne's stepfather before the war. But I had a friend whose brother had gone missing in the mud during a battle, in the region Corinne's family is from. I wanted to see if I could find evidence of him, for his family. Find a grave, perhaps, though that seemed a long shot. So many were lost in that mud." He closed his eyes, seeing what likely haunted his nightmares still, as it did hers.

And he'd poked through far more of it than she had, searching for friends and comrades-in-arms. She'd only ventured out to the field near their little cottage, hoping to find rations in some abandoned corpse's pack.

The hungry years.

"So I went searching for this one missing English soldier's grave, and what I found instead was a story of a man who miraculously survived months of infection and pneumonia, who spoke French like he was educated in London. Well, that intrigued me. I expected to find a stranger, never thought in a million years it would be Bastien, the very man I sought—but it was." His lips curved into a smile shadowed with memory. "And when he realized I knew his family—the family that believed him dead—he about went mad. I thought he'd kick me forcibly from the house. Might have done, if he'd had the strength. He'd already decided, you see, to stay dead. Because he believed his brother to be the better heir to their father."

Corinne grinned. Those years were more blur than clear memories, but she remembered that day, at least in fragments. Opening the door to Georges, a tired-looking young man, no older then than Liana was now. Hearing him ask for Pierre Bastien, saying he'd come from the priest in town. Hearing Papa—only *just* her Papa, two weeks before—explode when Georges admitted he knew Papa's brother.

She leaned over to bump her shoulder into Liana's. "He'd fallen in love with Maman by then, of course. They'd just married. Then this man claiming to have links to the past he'd relinquished showed up and put it all at risk."

Georges chuckled. "I thought I was doing his brother a favor. Turned out, I was doing myself one. I agreed not to tell anyone who he was—I knew what it was to have secrets, after all. And it was . . . comforting. Knowing there was someone else a bit like me nearby. My wife and Corinne's mother became close as sisters." Another shrug, this time with a single shoulder. "I count several brothers that aren't my blood. Bastien's one of them. Which makes this troublemaker more niece to me than my others"—he directed a fond, teasing grin Corinne's way—"given that I've had to keep an eye on her every day of her life to keep her from unleashing the very hounds of the netherworld."

Corinne laughed. Really laughed, like she hadn't done in months. He'd been there the day Papa read her the legend of Cerberus, and he'd declared then that she'd probably set him loose if they didn't watch her, just as she had old Madame Martin's pack when two boys from the village school wouldn't stop pulling on her curls.

He'd been proud of her for that quick thinking, she knew. The boys hadn't chased her home again. She wasn't so sure he approved of her quick thinking with Liana's family yet, but at the very least, he'd decided to draw them in, if only to test them.

It made tension unknot in her chest. Or perhaps it was the laughter that did that.

Liana was smiling too. "What a wonderful story—a wonderful family. I call my mother's oldest friend *tante* too, despite that she's no blood relation. It makes her no less family."

Corinne reached out and covered her uncle's calloused hand with her own. "Oncle Georges is the only family I have left in France. He's promised to watch out for me, never mind that I'm a grown woman who doesn't need a chaperone any longer."

Georges snorted a laugh of his own. "You,

Rinny, will *always* need a chaperone. Knowing you, you'll be slipping chocolate rations out of Nazi pockets and giving the stolen treasure as gifts for Christmas."

She made a show of pursing her lips. "Not a bad idea. Who knows what the shops may be like by then. And stolen chocolate *is* sweeter than any other on earth." She waited for their laughter to die down, gave a lazy stretch that allowed her to make sure no one was paying attention, and then said, "Liana has just invited me to a . . . poetry reading, Oncle."

He was skilled enough in hidden meanings to note that slight hesitation. To hear Corinne's unspoken request that he judge Liana's age, her disposition, her politics. He tilted his head, his smile soft and small and infinite. "Yes? I imagine it will be filled with young people eager to perform. But if ever you find yourself longing for the stylings of an old hand who has recited many a poem before . . ." He reached into his jacket pocket, pulled out a *carte de visite*.

It wasn't his home address on the card, nor his home telephone number. She didn't honestly know what flat or office resided at the location. She just knew that if ever she couldn't reach him at home, and it was an emergency, she should call him there and say, "The heel of my pump broke, some urchin stole my handbag, and I've a blister on my ankle after chasing him down. Can you come and pick me up, Oncle?" and then tell him wherever the emergency was.

A year ago, when he'd made her memorize the number and the instructions, it had seemed like one more game they'd play together while Maman and Tante Minette baked and gossiped in the kitchen. Nothing serious. Nothing she'd ever actually *need*.

Now she found herself reciting the words three times in her mind just to make sure they remained lodged where they belonged. Because too many of her other childhood games had already proven useful. Too much of her uncle's "silliness" had proven itself to be training for a world she hadn't thought would turn this way again.

Liana tucked the card into her handbag, a new light in her eyes. "Thank you, *monsieur*. I daresay we would love to hear the recitation of someone of your generation. Though . . ." Her expression shifted, twisted. "We are hardly organized yet. I don't know when the next reading will be."

Her uncle gave her friend a peaceful smile. "You'll sort it out, I have no doubt." He stood again, setting atop Corinne's novel another book that he must have had tucked into another pocket somewhere. "Here you are, *mon chouchou*. As promised. Happy reading."

"*Merci.*" It was another beat-up edition that he no doubt meant her to burn when she was finished decoding whatever message he'd scribbled into the margins—probably a response to the message from Maelie that she'd slipped into his letter box. Instructions to pass along to her friend.

He could have just *told* her the message, but he insisted she needed the training. The habit. The process.

Because the day might come when he was sending books from somewhere other than Paris, despite his promises to her mother to keep an eye on her. Or when they would be too closely watched, listened to, to speak freely.

He left with casual farewells, and though Corinne suspected Liana had a dozen questions for her, the thought of airing any more secrets on the street outside a café where anyone could hear made her stomach churn against the coffee she'd drunk. So she invited her to spend the night after dinner on Saturday, promising that they'd laugh and squeal like they were thirteen, and then she hurried on her way.

A few errands at the university, two stops at grocers that yielded only a can of *pâté* and half of her monthly sugar ration, and Corinne was on the train again, bound for home. And if she found herself studying the pockets of the Nazis she passed, wondering which of them might have chocolate inside them, she blamed Oncle Georges for planting the notion.

She could almost, *almost* pretend that the day wouldn't end as poorly as it was bound to do.

Knowing she had the time—the professor's car was absent from the curb—she took care of the code work first, burned the poor book her uncle had given her, and stashed the message she'd have to encode again into the margins of a book to send to Maelie in the safest place she could think of—her own letter box in the entryway.

By the time the knock sounded on her door, she was draped over her favorite chair, *Quinzinzinzili* in hand again. She only dawdled a moment before opening the door and offering Professor Bauer a nod in place of a smile. "Professor."

"*Mademoiselle*." He sidled past her, and she couldn't help but grant that he acted like, well . . . a professor. As she closed the door, his eyes went straight to the shelves of books, to a few titles he must have noted on his previous visit. Then his gaze dropped to the novel on her chair, and a grin split his mouth, making him look a decade younger. "*Quinzinzinzili*! How far are you? Have you got to the part where—"

"No!" Yes, she shouted it. Because spoiling what came next in a book was surely an unpardonable sin. Jesus had overlooked naming it as such, but that was only because novels hadn't been invented yet, she was sure. "I'm only on chapter two—don't you dare say a thing."

He laughed, and if she squinted just right, she could almost pretend he was some other professor, wearing a gray suit, taking off his hat and setting it on the table. One of countless colleagues who had done just that, laughed just like that, in their living room over the last fifteen years.

She blinked away the image, focused on the swastika on his armband. And asked, "What does 'interview' mean?"

He spun to face her, his amusement morphing into question. "I assume you aren't asking for a definition."

"Abraham Cohen." She folded her arms over her chest, as if he were nothing but an unruly undergraduate. "You said you 'interviewed' him yesterday. What does that mean? An interrogation? Was he harmed?"

Bauer's face softened. Indecision flittered through his eyes. And he sighed. "He is well. I promise you. He asked me to assure you of that fact, actually. When I mentioned that we had his name because of the library, he said I ought to assure his neighbor that he is unharmed."

Her mouth dropped open at the audacity. Abraham had always had a mischievous streak, yes, but to ask one's interrogator to deliver a message to one's friend? Papa would have called it *cheeky* and laughed until he was red in the face.

Corinne let her arms fall to her sides. "And you . . . did?"

He shrugged. "He is not a criminal—not yet. His books have been seized, and he will not be allowed to publish anymore. But he is still a person. Such common courtesies cost me nothing and clearly mean much to him. And to you." He lifted a brow. "You are . . . close?"

Her lips quirked before she could stop them. "The men of the library . . . as you know, my mother was there a lot—for her research as she was writing her thesis."

"So she *is* a doctor?"

Corinne paused. Why would he have wondered about that? "No, actually—she never defended it. She fell ill, and then she reconsidered the paper and . . ." Why was she telling him all this? She waved a hand and moved to the shelf farthest from him. "She got distracted with teaching, basically. Her plans were to revise it during her sabbatical and resubmit when she returns from her holiday." Whenever *that* would be—and as if her travels were only a holiday. "But at any rate, she spent many hours at the library next door, largely because of its proximity. I went with her, because what else was I to do? And so the other regulars, the directors—they became family, in a way. Abraham is like an uncle to me."

He nodded and turned his back to her, moving whole rows of books out, then back—checking behind them, she realized. "Did you know that those men were smuggling banned books back into Germany?"

"What?" She'd been trying to mimic him, but

she'd clearly reached for too many books at once—they all went tumbling, an avalanche of winces.

The rhythmic *shick-thump, shick-thump* of his own investigation paused, and she could feel the burn of his gaze on her as she stooped to pick up her fallen tomes. "One of the rooms at the library—it had a few copies remaining, and one underway. Banned material, rebound under innocuous, approved titles. I found an address book too, of places in Germany where these mockingbirds were shipped."

Juste ciel. Why hadn't they removed all such evidence?

Because they were rushed and harried and couldn't see to every detail, and too afraid of implicating her by association to let her help, that was why.

She stood again and slid the books back into their places. "I imagine whatever Ministry you work for will be glad for that information. Though . . . you do have to admit, don't you? It's rather clever." She chanced a quick glance over her shoulder.

Because even if he knew that, he'd never know she'd been the one to inspire the charade, when Maman had caught her reading a novel in the library one night, disguised behind the textbook she *ought* to have been studying. The others had all laughed.

And then grown sober. And then schemed.

Bauer didn't look away from his work. *Shick-thump. Shick-thump.* "I rather think the Ministry will be furious that such an operation went on for years and was only discovered after it had already, by necessity, halted." He'd already gone through the top two shelves of that first case. To better reach the third, he stepped back, bumping into one of the twin sofas. *Shick* . . . pause. "What have we here?"

Nothing that could possibly incriminate her—she wasn't fool enough to hide anything on her bookshelves when she knew he'd be coming to investigate them.

But the soft smile that overtook his mouth made her wonder what it *was* and had her all but running around the furniture to see.

"Oh—please no. That's just one of my horrid attempts at art." What was that old sketch even doing there? It was ancient, unskilled . . . and when she reached for it, he held it up, away, out of her range.

"I'm *looking* at this, thank you." He continued to do so, tilting his head back to continue studying the portrait.

Well, a candid portrait anyway. Of Maman, tucked into Papa's side on one of those very sofas. She vaguely remembered the day—one of their first here in this flat, after Papa had found it for them. After they'd moved everything they owned from the cottage in Pozières to this neighborhood in the City of Lights that felt so foreign, so strange, so hostile.

The sketch provided a poor imitation—though a hint, she granted—of the love between her parents. The way they curled into each other, both reading from the same book. Sometimes they would sit far too long on one page, neither wanting to move to flip it, each assuming the other hadn't finished yet.

What her drawing made no attempt to capture was the exhaustion back in Papa's eyes. The weakness once more in his limbs.

He'd never been *healthy* again, after she tripped over him in the mud and he sent her shrieking for her mother when he peeled his eyes open. He'd been better. For months at a time, he'd been good enough. Then he'd catch a cold or an ague and they'd wonder if this would be the one that took him, that overwhelmed his fragile lungs.

He'd called himself a shadow of the man he'd used to be. He'd joked that his injuries and illness had made him more like his brother, only he couldn't ever tell his brother so. For Remmy's own good, he said. Because he was the better heir to their father, the better man, the one who deserved to carry their name forward.

She couldn't imagine that, couldn't imagine a better man. She'd loved the shadows, because he claimed to be one. Loved the darkness, because he said it soothed him, to see the stars dancing over France just as they had over England, only he'd never paused to look up at them back then. She'd loved books, because they were the one thing he had the strength to do with her through long, cold winters when he could never seem to get warm enough.

"Your parents?" Bauer asked, voice as soft as the memory.

She nodded, though he wasn't looking at her to see it. "Right after we moved here. It was . . ." Was there any harm in saying it? None that she could see. "It was our last month together. We didn't know it then—but Papa died right after we moved to the city. As if, once he'd made a way for our dreams, he thought we didn't need him anymore."

Ciel—she hadn't meant to say it like that, so . . . truthfully. She'd meant to give facts, not feelings.

Bauer lowered the sketch, but he didn't hand it to her. No, he moved over to the row of photographs in their simple wooden frames atop the low shelves under the window, and he set it there against one. Among the faded, posed wedding photo, the one of her at her confirmation, the one of Oncle Georges and Tante Minette, taken the summer before she died in childbirth, along with their son.

So much sorrow, framed and frozen on that

shelf. So much love. So many reminders that life was never one or the other, but always both, twisted together like ribbons on a maypole. And now she was the only one here to look at them, and who knew if Maman would ever even make it home again?

When something tickled her cheek, she reached up, swiped, and jolted when she realized they were tears, not a stray lash or an escaped curl.

Bauer still didn't look at her. Perhaps he was too busy studying the photographs, or perhaps he was granting her a moment to collect herself. "My parents are gone too," he said softly. "Together—as I know they would have wanted to go—in an auto accident. A year ago. They would have wanted it that way, but I . . . I didn't. Not both, at once. Not then—as if there's ever a good time to lose the people we love best, *nein*?"

One more swipe of her cheeks, a sniff, and she pretended to be under control. "No, there isn't." She let silence stretch for a second, then asked what she would have had he been any other professor. Because just now, he was acting like one, rather than like himself. "Have you other family waiting for you? In Germany?"

He shook his head, back going stiff. "My brother didn't make it to adulthood. Grandparents, uncle—all gone. I had no cousins, no other siblings."

She shouldn't ask. But he wasn't a *young*

man, nor was he unattractive, so it seemed like a reasonable question. "Wife? Children?"

"*Nein.*" He faced her then, his smile small and tight, like any other professor's would be when the conversation was all the family they no longer had. "No one waits for me in Germany aside from a few colleagues and friends who have long ago given up on me providing good company anyway."

Like any other professor. It shouldn't make her smile go real. Shouldn't . . . but did. "Books? I imagine they miss you."

His smile went real too. "You have me there. I daresay my collection mourns my absence day and night." He motioned toward the novel on her chair. "Perhaps when you've finished . . . if it's a day you don't hate me for my uniform . . . you could tell me your thoughts. I'm afraid Kraus isn't much of a reader."

A laugh slipped out, and though she tried to smother it, it was too late. His eyes were already twinkling, his shoulders already relaxed. Letting her fingers fall from her lips again, she shook her head against the smile. "We'll see."

She'd visit Abraham first, see what he had to say about his "interviewer." If he'd treated her friend with respect, with kindness, then perhaps she'd grant him her opinions on the book.

If not, then she'd chuck it at his head when he walked by. Either way, a cause to smile.

EIGHT

26 July 1940

Christian had sent Kraus home, claiming that he meant to spend the evening at the library and that Ackermann had invited him out for dinner again with other officers. It wasn't a lie, exactly. He *did* intend to spend the evening here, among the banned books, and Ackermann *had* issued the invitation.

He did *not* intend to meet his superior for another meal. Not yet. He couldn't stomach another evening of the kind of talk those men preferred, of watching them ogle every woman who walked by, of listening to them muse as to what each one would look like without the dress or the blouse or the skirt.

Never in his life had he so missed the university world. He missed *conversations,* the kind where the talk wasn't just gossip about people or talk of the news, but about *ideas*. The kind that he left thinking about things in a way he never had before, the kind that stretched his mind, stretched his soul.

Here, at least, surrounded by books written by so many friends or acquaintances or literary heroes even if he'd never met them, he felt a bit of home. Once Kraus had finally been convinced to leave, he'd moved his things into the periodicals room, the one with the poster of the burning Reichstag. He'd been staring at it for several long minutes already. Remembering. Remembering the way his father's lips had pressed together with each new report that came in, remembering the worry in his mother's eyes.

He remembered the fear in his own gut when he heard that the Nazi Party had not only blamed the fire on their political opponents, but had used it as an excuse to arrest all those adversaries—anyone belonging to the old regime. Anyone who claimed to be—or was suspected of being—communist. Anyone, *anyone* in the government that wasn't part of the Nazi Party.

It had only been seven years ago—yet now people said "the Party" like it was the only one. Like any other political persuasion, any other beliefs were unthinkable.

They were, in a way. Because those other thoughts had been rooted out. Banned. Burned. When a people stopped entertaining opposing ideas, when they condemned the different as evil, then it was a short step from closed-minded to violently oppressive.

He shoved to his feet and strode out of the room, away from the poster of flames and accusations. First he simply meandered among the unruly stacks, pulling a few favorites down long enough to flip through their familiar pages, soak in their familiar words. To flip to the pocket glued to the back and see who else had read them.

The names of the regular patrons had grown familiar over the last two months. In part, yes, because one of his jobs had been to visit each one, to confiscate any forbidden books from their private libraries or at least to stamp them with a red *V*, to warn any Jews or communists that they would have to register—all with Kraus looking on over his shoulder, watching.

But the familiarity was more from *this*. From seeing their names not only in a record book or in the lobby of a building, but in the books they'd selected. Had they enjoyed this book? That one? Had they peeled back the layers of this satire or that poem? Had they gotten lost in the adventures of the novels? Argued with the philosophy in the treatises?

He wished he could ask them, could risk letting them all know that he was more one of them than of his "own." He wished he could knock on Abraham's door not as an officer but as a friend and slip inside for one of the talks they'd had in years past. Wished he could find Earnst, wherever he was, and see how his latest manuscript was shaping up. Wished that the next time he called at Josef's flat to see if he were back, the door would swing wide and . . .

No. No, he didn't want Josef to be in Paris. *Couldn't* want it. That was too selfish, too reckless. He prayed instead that the man who'd always been like a second father to him had gone to England, America, somewhere else.

He'd wandered back to the circulation desk, his gaze latched unseeing before him. Only when he blinked did he realize he was staring at the three books Corinne Bastien had given him nearly two weeks ago—those three strange books.

He hadn't opened them again, not with Kraus always present, always asking why he reacted to things as he did. Not knowing well that his aide, his supposed helper, gave reports of Christian's every action, just as Ackermann did.

His old colleagues, that blessed circle of scholars, were as lost to him now, here, as they'd been the last seven years. The ones that had remained in Germany were still there, out of reach.

But the library's neighbor had surely had time to finish reading that novel by now—and he *had* "threatened" to drop by again this week to see if any more books had turned up, to search somewhere other than the shelves.

Maybe she would talk to him, *converse* with him about something other than the news, the war, the work he was trying so hard to do as God would want him to do it instead of how Goebbels expected it to be done.

Before he could give it enough thought to talk himself out of it, he let himself out, the door still locked behind him, and swung through the gate, up the steps next to it, and into the lobby of her building. He'd left his jacket in the library, but it was too hot to care.

Only after he'd knocked on her door did he let the doubts creep in.

She likely wouldn't open it. Or if she did, she'd either try to turn him away with an insistence that the rest of her mother's books weren't there, or she'd let him in with that guarded, resentful look in her eyes.

The look that had faded into something else last time, as they searched the shelves. As they'd spoken like two human beings instead of occupier and dissident—which she most decidedly *was*.

Of course she was. She *should* be. No French citizen should subscribe to Nazi philosophy. He couldn't tell her he approved, of course, but he could fail to question her about the oddities in the books she'd handed him. He could resist pointing out that *no* book he'd pulled from the shelves next door had *her* name in them, despite all her talk of spending her evenings there with her mother. With Abraham, who clearly knew her well. With . . . the others? Earnst? Josef?

Did she know them? Did she love them, like she did Abraham? Had they ever mentioned him to her?

Clearly not, or she wouldn't have met him with such hostility—or at least not without challenging him on what would look like a betrayal. No, perhaps they'd mentioned the son of their good friend, perhaps they'd even referred to him as "little Chris" as they'd always done, but—

The door swung open. And while she *did* bar the opening, it was by leaning into the frame, arms crossed over her chest, and amusement—amusement!—on her face. "You are relentless, aren't you?"

He held up a finger. "It occurred to me—if your mother really *did* consider taking the books with her, she could well have decided against it when she tried to lift the luggage. Could she not have put them away somewhere in her room, then? Have you checked her armoire? Bedside table? Under the bed?"

Corinne rolled her eyes, but she also stepped back and motioned him in. "*I* think you're just starved for intelligent conversation."

"*Ciel*, yes." He chuckled with relief at her acknowledging it as he stepped inside. "If I thought I could get away with it, I'd enroll in a class at the Sorbonne just to hear talk of something other than this infernal war and the *glorious rebirth of the master race.*"

Not exactly a sentiment a Nazi officer should have expressed. Aloud. To a supposed enemy. But it was no secret that he wasn't a normal officer. "Or even better, I could offer to teach something."

Perhaps her laughter was only a snort, but he'd heard a real one, last time. Still remembered the music of it. "And what would you teach, Professor? German history? Aryan mythology?"

He winced. "Have you read any of that nonsense? It's as outlandish as the Greeks' tales of golden fleeces and minotaurs, yet it's being taught as fact." Another thing he shouldn't have said.

The lift of her mouth said she knew it. "Should I report you for speaking such blasphemy?"

"You could try, but given your affiliations . . ." He motioned in the general direction of the library. And grinned. "Did you finish *Quinzinzinzili* yet?"

They searched her mother's room as they talked about the novel, and it wasn't just the photograph on the bedside table of her parents in wedding attire with a young Corinne grinning happily up at the camera—all in styles straight from the era of the World War—that made him think she wasn't, in fact, as young as he'd first assumed her to be. It was the fact that she didn't talk like an undergraduate. She spoke like someone who had been studying, debating literature for far longer than a few years.

It was impolite, of course, to ask a woman her age. But he liked the thought that she wasn't twenty. More than he should. Liked the thought that maybe they were more peers than he'd first thought.

Dangerous territory. Unfamiliar territory. He hadn't longed for the company of a woman in years.

And he had no business doing so now, despite that she was the only one in Paris he felt like he could talk to right now. He shouldn't. Perhaps they had mutual friends, perhaps they shared interests, but she couldn't know that—about the friends. She couldn't know the truth. It would put at risk everything that mattered most.

He fished under the bedside table, fingers skimming over dust and a hairpin and then stopping when they brushed up against something hard. Clothbound. Paper. A book, without question. He got a hold on it and pulled it out, lips turning up when he saw the title. Full smile breaking free when the library card was present in the back. "There, see? I'm brilliant."

She laughed again and sat on the small chair stuffed into the corner. "And my mother is an absolute slob."

He didn't flip through it, afraid to find more eraser leavings that he'd just have to pretend he hadn't seen. Because she didn't seem exactly surprised that he'd found it there. And there had been swaths of clean floor in front of it before he'd disturbed the dust by pulling it out. "Only fourteen more. At the pace of one a week, we'll have discovered them all by the time the leaves turn."

She rolled her eyes. "I'll be too busy with classes to do much searching otherwise, so fine. Do your weekly search."

Did he wonder where it had actually come from? Why she'd hidden it for him to find? Of course he did. But he didn't want the answers. They were bound to be things he ought to report but wouldn't.

He settled for standing, stretching out the kink in his back. "*Aua*. I'm out of the practice of crawling about on the floor, it seems."

The pang traveled straight from his lumbar to his heart. How had that happened? A year ago, he had spent countless hours sitting cross-legged in front of the fireplace or—

Nein. Not thoughts he could afford to think. Not now. Not ever.

He turned to her instead, giving her a smile that would broadcast he was clearly fishing for information as he asked, "So what classes will keep you busy? Are they . . . graduate level? What degree are you pursuing?"

He was quickly coming to like that challenging glint in her eyes. "*Mais non*, Professor. You didn't answer my question about what *you* teach, so don't think I'll tell you anything about my own pursuits."

"I am an open book," he said, arms spread wide. It was true, once. Now . . . now he was more like those re-covered ones the library had been producing before the invasion. The inside and the out represented two very different things. "I teach literature, when I'm not in the library."

He expected that glint in her eyes to turn to a sparkle. He expected her face to light up, given her clear love of both things. Instead, her face shuttered like windows behind blackout curtains. "A professor of literature, sent to Paris to tell us what's *verboten*. I imagine you were one of the ones called on, then, to advise Goebbels on his list of books to ban? To *burn?*"

The desire to let her see the truth of him blazed so fierce, so strong, that he knew letting it burn free would leave him in ashes.

He bit it back. Doused the yearning with a reminder of a truth far deeper than his own thoughts, his own beliefs, his own philosophy—the truth that if he trusted anyone, *anyone* else with his secrets, it could mean death for the only person left in the world who really mattered.

How fortunate that he had so many years of practice at swallowing back the truth. At reciting the Party line.

He selected the smile he gave his colleagues when someone from the Ministry hovered nearby. "You act as though Germany is the first country to ever burn books it didn't like."

A spark entered her eyes now, but not the one he'd hoped for before. No, it felt more like one of the sparks of his own denial had drifted to her and set alight the dry kindling of her spirit. "This is a history you've learned well, I suppose? So you can teach it to your students? Tell me, Professor. Tell me why burning books is so acceptable."

Her mother's room felt too small, too close, too personal for words like these. He pivoted toward the door, knowing well she'd follow. The walls of books welcomed him, promising him forgiveness for whatever he would say. Because they knew. They knew the truth.

"It has always been a means for victors to control the cultures they defeat, for one thing. The burning of the Library of Alexandria, for instance—"

An incredulous puff of laughter. "Really? I have never in my life heard an intellectual tout that act of horror as a good thing."

Because it had been a massacre—not of people, but of knowledge. Of the wealth of it. The preservation of it.

He set the dusty book on an end table. "The Church has banned and burned innumerable works through the years. Books that teach heresies or pagan theology—there's even an account of it in Acts—"

"That is *hardly* the same—"

"More modern examples, then?" He spun to face her, now that he was certain his own false-title-and-cover were glued firmly in place.

"Perhaps one from your own beloved city? In 1242, twenty-four cartloads of Jewish writings were burned here in Paris. Pascal's *Lettres* were burned in the sixteen hundreds for being too free with the secular authorities."

Her jaw clenched tight.

His lifted. Just a professor, lecturing a wayward student. That was all. "Charles I of England declared the burning of books to be a way of suppressing opposition. John Milton, whose *Areopagitica* is so often quoted as being the ultimate denouncement of censorship, himself proclaimed that only *good* books ought to be above such treatment and that if a book *proved a monster, who denies but that it was justly burnt or sunk into the sea.*"

Her arms crossed. "Should I be taking notes, Professor?"

"Who decides what literature is 'good,' Corinne? Who decides what is to be censored, what is to be kept from our children, our impressionable, our easily swayed? The Church? The government?"

"The people!"

He'd known she'd say it that way—because that was the answer that fit the pattern. His smile felt sadder than he meant it to. He gestured out her darkened window, to the west, to Berlin. "I was at the first book burning in 1933. Do you know who led it? It wasn't Goebbels, wasn't

Hitler—they just showed up to cheer it on. It was the *students*. It was the *people*. They chose. They brought the books, they laughed as they dumped them on the pyres. They *rejoiced* at the thought of getting rid of the words they didn't want to have to consider anymore, the ideas that they said were harmful."

The people could be wrong. The people could get so caught up in their own ideology that they forgot that the love of wisdom wasn't about being *right*.

She trembled, but he wasn't fool enough to think it was from intimidation. She was furious. "Ideas cannot be *burned*. They cannot be destroyed just because a few copies of the books they're printed in are."

"It was never about the destruction." Where her tone had been hot, a bit too loud, his was soft. Quiet. "It was about the statement. That's all it's ever about. The people—the ones you say have the right to make such decisions—proclaiming that decision for the world to see. Goebbels has no impossible dreams of destroying every copy of the books they've banned. If he did, we wouldn't be issued all those stamps with the *V* for *verboten*. The idea is simply to tell the world, 'These ideas are bad. These ideas are useless. These authors are your inferior, so don't listen to them.' "

"But they're not!" Her voice shook now, too,

the fire raging in her eyes, a hand slicing toward the book he'd set down.

"Who decides?" he asked again, quietly. A shake of his head did nothing to dislodge the sorrow his own words lit in his soul. "If it's truly the people, then you have no right to your anger. But I think what you meant to say was 'each person.' You want the right to decide for yourself. As I do. As do we all."

Her chest rose as she sucked in a long breath, fell again as it heaved out. The fire died down as she no doubt retraced the conversation in her mind, realized how he'd led her straight into the answer that fit the pattern, rather than the one she really wanted. "That *is* what I meant."

"I know." He reached again for the book, not opening it or looking at it. Just holding it at his side to show her he'd leave soon. "And perhaps that's a right that we have in nature—the right to make our own choices. But it's one we give up, at least in part, when we form societies, when we give governments power, when we agree to abide by the laws those governments set out in return for their defense and administration."

Her lips twitched, though not in a smile. "A rather broad paraphrase of Rousseau, though your point is clear. But I did not agree to your government. I did not bind myself to that social contract."

"But *your* government did. If A equals B and

B equals C . . ." He shrugged and shifted toward the door. Paused. "In Germany, it was the people who willingly gave up that right. Who *asked* for censorship, who led the protests demanding it. If you're going to rail against injustice, then at least know what deserves your ire. Not that a few copies of books were burned—but that the people danced around the pyre."

He let himself out, not pausing until he was back in the safety of the library.

He should have gone to dinner with the officers. Perhaps he'd have had to play the same role, but at least then it wouldn't have been to deceive someone he wished were a friend.

NINE

12 August 1940

Corinne should have left five minutes ago, but how could she when she didn't know when she'd get to keep such company again? Not only had Abraham's wife, Mathilda, answered the door when she knocked this time and greeted her with a robust hug and assurance that her husband was home, but Alfred Kantorowicz was there too—Corinne hadn't even realized the director was back in Paris.

What she'd meant to be a half-hour visit to get Abraham's story of his interview—"It was just that, *ma petite*, I assure you! The *sonderführer* was not only polite, he was quick to dismiss me"—had stretched to an hour-long visit with two of the men who had encouraged her in her education and her dreams.

"I walked by the place this morning," Kantorowicz admitted on a sigh, eyes latched on to one of the books Corinne had brought for Abraham—from her own collection and approved by any Nazi censors who stopped by for an inspection. "Even from the street, I could see the disarray we left it all in. I wonder . . . I wonder if it could have been different. If, as we so blithely proclaimed at the start, we *could* have taken the library back to Germany, had we done things differently."

"Alfred," Abraham chided, low and long. "It was bigger than our choices. Bigger than our wants."

"But if I hadn't gone off to join the war in Spain—if we'd written more about books in our newsletter and less about politics . . . perhaps, if we'd been more like the other libraries and not just a place for shouting out our anti-Nazi ideals . . ."

Corinne shifted on her chair and glanced at her watch. If she didn't leave in the next five minutes, she'd be late for class. But the nostalgia in the man's voice had pulled her in. Made her remember those early years of the Deutsche Freiheitsbibliothek, when the shelves had been well-ordered, when the staff were all knowledgeable and eager to gather research sources for inquiring minds, when there was never any confusion about who had checked out what.

Maybe he was right. Maybe, if they'd kept on that way, it would have been too much of a neighborhood institution to be handed over so blithely to the Nazis.

But it had been an institution only for this limited circle—the German exiles still writing and publishing. Over the years, the public stopped coming to their grand events to celebrate the release of new books. Patrons had withdrawn their support. News coverage had entirely ceased.

And then the directors themselves got distracted, especially by the Spanish Civil War. The newsletter had stopped. Staff had been dismissed. Chaos had crept in, slowly and steadily, and no matter how Corinne and Maman tried to mitigate it, the point always remained that it wasn't *theirs*. They were just neighbors. New friends. They didn't belong, not like these men.

And the proof of it ticked its reminder against her wrist. She still had a job to get to. Work to be done. She stood, knowing her smile was small and sad. "I'd better hurry. Do you know if anyone else is back in Paris?"

Mathilda shot her a warning glance as she stood from her armchair to bid her farewell. "You need to stay away from all of us, *ma petite*. If the Nazis catch you fraternizing with a bunch of stodgy old dissidents . . ."

She gave the two men her cheekiest, most innocent grin. "They're *dissidents?* Why, I had no idea! I thought those nice old men were just writers. Of course, I couldn't read a word they wrote, it was all in German . . . but they kept chocolates on hand for me." She widened her eyes, made her full lips pout. "I haven't had chocolate in *ages*."

Beside the door, Abraham laughed. "You'll

have the gray-shirts shoving their rations at you if you give that performance."

She sent him a wink, hugged Mathilda tight, and then kissed each of the men on the cheek. They hadn't answered her question about their friends—but that was all right. She'd just keep checking each of their flats, one a day, like she'd been doing all of July. This was the first she'd actually caught Abraham and his wife at home, but it hadn't been for lack of trying.

Luckily, she timed the Métro just right, and then it was only a matter of darting across campus toward the linguistics building. She spotted Liana and a few of her friends in front of the library and waved a hello. No doubt her all-but-run cautioned them against hailing her.

The cool of the building welcomed her out of the August heat, and she smiled to hear the chatter of students in the corridors—a sure sign that she wasn't late quite yet. She wove her way through a few knots of them, glancing down at her watch as she turned toward her door.

She plowed straight into something. No, some-*one*, which she realized only when hands gripped her elbows. "*Pardonnez-moi!*" she screeched even as she reeled back a step.

Because it was gray wool before her eyes. Too familiar these days. Too dreaded. Not just the shirt of the *soldaten* who guarded the constantly moving checkpoints, but the tailored jacket of an officer.

Her stomach knotted as she followed the tie before her eyes up to a chin—an unfamiliar chin, topped by smiling blue eyes in a face that couldn't be a day over twenty-five. "Careful," the man said in German.

Given the sign on the door proclaiming this a class in *Deutsch* literature, he no doubt expected her to understand. So she forced a smile and backed up a step. The knot eased just a bit when she realized it wasn't Christian Bauer—the officer she saw most often. She didn't care to examine whether the ease was from relief or regret. "I apologize," she returned in the German that, according to the men she'd just left, held a flawless upper-class-Berlin accent. "I should know better than to barrel blindly through a door."

He released her elbows and stepped to the side, sweeping out a hand to welcome her in, as if this were *his* classroom.

The knot cinched newly tight in her stomach. Was it? Had the Nazis taken over this class? Was there a note waiting in her box informing her of it?

"No harm done," the man said. He was still smiling as he held out a hand. "Karl Gustaf—newly minted officer in the Ministry of Education." He looked proud as he showed off his insignia. "Just arrived in Paris yesterday."

Paris was full of newly arrived soldiers. Apparently Hitler had promised a Parisian holiday to all his soldiers at some point during their enlistment, and the carousel of them had already begun. She smiled, as if it weren't exhausting to be constantly stopped by smooth-cheeked boys in uniform asking for directions to the Eiffel Tower or Notre Dame. "I hope you're enjoying our fair city."

"It's beautiful! I think I spent most of the day yesterday walking around with my jaw hanging open as I tried to take it in." His chuckle didn't seem to hold any guile. "But to business today, of course. The Ministry has me sitting in on classes here and there, to observe what's being taught. Obviously this one is top of the list."

Sitting in on—not taking over. Good. Good. And honestly, she'd been expecting someone to observe them eventually. Especially, as he said, the German-language courses. They would want to be sure the untrustworthy Parisians were accurately portraying the Master Race and its tongue, after all.

From outside, the bell in the tower tolled the hour. Students pushed their way inside the classroom, sending Corinne back another step. She offered a polite smile to their guest. "Well, I hope you enjoy the lesson."

His smile went a bit tighter. "We'll see. I have

always doubted that any non-German could adequately teach our language or literature."

Of all the insufferable . . .

Then the grin again. "You didn't tell me your name."

He'd learn it soon enough. She gave him a too-innocent smile and gripped her bag. "Doctor Corinne Bastien—your professor for the day, it seems." Not giving him the chance to recover from his gape, she strode for her desk at the front of the room.

And nearly groaned when another new male face took a seat in the front row, eyes latched on to her in a way she knew too well. "Good morning," he said. "Graduate assistant? I thought the full professor taught this class. Is he sick?" A smirk. "Lucky us."

She cleared her throat and moved her gaze to one of the only other men in the class. "Mr. Boucher?"

Boucher was trying not to laugh. "Dr. Bastien has two doctorates, in linguistics and philosophy. She has been on staff at the Sorbonne for five years, since she defended her second thesis and graduated magna cum laude. And she is at *least* ten years older than you, Didier, so don't get any ideas."

"I don't really care for the emphasis on that *at least*," she said with an amused smile, "but *danke, monsieur*. Now. For those of you just

180

joining us, we have been discussing Goethe's *Faust: Part One*. I believe we left off yesterday arguing whether a translation of his verse ought to attempt to rhyme in French as it does in German, thereby preserving the art and cadence, or if accuracy of translation is the better choice. Mademoiselle Grandier, I believe you'd been about to weigh in yesterday?"

As the class progressed—eventually moving to actual translations and thereby giving her ample opportunity to provide lessons on the finer points of German thought and idiomatic usage—she made it a point not to glance at the Nazi who had taken a seat in the uppermost row, despite scads of empty desks on lower levels.

What he thinks of my teaching is none of my business, she wanted to think. *He could take my job,* she couldn't help but think. Still, what could she do but what she always did? She taught this class like she did her ones on Greek philosophy or advanced English—without any agenda but sharing her love of the subjects, the languages, the thoughts that had shaped Western society.

But that was all Abraham had ever wanted to do too, or any of the others. And she didn't have the savings those men had brought with them from Germany. All the money Papa had accepted from his brother had been for their educations, hers and Maman's. He *could* have accepted more, but none of them had wanted it. Even that much had been a gift they'd never dreamed of.

If their new overlords decided only a German-born professor could teach this class, would the university simply let her offer a different one in its place? Or would Karl Gustaf have her sacked altogether?

He was gone by the time the class ended and she finally granted herself permission to glance to the back row. A good sign or a bad? Try as she might to tell herself she didn't have time to worry over it, the coffee she'd sipped at Abraham's still churned in her stomach.

"Ça va?" Madeline Grandier asked in a whisper as Corinne trailed her toward the door. She glanced up at the empty back row.

Corinne pasted on a smile. "Ça va, Madeline. Such things are to be expected these days."

The girl screwed up her face. "They shouldn't be." She glanced around, leaned closer. "Some of us are meeting sometimes—to . . . read poetry."

Corinne held up a hand. "Not here," she murmured, quietly enough that even she barely heard her own words above the talk of the other students.

A good decision—Gustaf was waiting in the corridor, right outside the door. Still smiling, but she wasn't willing to trust such a thing, especially as he halted her with a brusque, "A moment, Doctor," and sent Madeline on her way with a shooing motion.

Arrogant, insufferable prig.

She smiled back. "Of course. I hope you found the class satisfactory."

"Satisfactory?" Was his laugh one of genuine humor, or was he mocking her? She honestly couldn't tell, not until he took her hand and pulled it through the crook of his elbow. No, not even then. Not until he said, "You must be German, at least in part. You speak like one, *think* like one. Your mother, perhaps? Or a grandparent?" His gaze moved to her hair, her eyes.

Gauging her Aryan purity, she would wager. Trying to guess how far from those supposed-gods her lineage had fallen. "Pure French, actually. Though I have been blessed to have several German tutors throughout the years." She wanted to tell him their names, just to see the look on his face.

She wouldn't, of course. That would be tantamount to shooting herself in the foot.

His hand still lingered on hers, fingers tightening now. "I have rarely heard professors debate translation so eloquently—much less a female. I am truly impressed, Doctor. I never expected to see a woman thriving in captivity quite this way."

Her feet jerked her to a halt, giving him little choice but to stop with her. "Did you say *captivity?*" She must have misheard. Or he'd misspoken. Or her German vocabulary needed some brushing up after all.

He motioned toward the building—or perhaps beyond it. "These walls, the city—grand as they are, it isn't what mankind was meant for. We're meant to run free in the countryside, to reacquaint ourselves with nature. Breathe fresh air. Don't you agree?"

She let him tug her forward again, but she wasn't about to fall into the verbal trap of yet another German officer. "I certainly won't argue against fresh air's desirability. Though I could quote several philosophers who would argue that a city is a very natural development of mankind and his need for community."

"To an extent, of course. Villages, towns, even cities of the size of the ancients'. But city life drains us. According to the latest statistics, city dwellers are less likely to marry, to procreate. And when they do, they produce fewer offspring. How are we to proliferate the master race under those conditions?" He shook his head. "No, Hitler's 'Back to the Country' campaign has the right idea. In a small rural village, you'd have had no trouble finding a husband by now, *fraulein*, to give you the family you must want."

She was *fraulein* again now, was she? No longer *doctor?* She ripped her hand out from under his, pulled it away from his arm. "Actually, Herr Gustaf, I could have had my pick of husbands ten times over—here *or* in the village I was born in—had that been my desire. But no rural village could give me the education I craved."

His smile now was patronizing. Condescending. "And it is important for a woman to be well-spoken, well taught. But women should not be constrained by concerns of politics or academics. You would indeed make a fine helpmeet for—"

"I have another class." She stepped away, offered a tight smile. "Thank you for your encouragement. I hope you enjoy your time in Paris."

She hoped he ate bad cheese and spent three days in the toilet, but *that* thought she kept to herself as she pivoted and stomped away.

Her next class wasn't, in fact, until after lunch, but after checking to be sure he hadn't followed her, Corinne let herself into her tiny cupboard of an office and indulged in a growl. Punctuating it by tossing her attaché case onto her chair helped dispel some of the frustration.

She had heard, of course, of Germany's "Back to Nature" campaign. She knew the prevailing Nazi sentiments on family, children, and a woman's "proper" role—in the home, nowhere else. She had butted up against plenty of men with similar opinions over the years, well before the Germans invaded.

But she'd won her place. Fought for it and secured it, by her own merits. She was one of only a few female professors, it was true, but she'd earned the respect of her colleagues, just as Maman had done.

At the burning in her eyes, she squeezed them shut. This was why she didn't even tell people that she wasn't just a student, she was a professor. They were willing, for whatever reason, to accept it of Maman—a widow, a mother. But for a young woman to pursue education above a husband? A profession above children?

It wasn't that she didn't *want* those things—but she wanted them *too,* not instead of. And thus far, she'd found no one to make her heart react like Maman's had to Papa. No man who would give up everything to give her her dreams.

A knock sounded on the door behind her. "Corinne? Are you in there?"

Liana. Corinne blinked the moisture from her eyes and opened the door for her friend.

Liana stood there with brows drawn. "I saw a Nazi striding from your building, and heard Madeline say something about one auditing your class. Are you all right?"

"I . . . don't know." It felt like defeat to admit it, but who else could she be honest with? She perched on the edge of her desk. "He liked the class. And then launched into how I should be some man's articulate wife, not *confined* by the *restrictions* of academia . . ."

Liana grimaced. "Same old rot we always hear, isn't it?"

"But this rot could get me sacked. What if women are dismissed like foreigners have been,

Liana?" Her friend already knew that she was alone, more or less, in Paris. Oncle Georges traveled too much, kept few resources to his name. "I have little savings. I could lose the flat. And then what? Where would I go?"

"To our house, of course." Liana perched beside her, bumping their shoulders together. "Or if you're feeling adventurous, you could poach some grand apartment that the aristocrats left behind when they fled."

Leave it to Liana to make her laugh. She thought, for just a moment, of Maman. Did she have a flat in London to herself? Or had she accepted an invitation from one of the in-laws who had been so surprised to learn she existed, that Papa had lived for years in France without telling them? Was she worrying, from wherever she was staying, about Corinne, and whether she'd be able to keep the place they'd called home for half her life?

Yes. Of course she was worrying about that. She was her mother. Just as worry for her kept Corinne up some nights.

It wasn't supposed to be this way. They weren't supposed to be apart so long. Corinne had never agreed to being alone for the indefinite future, with only her uncle occasionally dropping by, with all her old friends fled, with so many empty, hollow hours to fill with nothing but fretting and mounting hunger.

Then she turned her attention back to her friend. "I should probably say I can't impose upon a family I've known so short a time, but . . ."

Liana laughed this time. "But after Maman has made you help with the dishes, you cannot claim to be anything but family. Come." She took hold of Corinne's wrist and pulled her toward the door. "You don't have another class until two, do you? Let's have lunch at your flat, and we can rant in peace about overbearing men—German *and* French."

Michel, it seemed, had a few opinions that Liana didn't much care for either, and she made no secret of it as they walked to Corinne's flat. It felt blessedly ordinary, complaining about one's beau, about the social norms that they wanted to embrace yet bucked against.

"Why?" Liana demanded as they rounded the final corner onto Boulevard Arago. "Why can a woman not both pursue a vocation in the world *and* raise a family? Why are men the only ones who do not have to decide?"

Papa had been willing to grant Maman both. More, he'd helped her reach for them. Surely there were other men like him in the world. "Michel didn't actually say you couldn't write novels while you raise a family, did he?"

Her friend huffed. "He said I wouldn't have *time* to. That the desire to pen my thoughts would fade when I had a little one to tell stories to instead. And *then?*" She leaned close, eyes blazing, voice low. "Then he tried to tell me that *poetry* wasn't for females either. That we ought to leave it all to the men."

Corinne's lips parted in surprise. When General de Gaulle had called for every French citizen to hold fast, to keep fighting, to never surrender, he had called them *all* out—not just the men. She herself hadn't gone to any of the meetings—it would have felt too strange, being there with her students—but Liana had told her in whispers of the three they'd held. "You're not the only woman there, are you?"

A puff of breath. "No. But there are only five of us, out of twenty. Still, we can *help*. We can spread pamphlets like anyone else."

"Yes." But the word came out slowly as her gaze fell on the German auto parked in front of the library. Not so long ago, very different German men had been in that building. Using words, tracts, pamphlets, books to try to fight a war ... but there had been other voices too, voices that grew louder and more frequent as the years dragged by and words achieved little appreciable change. Voices that called for violence. Those voices were more likely to be heard now, when violence had already met them. She pulled Liana to a halt well away from listening German ears. "But what if they begin passing out bombs instead? Weapons? Will you still want to take part?"

The pretty bold slashes of Liana's brows drew into a *V. V* for victory. *V* for *verboten*. "It won't come to that."

"Won't it?" The gray-shirts patrolling Paris's streets certainly weren't enforcing Nazi rule with only posters and propaganda. They had pistols. Rifles. Bayonets. How long would it really take for fiery young men like Michel to decide they'd have to meet like with like?

Instead of it giving her pause, the question seemed to steel whatever resolve Liana had formed. She lifted her chin, cocked her head, and looked toward the library.

No—toward the two Nazis stepping out its door.

"Perhaps you're right, Corinne. Perhaps that's not my way—but there are other ways to help. Get information, perhaps?" When the men noticed them, Liana sent them a too-warm, too-inviting smile and added a flirtatious little wave.

Corinne gripped her elbow and pulled her arm back down. "Are you mad?" she hissed. "You know what the Parisiennes who fraternize with Nazis are being called! Your father will—"

"You know what?" Liana pulled her arm free and sent her a smirk. "You think too much."

Now *that* was a familiar accusation. And much as she'd like to huff over hearing it again from a girl ten years her junior, she couldn't spare the time. Liana was already sashaying toward Kraus and Bauer, putting all the sway into her hips that Corinne had taken from her own when the officers in the restaurant had been watching.

She had little choice but to scurry after her. "Liana!"

Kraus smiled, though it was guarded as he looked between Corinne and the pretty brunette —no doubt because he assumed any friend of Corinne's was an enemy of his.

He wasn't wrong.

"*Bonjour*," he said, the word awkward from his lips.

Bauer was frowning. He'd met Liana last week, when he'd dropped by for another surprise book inspection. Liana had been there to spend the night with Corinne. She'd expected him to leave again within minutes when he realized she had company, but instead, he'd asked Liana polite questions . . . which had turned into more intentional questions when he learned she was a university student, studying literature. By the end of his hour-long visit, he still hadn't found the book she'd planted for him to discover in Maman's closet, but he'd encouraged Liana to chase her literary dreams and even recommended a few French publishers who favored work like what she described wanting to write someday.

Why did he have to be so . . . *nice?*

"If he weren't so old," Liana had whispered when he'd left, "I'd declare myself in love."

As if his age were the real problem—and besides, he wasn't that old. Perhaps, what, three or four years older than Corinne? That was *young,* thank you very much.

Bauer shifted his questioning gaze to Corinne, and she had no trouble decoding it. Liana, he already knew, was no senseless flirt, nor was she in a situation desperate enough to warrant giving in to the advances of a Nazi, like other Parisiennes. So what game was she playing?

Corinne shrugged and shifted closer to his side while Liana draped an arm over Kraus's shoulder and asked him if they were about to go to lunch. "She is . . . upset with her beau." It was the only semi-reasonable explanation she could devise on such short notice. "He was trying to tell her that her dreams of writing would fade away once she was married and had children."

Professor Bauer sighed. "I would offer to have a talk with the young man, but I suspect he would do the opposite of anything I said. Perhaps if I show up dressed like a Parisian?"

She shouldn't joke with him. Shouldn't laugh. But a smile twisted her lips anyway. "I am trying to imagine you in a beret . . ."

"I look ridiculous." His lips twitched too. "I tried. But I cut a dashing figure in a fedora, I'm told."

The style would certainly suit him better than the Nazi cap—but she wasn't about to say so.

Especially since Liana was inviting Kraus and Bauer both up to Corinne's flat for lunch, and Kraus was, for some reason, agreeing. Corinne cursed herself for getting distracted. "Oh, Liana, I don't think . . . we don't really have enough to offer them, certainly not the fare they're used to."

Kraus didn't take his eyes off Liana. "We have our own food. We can bring it. Isn't that right, Professor?"

Bauer looked to be tamping down another smile. "Of course."

Corinne was going to have a few choice words for her friend when they were alone again. Liana hadn't seemed to consider that the flat might not be prepared for another surprise inspection by the Nazis. The professor only ever came in the evenings, giving her ample time after class to put away anything she didn't want him to see.

Or, given that he'd sifted through nearly the entire flat at this point, at least put away so it wasn't obvious she'd been using it.

The last issue of *Marianne* magazine still sat on her end table, but Corinne's quick perusal of the space as they entered didn't show anything else incriminating, at least. She always changed the dial back to Radio Paris before she switched it off, and she never left out anything from Oncle Georges. And while she didn't dare assume that the professor wouldn't recognize *Marianne* as one of the periodicals that had been dismantled when it refused to accept Nazi oversight, Kraus probably wouldn't.

And she was beginning to think that the *soldat* was more the menace than the professor. Bauer had pulled several banned books from her shelf and, rather than confiscate them or even stamp them with that horrid red *V,* he'd simply talked about the stories with her as if they were two patrons in any fiction section. He'd even recommended other works by the same authors.

She couldn't discount the possibility that he was trying to set a trap for her. Lure her into purchasing *verboten* books. Tracking her movements and then arresting the bookseller, her, everyone.

But Abraham's words from that morning kept rattling around in her head as she accepted the bread, meat, and cheese—Bread! Meat! Cheese!—from the men and added them to her own provisions.

The professor had been perfectly polite, he'd said. He'd let him go at the first possible moment, he'd said. He'd even made book recommendations, provided him with a list, he'd said.

He'd pulled out the list to prove it. She'd only scanned it, to be sure, but now . . . it was an odd list. A strange mix of German, French, and English titles. Some of which were obscure, some of which weren't really even *good*—and having heard, at this point, Bauer's opinion on dozens of books, she didn't think he'd disagree with her about those.

So . . . why? Why those books? None of them were banned, it was true, but . . .

And why had he taken the time to make up a list to give him anyway?

"Need some help?" He slid into the kitchen with so much ease that her back went straight. Two weeks ago, they'd searched this room, and he'd found another book that she'd hidden behind an old, dented pan they never used anymore. It had been strange, seeing him poking through the cabinets, laughing when he pulled out the book. It was strange now to watch him move to her cupboards with complete comfort and pull down plates, freshly washed serviettes, and silverware enough for the four of them.

"Oh, I just met her when classes started back up," Liana was saying from the living room, the tone of her voice putting Corinne on edge. It was . . . sultry. Inviting. And she apparently had already realized that if she meant to win Kraus's trust, she had to pit herself against Corinne somehow.

The professor set the service onto the table, and she jumped.

He frowned. "Are you all right, *mademoiselle*?"

He hadn't called her Corinne again, not since that night when he'd talked about the book burnings. She hadn't expected him to even come back after that, honestly. And if he did, she'd expected the return of the strict Nazi officer, going about his business.

Yet he'd returned four days later. And five after that. And then within three. Less to search, she'd definitely come to realize, than to talk about whatever book he'd been reading, and to ask her about hers.

She pulled the bread knife from its block and moved to the baguette. *Juste ciel*, it had been far too long since she'd actually sliced a loaf of bread. She never got a whole one these days, always forced to share with someone else, and she never even bothered cutting it. Tearing hunks off to eat with a few grams of cheese sufficed most days. "Do you know Karl Gustaf?"

He put a plate before each chair. "I don't think so. Should I? Is he a writer?"

A snort escaped before she could stop it. "Everything's books with you, isn't it?" It came out too teasing.

He shot her a grin. "Guilty. So if not a writer . . . ?"

She settled the knife an inch from the end, sliced on the diagonal. She'd been careful, so careful to let him think her a student. The less any Nazi knew about her, the better.

But one Nazi—the one who mattered—already knew. "He's . . . from the Ministry of Education, apparently. He audited one of my classes today."

The professor's hands went still, and his frown went deep. "I knew they were sending men for the job—I thought I'd know them. Foolish, I suppose. There are many universities other than my own in Germany." He reached for the silverware. "Are you merely unsettled by his presence, or did he do something in particular?"

The words sounded careful to her ears. Too casual. His movements too precise. She sliced another piece of bread. "Both. He first praised my teaching, insisting I must be at least part German—and then all but apologized for the evils of the city forcing me to work instead of finding a husband as is fitting."

"Teaching?" Silverware clattered to the table. He spun to face her.

She expected outrage. Disapproval, like Gustaf had shown. Anger, at least, that she'd never mentioned it before, despite his regular visits over the last few months.

She saw only . . . delight. Absolute, pure delight. He grinned. "I ought to have known. What do you teach? Which class was—*dummkopf*!" He slapped a hand dramatically to his head. "*You* are Dr. Bastien, not your mother!"

The secretary in the registrar's office had already admitted that he'd come looking for Maman, and that she'd nearly pointed him Corinne's way instead, but he'd barreled out too quickly. Claire had meant to apologize for it.

Corinne had assured her no harm was done, that he already knew she was Yvonne Bastien's daughter. Now, she lifted one shoulder and cut another slice. "He visited my class on German literature." No point in hiding that either. It would soon be in whatever files they kept on her. "We're translating Goethe's *Faust*."

He leaned onto the table, laughing softly. "Of course. You speak German. I shouldn't be surprised, given your neighbors." His grin was crooked. It made him look closer to Kraus's age than his own. "What is your doctorate in?"

"Linguistics." She paused. Cut. "The first one. My second is in philosophy."

"Two doctorates." He straightened, and though he shook his head, he was still smiling. "I'm outranked. May I be terribly rude?"

This time she turned to face him, abandoning the bread for a moment. "Rude?"

"How old *are* you?" He lifted his hands. "I know, I know. One should never ask a lady such a thing, but . . . I thought you no more than nineteen or twenty when we first met, and I've been recalculating every time we have a conversation. I can't decide if you're eighteen or eighty."

She smirked and returned to her work. "Eighty, naturally. Don't I look marvelous for my age?"

"That part was never in question, whatever your answer."

Only narrowly did she avoid slicing into her

198

thumb. Had he meant it as the compliment it sounded like? Probably not. He was simply a kind, polite man, despite his uniform. His mother—no doubt a proper German *hausfrau* who never worked a day outside the home in her life—had probably taught him always to compliment a woman. "I will turn thirty-one next month."

"*Danke Gotte*. If my new best friend was fifteen years my junior, I was going to have a good cry."

This time she set down the knife to avoid risk to life and limb. She had no name for the torrent of emotions churning inside her. Disbelief, fury, joy, panic—all of them and none of them. "We are *not*—"

"Relax, Doctor." It wasn't right that a Nazi should have a smile like that. Teasing and self-deprecating and twinkling and wise. "It is just between us and the books. Hush-hush."

She yanked another plate from the cupboard and arranged the bread on it. "Do I get no say in this?"

"You've had plenty of say! You said that *Don Quixote* was an exploration of Cervantes's alienation, that St. Augustine hilariously inspired you *to* steal as a child instead of warning you of the evils of it, that Kant's moral imperative changed the way you thought of both morality and Kant."

Her cheeks were on fire. Had she really said all

that? So many of her thoughts—her true, inmost thoughts?

She had. Of course she had. Because they'd just been discussing books, that was all, and she'd never trained herself to withhold her thoughts on such subjects. She'd rather trained herself to explore them, express them, and defend them.

"Don't look so woebegone." He'd moved to her side and reached now for the plate of bread, nudging her playfully. "I didn't say I was *your* best friend. You're free to keep hating me if you like, but I feel no such obligation."

She squeezed her eyes shut and let him call the younger two in to eat.

TEN

19 August 1940

It had taken Christian a week to track down Karl Gustaf. One would think that after months of slow and methodical work in Paris—following a decade of it in his own professional life—he'd have learned some patience. And when it came to classifying books, teaching, or doing research for his next paper, he had it in spades.

For some reason, though, he found his patience greatly lacking in a few key areas now, and all of them revolved around the people he most wanted to see and was most afraid of finding.

Alfred Kantorowicz had been stopped at a checkpoint two days ago and, hence, brought in for questioning. He didn't know the man personally, but Christian was well aware that he was the director of the Library of Burned Books and that, as such, he ought to be treated more severely than the other exiled writers Christian had interviewed thus far.

He'd asked what he was supposed to ask. He'd given the usual orders for registry and had directed the search of his flat, removing any *verboten* texts. He'd then dismissed Kantorowicz, as expected . . . without asking the questions whose answers he really wanted.

Where was Earnst Yung? Josef Horowitz? Kantorowicz had been stopped not at one of the checkpoints leading into the city, but at a random one near his old address, which meant that he'd somehow slipped back into Paris undetected. Who else had done the same? What other friends were here? So close? So out of reach in all but the worst ways?

He strode toward one of the many hotels that had been pressed into use by the Reich, one he hadn't visited before, briefcase in hand and face as neutral as he could make it. So many members of so many departments had been sent to and then called from Paris since they "liberated" it that trying to find one particular officer proved ridiculously difficult. At first he'd wondered if Gustaf had already been recalled, perhaps even replaced . . . but then a reply had come to one of his many inquiries yesterday.

The anxious knot in his stomach hadn't been at the thought of finally meeting the man who had put the creases in Corinne Bastien's brow—it was the fact that the message had been waiting for him when he returned from knocking on Josef's door.

There'd been no answer. Just as he'd prayed. Just as he'd feared.

But he had to keep knocking. He called at the last known residences of every member of the Deutsche Freiheitsbibliothek at least once a week, just in case they'd managed to avoid all the random checkpoints. Because if he left anyone out of the rotation, Ackermann would notice. Note it. Report it.

Perhaps just rebuke him for the oversight and order him to correct it . . . or perhaps he'd decide that Christian had better be sent back to Berlin and whoever was next on the list be brought in to finish his job.

It would be easier to let that happen. Be dismissed. Return to his quiet life, where fear of the Gestapo knocking on his door would at least only put *him* at risk, no one else. And at least with the Gestapo in Berlin, he had a friend who could possibly help mitigate any consequences.

But what if it hadn't just been some strange chance, or even Erik Reinholdt's conniving, that had led him here? What if it was what God wanted? What if the Lord had sent him here to try to mitigate some of the damage being done, to help those he could?

What if this was his path to atonement?

"That isn't the way it works," the priest had said last week when he'd finally worked up the courage to go to reconciliation at the small church nearest to the Library of Burned Books, after he'd dismissed Kraus one evening. "You do not choose your own atonement, especially when there has been no sin."

"But there *has,*" he'd insisted. Otherwise, why

would he feel this crushing guilt, this emptiness? What was that, if not separation from the Father?

"You did the only thing you knew to do in an impossible situation," the faceless priest had said. "The sins of pride you have confessed, of selfishness, of lack of trust in our heavenly Father—those I can forgive. For those I can ascribe penance. But not for the other."

He knew, intellectually, that the priest had been trying to tell him that his decision hadn't been a sinful one. But what it felt like was that forgiveness was withheld, when he craved it so deeply.

He pulled upon the door to the hotel, remembering walking into the church for Mass yesterday, for the first time in nearly a year. He'd chosen a small but not too small church for that, in an *arrondissement* he otherwise never visited. No great cathedral, no tiny community. Somewhere he wouldn't be noticed. He'd worn his civilian clothes, his fedora pulled low over his brow until he made his way inside, and then he'd chosen one of the back pews, where he could scarcely hear the Latin intonations, but where the rhythm of them could still tug at his soul.

Should he have taken Communion? He hadn't been sure. Despite the priest's words, he hadn't felt clean enough, worthy enough. He hadn't been certain that the wafer wouldn't choke him, holy fire strike him down.

But his mother's words had echoed in his mind and urged him into the aisle with the others. *His perfection is greater than our imperfection. We are not capable, by ignorance or pride, of defiling his holiness. But his holiness is capable of cleansing us, working in us, even when we don't fully believe it. Do not deny it the chance.*

He didn't dare wonder what his mother would think if she realized he'd avoided Mass for so long. True, being a Catholic in Nazi Germany came with risks—priests were among the murdered on the Night of the Long Knives, the church's property had been stripped, all schools and societies closed. Private citizens weren't forbidden from practicing their faith, exactly . . . they just knew that if they vocalized any critique of Hitler based on those beliefs, they'd pay for it.

But being a German Nazi Catholic in occupied Paris? That was a new sort of risk. The same one, though, that he risked in every other part of his life. So if he was walking the tightrope anyway, he'd better do it fortified by the Savior.

A *soldat* manned the front desk, saluting when he saw Christian's rank. "Sonderführer. How may I be of assistance?"

Christian pasted on a smile—the one made for secretaries and office workers. "I have an appointment with Sonderführer Karl Gustaf."

"Of course. You'll find his office in room 402, sir."

"Thank you." A quick ride on the lift, a short walk to the room in question, a polite knock on the door, and then he was being ushered inside by Karl Gustaf.

"Bauer!" the younger man greeted him with an enthusiastic handshake, blue eyes alight. "I've been hearing of your work since I hit Paris. From the University of Berlin, aren't you? I'm a Munich man, myself."

Christian forced a smile—the one reserved for university rivalries. "I'll forgive you for it."

Gustaf laughed and motioned him to one of the wooden chairs set up at the cramped desk. "I admit I was surprised to learn that a professor was given your appointment rather than a librarian by trade."

So had he, but it probably wouldn't serve him to say it. Christian shrugged. "I am director of the university library in addition to being a professor. I in fact served on the committee that compiled the list of banned books."

One of the most frustrating appointments he'd ever experienced, until he'd come to Paris. At first he'd tried to argue for so many books, so many authors . . . then he'd wondered if doing so would get him labeled as a dissident too. Put his whole family in danger.

Was it better to speak up and be permanently silenced or to work silently, doing what good he could? It was a conversation he and Erik had

had on several occasions. Christian, as he was recruited to this ignoble work; Erik, as the police force he'd served on so happily was absorbed into Hitler's Gestapo. They'd both felt like cowards by choosing the second, but they'd reasoned they could do more good hidden among their enemies. Christian had managed to save more books that way than if he'd been arrested. Perhaps, through them, saving people too. And Erik—banished to a desk and the Gestapo's files because of his hesitation in joining the Party—could now alter those files here and there, to help people avoid punishment for their beliefs.

Gustaf leaned back in the chair he'd selected, impressed. "What an honor. I was a student at the time. I suppose that gives you unique qualifications though, yes? You probably don't even need to consult the list as much as the rest of us would, if you helped compile it."

"Indeed. Sometimes I think every author's name is branded in my memory." So many friends, heroes, favorites. He leaned back too and hooked an ankle over the opposite leg. "Though I miss the university world. When I heard that the Ministry of Education had sent representatives to oversee the French universities, I was a bit jealous, I confess. How has your work been going?"

Gustaf's smile was open, not a hint of suspicion in his eyes. He had no reason to think, after all, that Christian was asking with ulterior motives. No way of knowing that his intentions weren't to make a friend, but to protect one.

Because she *was* a friend, even if she didn't want to be. The only one he could risk talking to about books, art, philosophy. He didn't know if it was within his power to protect her position at the university—but if it was, he'd do it. And by his calculation, it began here.

His host poured coffee from a carafe into a cup. "Care for some?"

"Yes, thank you." He took a cup, sipped.

Gustaf settled back in, looking perfectly at ease. "I confess it has its moments of overwhelm, though I am hardly the only one assigned the task. My French is rustier than I thought, and that is, of course, what most of the classes are held in. Makes it difficult to know what they're saying."

"Mm, understandable. And the French we learn for ordering in restaurants or even translating Racine and Molière does not give us the vocabulary we need to observe a lecture on physics or economics, does it?"

"Exactly so." Gustaf paused for a drink and then set his utilitarian white cup back on its saucer. "Some things are easy, of course—making certain all the foreigners have been dismissed as ordered, checking the professors against the list of those registered to the communist party or registry of Jews. Other decisions are trickier."

Christian nodded, hoping his eyes projected understanding. "I've been curious about that. There are female professors at some of Paris's universities, aren't there? If I recall correctly, Marie Curie was the first, at the Sorbonne around the turn of the century."

"There are four on the record at the Sorbonne now, only two still in Paris." Gustaf's eyes lit in a way that Christian didn't much like. "One a stodgy woman who has been teaching English since 1923, but the other—she is an interesting case. I cannot recall mention of another unmarried female professor, at least not currently. It doesn't seem quite fitting—but she is a remarkable teacher, I grant you that. Even I learned something about Goethe in her class, and I've taught it myself four different times."

Though it took effort, Christian kept his smile small, only mildly interested, rather than demanding to hear those insights.

Perhaps if he shared his lunch again, he could convince her to give him her lecture.

"Well, at least the French weren't overly welcoming of women in academic circles—not like the Americans or British. So you shouldn't run into too many of those dilemmas here."

Gustaf sighed. "There are female entrance exams to higher education, but not many who pass them, from what I've seen. I certainly didn't expect to run into the question on my first day here. I am torn. On the one hand, it sets a bad example to have a beautiful young woman thumbing her nose at our way of life. On the other hand, I interviewed the other professors on staff who have taught the German-language classes, and I am not convinced they would do the job half as well. And if a pretty, talented professor can bring more students to learn German . . . does that offsct her bad example?" He shrugged. "I would welcome your opinion, Professor."

"I do understand the need to set the right example." He set his cup on the desk, fingers lingering on it as if he was only now giving it thought. "But I would say that winning the hearts and minds of the students is our top priority, and if she can aid us in that cause . . ."

Were she here, she'd likely have stomped on his foot for accusing her of such a thing. He'd seen the magazine she was so quick to put away last week, and the peek he'd snuck showed him that the page she'd had turned down was a rather rousing essay by Jean Guéhenno about "the France that cannot be invaded."

He'd read it already. Had committed a few passages to memory. Because they weren't just true of France, those sentiments about how one's true home, one's true country wasn't just the land that could be occupied by an enemy—it was the heart and soul of a people, the part that couldn't die, couldn't surrender, couldn't just be taken over by another.

They were true of Germany too. He had to believe that. Had to believe that Hitler's regime hadn't stripped his people of everything—that though Germany too was occupied by Nazis, it didn't *make them* Nazis, not all of them. No more than the French were, just because the swastika flew from every government building.

The true France, Guéhenno had said, was worth fighting for.

The true Germany was too.

Would Corinne understand that, if he tried to explain it? Or would her eyes fall to his uniform as they so often did, and her expression close off? Would she grant that not all Frenchmen agreed with Pétain and his puppet regime, despite the fact that most obeyed the dictates publicly, but deny that anyone in a Nazi uniform could be someone else beneath it?

Across from him, Gustaf considered the point with a long inhalation. "She held the students in thrall, it's true. And her teaching—I thought for sure she must have a German mother, but she said not, only tutors. She has the spirit though. The understanding of the Aryan soul."

The *German* soul. But he pressed his lips against the correction. He had no desire to get into a debate with this young devotee about Aryan mythos. Nor to point out that the tutors who had instilled it in her were the ones deemed not German enough for Germany. "I would say then that you oughtn't to rush into any decisions. Perhaps keep an eye on her, and a pulse on what her students are saying. But if she isn't corrupting the youth—" He paused to see if Gustaf would smile at the reference to Socrates, but his expression didn't so much as flicker. He cleared his throat to make up for the pause. "Then I see little harm in maintaining the status quo. For now, at least."

The younger man nodded, all enthusiasm and relief. "That makes sense. And I can attempt to persuade her, in the meantime, to mitigate the marks against her. If she were married, especially to someone else in academia whose work hers supported . . ."

Christian chuckled and lifted his coffee again. "Perhaps she has a great story of a lost love that you could present as her excuse. A fiancé who died tragically and whose work she is carrying on out of eternal devotion."

A father's love, a father's dream, in reality. But they were writing fiction here, not fact.

"Not a bad idea," Gustaf said with a chuckle of his own. "I'll talk to her again soon. Get her story. See if she would perhaps be inclined toward working with us."

If this man's French weren't so rusty, he probably would have heard the way Parisians spat the word "collaborator" at any politician, lackey, restauranteur, or functionary who had embraced their occupiers. The special sneers they reserved for the young women who went out on the town with Nazi officers and *soldaten*.

He had only to see the horror in her eyes when her young friend had flirted with Kraus last week to know Corinne's opinion of such things. And the fact that young Liana had most decidedly *not* been seen by them again on Boulevard Arago. "Perhaps." He checked his watch, sighed. "I'm afraid I have another appointment—I only wanted to introduce myself, offer a listening ear whenever you need it. We academics must stick together, after all, among this sea of military men."

Gustaf leapt to his feet as Christian stood, hand held out to shake again. "I'm glad you did, Professor. And how right you are. Perhaps we could arrange a standing time to meet each week. Lunch? Dinner?"

Would Ackermann forgive it if he gave Gustaf the Saturday dinner time? Probably not. His superior seemed to like bringing Christian to heel at least once a week, filling his ears with things he'd rather not hear. "Perhaps Friday dinners?"

"Perfect."

"I'll send round a list of restaurants you might enjoy." He fished a card from his pocket with his official hotel-office direction, though he only ever collected his mail once a day and otherwise ignored the desk in favor of the library. "And if ever you need to get in touch, just send a note round here. I'm out most of the day at the various libraries and doing interviews and the like, but I do collect my messages."

Gustaf stared at the card a moment as if committing it to memory then and there. "I will, thank you. You can't know how glad I am to have a like-minded man of letters to keep company with here."

Christian put his cap back on and smiled. "I believe you mean that *only* I can know. I look forward to a longer visit soon, Gustaf."

"I'll mark it on my calendar now."

He held his smile in place as he let himself back into the corridor. Let his expression drop into neutral as he traveled back down to the lobby and then onto the street. Wished he could let it fall then, wished that he dared to feel his real feelings anytime other than when he was locked away inside the stark, unwelcoming hotel room he slept in each night.

He moved to the car Kraus waited beside, knowing that wish would remain ungranted.

Perhaps he could at least make the home visitations to the exiles on his own. Make it sound like he was doing his young aide a favor, not forcing him to come along on what were always fruitless calls anyway. Claim he wanted to walk, stretch his legs, that all this being-chauffeured-about was making him too soft. He was used to walking everywhere in Berlin, after all. It was what had always kept him in shape.

Then maybe, just maybe, if he ever caught one of them at home . . . maybe he could actually be *himself* for an hour or two.

ELEVEN

28 August 1940

The birds had gone silent. It took Corinne half of her walk to pinpoint what was wrong—to realize that when she cut through the park nearest her flat, there'd been no cooing pigeons flocking her, that none fluttered overhead, that the birdsong usually filling the air was absent. It made the already quiet city eerie in a way she'd never experienced, not even in the two and a half months since the invasion.

On every new street she turned, she looked for them. The most she saw were a few carcasses in alleyways, making her stomach go tight. Making her nose and mouth burn with the memory of the choking clouds of noxious fumes when the fuel reserves had burned.

She'd already experienced Paris without its artists. Paris without its readers. Paris without its students. But Paris without its pigeons? That, more than all the others, somehow said "Paris without its freedom" to her.

A shiver overtook her despite the heat, and she checked again the address she had scrawled into her book. She'd visited many of the regulars of the German library at their home over the years, but Josef Horowitz lived a bit further away than the others. And had always come to the library so regularly that she'd never *needed* to visit him at home. And then after his grandson arrived from Germany last year, she'd known he was spending all his spare time with the lad and hadn't wanted to intrude.

This was the right building though, assuming she'd read the messy scrawl correctly when she'd copied it from one of the library's record books before the government locked everything up.

She still got twitchy when she thought of the books locked away next door that she hadn't had a chance to gather before the place had been shut down. At this point, though, she had to think that Bauer hadn't found them. He surely wasn't flipping through each and every volume. And if he had, he wouldn't know what it was.

Who, after all, would expect encoded instructions for espionage to be in the pages of random books?

Even so. She strode toward the front doors of the building and studied the numbers on the board within, so she knew which floor to go to. She should have used her own books, like Oncle Georges had suggested. Approved books. And she was, now—if the parcels were opened, those were less likely to be confiscated.

The poetic justice had been irresistible though, when they devised the plan. And she hadn't thought Paris would fall, that *France* would fall so soon. She hadn't thought those books would be a red flag to the enemy, just a rude gesture to them from afar.

There—number 42, J. Horowitz. Knowing she was in the right place made her shoulders relax. Not that he was likely back in Paris—Abraham was fairly certain he meant to keep his grandson out of occupied territory if at all possible—but she couldn't stand having his name on her list, not checked off.

She didn't mount the stairs quite as jauntily as she was forced to do when Liana was with her, but still she reached the fourth floor in good time. A glance at her watch told her it was still only seven, giving her two full hours before she had to be safely back inside her own building.

A brass 42 pulled her toward the right door, and she knocked, humming a bit of "*Parlez-moi d'amour*" that Liana had been singing earlier. She jumped when the door swung open, plastering a hand to her chest.

Josef filled the doorway, his gray hair perfectly combed, his gray eyes twinkling at her reaction. "Expecting somebody else, Corinne?"

She grinned, dropped her hand, and leaned in to kiss his cheeks. "Expecting no one, honestly. What are you doing back in Paris?"

He smiled, pressed a finger to his lips, and motioned toward a closed door as he ushered her in. "My grandson just went to bed."

"So early?" The moment she said it, she called herself a dunce. *Was* seven early for a boy of . . . however old his grandson was? She'd yet to meet him, which had given her no few opportunities to complain to Josef before the invasion. But now? "Sorry," she whispered, eyeing the closed door. "I won't stay long. I'm only checking on everyone I can."

"No, please. Come in, sit." He motioned for her to put her things on the entryway table. "We've had a long few days." He sounded weary enough to want to be in bed himself. "We just got home last night—and dodging the checkpoints was quite an adventure, I might add."

She squeezed his elbow and followed him to the sofa. "You shouldn't have returned." It was true that he wasn't Jewish, wasn't communist, but he was still an enemy of the Nazi Party—first because his grandfather had been Jewish, and that was enough to make a man inferior, apparently, and secondly because he'd been rather vocal in his criticisms of the Party back in Germany, and it had landed him on the banned list.

"I know but . . ." He glanced toward the closed door to his grandson's bedroom and sank onto the couch beside her with a smile. The smile he mustered looked frayed around the edges, but still he reached for her hand and gave her fingers a squeeze. "It's good of you to come and check on us all, but you know you shouldn't, *schatzi*."

He'd been the first of the German exiles to start calling her his "little treasure," like he would his own children or grandchildren. She'd certainly not been a child when she met him seven years ago, but since he was old enough to be her father and she missed hers so, she'd accepted the endearment with a smile.

She smiled again now, hearing it from his lips after months of silence. "It seems life is full of *shouldn't*s, isn't it? Yet here we both are. Although . . ." She'd already been whispering in deference to the sleeping child, but she pitched her voice even lower and leaned in a bit. "You need to be careful. There's a Nazi *sonderführer* who has been charged with interrogating everyone associated with the library, and he's been making house calls too, according to Abraham."

Panic lit, banked, sputtered. He nodded. "I should expect nothing less. But it is, I hope, all right. I managed to secure false papers, and I will be moving flats soon. I do not know how well our documents will hold up, but hopefully enough. New names, new history. Much as I hate to lie—"

"There is no shame in guarding your grandson's life. Thus far they are only making foreign nationals register and banning them from employment, but there are whispers that soon they'll start arresting whomever they like, for whatever they like."

"They have been doing the same in Germany—I don't know why they'd stop now." He leaned into the cushion, the lines on his face so much deeper than they'd been when she'd last seen him in May.

Her every instinct said to fret. She made the effort to smile instead. "Don't forget to change your name on the placard in the lobby, if you're going to be going by a different name altogether. If you intend to be here more than a day, at least."

"Ah. Yes. I'll be getting that new flat next week, but in the meantime, I made a new name plate. I just haven't had time—"

"I'll change it out for you when I leave."

He patted her hand where it rested on the cushion between them. "You're a good girl."

She wanted to ask where he'd gone, how he'd found someone to give him false papers, why he'd decided to risk coming back and how he'd managed the journey with a child, yet remained undiscovered. She wanted to ask if he meant to reestablish communication with the others, if he'd intended to let *her* know he was back.

Before she could ask any of them, another knock sounded on the door.

Josef sighed and pushed back up to his feet. "I saw Mathilda at the grocer's today. She said Abraham would be by later—I assumed it was him when you knocked."

The shoulders that had gone instantly tense at the knock relaxed a degree. Even so, she was going to suggest a quicker move than next week the moment he'd let Abraham in and greetings were out of the way.

She glanced toward the bedroom door. The little one must have been exhausted indeed to be sleeping through all this knocking and not coming to investigate. When she was a child, Maman had always teased that she had the ears of a wolf, capable of hearing even the faintest of whispers if they said anything interesting. She'd all the time gotten out of bed to greet late-arriving guests or interject herself into a conversation that was meant to be just between her parents.

Ciel, it was a wonder they hadn't lost their tempers with her eight times a day.

The door squeaked open again, and Josef's sharp inhale not only brought her head back around, it brought her to her feet. "Chris?"

The name meant little to her. But the gray of the uniform, the shape of the hat had her stepping forward. It was a Nazi at the door, not—who was *Chris?*

She saw in the next moment, when Christian Bauer stepped around Josef, consternation on his face. "What are you doing back here?" He didn't sound like a Nazi officer as he said it—he sounded like an outraged friend, his gaze locked on the older man's face. "You were supposed to be on your way to England. America. Anywhere but here."

There were too many pieces coming together at once.

They knew each other, these two. Josef called the professor by a nickname. Bauer chastised him like a friend.

And with *concern.* The same concern she herself had felt, had expressed.

It made sense, in a way. Josef was part of the Berlin contingent. The *University of Berlin* contingent. It wasn't unthinkable that he and Bauer had crossed paths, or even that they'd once been friends as well as colleagues.

But their friendship clearly wasn't past tense. Not if Bauer had known that Josef had left Paris and was "supposed to be" bound for England or America.

Josef shut the door quickly behind them, his own expression just as fierce as he faced Bauer, faced Corinne. "England has rounded up all German expatriates, especially Jews, and interred them on the Isle of Man. And am I really to trust an ocean filled with U-boats?"

"So then you stay in Free France or other unoccupied territory. Anything would be better than here!"

"He wanted to come back." This Josef pronounced coolly, evenly, calmly. A glint of challenge in his eye. "Because it's where we said we'd be."

Corinne wobbled forward another step. What *he?* Who—?

"Vati?" The new voice was high-pitched, reaching her ears a split second before that closed bedroom door burst open and a little boy flew out. "Vati!"

More pieces. Too many pieces.

The boy wasn't in pajamas. He didn't look sleep tousled.

And why should that be the first thing she noted, instead of the fact that he darted across the floor, around the chair, straight for Bauer, calling out that word over and over again?

Vati. Vati.

The old German lessons clicked belatedly into place. *Vati*: Daddy. Papa. The diminutive form of *father,* usually used only by small children.

As the professor turned, he caught sight of her. She saw the flicker of it in his eyes, too quickly gone for her to determine what else colored the surprise. Anger? Fear?

But she wasn't his focus. He spun to face the boy. Dropped to his knees. Opened his arms just as the little one barreled into him.

And wept as he held his boy tight.

Corinne sank back down onto the sofa. Christian had a son. A son who lived with a

German exile, part Jewish, who claimed the boy was his grandson.

Pieces. Fragments. Snippets. She could see them all, but they made no sense, like lines of poetry taken out of context. Like a language for which she had no lexicon.

Then one more piece, as the little boy rested his head against Christian's shoulder, revealing his full face to Corinne for the first time.

He had a scar on his lip, no left eye, a malformed ear on that side. And he held on to his father as if he never meant to let go again.

Christian heard the words whispered from the sofa as if through water, through a tunnel, through fog.

"I don't understand. You know him? Professor Bauer?"

"I am his godfather. His father was my dearest friend."

"The boy? You said he was your grandson—"

"Chris has been like a son to me. Felix like a grandson."

"*Chris?* He is a Nazi officer—"

"There is much you don't understand, *schatzi*."

"So tell me!"

"It is not my story to tell."

One part of Christian's mind said he should get up from the floor. He should answer her questions. He should swear her to secrecy.

That part would have to wait its turn. Right now, all that mattered was that his very heart had been restored, and for the first time in his life he knew how Felix must have felt when Dr. Schwerin repaired his cleft palate, though he'd been too little to put words to it: like something too long missing had been restored. Something broken had been fixed. Some disorder he'd grown so accustomed to that he didn't even know it was a disorder had been righted.

It *hurt.* It hurt in every cell of his being, hurt like feeling returning to a frozen limb. It hurt so beautifully that he clung to this moment as long as he possibly could.

His baby's arms were around him again. Felix was safe, and he was here, and even though he shouldn't have been, he *was,* and Christian was too. And at this moment, he was going to accept that as a gift from God. Later, he could think about the consequences. Later, he could argue with Josef.

He had no capacity for words right now anyway, couldn't work anything but "Felix, Felix, Felix" through the sobs. He shook all over. Trembled so much that he had to sink from his knees to a seat on the floor, gathering his boy close.

Felix wrapped around him, just like he'd always done. "It's all right, Vati," he said into Christian's ear. "I missed you. I'm all right."

Christian rested a hand on his son's head, burying his fingers in the blond curls. There, the indentation that they all said shouldn't be there, was a malformation, but which had always seemed purpose-built for his thumb to rest against, letting him cradle him so perfectly. "Felix," he murmured again. "I missed you like air."

"Are we going home? You said you'd come when it was safe, that—"

"No." He kissed his head, his cheek, the nub that should have been an ear but was instead the sweetest little curl. "It's still not safe, *mäuschen*. I'm sorry. I'm so sorry."

Little fingers rested on his cheek in that way he'd been doing since he was just a baby, then stroked down over the scruff of his jaw. "Don't leave me again, Vati." Tears clogged Felix's voice too.

It made Christian's throat close off again. He couldn't answer—what answer could he possibly give? So he held him tighter, tucking his head under Christian's chin, and squeezed his eyes shut.

They had now. This moment. This hour. That was all they were ever promised, that's what Mutter had told them when Dr. Schwerin explained the birth defects and said he didn't know if the child would live. "We never know who will live, or for how long," she'd said. "But he's alive now. So love him."

It's how he'd viewed every moment of Felix's life. There was only now, so he would love him. Only now, so he would protect him in whatever way he could. Only now, and he wouldn't let anyone steal it from them.

Even when it meant sending him away, devastated in the certainty that he'd never see him again, but trusting that his boy could still *live,* even without him.

And then now. This moment. Even if it was only this moment, he would treasure it forever.

"Chris." Josef's voice was soft, gentle, and the pain in Christian's backside and bent knees said he'd given him ample time to just sit with his son.

Not enough. It was never enough. But he sniffed, and he stood, lifting Felix as he did so, just as he'd done so many times before. He sat with him in the chair at right angles to the sofa Josef and Corinne occupied.

She stared at him like she'd never seen him before.

Fair enough.

Josef sighed and motioned to her. "You had better explain yourself before she invents a story of her own."

His eyes slid shut, giving him a whiff of the shampoo from Felix's hair. He didn't even know where to begin. With her questions, he supposed. The ones she'd asked through the water and the tunnel and the fog. "I am not . . . I didn't want to join the Party. I only did because I thought . . ." He glanced down at Felix, who still gripped Christian's collar in one hand, the thumb of his other in his mouth.

It should have made him frown—he'd broken him of that habit a year ago. But then his whole world had been uprooted, so who could begrudge him his comfort? The sight gave Christian a strange comfort too.

He was still the child he'd been. Still his little boy. Not all grown up. Not so long separated that he didn't even remember him. He'd still called out his name the very moment he heard his voice.

But how could he say in Felix's hearing that he'd joined the Nazis to try to save his life? That he'd thought it was his only hope of getting the medical help he would need?

How wrong he'd been.

Corinne's golden brows drew together. "Why in the world did they entrust you with this role if you're not a dedicated member of the Party?" Her German was flawless, her accent no different than his own. Only when she replied in it did he realize that he hadn't shifted back from his mother tongue.

As for her question, a snort slipped out. "I have no idea. They shouldn't have. When they called me in to the Ministry, I thought I was being arrested—there were several times in my classes that I spoke what I really thought instead of what they wanted me to say. I know very well it had been reported. And yet, instead . . ." He could only shrug. "The only thing that makes sense is that an old friend of mine helped arrange it—he was a police officer before, which means Gestapo now. He works in the filing room, so perhaps he made changes to my files. I can only guess about that. But since I'm here, I'm trying to do what good I can."

Her breath blew out, her gaze shifting to Felix.

He knew the usual looks his son got: pity, disgust, curiosity. He knew the usual questions: *What's wrong with him? Was he in an accident? Was he born that way?*

Corinne only asked, "How could you stand to be away from him? How long has it been?"

He brushed Felix's curls back again, just to watch them spring forward once more. "Ten months now. I . . . had no choice. It wasn't safe in Germany."

She was clearly about to ask why, but that explanation would have to wait. So he offered instead, "His mother died when he was just a baby. Cancer. It's been just the two of us all these years, hasn't it, *mäuschen*?"

Felix nodded against him, fingers curling tighter into his shirt.

"Ilse would be so proud though," Josef said. "So proud of how her boys have thrived together."

Christian's smile was barely a lift of the corners of his lips. Ilse had been so scared to die—not for her own sake, but because she hadn't wanted to leave their "little mouse" behind, hadn't trusted anyone to protect him like she would. Even Christian. The last words she'd spoken had been, "Promise me. Promise me you'll take care of him. *Promise me.*"

He'd sobbed then like he had moments ago—not just at the loss of his wife, not at the tatters of a life she'd leave him with, but because she hadn't trusted that he'd do it without that promise. What had he ever done to make her doubt him? He'd loved Felix every minute. Loved *her* every minute, even when they realized a month before the birth that she was sick.

Her image had faded from before his eyes over the years. They'd had only two together—six apart. The memories had bleached out like cotton left too long in the sun.

The hurt had eased. Forgiveness had come in its place. And guilt, somehow, at the thought that he needed to forgive her.

Was it wrong for a mother to love her baby so fiercely? To love him more than her husband? Of course not.

Yet why hadn't she been able to see that a father's love was no less consuming?

Corinne cleared her throat. "I'm sorry. For your loss."

She'd be realizing he hadn't lied when he said he had no one left in Germany. Realizing why his back had gone stiff when she'd asked if he had a wife and children. She'd be sifting through every conversation, looking for hints he'd dropped.

If he'd been careful enough, then there wouldn't have been any. He didn't dare even think about Felix when he was around anyone else. When around her, he'd had to play the role he'd been given. And all his supposed colleagues thought he was not only widowed, but that his child had died.

It was the only way to keep his promise.

"I . . . had to bring him back, Chris. This is where you'd told him you'd find him. He was inconsolable in the country, and when I mentioned America, he . . ."

Felix curled into a tighter ball against him. "Not going to *Merica*," he spat out around his thumb. "I'm staying with *you*."

Josef lifted a helpless hand. "I didn't know you were here. That you'd knock on the door. Last I heard, you were still in Berlin, still teaching—how was I to know they'd send you here?"

"It's all right," he crooned, more for Felix than for Josef, though he certainly didn't blame his godfather for his decisions. He knew better than anyone how insistent—and *loud*—an outraged Felix could be. And given that they'd agreed that, as much as possible, he would keep the boy and his distinctive features out of sight . . . loud could get dangerous, quickly. "We're all here now. This is a gift from God, *ja*? We'll find a way. I can visit."

Josef shook his head, face pained. "Chris . . . how? A Nazi paying me a visit like Corinne warned you would do, yes. Once. Maybe even twice. But no more than that. And even that will draw attention. You think my neighbors won't see you?"

"Out of uniform then—"

"That would make it even worse if you were caught, I'd think. You couldn't claim it was part of your duties." Corinne tapped a fingernail on her bottom lip. Calculation clicked through her eyes. "You can meet up at my house."

"What?" Josef turned back to her, but not before Christian saw his look of incredulity.

Not before Christian felt it himself.

"It's the simple answer. It's no secret that you're an old friend of mine, Josef. If any of the neighbors ask, I could say you need a few hours' help now and then with your grandson, while you run errands. I don't have class on Tuesdays or Thursdays. You could come then. And Christian has been stopping by on random evenings anyway—he set his office up at the library, you know. Though I'm only just beginning to understand why."

"*What?* Were you trying to terrorize the poor

girl?" Now his godfather spun back to him, ignoring the bit about the library. That would surely come as no surprise to him. Where else in Paris could he possibly go to feel at home?

And the accusation shouldn't have made him laugh, but never in his life had anyone accused him of being terrifying. Brazen, yes. Occasionally courageous to the point of foolhardiness when it was to defend someone he loved, certainly.

But as his favorite childhood bully could attest, his attempts were more comical than terrifying.

"It's her own fault, for being the only one in Paris I've been able to have an intelligent conversation with. If she'd just played dumb, I'd have given up on her mother's library books months ago."

Corinne smirked.

Josef frowned. "What books? Yvonne hasn't checked any books out in years."

"Years?" Christian's gaze snapped back to Corinne. Narrowed.

She gave an innocent bat of her eyelashes. "Well we never saw the point in paying for *two* memberships to the library . . ."

Josef glanced from one of them to the other, eventually waving it all away and leaning back again. "Foolish of me. When is Corinne Bastien *ever* afraid of the things she should be? So you are already acquainted, clearly. And meet regularly enough that its continuing will not draw undue attention. Although . . ." A new frown. "Has gossip not already been at work over that?"

Corinne chuckled. "Given the things I say about him to all my neighbors after one of his searches that ought to be illegal?"

Perhaps Christian would have winced over it, had it not been exactly what she ought to have said to them. If it didn't mean now that he could see his son. Hold him. Hear about his day. He rested his lips against the satin-smooth curls. "I know it isn't every day, Felix. But twice a week—that is a blessing, isn't it? I can see you every Tuesday. Every Thursday. But still we'll be safe."

As safe as any of them were in Paris right now.

For the first time, Felix turned his head so he could look at Corinne, repositioning himself in Christian's lap to better accomplish it. He studied her so long, it was a wonder she didn't shift uncomfortably under the perusal.

She only leaned forward, resting her elbows on her knees. "Do you have questions for me, Felix?"

No baby talk, no lilt in her voice like most adults used with children. Did she know that it was the same way Christian had always spoken to him? Like an equal, just of smaller size?

Felix let his thumb slip from his mouth. "What kind of house do you have?"

"It's a flat, much like this one, but about twenty

minutes' walk from here. I'm on the third floor. One of my neighbors still hasn't returned from the country, but there's another family two doors down with a little girl who's eight. Her name is Desirée."

"Do I have to do chores at your house? Grandpapa Josef makes me do chores."

Corinne repressed a smile. "I *do* expect guests to clean up their own messes, if they make one, but I don't imagine you'd have to do any other chores while you're there."

"Do you have a radio?"

"I do."

"Chocolate?"

She pursed her lips. "I don't. But I think your *vati* can help you with that."

He hadn't used any of his chocolate rations, honestly—it reminded him too much of Felix. "I do indeed. A perk of this very ugly uniform."

Felix frowned at him and twisted around to run a finger over one of the buttons. "It's not ugly."

Only because he couldn't understand what it stood for. Christian leaned forward and pressed another kiss to his son's brow. "It's past your bedtime, young man. Let me tuck you in, and then I'll have to see the *mademoiselle* home, or she'll be in trouble for breaking curfew."

"Oh!" Her gaze flew to the clock on the wall. "I didn't realize it was so late."

But another perk of the uniform—curfew didn't

apply to him. Nor to whomever he was with. He stood with Felix, shooting her a look. "Wait for me. Ten minutes isn't enough for you to get home."

She held up her hands in surrender. Or, more likely, because she wanted more answers on the walk back to Boulevard Arago.

And he'd be happy to provide them—after he tucked his little boy into bed and lingered there to watch him fall asleep.

TWELVE

Corinne hadn't realized how much she'd missed the night. Watching from her window wasn't the same as walking through a warm summer evening—and these summer nights were especially beautiful, with no light from streetlamps or windows. Stars actually twinkled down on Paris from the heavens—something rarely seen when the city was free and glowing with electric lights. Blackouts had been in effect for a year already as they feared invasion, but not until the Nazi curfew did she realize how much she'd always loved nighttime walks. To have one again restored some small part of her soul.

One small, unexpected blessing in a ravaged world. She'd have to learn how to count such things. How to relish them. How to thank God for them.

Beside her, Christian drew in a long breath. Neither of them had spoken yet—it seemed too dangerous. The streets were too quiet, too empty. It felt like any word they spoke would be picked up and passed from hand to hand in the shadows.

But the song of the stars, the dance of the wind had been conversation enough during the walk, and now her building loomed before her.

She didn't ask if he wanted to come up. He

didn't ask if he could. They both knew there were still answers she needed.

And the moment they were safely in her flat, Radio Paris switched on to drown out their voices, she spun to face him. "Tell me. Tell me the real reason you sent him away."

Had she ever even looked at him before? Really looked?

She'd noted the sandy hair, yes, that had probably once been as blond as Felix's. The average height. The spectacles that he'd take off halfway through a debate and toss to the nearest table as punctuation for whatever point he'd been making.

But she wasn't sure she'd ever really noticed how blue his eyes were behind the lenses. How beautiful he was with tears dried on his face. How compelling the line of his jaw was as he rubbed a tired hand along it, as if remembering the feel of tiny fingers there half an hour before.

She couldn't recall the last time she'd seen a man cry. She never would have guessed that it would break her heart in one second, and then knit it back together in the next.

He'd shattered her tonight. Shattered every idea about him she'd had, every thought, every assumption. Shattered her and left her . . . free.

He shrugged out of the uniform jacket he apparently hated as much as she did and slumped into his usual chair.

He had a *usual* chair. What had happened in her life, that he had a usual chair—and why hadn't she even noticed it? She perched on the arm of the couch, not quite ready to fully sit.

He had long fingers—a scholar's fingers, perfect for flipping through books, taking notes, writing essays. He ran them through his hair and then rubbed them over his eyes. "His . . . features."

She nodded, debating how to politely ask. "He was born with them?" She'd seen children with cleft palates, ones who had undergone surgery to attempt to correct it. But the eye, the ear, the strange shape of his skull . . . those she'd never seen before.

Christian's nostrils flared. He nodded. "They didn't know, when he was born, how extensive it might be—inside, I mean. Whether he would ever walk, ever talk, whether his brain was correctly formed or not. Whether it would affect his breathing as he grew, his balance . . . they had no answers. The surgeon didn't even want to correct his cleft palate, he said it was useless, given the extent of the other malformations."

Corinne winced at the word just as he did. And melted onto the cushion. "But he seems fine—I mean . . ."

"He is smart as a whip, quick, strong—he *is* fine." His eyes slid shut. "Just missing an eye. Missing an ear. Missing the right shape to his skull. But it makes him no less a person."

"Of course it doesn't!"

His gaze met hers again. He swallowed. "When he was still a baby, the letters began. His birth defects had been recorded, you see. But the government . . . the government wanted me to know that I didn't have to shoulder the burden of a malformed child. That there were institutions to help, that specialized in children like him." His fingers dug into the arm of his chair. "I had just buried my wife, just nursed my son through the wounds of his first surgery, and they wanted me to hand him over."

Corinne dug her own fingers in, to keep from reaching across for his. "What sort of institutions?"

His laugh lacked all humor. "I didn't know, at first. I imagined them to be like schools or orphanages. I actually said, to one of the kind-eyed women who came by when he was three, that perhaps I'd consider it when he was a little older. I reassured her—because I thought she actually *cared*—that my mother kept him during the day and loved him to pieces, that he seemed to be developing like a normal toddler, that he was no burden. I told her to drop by again in a year. Before I knew. Before I knew that the children they took didn't ever go home again. Before our family doctor told me in a whisper that a colleague of his had been called to one of these places to euthanize them."

"No." She wanted to shout it, but she couldn't. Could barely work even that breath through her throat. How could anyone look at that sweet boy, at any child, and want to kill them, just because they were different?

Christian stared straight ahead, and she wondered what he saw. His son? Their doctor? That kind-eyed woman who'd come to his door and tried to deliver his boy to his death? "Gradually, the messages changed. They went from *we can help* to *we can get rid of him for you.* Parents, you see—good, Aryan parents who were ashamed of their disgraceful offspring, the ones who demanded time and energy and cost them their pride—they were *begging* for help. Asking for the government to do the 'kind' thing and end their children's 'misery.'"

Her stomach rolled. She leaned forward, bracing her elbows on her knees and resting her head in her palms.

"I joined the Party, because they were always kinder to their own. I thought it would make it easier to get medical help. I thought they'd stop harassing me if I said I was one of them. But it only got worse. And then—then it wasn't optional anymore. Children with facial deformities *must* be delivered to the government."

She sucked in a breath and looked up, because she felt his gaze return to her.

He looked haunted. Empty. Tormented. "What

was I to do? What was I to do but get him out of there? They would have *killed* him."

"Of course you got him out." Her hand lifted of its own accord, reached for him. Settled over those fingers threatening to rip the upholstery on her chair. She didn't much care if he did. "Only . . . why didn't you come with him?"

His face twisted, and two more tears slipped out of his eyes. "They were watching me. I—I was too vocal in my arguments. I tried to appeal the order, I gave a lecture about the sanctity of life—*all* life—that had the Ministry breathing down my neck. I tried to just take him on holiday, get out of the city for a while so I could think it through, and we were stopped by the Gestapo and turned back around. But it was me they were watching. He was just a boy—he was no threat. I was the one they kept their thumb on."

She stroked her thumb over his knuckles. Paltry comfort, but all she knew how to give. "All right. That makes sense then, that you would send him away. To Josef. But didn't they suspect you all the more, then? Why wouldn't they have arrested you?"

For a long moment, he was silent, just letting the tears slip unchecked down his cheeks. Then he drew in a long breath. "It was Dr. Schwerin's idea. We would fake his death—and make it a medical issue, not an accident. He created a fake death certificate, performed a fake autopsy, and filed a report saying that a recent growth spurt had triggered the collapse of his lungs, which had indeed been underdeveloped. That friend of mine I mentioned, who was a police officer—Reich Security, now. He helped us sneak Felix out of Berlin during one of his holidays. Josef met him in Strasbourg."

Her breath shook. "Those are good friends."

"The best. The doctor had treated Ilse, had tried so much for her—he had fought so hard, so long for Felix. And Erik—" He paused, breathed a laugh. "Erik Reinholdt is so different from me on the outside. He scorns the church, he skirts whatever rules he can, he *tormented* me when we were children." He shook his head, fondness in his eyes. "But somehow, by the time we grew up, he was my best friend. He still lives in the house he grew up in, after his parents retired to the country. Two doors down from my parents. But since I got married, we really only saw each other there in the old neighborhood. My colleagues didn't know him. His didn't know me. No one ever drew the connection."

Another pulse of silence, his gaze dropping to their hands. "And so . . . I lived out my part of the tale. Contrite, horrified that I had argued that my son was healthy when clearly he wasn't. I said what I was supposed to say. Taught what I was supposed to teach. Let them think they'd won, that I'd seen the light. Hoping, praying every day that even if I lost my soul, it would save my son's life."

"Christian." She didn't know what else she meant to say. What could she? What words could change even a whisper of that horror. "Were you . . . eventually, I mean? Planning to come here?"

His lips turned up, but it was more grimace than smile. "Honestly, I thought I'd be arrested and killed long before now. But I said I would, after a year. That was the plan—before we knew that France would be occupied territory by then. I was going to request a leave, a holiday, and come here. But then war made everything uncertain, and . . ." He shook his head. "I thought it was all over when they called me in. Schwerin had been brought in for questioning a month before, when he was caught treating Jews—I thought they'd found us out, somehow. That I'd be sent to one of those camps."

"Camps?"

"They call them concentration camps—prison camps. They had to build them when the prison system was overburdened with political prisoners. Now . . . they're everywhere. They send the Jews, the Gypsies, the homeless, anyone who gets on the wrong side of the Gestapo." His eyes had gone unfocused. He took his glasses off, tossed them to the table as he always did. "I thought I'd never see my boy again. And then . . . this." He motioned to himself.

To his uniform. Corinne had to shake her head. "I still don't understand why they gave you this position if you'd been in such trouble with them before."

He moved his head slowly from side to side, gaze still on the past. "Different divisions. Usually their files are impeccable though. I have heard so many stories of people brought in for questioning, their whole lives seeming to be laid out in their files, things they couldn't think how the Gestapo knew. Yet when I sat before them, they had none of it. None of the inflammatory lectures I'd given were noted. None of my arguments over Felix. My file was *clean*. Glowing, even. As if I'd always been an enthusiastic Party member."

She squeezed his hand. "The work of this friend of yours?"

"That's my best guess." He snorted and turned his hand under hers, so that their fingers wove together. "He kept telling me to leave, to go to Paris while I still could. He warned me that when the army took over, my chance would be gone. That Josef would do what he promised and take Felix to safety. But I was so afraid—so afraid that if I moved too soon, I'd lose him forever. And I was convinced that the mighty French army could hold Hitler at bay."

"We all thought so too." When was the last time a man had held her hand? Papa had, of course. And Oncle Georges. Once in a while, their mutual friends from the library would give her fingers a squeeze or a pat. But they never held her hand like this, fingers entwined through hers. And never had she let a man her own age do so. She hadn't been ready for such a distraction.

But it didn't distract, not as he held on as if she were an anchor in a storm. It focused. "However it happened, you *are* here now, and so is he. Together. And for now, meeting here should work. I'll have Josef bring him by every day, say I'm helping him in the afternoons after class so he can attend his own business, so that you and they aren't always coming only on the same days. But we should make long-term plans—plans to get you both out of here."

She could call on Oncle Georges for help. Send them to Maman and Papa's family in England, perhaps. If such things were possible—if England could keep Hitler at bay. Get them false papers, so they wouldn't be sent to the Isle of Man or forbidden entry in the first place.

"Maybe." He sat forward, not letting go of her hand but using his free one to pinch the bridge of his nose. "I don't know. I will have to consider everything carefully. The uniform does grant me certain privileges . . . but I'm still just a lackey. I have no authority outside of the libraries and literary circle. And Ackermann watches me carefully. I know well that Kraus reports everything I do to him." For the first time since they sat down, since he started his tale, he looked her in the eye. "I can't risk losing him forever. I can't . . . I can't bear it. Staying here, playing the game—if that charade will keep him safe, then I'll wear this blighted uniform forever. If trying to escape it would put him at risk, then so be it. God knows who I am beneath the insignia. It will have to be enough."

She wanted to say it wasn't—that being a secret godly man wasn't nearly good enough, that he ought to shuck the dressing of evil, hold his child close, and run for freedom.

But how could she tell this broken father to put his son at even greater risk? She had a feeling that the Nazis wouldn't deal kindly with one of their officers trying to defect to England. He was right about that. If he was caught—the chances of which were higher than she wanted to think, if what he said was true—then they'd likely execute him. Him, and Felix with him.

She blew out a long breath. And could admit, silently at least, that it was a selfish thing, to want him free of that uniform. Because she liked the feel of his fingers wrapped around hers. She liked the way he was looking at her, as if he hadn't just let her begrudgingly into his secrets, but as if he welcomed her there with joy. With relief. Because it would be so easy to really like this man, now that she knew what was true and what was facade.

But she didn't want to be one of those women. One of the collaborators who smiled at their Nazi paramours and ignored the voices of their own people condemning them for it. She didn't want anyone to think she was like that. To catch her looking at him like she knew well she was doing right now—wondering what would happen if he leaned forward just a bit more, over, and pressed his lips to hers—and brand her with the same iron.

She didn't want to fall in love with a Nazi— even one who hated the Nazis as much as she did. Yet if he defected, left Paris, how would that be any better? She couldn't leave, not if she meant to see through the role she'd assigned herself in this war, gathering the information from her students.

But was that effort even worthwhile? Or was it just delusions of grandeur? Would the information they gathered do a lick of good anyway? Maybe she was a fool to risk so much for it all. She was no better than Don Quixote, tilting at windmills.

Maybe . . . maybe, if he were free of the uniform, it would be worth the sacrifice. Maybe . . .

Perhaps he read those thoughts in her eyes as clearly as he seemed to gauge all her others. He pulled his fingers free, cleared his throat, and stood up. "I appreciate your willingness to help in all this—but I won't hold you to it. Think it through. Weigh the options. I know you won't want the neighbors to talk, to assume things, and . . . how long will they really believe I'm only coming to search for books?"

Should she have felt rejected? She could imagine Liana assuming he didn't *want* to spend more time with her and was making excuses.

But Corinne had seen more of the world, more of *people* than Liana had. She knew very well that Christian spoke from his sense of honor, not from his own desires. She smiled. "Oh, they were already suspicious of that. I had to tell them that poor Kraus was all but illiterate, and that it seemed you mostly stopped by to spar over books. Which debates, of course, I let you win, because you occupiers are notoriously bad-tempered when you lose."

There—a hint of a smile. "Let me, do you? Strange. I don't think Corinne Bastien has ever purposefully lost a single argument in her life."

She lifted a shoulder in a shrug and stood too. "There are many things about Corinne Bastien that you have yet to discover. But." She stepped closer, into his space. Just to test—to watch the way his eyes shifted, his pupils dilated, his breath hitched. "It seems you'll have the opportunity to learn a bit more, at least. Because I'm not going to change my mind about the offer."

His breath whooshed out. "Has anyone ever mentioned that you're impulsive? And that such tendencies can lead one into trouble in this day and age?"

She chuckled. "Trouble and I are old friends. When she doesn't come to call often enough, I go out and seek her. Such an interesting companion, after all."

He didn't smile, didn't laugh. Just regarded her long and evenly. "I don't want you to regret this. To land yourself in danger for us—veritable strangers, after all. Who you never would have met were it not for this horrible war."

"Strangers?" Incredulity seeped into her words now, and she gestured toward the building next door. "Your godfather is like family to me! You think if the war had held off, if you'd come to Paris in a few months like you originally planned, that we wouldn't have met? You think if I'd realized all this time that *you* were the *Little Chris* they speak of so fondly, I wouldn't have treated you differently from the start?"

She wanted to ask about the moniker—but she already knew the reason. His father, too, had been Christian. But when she'd heard the men talking about *Little Chris* over the years, she'd assumed he was still a teenager, a student. She certainly hadn't realized he was older than she was, that he'd been married, widowed, was raising a child. She'd had no way of making the connection between their favorite "upstart intellectual" whose surname she'd never learned and the Nazi officer who'd taken over their world.

Abraham could have told her. But no doubt he knew how precarious was the line Christian was walking. What was at stake if any of them slipped. She wouldn't begrudge them, any of them, their secrets.

How could she, when she had her own?

Again his eyes shifted, this time turning soft. "That is a happy thought, isn't it? That for the past seven years, my friends have been yours. That when they left me, they found you. When you look at it that way, it doesn't seem so odd anymore that I knew immediately that I liked you better than anyone else in Paris."

Ciel. She eased back a step, lest she do something stupid like wrap her arms around him. "You did not. You thought I was an impudent teenager hiding her mother's books."

"I've dedicated my life to impudent teenagers." He smiled, but it faded. His gaze dropped. "I thought . . . I thought I could make a difference there, with them. That if I could just help them see that these ideas are mad, convince them to keep their minds open . . . Perhaps if I hadn't been so distracted with my own family problems. Perhaps I'd have done a better job of helping them see how dangerous the path they'd chosen is."

"Don't." Her fingers reached out again before she could stop them, found his. "You cannot shoulder the burden of this. It is so much bigger than you. Rooted in bitterness and discontent that fed generations before you ever got up to try to teach them."

He nodded, his eyes flicking to the copy of *Marianne* still sitting on the table, under his glasses. She hadn't had the heart to toss it out—she kept opening it up to that article, rereading the words. *The France which cannot be invaded.*

Had he read it? Suddenly she suspected he had. Especially with the way his larynx bobbed as he swallowed. "There is a Germany that cannot—has not—been invaded too. I must believe that. I have been living for seven years in an occupied country, but the madness of the loud and the few and the violent will *not* be our legacy forever. It cannot."

Oh, forget all the reasons she shouldn't. She stepped closer and wrapped her arms around his waist. "It won't. We'll win, somehow. We'll win this war. We'll keep fighting, keep resisting, keep thinking and believing and praying—and someday, you'll go back there and help rebuild. You just have to survive until someday, Christian. You and Felix and Abraham and Earnst and Josef."

"Until someday." He sighed, but his arms came around her. It wasn't an embrace of passion or desire or attraction. It was just two tired people who realized they were allies after all, holding each other up. His chin rested on her hair. "How I pray we'll all live that long."

THIRTEEN

1 October 1940

Christian switched on a lamp and hummed a snatch of "*Ode an die Freude*" as he moved to the next shelf of books awaiting his attention. He moved them to his worktable, making the stacks large enough that Kraus, when he came in from his cigarette break outside, groaned.

"Again, Professor?" he asked.

Christian smiled into the pages. "It is my job, *soldat*."

"No other officer works so much overtime. It is nearly time for supper."

So it was—and he would take it next door, with Josef. With Corinne. With *Felix*. He flicked his gaze up toward his aide, careful to keep his eyes blank. "You might as well go home."

They went through this little dance four of seven days of the week—even on the nights when Christian *didn't* knock on Corinne's door, because it wouldn't do for Kraus to notice the pattern.

The younger man sighed. "Ackermann doesn't like me leaving you here unattended."

That was new. Usually Kraus argued about his duty and Christian's overworking, but he'd never actually put such a fine point on it. Christian frowned, spun to face Kraus fully, and let his perplexity settle on his face without a mask. "I beg your pardon? Does my superior not like the idea of me being without help or does he think I need a babysitter?"

They both knew the answer, but Christian had never dared to call it out so baldly before, never forced his young aide to admit to his true purpose.

Kraus winced. "It is only that you aren't a soldier, sir, and—"

"And these *books* are not enemy combatants. They are *books*. They do not put up a fight when I stamp them or sort them or store them. So why, pray tell, would I need a soldier overseeing the process?"

Kraus flushed. "It is just—"

"Allow me to tell you what it *just* is." Christian straightened to his full height. He was no giant, but he had a couple inches on the *soldat*—who was probably still growing, young as he was—and he utilized them now. A professor dressing down a wayward student. "It is *just* a military officer uncomfortable with what he doesn't know. Ackermann is a fine officer—and please, tell him I said so when you report this conversation. He is exceptional at his job. But if he were capable of *this* job, then I would not have been recruited into the army and brought to Paris as the *bibliotheksschutz*. Is that not so?"

Kraus's flush deepened. "Of course, Professor—and no one doubts that you are an excellent library protector, but—"

"But some military men have an innate distrust of academics. He does not trust me because I did not volunteer, because I did not join the military of my own volition. Isn't that so?"

Kraus cleared his throat and looked away.

"And yet the very fact that I am here *now*, fulfilling a needed position that a purely *military* man is incapable of doing does not settle well either. When the simple fact is that no one who had spent his career following military pursuits would now be qualified for the job *I* have been assigned. So instead of second-guessing me and my authority at every turn and feeling the need to stand around watching me read, I highly suggest that you report back to Ackermann and tell him that I said that if he feels the need to watch me so closely, he can petition Goebbels to replace me here and now, because I will *not* suffer this a moment more. I have been patient for the last three and a half months, but this cannot continue."

Strength, he told himself. He must show it even when he didn't feel it. Blustering before a bully.

No, not blustering. He must actually face them all down, just as he had Erik and his gang when he was a boy. It didn't matter if he was weak and destined for a black eye. Vater had taught him the importance of knowing which fights to choose, hadn't he?

Christian needed to plant his feet now, make his stance clear, or he would be bulldozed over—and at this point, that meant danger for far more people than just *him*.

Josef. Felix. Corinne. All their safety now relied on him maintaining the trust of his higher-ups. He squared his shoulders, lifted his chin, and did his best imitation of a too-proud scholar. "I am a tenured professor of the most prestigious institution in Berlin. I am the chosen and trusted emissary of Goebbels to Paris. My work in the university library has made it the premiere example in all of Germany, my assistance creating the list of banned books has been applauded by Hitler himself, and I have had enough of this constant hovering, *soldat*. I am a man of letters. I am accustomed to working in peace. Do I make myself clear?"

Kraus edged back a step. "Of course, sir. I'll . . ."

"You'll go immediately to Ackermann and tell him that if I cannot be granted quiet evenings after working all day in the public libraries, then he should write to Goebbels immediately and have me replaced." He cracked a grin, and it went genuine when he saw the way Kraus startled at the change in his expression. "It's a matter of my sanity, Kraus. I am a solitary man. If I don't have a few hours of quiet each week surrounded by nothing but books, I'm liable to start snapping at everyone."

Kraus relaxed, a smile of his own overtaking his lips by millimeters. "I'd say I understand, Professor . . . but that sounds about like the worst punishment in the world."

Christian laughed. "Yet another example, then, of how our differences make us uniquely suited to our tasks. Go, *soldat*. *Please*. Before I assign you an essay to write to get you out of my hair."

Kraus's eyes went wide, and whether the panic in them was exaggerated for the joke or genuine, he took off toward the door at a comically quick pace. "I'm going!"

After the door had shut behind him, Christian sat, drawing in a long, slow breath as he did so. He would give Kraus forty minutes to be well and truly gone, as he always did. Time to do the actual work he said he was doing, though he didn't require nearly the time for it that he claimed.

It was a simple matter, really, given the nature of this particular library. Many of the titles in here were already known by the Party and banned. It was merely a matter of cataloguing them—because the library's records were not to be trusted—stamping them with the wretched red *V* and putting them where they should have been on the shelves all along.

Once in a while, he came across a book that hadn't been on the original list, because it was too new—but whose author was banned. These he took more time with, skimming through each one and making notes that he would send back to Goebbels on the contents.

Much as he'd like to leave out reference to anything inflammatory, he didn't dare. It would be too easy for someone to check his work and look up the books themselves.

Facts. He was only recording facts, which anyone could find on their own. It wasn't a betrayal. Wasn't a selling out of the men and women who had written the words. Most of them were well out of reach of the Nazis at this point anyway, safe in England or America, other copies of their work circulating freely in the part of the world that welcomed their thoughts.

He pulled forward a copy of Helen Keller's autobiography and sighed. Perhaps her words weren't *welcome* in Germany—but they were needed. His people needed to see that someone could be born different, could be born "less," could be born with defects that would have them killed now in Germany, but it didn't make them weak. It made them *strong*. It didn't make them a mark against their race—it made them the triumph of it.

Civilization wasn't just built on raw physical power. It was built on strength of character that made people overcome the worst of circumstances. He traced his fingers over the gilt lettering on the cover and prayed that Felix would have Keller's kind of strength. Her courage. Her ferocity in the face of limitations.

This title was already on the banned list, so he didn't need to flip through it—but he did, his eyes soaking up a few familiar, beloved passages.

On page 35, he paused. Frowned.

Keller's weren't the only words in these pages. In the margins were light pencil markings, random French and Latin and even German strung together.

The words themselves made no sense—none. He knew them all, and they were nothing but gibberish. Not just some rude lender's notes made in the margins. They had nothing to do with the text.

But the fact that this was the fourth book he'd found with such notations, all in the same hand . . . He flipped more carefully through the pages, reading the handful of places with writing. Several of the words repeated.

Some sort of code?

He tapped a finger against the time-softened trimmed edge of the book block, considering. It could be nothing—someone's strange and indecipherable shorthand. It could be more.

Either way, he closed the book and slipped it into the crate he kept well buried under other piles of books, with the other three tomes he'd found with similar markings.

He made no note of it in his records. And when he flipped through the master records of the library and found its entry, he wrote "Poor condition, destroyed" in all caps, as he had the other three—and several copies of books that really were in too bad a shape to be sent anywhere but to a burn pile. The mold infesting them would spread to other books if he stored them together and destroy the whole lot.

He worked until the emptiness of his stomach prompted him to look at his watch. Two minutes until his designated time to abandon the library and knock on Corinne's door. Perfect. He left himself a few notes on where to pick up tomorrow, switched off the lights, scooped up the three newly purchased books he had waiting by the door, locked up, and moved a few steps into the warm October evening.

Parisians still bustled up and down the streets, enjoying the hours before curfew. Already, though, he noted that the familiar residents of the neighborhood were growing thinner. Rationing had officially begun two weeks ago, and he'd overheard plenty of grumbling about how everyone had to stand in three different queues for five hours apiece to collect their different tickets, only to then stand hours more in line for bread or meat or pasta, only to be turned away when the grocers ran out—assuming they had anything to begin with.

Already he felt guilty for his full plates three times a day, and he knew well this was only the start. That the shortages would only get worse, not better, because no matter how much food France produced, it wouldn't go to the French anymore. It would go to Germany. Sent back to feed Christian's countrymen, to feed the military machine, to supply what their own farmers couldn't because their men were fighting this wretched war.

His eyes scanned the street as he walked, searching for any German faces, any Nazi uniforms, any autos belonging to them. He half expected to see Ackermann steaming his way, fury in his eyes, ready to call his bluff and have him sent back to Berlin.

Please, Lord God. He hadn't wanted to come here like this. Hadn't wanted to risk his son and Josef. But now, now that he got to hold him again twice a week, he couldn't bear the thought of leaving, any more than he could bear the thought of them being found out.

What would the Party do, if they discovered that Felix was still alive?

Even as he asked, he knew. They would kill his boy, just as they'd wanted to do in Germany. They would kill Christian—which he wouldn't fight, not if they'd taken Felix. But it wouldn't stop there, he knew it wouldn't. They would kill Josef for harboring him. They would kill Schwerin for faking his death. They would kill Erik for smuggling him out. They would kill Corinne for offering them a safe refuge.

So many good people, caught up in protecting his family. So much blood that would be on his hands if anyone caught him with his son.

He knew he'd taken a risk by issuing the ultimatum. But better to be sent back to Berlin for insubordination than to get caught and be responsible for the loss of so many beautiful lives.

Another check over his shoulder before he knocked on her door.

Eight. This would be his eighth visit to Felix in these rooms. Eight evenings spent with Felix in his lap or climbing over him, watching him build with the blocks Corinne had unearthed from somewhere, exclaiming over his drawings, listening as he shared what Josef had been teaching him in his private schooling in their new flat whose address Christian had refused to be given. Corinne had apparently been adding to his learning as well.

His little boy was going to be better educated than any other child in Europe, despite no Nazi-run government ever allowing him to step foot in a school.

Corinne opened the door, making a show of sighing. "It must be Tuesday again," she said at a volume loud enough to be heard by any neighbors who cared to listen. "I would threaten not to be at home if I thought you'd do something other than stand here and knock incessantly and destroy the peace of the whole building. Again."

They'd staged such a thing one night, just for show. To make certain all her neighbors knew that she didn't want him there, and that he was relentless. He held up the three books. "I bring you gifts of newly published literature and still you're so cool?"

She lifted her chin, eyes as cold as ice. "I could buy my own books."

"But who's to say you'd buy the ones I want to discuss with you? Let me in, Mademoiselle Bastien, if you please."

She stepped aside, a growl of annoyance in her throat.

He heard a soft *click* of another door—perhaps her other neighbors, recently returned from the countryside? Good. Let them all see and hear.

Not until she closed her own door behind him did he let himself grin. "And here they're the very ones you requested."

Corinne took the books from his hand with a quiet chuckle. "I certainly hope so. Felix is in the kitchen."

He paused, waiting for her to lock the door and slide the chain, before tossing his hat and jacket to a chair.

He wanted to shout his son's name as he used to do, when he'd come to collect him from his parents' house. He wanted to hear that laugh as Felix came bounding into the room, throwing himself into Christian's waiting arms. He wanted to roar like a lion and scoop him up, spin him around until he roared too.

He didn't dare, of course. They did their best to keep the neighbors from realizing that Felix was even still here while Christian was. So instead he moved softly into the kitchen, merely dropping to a knee and opening his arms as his son scurried toward him. Felix, too, had learned the value of silence in his months of exile. Not since that first night had he shouted "Vati!" or come running.

It didn't matter the volume. Didn't matter the speed. He folded his son into his arms, let his eyes slide shut, and held him close. "Hello, Felix."

"Come look what I've made, Vati." Felix gave him one more squeeze and then ran back to the table, tugging him willingly along by the hand.

Dinner, such as it was, simmered on the stove. He knew well that it would include some of the rations he'd slipped to Corinne, and which she had tried three times to refuse. *I know you don't want Nazi food,* he'd said at last, exasperated. *So don't eat if you don't want to. But you're feeding my son, and I will give him whatever I can, to spite them if for no other reason. Let me feed him, Corinne.*

266

She'd relented, but with that set to her mouth he was coming to know so well. The one that said she had many more objections she'd swallowed down, and that he hadn't really won, even if it looked like he had.

Every time he learned one new facet of her, the light would shine on a dozen more. Like this one—the way she squeezed past them to reach the stove and reached out to run her fingers through Felix's golden curls. The way his little boy smiled up at her with pure adoration and she smiled back with the same.

Eight visits he'd had with Felix—but she'd had more. She saw him nearly every day, watching him while Josef ran errands or enjoyed a rare solitary hour.

"Look, Vati." Felix shoved aside a few drawings of stick-figure dragons and robots and pulled forward a page with careful handwriting on it, in two different hands. The first, confident bold lines proclaiming *I am the way, the truth, and the life* in a feminine print, and the second the overlarge, clumsy imitation of a child.

Christian rested a hand on Felix's shoulder and grinned down at his eager face. "Beautifully done, Felix. And can you read it?"

His boy nodded eagerly and sounded out each word.

After exclaiming over the remarkable job he was doing, Christian glanced again at the lines of instruction. They were overcareful, as his own would have been had he been writing letters for his son to trace and follow. But even so, a bit of her own personality came through in them.

He glanced at the notepad she always kept on the counter, with her errand list scrawled far less neatly across it.

Familiar script, and not just because he saw it all over her house and library. But because it was the same hand that he'd just seen in the margins of the book next door.

"Christian? Are you all right?"

He blinked, refocused on where she stood by the stove, and realized that she'd said his name three times already. She stood with an old, stained apron tied over her neat skirt and blouse, her curls pulled back in a messy tail that he knew she wouldn't have worn out of her flat, and a spoon held out.

He smiled an apology. "I'm afraid my mind was on Felix. What did you say?"

"I've never made *gulaschsuppe* before, but Felix wanted it. Josef tried to remember what's in it, but he's clearly no cook. Tell me how close I am."

She was making his son's favorite soup? Of course she was. He shifted closer and took the spoon from her, blowing on the steaming broth before taking a sip. It wasn't bad, though it certainly didn't taste like his mother's. "I don't suppose you have Hungarian paprika?"

"Paprika." Her lips said she was irritated. Her eyes said she was amused. "Josef failed to mention paprika entirely."

"Where is he, anyway?" He hadn't seen him in the living room, but sometimes his godfather used this time for his own chores or errands.

"He isn't feeling well. I sent him home and told him Felix could stay here tonight. I'll drop him by on my way to the Sorbonne tomorrow."

Christian frowned. "Sick?"

"Just a cold. I daresay a good night's sleep and he'll be on the mend." She rummaged through a cupboard. "There we are—paprika. I doubt mine is Hungarian, but I have both sweet and spicy versions. Which does it take?"

"Both, actually. And lots of it—a tablespoon of the sweet, and then the spicy to taste. It's the key ingredient of the goulash."

She reached for two matching jars filled with red powder. "Clearly I should have asked *you* for the recipe."

"Clearly. Josef's wife did all the cooking, and since her death, he has eaten simply or with friends. I, on the other hand, decided years ago that I'd rather spend my evenings at home with Felix, and so I had better learn how to feed us."

"Oma gave him lessons," Felix put in as he strained up for a taste too. Christian blew on another spoonful of broth and gave it to him. "Definitely more paprika," he said.

Christian chuckled, highly doubting that his son would have been able to say anything beyond "No, that's not right" if he hadn't just heard their exchange. "And she gave Felix many lessons in cookie baking, isn't that right, *mäuschen*?"

Felix grinned, though it faded a moment later. "We can't make cookies here. Sugar and butter are rational, Tante Corinne says. And there's no chocolate."

"Rationed," he corrected by instinct, then reached to those sweet curls much like she'd done. "And she's right. But I daresay I can find one for you at a bakery for next time, all right?" Generally speaking, cafés and restaurants and bakeries were still granted enough to stay in business—though prices had soared to the point that few Parisians could afford the offerings. Only Nazis sat at their tables now most days.

"And we'll save up our sugar and butter whenever we get some," Corinne promised as she stirred in the paprika. "Perhaps there will be enough for some Christmas treats."

Saving up rations for three months, just in the hopes of having one or two batches of holiday sweets . . . and that was assuming she could find the supplies her coupons entitled her to. Christian shooed Felix back to the table and stepped closer to her, pitching his voice low. "And was there anything left by the time you got off work this week?"

She waved his concern away. "I wait in the queues on Tuesdays and Thursdays."

Except that she had to be here to meet Josef with Felix at noon, and sometimes she hadn't made it to the front of the lines by then. "Corinne..."

"I'm certain your good friend Gustaf would love it if I resigned so that I could wait for food with all the other housewives every day, but alas. We make do with what they have those two days."

Her "making do" had already resulted in her cinching her belt in a notch, but he knew better than to argue it again here and now. Instead, he'd be grateful she'd taken the meat he offered her for the goulash.

He couldn't begrudge her pride. He couldn't begrudge her desire to share in the hardship of her neighbors and friends, colleagues and students. He couldn't begrudge her the story she lived for them to see, that he was just a benign enemy she tolerated.

But his gaze dropped again to her notepad as he moved to help Felix clear the table so they could set it.

She knew all his secrets now—Felix, Josef, his opposition to the Nazi Party. She not only knew, she was a coconspirator, providing a place for them to meet.

Yet he knew none of hers. He hadn't asked.

He wouldn't. He owed her that privacy, that

protection. If ever he was caught and she somehow escaped implication, he didn't want to know anything that they could torture out of him, anything that could get her in trouble.

"Is my list really that interesting?" She'd come closer and glanced down as if expecting the list to suddenly say something more incriminating than "Return Liana's floral scarf" and "Adoration Friday at 5."

He shrugged. "It has been ages since I have attended Adoration. Our churches in Germany aren't technically closed, but they were stripped of everything, including every monstrance, cross, and crucifix. It was all melted down. For the war effort." Nothing left to hold the blessed sacrament, as if that meant the Nazis could rid Germany of those who adored Christ above Hitler.

As if their priests who had escaped arrest and murder weren't still blessing the host and preaching about loving one's neighbor, no matter the danger.

Corinne let out a long breath. "And if you were to attend such a thing here?"

He gathered the bowls and spoons from her cupboard and drawer. "I have ventured to Mass a few times, in my civilian clothes, and far from where I'm billeted. Even so, it feels like a risk. Perhaps I'm just paranoid but . . ."

"But for good reason." She sent the good reason

to the lavatory to wash up and then stepped closer to Christian, bringing with her the floral scent of her shampoo. "Desirée saw him today when Josef was bringing him up—he pretended to be asleep on Josef's shoulder, but she was so excited to see another child in the building . . . I told her a bit of the story we agreed on."

That Josef was her mother's cousin from Pozières and Felix was his grandson, that they had come to Paris for Josef's work and he needed help with the boy, who was hard of hearing—to account for the muteness they'd demanded of him. He knew to keep his face resting against Josef's shoulder, his missing eye and ear out of sight, and to keep from speaking lest someone detect a German accent or he slip up and say something he shouldn't.

Christian nodded. "We knew it was only a matter of time."

"I know, but . . . he's getting too big for Josef to carry him up all those stairs. And he cannot simply remain unseen for years on end, can he?" Her eyes glimmered—clearly an idea was brewing in that clever mind of hers.

Christian leaned against the workbench. "All right, out with it. You've obviously thought up a better story."

The beginnings of a smile played on her lips. "Have I ever told you of Old Jacques?"

He merely lifted his brows.

"He lived in my village, in Somme. One of the cantankerous old men that we children all avoided—and him especially because he was missing a leg from the knee down. Once, when I was ten, my friends and I were talking about how he'd run someone's brother out of his garden, and someone asked how he lost his leg. Another said it was the war, her mother had said so, and we all took her at her word. In fact, most of the village told that same tale—that he'd lost his leg in the World War, like so many others who came home with missing limbs."

Christian nodded. "A tragedy that both sides suffered."

"Yes, but . . ." She leaned in, eyes alight. "He didn't serve in the war—he couldn't. Because he lost his leg as a boy, jumping the tracks. He fell and was run over."

Christian sucked in a breath, shocked. "That's horrible."

"Of course it is, but that's not my point. My point is that the people who knew the truth had died or moved away, and the few remaining who did know it never paused to think about it, so the *expected* story was given about him. No one asked him, no one said it in his hearing, it's just what was assumed by an entire generation. I would probably still think to this day that he'd lost his leg in war if Maman hadn't heard us one day and corrected us."

He was beginning to see the direction she was going, though what particular door she meant to take him through he could only guess. "So you recommend a different story for Felix?"

She reached into a drawer and pulled out a small something, black and soft looking. When she unfolded the elastic band, he realized it was an eye patch. "Haven't you seen some of the families come in from the countryside that was bombarded? From Dunkerque? Plenty of civilians were caught in the melee, even children. Plenty are entering the city now with missing limbs. It is sad and horrible, yes—but it's also camouflage for Felix."

He took the miniature eye patch from her. "So we cover his missing eye and let everyone think it was caused by an accident."

"Let his hair grow—it's getting long anyway—to cover his ear, and the curls themselves will cover the shape of his skull. Any other abnormalities will be attributed to whatever accident people think befell him."

The fabric was soft, but something stiffer rested inside it—cardboard? No, more flexible. Perhaps leather. The elastic would all but vanish beneath the mass of golden curls.

Hide it. He'd never wanted to make his son so conscious of his differences that he felt the need to hide them. He wanted him to be like Helen Keller, to embrace what God had given him and be stronger for it. To write himself a life story worth telling to others.

He didn't want Felix to ever feel ashamed of what the world perceived as *missing*. Not when he had so much, so many gifts of spirit and heart.

But at the same time, they had to fight for his right to live. And if they could do that better by using a disguise as long as the Nazis were in power, by making Felix look more like a French boy caught in crossfire and not like a German boy running from the authorities, then he'd be a fool to refuse on principle.

He nodded, his swallow feeling hard in his throat. "We can ask him. I will not force him to wear this, but—"

Little steps ran their way, and, ever curious, Felix's gaze went straight to the eye patch. "What's that, Vati?"

Well, no point in wasting time. Christian held it up. "It's an eye patch that Tante Corinne made for you, if you'd like it."

Felix's mouth dropped open. "Like a *pirate?*" He snatched the fabric from Christian's hand and immediately tried to put it on.

Corinne laughed and reached to help him arrange it. "Josef has been reading him *Treasure Island*."

Of course he had. Christian smiled as Corinne settled the elastic under Felix's curls. She was right—his hair was longer than Christian had ever let it get . . . lest he be mistaken for a girl, which had always made him furious when he was four and five. But Josef had clearly not prioritized finding a barber. Or braved cutting it himself, given Felix's inability to sit still for more than ten seconds at a clip.

It could work. And per Corinne's story, they wouldn't even have to lie. Just to let people assume whatever they wanted.

Christian bent to a knee and made a show of surveying Felix from left and right. "Why, I do believe it's Long John Goldenhair himself! The most dreaded pirate of the Seine!"

Felix giggled and thrust forward an invisible sword. "Yo ho ho!" He went dashing off, no doubt to christen one of Corinne's sofas or chairs as his pirate vessel and set sail on the high seas.

"Dinner will be ready in just a minute, Felix," she called after him.

She sounded so . . . *normal*. Looked it, as she'd stood there with his boy, their blond curls matching every bit as much as their blue eyes. In some ways, she looked more like his mother than Ilse had with her dark hair.

He squeezed his eyes shut and braced a hand on the table after he stood again. He knew it wasn't fair of him to let her help them like this. To not only trust her with knowledge of Felix, but to weave her into their lives. To watch her smile with affection at his son and wish, wish, *wish* things were different.

For the first time in six years, he wanted to wrap his arms around a woman. He wanted to press his lips to hers and just *be* with her. He wanted to know he wasn't alone, that someone else loved Felix like he did. He wanted to come to this flat every day and find her here with his son and slip into that world and rest there.

He was a fool. Worse. He was selfish and cruel to even want such things. Such impossibilities. Such temptations.

"Christian." Her fingers brushed his cheek, as they'd done the night she learned of Felix—as they hadn't done since. His eyes opened, and he found her standing close, too close, concern making her frown and teasing out the tiniest of lines around her eyes, proving the age that seldom showed. "What's wrong? If it's the eye patch—"

"No, that's brilliant. It's just . . ." What? He couldn't tell her that he wanted to love her but didn't dare. He couldn't tell her that he wanted a life that would be her ruin. He had to find another truth to offer her. One that wouldn't ask her to risk anything more than she already had for him, for them. "I . . . may have issued my superior an ultimatum, via Kraus."

Her hand dropped, eyes going wide. "You *what?*"

He told her as they dished up bowls of soup and set them out to cool, and by the end of his tale, she was nodding. "Smart, I think. Men like that only respond to shows of strength."

He sighed and turned to call Felix in for supper. "Let's hope so."

FOURTEEN

23 October 1940

Corinne shut the door with a soft *click,* trying to ignore the way her chest squeezed every time Josef and Felix left her apartment. She knew that what she *ought* to do was spin away and remove the evidence Felix always left of his visits—colored crayons scattered over tables and to wherever they rolled on the floor when he abandoned them to act out some scene from whatever story Grandpapa Josef had read to him the night before, small cups half-filled with water in every room, wooden blocks teetering in impossible towers.

What she *wanted* to do was stand here for another long minute, rest her head against the wood, and savor the feel of Felix's little arms around her, hugging her close and bidding her farewell.

She'd never thought she was the most maternal of women. For so long she'd been focused on her education, and then on attaining a professorship when the odds were stacked against her. She'd dedicated so many years to fighting for the right to chase her dreams, knowing very well that she was sacrificing the chance for a home and family of her own.

Never before had she thought she'd minded. When parishioners made prod after poke after pointed comment about how her best years were wasting away and if she didn't get started soon, she'd never have a family, she'd shrugged it all off. She had Maman. She had her friends, her colleagues, her students. And since no man had ever made her heart pound the way Maman had described her own doing for Papa, Corinne had been content to say, *Later. And if never, then so be it.*

But she didn't have Maman now. Most of her friends, colleagues, and students had left Paris, and the new ones to take their places weren't exactly the same, even if they were precious.

And a man was making her heart pound, even when he wasn't here. Even when it was only his godfather and his son laughing with her in the autumn afternoon. He didn't *have* to be here—she saw him in Felix, and in Josef, and in the chair he always claimed. She heard his voice in the lines of conversation he ought to have spoken, in the stories Josef told, in the love in Felix's voice.

She wasn't just falling in love with the German professor—she was falling in love with his son, and this was bound to end poorly.

"Ah well," she said to the door. "Some of the best literature is tragedy, after all. That's no reason not to experience the story."

Her gaze fell to the small table she and Maman

had always kept by the door, which was, at the moment, empty of post. She'd meant to get it on her way up after her last class of the day, but she'd spotted the Pirate Goldenhair and his laughing guardian bounding through the building's front door as she approached so hadn't paused to take the time.

Now, however, she grabbed the small brass key and hurried down to fetch it. She had plenty of time to sort the post and *then* clean up the whirlwind of chaos Felix always left in his wake.

Liana was supposed to be coming by tonight after her "poetry" meeting. And while her friend knew that Corinne had been helping out with her "cousins," even she didn't know the truth. No one did, other than the four of them. And in Corinne's mind, the best way to keep the secret was to make certain she left no details out to be seen in the first place.

The breeze that drifted in through the door in the foyer when Madame Dardenne entered smelled of turning leaves and coming frost. It made Corinne smile as much as her neighbor did. "*Bonjour*," she said in greeting, moving to the row of shining brass letter boxes.

Madame Dardenne smiled and moved to her own box. "*Bonjour*, Corinne. Was that Felix I saw bobbing along with your cousin? Desirée will be sorry she missed him. She is still talking about their last game of pirate and island queen."

Corinne chuckled, pushing aside the anxiety she and Josef and Christian had all shared when Felix and Desirée had finally been officially introduced three weeks ago. At least once a week, the children played at Corinne's flat now. "It was, but his grandpapa still had a few things to get done and wanted to be home before dark."

Madame Dardenne shivered. "I am not looking forward to the winter and its lack of daylight. It is terrifying enough, going through their checkpoints in the light of day, even when I know I have nothing *verboten* with me. But at night?" The woman paused, her eyes widening a fraction, and then she rushed on to say, "Not that I think the Nazi men would do anything untoward, of course—I would not want to go through a checkpoint of French soldiers after dark by myself either. It's—"

"*Madame.*" Corinne reached over and rested her fingers on her neighbor's arm, giving her a comforting smile. "We are *all* uneasy passing through checkpoints. And no woman is likely to feel quite as safe as she once did walking the streets of Paris after dark, with the shift in our residents. As you say, we would feel no more secure if it were French soldiers teeming. Too many men in one place can lead to bad things, we all know that. They need our feminine influence to keep them gentle."

Her neighbor chuckled, though she didn't relax much.

Corinne couldn't blame her. This was the way of things now, and she was as guilty of it as anyone else. You never knew what neighbor might decide to report you for something. What friend actually thought as you did and which ones had decided that they didn't care what regime ruled over them, they just wanted to go on living their lives as best they could.

No one could speak their mind these days.

They each pulled their post from their boxes in silence, then both turned to the stairs. Once upon a time, the silence either would have been comfortable or easily broken by meaningless, peaceful chatter—who saw who at the bakery, what Desirée had said that had them laughing, a ridiculous line in a student's essay.

These days, the silence stretched tight, and Corinne had no idea how to break it without it snapping around and lashing her face.

Somehow, mines had infested her life. One wrong step, and it could all come shattering down around her.

She paused at her own door, a bit surprised when Madame Dardenne did too. "Corinne," she said softly, slowly, a furrow in her brows. "I know you've said repeatedly that I oughtn't to worry—about that officer from the library next door, I mean. But . . . I saw the way he looked at you last week, when you arrived home and found him waiting at your door. Say what you will, his interest isn't just in books."

Juste ciel. Good thing she had years of practice controlling the instinct to blush—she'd had to learn it to excel in the patriarchal world of academia, and it served her well now too. She tamped down the instinct to demand, "How was he looking at me?" and instead huffed. "I shouldn't be surprised—it's difficult to keep a man focused on what I have to say at the best of times. All my mother's fault for passing along these curls."

Her neighbor chuckled, easing onward a step. "And the lips, and the eyes, and the figure—but I am serious, Corinne. Perhaps books are his excuse, but they are not all he thinks about when he's with you."

No—he thought of Felix and Josef and the tightrope on which they were all walking. Corinne sent her a smile. "Not to sound arrogant, my friend—but I have plenty of practice with such things. I know how to keep him on the other side of the room. And given that plenty of our conversations have been about his wife, Ilse, it is always easy enough to steer him back that direction. He may be a Nazi, but he isn't without *some* morals, praise be to God."

Madame Dardenne chuckled and half turned away, toward her own door. "Good. But even so . . . I heard too many stories of too many men in past wars who missed their wives so much they sought comfort elsewhere."

"Well, lucky for us all, I've never been accused of being a bastion of comfort."

They chuckled together, and the jest did its job. Some of the tension eased, and they each opened their doors and said a friendly farewell.

Corinne wasted no time in throwing the bolt and sliding the chain once she was inside. There was a book in her post. She dropped everything else onto the table and tore into the brown paper wrapping it.

The Count of Monte Cristo, which meant Rosette in Pas-de-Calais—the informant Oncle Georges was most interested in hearing from, given the German presence in the coastal region near the English Channel. This was the third book she'd sent back to Corinne, and its margins were burgeoning with secrets.

After pulling forward the dictionary they used as a key, she quickly decoded the seeming gibberish, turning it into information on Luftwaffe movements and conversations she'd overheard at her family's café while pretending she didn't know a word of German.

As she scrawled the last of it out and reread it, Corinne's stomach twisted. It had been bad enough, knowing in advance that the *blitzkrieg* of England would start when there was nothing she could do to stop it, when the warning Oncle

Georges sent to London had been met with an assurance that it was expected, that they were as prepared as they could be. That children had been evacuated to the country and the Royal Air Force was poised to defend England's skies.

Still Corinne had glued herself to the radio every possible moment, the BBC turned down low so she could hear the reports of both the French and English broadcasters, painting a picture in words for her of a bombed-but-not-broken London.

She'd still wondered after every night of bombing if, this time, they'd hit her mother. If the one blood relative she had left in the world had been snatched from her, and how long it would be until she'd know it, if so. She'd never known her insides could twist so tight, that an empty flat could weigh so heavy.

This new information, though—it didn't *change* things, not really, but it made it all the worse.

She hadn't thought it could get worse than bombs raining down on the city where her mother was living. But it turned out, all that was needed to achieve such a thing was a crueler bomb.

She granted herself one long breath and then moved to the phone, dialing her uncle's home number first and, when there was no answer, resorting to his secondary one that he put on his cards. It was on its fifth ring when there was a knock at her door.

He didn't even grant her time to panic before calling out, "It's me, *mon chouchou*."

She let out a huff of relief and put the receiver back in its cradle, hurrying to let Oncle Georges in. "Are you a mind reader now? I was just trying to call you."

"Oh?" He flashed her a grin and stepped inside. "Good to know I'm keeping up my knack for being in the right place at the right time."

She closed the door behind him, frowning at the suitcase he was carrying. The weight in her stomach increased threefold. "You're leaving Paris?"

He did it frequently, for a day or two, for reasons she never dared to ask. But for those quick trips, he never carried a suitcase, just an old rucksack from his military days, over his shoulder.

His smile made no sense at all. It was full of mischief—delight even. "On the contrary. I've just brought you a present."

She narrowed her eyes, given that the *last* present he'd brought her had been black-market sweets. "It's not illegal *bonbons* again, is it?"

"Oh, Rinny. You couldn't be further from the truth." He strode toward the kitchen, pushing her things aside unceremoniously so he could set the suitcase on the table. A few quick movements and the latches were undone, the suitcase open, and neatly folded clothes in view.

She shifted into place at his side, curiosity compounding into something more like wonder as he did something she couldn't quite catch, but which presumably released some other locking mechanism—because in the next moment he lifted out a tray that the clothes rested on, and then undid the lining in the top too.

Revealing . . . mechanical things. She didn't know what they were, but they looked almost like . . . "What is that?" Her voice was low as a hiss, stealthy as a whisper.

"Suitcase wireless set," he replied, voice low but casual. No, not casual—*bright.* Like a boy with a new toy. "Something else, isn't it?" His words had shifted into English, which they rarely did unless it was for a purpose. "They've been working on this sort of technology for ages—I volunteered to do a field test for them. Could be months or years yet before they're ready to send them out with agents, but we have to be sure the technology will work at such a distance, with interference from Nazi radios."

Corinne dropped to a chair, ears buzzing. He had a wireless set? In a suitcase? In her *flat?* "Have you gone mad?" She made her words English, too, since he had. "If you get caught with that—"

"Please." A condescending look for a single beat, then another grin. "Though if you don't *want* to speak with your mother—"

"What?" She snapped up straight, gaze pinballing from him to the contraption. "Maman?"

"This comes to us courtesy of Bletchley Park, Rin. With instructions saying that she and David will be listening specifically for our messages at four each afternoon."

She checked her watch—five minutes until four. Then studied the equipment again. "Is it telegraph or—"

"Radio." In proof, he unhooked one of the pieces and pulled it out—it looked more or less like a telephone receiver.

Tears clouded her eyes. "You mean . . . I can really *talk* to her? Hear her?"

He offered the receiver. "Don't count on it sounding quite like the BBC, but yes." He fished headphones from their nest and handed those over too. "I'll get it set up." But he paused a second later, eyes finally falling to the book and papers he'd moved aside. "Is that something of interest to report? Is that why you were calling?"

She tried to blink back the tears, but the blighted things kept burning. She nodded and handed him the decryption, watching his mirth fade into the serious facade she was more accustomed to seeing these days.

He muttered a word she didn't care to translate and rubbed a hand over his face. "Delayed detonation—that will let the bombs penetrate deeper into buildings. More destruction."

"I know." She positioned the headphones over her ears. "I don't know how knowing it will help them, but . . ."

"But it's always better to know. Even when knowing can't mean action." He set the paper in front of her and went about powering up the set with a few flips of switches. "Go ahead and report it to them, but be certain to use the code names we've devised for every person and place."

"I remember." How could she forget, when saying a name could mean getting that person captured and killed? "Is there risk of the signal being intercepted?"

"Always—but as long as you don't give away locations or people, it's just more babble in the air that means nothing to anyone but us. And so far as I know, the Germans are still behind us in interception technology. Even so, if we can do it, we'd better assume they can."

Corinne nodded, jumping a bit as a crackle filled her ears. Just static for a minute, but then precisely at four, she heard a masculine voice.

"This is Atlas One, for Blanche and the dragon slayer. Atlas One, over."

Her eyes slid shut. *David.* She'd only met him once, briefly, and wouldn't have recognized his voice under any other circumstance—but she knew it now. David, Papa's nephew who had grown up across the Atlantic, spending half his life in America and half in England. A regular Atlantean, she had called him—*Atlas One*, he'd dubbed himself.

Her call sign was more a joke—a play on her favorite childhood fairy tale, Snow White. *Blanche.* And of course, Oncle Georges had opted for the saint who bore his name and supposedly slayed a dragon. "This is Blanche. Go ahead, Atlas One. Is Evergreen there? Over."

Yvonne, a feminization of *yew,* an evergreen tree. "This is Evergreen. Over."

Maman! Corinne had to cover her mouth to hold back the sob that wanted to burst free. It didn't sound clear as if she were in the room with her, or even quite like if she was on the phone somewhere in Paris. There was static and background noise and a distortion that made her mother's voice sound a bit too high.

But it was *her.* "Evergreen," she finally whispered. "It is good to hear your voice. Over."

"I was just thinking the same, Blanche. You are well? We've heard horrible things."

"*You* have? This Blitz—"

"Radio protocol, Blanche," her uncle chided as she and her mother spoke over each other, creating crackling chaos.

She nodded. Gripped the receiver. And let her eyes slide closed.

Her mother was alive. Her mother was well. Annoying as all the "over" business was, if it meant hearing her more clearly, she'd rein herself in.

They could only speak for a few minutes, so it was all basic updating and assurances, and then she passed along the news from "Little Egret" about the new delayed action bombs that the Nazis had been bragging about. All too soon, they were signing off, and Oncle Georges was powering the radio down again.

"We can't use this often," he said as he quickly packed it all up and away again. "And not from the same place twice in a row. Next week, we'll call from my flat. The week after that, from the office. Then perhaps here again. Understand?"

She didn't, really—she knew it had something to do with tracing signals, though the science of it was beyond what she'd bothered to learn. But his point was clear enough. "All right."

"I'd better go. If I'm caught with this thing, I don't want it to be anywhere near you." He took two strides, out of the dining area and into the bookcase-lined living room. And then he halted.

Only then did she realize what he'd be seeing—what it was a miracle he hadn't spotted the moment he entered, and he'd be kicking himself for being so distracted.

The blocks. The crayons. The papers with "Felix the Pirate" scratched crookedly onto them because "Goldenhair" was too long to write, he'd said.

"Corinne . . . have you been babysitting?"

She'd known it was only a matter of time before he found out, given the way he dropped by unannounced. But when week after week had slid by without him crossing paths with them, she had dared to hope it could continue.

No—she wasn't that naive. She'd just decided she wouldn't invite that particular trouble until it came pounding on her door. "You remember Josef Horowitz?"

He turned slowly back to face her. "Of course. I didn't realize he was back in Paris though."

"He is, but under a new name—a French name, with French papers. For him and his grandson, Felix. He's keeping a low profile though, of course, and needs help now and then with the little boy."

A perfectly reasonable, logical explanation. And true, every word of it.

But Oncle Georges's eyes still narrowed. "And since when do you volunteer to help with children?"

Her mouth dropped open. "I have watched Desirée plenty of times for Madame Dardenne!" Well, twice. But he didn't know that. "You act as if I'm *opposed* to children, when all I've ever said is that I'm in no hurry to have them and have no interest in teaching at that level."

His face shifted back to neutral, but his gaze stayed locked on her. Reading. Deciphering. Decoding. "What aren't you telling me."

Not a question. And she knew better than to give him anything but the truth. Even so, he'd have to settle for *part* of the remaining truth. "The little boy, Felix—he was smuggled out of Germany because of facial deformities. They wanted to euthanize him."

Her uncle winced, but she could see the suspicion turn into compassion. "Monsters."

"We've fit him with an eye patch to cover the missing eye, and his hair is long enough to cover the deformed ear. Everyone thinks he was hurt at Dunkerque when their hotel was bombed."

The corner of his mouth pulled up. "Like Old Jacques, eh?"

"Exactly. He speaks French like a native at this point, and you know Josef does too. They've moved flats, away from the neighbors who knew them as the Horowitzes. I know it's a risk for them to come here, so close to the library, where people might recognize Josef, but he needed help, and Felix took to me."

It was an over-explanation, but he'd expect as much from her when he thought she'd be afraid of him telling her to cut off her friends.

Round and round the deception swirled—deceiving even with truth. No lie, and yet the most important fact, withheld.

He couldn't know about Christian. *That* would be a bridge too far.

He eased closer to her again and pressed a kiss

to her brow. "I always knew you had a soft heart buried somewhere underneath all the mischief."

She puffed out a breath and gave him a friendly shove. "Take it back."

He chuckled and turned away again. "I trust you to be cautious, *mon chouchou*. And I trust Josef to be too. For now. But if restrictions increase, they may need to leave Paris again. I can try to help if you need me to. It's becoming increasingly difficult to move in and out of Nazi territory, but I have a few tricks up my sleeve still."

He had a soft heart too, buried under the decades of secrets. "Thank you, Oncle. Let's hope they don't need it."

The look he sent her as he let himself out the door haunted her the rest of the night. A look that said, *They will.* And pitied her for thinking otherwise.

FIFTEEN

1 November 1940

There had been a book in the return bin that morning, clearly pushed through the slot sometime after Christian had locked up on Thursday night and before he'd arrived Friday morning. He could still see its outline there in the bin, even as he sat at dinner with Ackermann and Gustaf and one of his superior's cronies hours later, a plate of steak before him.

Steak, when his son was lucky to have soup with actual bone broth in the weeks when Christian couldn't smuggle them meat.

He could still see the autumn sun catching on the gilt lettering, could still feel the hammering of his heart as he prayed Kraus *wouldn't* see it. Could still feel the way the world had slowed as, praise God, his aide moved straight for the lavatory, like he did most every morning. He could still taste the bile that had stung his throat as he bent down to pick it up and hastened to move it to the stack of other books awaiting his attention at his table.

Because it had to be either from Corinne or Josef. And neither would risk slipping him a book, and presumably a message within it, if it wasn't an emergency.

He'd been right—and he'd been wrong. As evidenced by the note slipped between pages 102 and 103, which he had read four times and then folded and slipped into his innermost pocket, throwing it away with his lunch rubbish, despite it being full of nothing but vague pronouns.

Josef, who had never quite got over the cold of weeks before thanks, he was sure, to poor nutrition, now had the flu. Corinne had kept Felix at her flat again last night, which he'd already known. But this morning's note from her had said that he'd come down with it too, and that he was inconsolable, and if Christian could find even a moment to slip away today, even if it was late, she knew Felix would appreciate it.

Not an emergency. Not truly. But he knew how his son got when he was sick. He wanted to be held, and he would whimper even as he slept, and Corinne—who had likely never dealt with a sick child before—would be wondering at every moment if he was ill enough to need a doctor. Because Felix would look, sound, and seem *miserable*.

No doubt he *was* miserable. But if it was just the flu, then he would bounce back quickly. He probably felt better already. He always got better so much faster than any of the adults who caught the same thing.

That was what he'd been telling himself all day, as Kraus shadowed his every move until now, when he had his standing dinner with Gustaf. Corinne knew he had this commitment, of course. She would know that he would have canceled it if he could have—but when Ackermann had invited himself along, he hadn't dared.

His fingers flexed around his fork, yearning to brush over his son's forehead. Was he feverish? How hot? Did Corinne have a thermometer?

"You seem distracted tonight, Bauer." Ackermann took a swig of his beer, though he barely spared Christian a glance despite the observation. He had, as usual, requested a table near the window so he could "people watch." By which he meant ogle every Parisienne to walk obliviously by.

Gustaf chuckled. He and Ackermann hadn't exactly hit it off—his superior truly wasn't fond of *bücherwurms*, it seemed. But it hadn't taken Gustaf long to learn that if he responded favorably to whatever blonde, brunette, or ginger Ackermann pointed out, he'd earn himself a bit less taunting.

A lesson Christian had pointedly ignored, each and every time he was forced to dine with his commanding officer.

Meals with Gustaf he didn't actually mind. Despite the fact that his fellow *sonderführer* was far too much a true believer in Nazi propaganda, he was still a learned man, capable of intelligent conversation on a variety of topics close to

Christian's heart. Their weekly Friday dinners couldn't hold a candle to the time he spent at Corinne's flat, of course, but Gustaf had quickly become the closest thing Christian had to a friend among the Nazis in Paris.

"I daresay he's just distracted by thoughts of my favorite professor at the Sorbonne."

Christian snapped his gaze to Gustaf, who was grinning at him.

He took it back. They weren't friends at all.

Ackermann frowned. "What, did he get in a debate with a stuffy old French scholar?"

Gustaf, blast him, laughed. "Quite the contrary—when he stopped at the university to pick me up, he caught a glimpse of one of the few female professors on campus. And she is quite worth looking twice at."

Blast, blast, blast. He'd *tried* to school his expression when he'd caught an unexpected sight of Corinne—but he'd been too caught off guard. He'd thought, given her note, that she'd taken the day off to tend to Felix. What was she doing on campus? Did it mean his son was better? Had she taken him back to Josef's? Had he been *there,* in her office? Or had she left him for a few minutes with Madame Dardenne while she took care of something important?

And then, yes, there was the more obvious bit too. Seeing her in her native environment, striding those university paths as if she were the queen of academia. Gorgeous and confident and deserving of the acclaim she'd achieved, gaining a position at such a young age, and being a woman.

Obviously Gustaf had noticed. He'd just made the reasonable assumption that Christian had been floored by the beauty of a stranger. Nothing to worry about, he'd thought.

Until now.

Ackermann's brows clashed like thunder, and he leaned forward. "Did you say a *female* professor? And you've let this continue—a woman in such a position?"

Christian could read the panic in Gustaf's eyes. He probably would have helped him even if it didn't mean protecting Corinne—at least, he liked to think he would have, though he was none too pleased with Gustaf just now. "We've spoken of this particular professor before, sir," Christian said calmly. "Quite a predicament, given that she teaches German literature as I myself would, certainly better than any other Frenchman we've encountered. We decided it was more important that the students learn the true heart of Germany than that they be spared a woman's thoughts."

Ackermann looked from one of them to the other. "No Frenchman can know the heart of Germany."

"Oh, but you should hear her sometime!"

Gustaf was far too quick to say. "Listening to her speak of Goethe makes me fall in love with the Fatherland all over again."

"I am not inclined to listen to *any* lectures, especially from a woman," Ackermann growled.

Good. Good.

But Gustaf, the idiot, opened his mouth again, laughing this time. "If you don't want to come for the literature lesson, then come to look at her. I'm telling you, sir, she puts all those women strolling along out there to shame—she must, if she drew stoic Bauer's stare, eh?"

If he weren't a pacifist, he'd seriously consider plucking out every one of Gustaf's hairs and stuffing them in his overactive mouth. "I was hardly staring. She reminded me for a moment of someone I know in Berlin—you know how it goes, expecting to see neighbors and friends even in foreign cities. And I didn't realize it was the professor you'd mentioned until you said so."

Ackermann chuckled—a grating, chafing, patronizing sound. "Well, well. Now I'm interested. What does she look like?"

"Like the epitome of a perfect Aryan woman. Blonde curls, blue eyes, these lips that just beg to be kissed—she could be a movie star."

Ackermann narrowed his eyes. On Christian. "It seems our friend has a type. The only woman I've ever caught him staring at also had blonde curls. Quite the looker that one was too—she strode by right out that window our first time dining here."

Christian forced himself to take a bite, chew, swallow as they goaded him. As if he hadn't a care in the world. "I do in fact have a type—but not that. Shall I show you a photo of my wife?"

"Wife?" Gustaf frowned. "You're married? And haven't mentioned it in all this time?"

"Widowed." Still, he reached into his wallet and pulled out the old, dog-eared photo he'd been carrying there for the last decade, since he and Ilse first began seeing each other. Since the night she'd slipped it to him with a pretty blush, *just in case he wanted it.* He'd made a show of sliding it into a place of honor after praising how pretty she looked in it and had never removed it but to draw it out to look at. "This is Ilse. Beautiful, wasn't she?"

They couldn't argue with that, though Ilse's beauty had been a more understated kind than Corinne's. Still, the photographer had caught her at her best, giving the camera a long look from under her dark lashes.

Ackermann grunted and passed the photo to his friend, who in turn passed it to Gustaf.

Gustaf's face softened as he looked at it. "Sorry, old man. Didn't realize you were still grieving your wife. How long were you married?"

"Not long enough." The answer he always gave, because when he confessed they'd been married only two years before she died, people expected him to have moved on just as quickly.

"Children?"

And *this* was the question he truly hated answering. He knew well that God detested a lying tongue—but he also valued life, and even the priest had told him it was no sin to protect it, not in the face of a government that denounced God and all that was holy and would have stolen that precious life. "One, but I'm afraid I buried him nearly a year ago."

He'd buried a coffin, anyway, in the family plot, beside his parents and Ilse.

"I'm sorry." Gustaf handed the photo back, expression somber. "I didn't realize."

"It isn't something I like talking about." But in this case, it effectively put an end to the talk of beautiful women, and for that, he was grateful. Ackermann's friend turned the conversation to how their boys were giving the RAF a run for their money and would soon have Londoners begging Churchill to surrender, and he and Ackermann mused on how long the English could hold out. Not long, they all agreed.

Gustaf, after giving the other two a few minutes to settle into their boasting of the Luftwaffe, leaned toward Christian. "I really am sorry, Bauer. I didn't mean to dredge up painful memories."

He forced himself to smile. "Quite all right. You couldn't have known."

And besides, it made it so that he could make his excuses soon after, and no one tried to stop him or cajole him into dessert. He was able to hurry into the car that Kraus had left him with and drive back to Boulevard Arago. He parked in his usual place in front of the library and stared for a moment at the door to Corinne's building.

First, the library. He let himself in and gathered the books he'd been stashing in the covered box, slipping them all into a tote. Darkness was falling outside, and though there was still an hour before curfew, few Parisians were out.

Good. No one saw him as he turned into her building, and he kept the door from banging behind him. He'd learned the noises of the stairs by now and kept his steps quiet as he ascended to her floor. At the door, he scratched instead of knocking. This was one time he didn't really want anyone seeing him come in. It was too late for a social call, a conversation on books—and without the excuse of seeing her safely home like the night they'd met at Josef's. Too late for the sort of visit she could admit to her neighbors. Though if she didn't hear his scratch, he'd—

The door swung open, and Corinne motioned him inside, closing the door silently again behind him. "I'm so sorry to have alarmed you," she whispered the moment the latch released under her palm. "I knew I shouldn't have, but he was so upset—and I couldn't risk a second note to call you off."

"It's all right." He whispered too, even though the low drone of the radio would have drowned out any risk of the neighbors overhearing. "How is he? I didn't know what to think when I saw you on campus this afternoon."

She winced and took the tote when he offered it to her, not even glancing inside, just setting it down by the entryway table, like she always did the books he brought her. "There were a few things I had to do before Monday. Madame Dardenne sat with him for an hour—I think Felix caught it from Desirée anyway, and gave it to Josef, though of course the children seem to succumb last and recover first."

"And praise God for it. Fever?" He moved toward her mother's bedroom, the one Felix had slept in before when he stayed here.

"Low-grade when he went to bed." She followed him inside. A small lamp glowed, bathing Felix in golden light. "He vomited twice, but not since lunch. He's eaten a bit since then and kept it down. Desirée had it yesterday but is nearly back to normal today, so I pray he'll be better tomorrow."

"No doubt he will." But he sat on the bed and brushed his fingers over Felix's forehead, as he'd wanted to do all day. Cool, though he had shadows under his eyes to prove the day he'd had.

His lashes fluttered open. "Vati?"

"Shh. I'm here, Felix. Tante Corinne tells me you didn't feel so well today."

"Belly hurt," he mumbled around his thumb, his eyelid falling closed again. "Better now though."

"Good." Christian brushed his too-long curls away from his face, traced the tiny shell of his unformed ear and, when Felix rolled onto his side as he always did, he rubbed circles over his small back with the tips of his fingers. He knew what that back felt like when it was flushed with fever, knew how clammy it would get, how his whimpers and moans would make everyone wonder if something really was wrong, if some unforeseen lung or heart condition was developing. If this was the time they'd realize there was something malformed on the inside too.

He knew the fear of nursing his child when he was sick. And he knew the relief when the fever broke and the aches ceased and he turned into his happy, if tired, little fellow again.

He moved his gaze to Corinne, who had sunk to a seat in her mother's dainty little armchair. She looked exhausted, and he prayed it was merely from worry and not because she, too, had caught the bug. "Thank you." Two little syllables that couldn't begin to hold all the gratitude in his heart. "You didn't have to do this."

"Don't be silly. Josef couldn't have cared for him, and it is no great thing for me to miss one class—Dr. Tessier was perfectly capable of filling in for me, as I've done for him from time to time."

He caught the flare of her nostrils though, the way her lips quavered a bit. He saw the way she swallowed hard as she watched Felix shift in his sleep. "Does it get easier?" she whispered, voice strained.

He breathed a laugh. "No. Never. Perhaps it will, someday. But it hasn't yet, not for me." He eased his hand off his son's back, and when Felix didn't budge, he leaned forward and pressed a kiss to his temple. "I love you, *mein mäuschen*."

Felix's lips moved against the thumb dangling just outside his mouth—a sleepy reflex of a response.

He knew he should let him rest. Even so, it took him several more minutes before he could convince himself to get up. He moved slowly back into the living room as Corinne followed him out. She left Felix's door open, the little lamp on. She would all night, he knew, so that if his son woke up, confused as to where he was, she could hear him, and he would see the increasingly familiar surroundings.

She didn't sit, but she leaned against the sliver of open wall with a sigh. "I'm sorry I worried you," she said again. "He was just so—"

"I know. I know how he gets. I wish I could have been here." In Berlin, he could have called in at the university, as Corinne had done today. But now, here? He would have had to feign an illness, to convince Kraus to go home. And then one never knew if a fellow officer might take it upon himself to knock on his hotel room door and make certain he didn't need a physician. They took health seriously in the ranks, since contagions could spread so quickly among them.

Her smile was self-deprecating. "I know he wished you could have been too. But Madame Dardenne assured me I was doing everything I could do, at least. And the worst of it passed by noon. We got through. It was just a day."

A day that had no doubt dragged on, feeling twice as long as it really was. He moved toward the door.

She pushed upright, brows drawn. "Are you leaving already? I mean—I know it's late. But I hate that you came all this way for a ten-minute visit, and him asleep."

He'd travel much farther for a much shorter visit, if that was all he could get. But he'd not been reaching for the doorknob, just for the tote of books. "I brought you something."

This time she breathed the laugh. "Let me guess—books?"

"I am so predictable." But as he pulled the four from the bag, something flickered in her eyes.

Because they weren't the new books he usually brought, or even used copies of unfamiliar tales. She'd know these. She'd know them because she had no doubt bent over them at one of the desks in the library next door and scratched those words into the margins. He held them out to her.

She met his gaze and didn't move.

"Take them," he said, voice sounding gruff in his own ears. "I've marked them all as destroyed due to mold."

Slowly, cautiously, more timidly than he'd ever seen her move, even when he caught her in the library that first day in June, she eased forward and took the books from his hands.

Once their weight transferred from his palms, he rallied a smile. Small, but the best he could manage. "Someday, when this is all over—when France and Germany are both free—you can tell me all about it. For now . . ." He shrugged. "You're keeping my secrets. The least I can do is hand you back your own."

"Christian." She pushed the books onto a shelf in front of the tidy row of her own titles and stepped closer. "It's not . . . you could probably guess—"

"No." The shake of his head was fierce enough that he had to reposition his glasses. "I don't want to know or to guess or even to speculate. The books are damaged. That's all. I'm removing them permanently from the library. Consider this my rubbish bin."

For a moment, she grinned at the idea—her flat being his rubbish bin—but then it shifted into something so much deeper. So much softer. And her hand found his cheek again, in that way he'd dreamed over and over of her doing.

He didn't mean to slip an arm around her waist, to anchor her there. He certainly didn't mean to tug her closer, so that her stomach touched his and reminded him that, despite it all, he was *alive,* and he was capable of yearning for more than safety for his son, and that his heart was still beating, beating, beating.

Her fingers traced his jaw, feathered over his ear, and slid around his neck. "Why must you be so *good?*" she whispered. "Why must you be everything I've ever wanted when you're nothing I dare to have?"

He leaned down until his forehead rested on hers. "Why must you be so clever and so fearless and so much a part of the world I can't claim?"

"Why couldn't you just have come with Felix, months ago?"

"Why couldn't you have just returned to Germany with Josef, triumphant, when Hitler was forced out of power by the return of sane-minded people? You could have come for a visit and fallen in love."

"With Berlin?" Her eyes were so close to his

that he could barely see their color. Yet the blue scorched him like the heart of a flame.

"That too." His other hand had, somehow, moved up to touch her curls, as he'd wanted to do since he first realized she wasn't so much younger than him. To test whether they were as silky as Felix's—they weren't, not quite—whether they would wrap around his fingers—they did. "Someday the world will be right again. It will be right, and you can tell me about the books, and all the impossibilities won't matter anymore."

"And in that day?" Her other hand had lifted too and rested against his chest. No doubt showing her how his heart was beating, beating, beating.

He let his eyes slide shut because he didn't dare to look at her, because already it was too overwhelming. Because her scent—lilacs and Paris and spring rain even though it was autumn—wrapped around him and made him weak in the knees. "In that day, I'll tell you how I feel as I watch you love my son. And I'll kiss you like I've been wanting to for ages."

At her *tsk*ing sound, his eyes opened again, and he found hers dancing. "Wrong again, Professor. In *that* day, you'll offer to apply at the Sorbonne or I'll say I'll apply at the University of Berlin, and you'll get down on one knee very romantically, and then we'll sort out how to get Felix to call me Maman instead of Tante. *This* is the day that you kiss me and tell me you love me."

His throat was dry as the Sahara. A striking contrast to his weak-willed eyes, which went wet as the sea. His fingers pressed into her waist. "I can't. I can't love you when you can't love me back, Corinne—and you *can't* love me back, not yet. Not now. Not as I am. Not in this uniform."

Her hand curled around his lapel. "You know, there's something you should understand about me. When someone tells me I *can't* do something, I feel it's my God-given duty to prove them wrong."

He smiled because he couldn't help it. "Now that you mention it, I'm pretty sure I surmised as much the moment we met. One of the many things I . . . love about you."

She tilted her head, both letting their eyes meet better and putting her mouth but a tantalizing inch from his. "That was close. Try again. A simple rearranging of the words and you'll have it."

He touched his lips to hers first, because he couldn't not, because he needed the strength she gave him, because his heart wasn't just beating but was pounding, pounding, pounding in his ears so that he couldn't hear his own thoughts above it. A soft touch, a gentle press.

All you get, he told himself. "*Je t'aime,*" he whispered against her lips. "*Ich liebe dich. Te amo.* I love you."

She'd understand the words in any language he could toss at her—but she clearly hadn't heard his command to himself to stop at one touch of their lips. She pulled him closer, lifted onto her toes, and held him there as she kissed him again—nothing soft, nothing gentle, nothing light. Her lips were fire and weight and demand and need.

Promise. Her lips were promise as they melded against his, as they parted and drew him in. They were faith in that tomorrow he had to believe would come someday. They were hope in a world filled with despair.

When at last they broke apart for breath, he realized he was holding her two inches off the floor and he set her back down, knowing well his cheeks and neck looked every bit as red as they felt.

Corinne, arms still wrapped around him, didn't let go. "I guess I should have listened to Madame Dardenne last week. She *told* me you were interested in more than just books."

He laughed. And kissed her again, because his lips had a mind of their own now. "She is a wise woman. Perhaps someday she won't look at me like I'm a monster."

"Someday." She pressed her cheek to his chest, one of her hands running slowly down his back, over the wool of his uniform. "I love you, Christian. Even now, when I can't."

"That'll just have to be enough." He held her

tight. And then he set her away, stepping back toward the door. "Until we're free . . . no more of that. Just books and Felix and Josef."

She wrapped her arms around her middle, but it was mischief sparkling in her eyes. "You can't put the genie back in the bottle, *mon amour*."

He settled his hand on the knob. "But when you make your three wishes, you can't get him back out again. I'd just as soon save my other two for when I really need them."

Her laughter followed him out into the hall.

SIXTEEN

7 November 1940

Josef was worrying her. Oh, he'd got over the worst of the flu after a couple days, but it had been a week, and still he was so tired, so weak. He needed a doctor—but of course, he didn't want to risk seeing one. Didn't want anyone to ask him questions or get a good look at his face or, God forbid, recognize him from one of the lectures or book signings or readings he'd done over the years. He didn't want anyone to detect the slight German accent that emerged when he was tired and realize he was no native Frenchman, regardless of what his papers said.

Corinne strode beside Liana down the walkways of the Sorbonne, fingers worrying the strap of her bag. She'd called him before she left home this morning, and he had sounded so *tired*. Of course, when she'd mentioned it, he'd scoffed. "You sound like Chris," he'd said. "Who is also risking far too much by calling to check up on me, and you had better tell him to stop. Perhaps he'll listen to you."

Unlikely, in this case. Christian still refused to let anyone tell him where Josef's new flat was, but he'd finally agreed that his phone number wouldn't hurt . . . because he couldn't stand having no way to reach out in case of emergency. "He won't."

Josef had only grunted at that, and he had agreed—though he'd sounded none too pleased about it—to let her come and pick up Felix again after class, bring him home with her for a few days. Madame Dardenne would watch him tomorrow while she was in class, and then they'd have the weekend together, and Josef could rest.

"Are you all right?" Liana asked as they turned toward Corinne's building. Concern dug grooves into her usually flawless brow as she watched her. "You've been awfully distracted this last week."

Corinne summoned up a smile. "Just worrying over a friend who's been ill." She didn't say who. Liana didn't ask. Just as Corinne never asked who was at their poetry readings or what "work of literature" they had discussed.

It was a strange friendship, in some ways. Both knowing the other was protecting secrets. Both knowing they'd approve of them, more or less. Both keeping their lips sealed though, because any stray word could spell the end.

Although if she planned to keep Felix all weekend . . . She cleared her throat. "Could you ask your mother if it's all right if I bring a guest to dinner on Saturday?"

Liana came to a halt. Eyes blinking. Lips

seeming torn between a smile and a frown. "A . . . *male* guest?"

Corinne paused too. And rolled her eyes. "Yes, actually, but—"

"Ah *ha!*" Liana poked a finger into Corinne's shoulder. "I knew it! I knew there was a man—that's what's put the twinkle in your eyes lately. Only . . ." Her face fell all the way into consternation, and she stepped closer. "I rather thought it was a certain professor who has poor taste in clothes. But you wouldn't bring *him* for dinner—"

"No." Secrets, so many secrets. She put her professional face on, covering any trace of emotion. "I wouldn't, and no, there's no man. If you've seen any delight in my eyes lately, though, it *is* for my guest—Felix. You remember the cousins I said I've been helping with? The grandfather has been ill. I volunteered to watch the little one for a few days."

"Oh." Liana blew the bangs of her hair out of her eyes. "Boring."

Corinne snorted a laugh that slipped right through her facade. "You won't say so after meeting the dreadful pirate Captain Goldenhair. He'll have you rolling with laughter within ten minutes."

Liana's lips curved up again even at the mention of it. "I'm sure Maman won't mind, but if Papa has failed to bring enough goodies home courtesy of the clientele, I will ring you up and let you know to stay home—or supplement our offerings. How are *your* contacts these days?"

She meant Oncle Georges—who didn't, for some reason, share Corinne's compunction against spending money in the black market—but that only made Corinne wince. "Better than I'd like in that particular way."

But she'd gotten to speak to her mother each week, if only for a few minutes at a time. To hear her voice and assure herself that the renewed Blitz on London, with its even-more-devastating bombs, hadn't laid claim to the indomitable Yvonne Bastien.

Given that, she could forgive her uncle his taste for black-market meat and sugar. She could thank him for making her feel useful, even as she knew well the information she passed along so far hadn't actually *done* anything.

She didn't know if it ever would. Didn't know if it was truly worth the risk to her dispersed students. But they, too, needed to do *something* to feel useful. So she would continue to gather whatever they sent her, continue to pass it along. Continue to pray that the Nazi invasion of Britain would hold off just a little bit longer, that her mother would be *safe* there, that every single thing in life hadn't spun completely out of control, much as it felt like it most days.

"Dr. Bastien!"

At the too-familiar voice, Corinne groaned, turning to see which direction Professor Gustaf would be coming from this time. She knew that Christian had developed a friendship with the man—and suspected that was why she hadn't been sacked already—but couldn't bring herself to like him even a little. He was a parasite, always showing up to her classes when she least wanted him there.

Which, granted, was any time.

When she saw that he had another Nazi officer beside him today—this one with the insignia of an *oberstleutnant* on his shoulders—she gave Liana a nudge away, hiding the movement behind her back. "Go, quickly, Liana," she muttered.

Theirs was, after all, a strange sort of friendship. One in which they'd learned to trust each other implicitly and obey each other's muttered warnings without question. Liana flounced away as if simply in a hurry to get to class, calling out a farewell to Corinne in one breath and a hello to a classmate in another.

Corinne held her ground, mask firmly in place, chin raised, letting her impatience waft off her even as she offered the iciest skeleton of a smile. "Good morning, Sonderführer." She shifted her gaze from Gustaf to his companion. "Oberstleutnant."

The *oberstleutnant* reached for her hand, his eyes hard as the entrance exams and every bit as questioning. "Good morning . . . Doctor." He said it like the word tasted bitter on his tongue.

She knew the type. She met it with a sweet little smile.

Gustaf cleared his throat. "Doctor, allow me to introduce Oberstleutnant Ackermann. He's the commanding officer of a friend of mine, the *bibliotheksschutz*."

"Ah," she said as if she'd never met the library protector—as if he hadn't warned her about Ackermann. "How good to meet you, sir." She motioned toward the building. "My class is starting soon. Will you be observing this morning, Sonderführer?"

Please say no, please say no, please say—

"We both will." Gustaf beamed.

Ackermann sent her a scowl she had little choice but to classify as predatory.

Corinne nodded and turned. "Then I'll invite you to walk with me instead of tarrying out here, so I'm not late."

Gustaf prattled as they walked, telling her things she already knew but shouldn't have—that he and Ackermann had met two weeks ago, that their foursome had taken up dining together every Friday evening, and how lovely—not Christian's choice of word—it had proven for all of them, to spend time with men from other walks of life and different perspectives . . .

She tuned him out as they entered her lecture

hall, where most of the students had already taken their usual seats. Gustaf started toward the back row, as he always did, but Ackermann ignored his example and took a place front and center—going so far as to order a student out of the seat he wanted.

Corinne set her bag on her desk, not shrinking from the gaze he leveled at her.

Just another bully, like so many she'd met before.

What gave her pause was when two more Nazi uniforms hurried in as the final bell of the hour tolled over the campus—Kraus and Christian. The younger looking a strange combination of eager and out of place, the elder looking as though he were trudging through molasses.

Ackermann had ordered him there. She knew it even before he took his seat in the back beside Gustaf and widened his eyes just slightly then glanced at his superior.

So be it. And praise God they were still working through their translation of *Faust*—Goethe was so well loved by Germans and so well respected by the French that he was some of the only common ground they could claim.

Her students had grown accustomed to Gustaf's presence over the course of the semester, but the additional visitors clearly had them on edge. A few shifted and fidgeted far too much, others sat so perfectly still that they put her in mind of animals trying to avoid the attention of a hunter.

Lord, give me confidence and peace. She silently added the St. Michael the Archangel prayer—this was the battleground for her, after all—and drew in a breath. Pasted on a smile. "Special welcome to our visitors this morning. I hope you all enjoy our continued discussion on *Faust*. And now if everyone would turn to where we left off on Tuesday. For those who are just joining us, we're in part one, scene four, in the study with Faust and Mephistopheles. I believe we left off at line 1712, when Mephistopheles is begging Faust for a few written words on life and death . . ."

Christian had to stifle the urge to elbow his aide when Kraus leaned over and whispered, "She's a *professor?*"

Gustaf only chuckled—because this was obviously a standard reaction to the too-young-looking Corinne—but Christian cut him what he hoped was a quelling look and said, "Shh."

He then spent the next five minutes praying that, somehow, Kraus wouldn't ruin it all. He wouldn't point out in the hearing of either Gustaf or Ackermann that this professor was none other than the neighbor of the Deutsche Freiheitsbibliothek, whom they had met multiple times, whose flat they'd had lunch in one day—only one, so far as Kraus knew. That Christian wouldn't be caught red-handed in the careful story he'd been trying to maintain to protect her.

It was all crumbling to pieces. Every bit of it. And while part of his mind spun, trying to find answers truthful enough to satisfy them all, the larger part was too tired after a sleepless night worrying for Josef. All he could do was close his eyes for two blessed seconds and give the entire mess into the capable hands of God.

If I overstepped, forgive me. If I shouldn't have tried to protect her through my own power, then correct the mess I've made. You be her protection, O Lord. Be her salvation. Be her provision.

What would she do if she lost this position? Could she find another somewhere else? If not here, then in another city?

Perhaps his heart split into innumerable splinters at the thought—but that didn't matter. It didn't matter if he got in trouble for withholding this detail about her identity. What could they really do to him? It wasn't like anyone had asked him about her and he'd lied. He'd simply failed to connect dots for them, dots that he could claim he thought were irrelevant.

But Corinne—*Corinne.*

After a few minutes, though, the frantic litany whispering through his mind had little choice but to quiet, given the cadence of her voice as she read the German words. He fell into rapt attention as her students would pipe up with their questions and thoughts and translations—eventually seeming to forget Ackermann's unwieldy presence—and she would not just answer but lead them into further thought.

He'd known that she would be good at this. He hadn't had to see her in action to know it. But now that he was, he fell even more in love with her. *You could apply at the Sorbonne . . . I could apply at the University of Berlin.* In another world, the world that should have been, they could have. One or the other or both. They could be happy. Together. Both doing what they loved. He could imagine slipping into her classes whenever he had the time and listening to her. He could imagine looking up and finding her in his. He could imagine walking home together, talking over their students and the essays they had to grade and the research they wanted to do, the papers they wanted to write and publish. He could imagine pulling her between the shelves of his library and showing her a book.

He could imagine ending every day, starting every day, punctuating every laugh with a kiss. He could imagine the freedom to actually look at each other and admit to knowing each other. To being friends. To being more.

Frustration—no, sorrow—twisted through his stomach. Would that world ever come? In his lifetime? In Felix's?

"Ah, so then, I think we have a translation of that line we can embrace." Corinne set down her worn copy of the book and moved to the blackboard, scrawling the line upon it. "'Happy the man who has pure truth within him.' But let's talk through the next line. We have two offerings here—'and who will never deign to sacrifice it' versus 'he will regret no sacrifice made for it.' Those are two very different meanings. What are the implications of either? Consider it in context of the rest of this speech, mind you—Faust is speaking of how, when one has written one's words down on paper, they take on a new power. A deadly power—he goes so far as to call the written word a spirit of evil. So is he commenting in 1724 and 1725 about *not sacrificing* truth or about not regretting any sacrifice made *for* truth?"

"I'm more interested in how that truth is lost in the process of putting it to words—specifically *written* words." It tumbled from Christian's lips before he could remind himself that he was just an observer, not a participant. That he wasn't here to be part of the conversation, only to follow an order and try to mitigate any damage.

But Corinne smiled up at him. "An insightful question from our guest. Class?"

Kraus sank down in his seat as heads craned around to look their way, as if attention in a classroom were his gravest fear. On Christian's other side, Gustaf chuckled quietly. "Didn't I tell you?" he murmured.

The students had forgotten them again in light of the discussion. "Can't we all relate to that?" a young woman said. "We have an idea, a thought, and it's bright and beautiful—until we try to put written words to it. What we write never captures the heart."

"And that's why words are so dangerous," a young man added, leaning forward in his excitement. "Because when we write them down, we lose the nuance of intention so easily. We lose the inflection in our voices. And the words themselves are but an imitation of the idea—imitations that can be twisted and used against us."

"Not just dangerous," a new voice said. "But powerful, as Dr. Bastien said. The written word can be gone back to over and again. It can be studied, like we're doing now. It can be debated. The written word can build empires or tear them down. Just look at the influence of texts like the Bible, like Rousseau, even *Mein Kampf*." The student darted a glance toward Ackermann. "No one can say those words haven't changed the tides of history."

Hence why power and danger were so closely united. And why Goethe had, through Faust, so wisely observed that truth gets lost when pen meets paper. No matter how writers might strive to capture it in bits and pieces, they all knew that their words could cut both ways.

Ask Josef. Ask Abraham. Ask Wells or Keller or Einstein. Sometimes the very act of bravery that writing represented was the noose one put around one's own neck without realizing it. The words they hoped would liberate, educate, and empower could be used as evidence against them when they failed to move enough people.

"A very good point. And one must say this of Hitler and Goebbels—they understand the power of words. That is why we have guests here today from the Ministries of Education and Propaganda." Corinne nodded toward them. "It's also why we have a Library of Burned Books in my own neighborhood. When Faust and Mephistopheles talk about signing one's writing in blood, it's more than hyperbole. And the students of Germany recognized that." She turned to one of the few male students in the class. "Monsieur Gregory, you have made no secret about your dislike for this text, though it is only because you don't like poetry. But let's pretend that it is because you think Goethe's ideas were dangerous. That they opposed all you believed in. Would you be sitting in this class still? Or would you have walked out and decried the text?"

The young man shifted in his chair but didn't answer.

She turned to another. "You are an atheist, Monsieur Laurent. I have heard you talking about how Christianity is not just wrong, but dangerous—that the greatest atrocities of the Western World were done in the name of religion. So then—perhaps you might decide to burn the Bible. I have heard each and every one of you trying to convince a friend to read or not read a book based on how *you* felt about it. Why?"

A beat of silence, but only one. It was a girl on the left who spoke up. "Because we want people to agree with us. We want them to say we're right. We want to foster that, and make certain they're exposed or not exposed to things to guarantee it."

Corinne nodded. "And that is what the students in Germany decided they would do. That they would make a statement for the world to see about what ideas they thought were worthwhile and which they thought weren't. But don't forget the line about signing in blood—they took it a step further. They decided not only what *ideas* they would engage with, but what *voices*. It is irrelevant, then, whether Wells said anything objectionable in *The Time Machine*—he spoke out against their ideals. It doesn't matter what theories Einstein puts forth—he is a Jew. Now—is this wise or foolish, Oberstleutnant Ackermann?"

Gustaf hissed out a breath. Kraus sank lower in

his chair. Christian couldn't have breathed if he'd wanted to.

Ackermann's shoulders curled back. "Wise. You cannot let children read garbage or they will become nothing but trash."

Corinne tilted her head, consideration in every line. "Ah, a very good point. One any parent would agree with you on. When it comes to children, we can and must censor what they read, yes. But are you arguing, then, Oberstleutnant, that all German citizens are children, incapable of making their own decisions on their reading material?"

Christian didn't know whether to wince or to cheer.

"Of course not!" Ackermann sneered—Christian couldn't see it, but he could hear it in his voice. "But adults must set the example. We must live what we hope they will emulate. And as no parent has the time to read every book in print to know what to keep out of their homes, it is a service to provide them with a list."

"But when you tell someone what to read, you're telling them what to *think*," the first girl said again, fire in her tone. "And it's one thing to try to influence your own friend. It's a whole different thing when it becomes law. Frenchmen know that better than anyone, don't we? The revolution that gave us life was also a terror. When you make it illegal to be something or think a certain way, then it's only a matter of time before *everyone* is at risk of the guillotine. That's not society, that's tyranny."

Christian held his breath as Ackermann's head snapped to the left. He could only pray he didn't have a clear view of the girl from his seat.

Corinne edged forward, into his line of sight. "An interesting point, *mademoiselle*, but for now, let's focus on your earlier observation, that it's the words we read that determine what we think. True or untrue, class?"

The argument went on, but Corinne didn't stray back to the desk or to her chalkboard, and he wanted to applaud her for it. Much as he wanted to do when, as the end of class drew near, she raised a hand to halt the conversation and spoke again.

"What we can all agree on is that words are powerful, *written* words especially so. And so it is a natural instinct of humanity to guard them—both to preserve the words and protect people from what could be construed as dangerous or harmful. Keep all of that in mind as you translate the rest of this scene, paying special attention to line 1788. *Die Zeit ist kurz, die Kunst ist lang.*"

Time is short, and art is long. One of his favorite lines. Christian stood as the others did, extending his mental applause to the students who absorbed the girl into their midst and all but carried her from the class while Corinne said something with a smile for Ackermann that he wished he could hear.

He couldn't, though, over the babble that sprang up. But what was she doing—tapping his arm? Lifting a brow . . . was she *flirting?*

Gustaf laughed and smacked him on the arm. "What did I tell you—I bet you'd like to come back on Tuesday, wouldn't you, to see how she leads them into the 'time and art' line? Aside from the fact that they're talking about translation along with the ideas, it's like one of my own classes."

"Indeed." He made himself grin at his friend.

Kraus edged forward. "Mind if I wait at the car, Professor?" He was surveying the room like it was trying to suffocate him.

"Go ahead." He prayed that his own relief at the request wasn't in his voice. But for Gustaf, he had better offer another morsel of truth. He nodded toward Corinne. "When she mentioned the Library of Burned Books—it's no wonder she looked familiar, if she's in that neighborhood. I've met her before. Didn't realize at the time that she was a professor, of course."

Gustaf laughed at the coincidence and motioned him down. "Well come, come. I'll make proper introductions—and we'll rescue her from the muscle, eh?"

He would have declined the introduction, but the rescue he wasn't about to withhold. Especially since, as the students cleared the room, he could finally make out what she was saying to Ackermann.

"The same is true in intellectual pursuits, Oberstleutnant. Just as you must spar and engage your muscles with resistance to build them, so we must do with the mind. Without lively debate, the ideas that you most treasure never would have developed. People *don't* just need to be handed something to believe in—they must wrestle with it, against it, and for it before they can truly claim it as their own."

Gustaf leaned close. "I think I'm in love—if only my family wouldn't disown me if I brought home a French girl, eh?" His chuckle, along with the lightness in his eyes, proved him joking.

Still, Christian had to suck in a long breath.

Ackermann was grunting and turning toward them, and from the look on his face, Christian couldn't tell if she'd won his respect . . . or consigned herself to unemployment.

SEVENTEEN

The collision of his worlds had left Christian on edge—every time he turned a corner, he swore someone was watching him. It hadn't helped that he'd escaped Ackermann at the Sorbonne only to have him show up at the library he was visiting later in the day, demanding to know if he'd conducted any more interviews of German ex-pats.

There'd been a look in his eye that Christian hadn't liked. One that said he was waiting to catch him in something.

It could have been paranoia, yes. But as Vater had taken to saying before his death, after Hitler rose to power, *Just because I'm paranoid doesn't mean no one's watching me.*

They were—they always were. That was the lesson he'd learned in those last months in Berlin. The Gestapo was always watching. One's own *neighbors* were always watching. In some cases, one's own *family* was watching—all too eager to prove their own loyalty by turning someone in.

Reich above blood. Reich above neighborhood. Reich above all.

He looked down again at the slip of paper. He'd deflected Ackermann's question by asking if he had news of any who had come back to Paris, insisting he'd questioned all the names with which he'd been provided—true.

This had been his superior's answer. An address scribbled on a piece of paper, along with a time. "There will be men there to bring him in. Why don't you oversee the escort this time? I got a taste of your side of things this morning. High time you *bücherwurms* experience *my* side."

He'd been unable to contain the mockery of a smile. "Oh, I have plenty of experience with your side, Oberstleutnant," he'd said. "I have a good friend in the Gestapo in Berlin."

Perhaps he shouldn't have taken that momentary delight—or mentioned Erik Reinholdt, even obtusely. But everyone, even military men, had a healthy fear of the Gestapo. And it had been gratifying to see the flicker of acknowledgment in his eyes.

He hadn't dared to refuse the order though. Since his ultimatum, Ackermann had granted him breathing room, yes . . . but he'd also taken to dropping by his hotel room without notice, always with invitations to this or that which they both knew he'd refuse. Just to check and make sure he was there.

How often did he knock when Christian *wasn't?*

He'd never questioned him on his absences, but he always had his whereabouts ready—at the Deutsche Freiheitsbibliothek. Sharing a meal with Gustaf. Touring this or that historical site, always careful to be seen in any public setting, to be friendly, to be remembered in case Ackermann questioned clerks about him. Visiting famous cathedrals . . . when a Mass just so happened to be underway or a priest was in a confessional.

Though for reconciliation, he inevitably returned to the same smaller church within walking distance of the Library of Burned Books. The one with the priest who had told him it was no sin to save his son's life from a bloodthirsty tyrant or his minions. No sin to lie in those circumstances. That it was bravery. That it was righteousness, like the midwives in the day of Pharaoh.

He knew which building it was the moment he turned the corner, given the cluster of soldiers waiting at the front door. They were joking with each other, shoving, laughing, paying no attention to the citizens that moved to the other side of the street to avoid them.

They all snapped to attention as he strode near. He gave them a salute. "Good evening, boys. Just starting your shifts, or as eager to be done with them as I am mine?"

They laughed, looking so blastedly *young* with their smooth cheeks and bright eyes and ready mirth. He felt like an old man, catching children skipping class. He wanted to say, *Why aren't you in school? You still have so much to learn. So much I could teach you, if only you'd listen.*

"Just coming on, sir," one of them said. "We can take care of this, if you're clocking out."

"Would that I could." He motioned them to fall in behind him. "But alas. I too have a superior, who seems to think I need to get out of libraries and conference rooms and see our fine soldiers in action."

Another of them snorted a laugh. "Hardly action, sir. No one ever does more than complain when we come to fetch them for an interview."

"Yeah, the hardest part is communication, generally speaking. They don't always speak German, and we sure don't always speak French."

He let himself smile at the self-deprecating humor. "Well, I do, if necessary. Though I don't even know to whom we'll be speaking."

"Here." Another of the four handed him a slip of paper much like the one Ackermann had given him—except this one had a name, not just an address.

Joseph Henriot.

His blood turned sluggish. Perhaps his feet would have too, had the soldiers behind him not kept him moving.

It wasn't just the fact that it was Josef's name that was on the paper—it was that it was his *new* name. At, presumably, his new address.

How? How had they learned his new identity—and so soon?

And why had Ackermann insisted that *Christian*

be there to collect him for interrogation? Did he know there was some link between them? Or was he simply intending to rub in the fact that he had found one of Christian's "missing ex-pat writers" when he'd failed to do so?

Don't overreact, he told himself. *Don't assume. If you assume, you'll give away more than they may know.*

It could be coincidence. It could be nothing. Someone could have reported Josef for something altogether different—a new neighbor, suspicious of a stray word or phrase or accent. They may not know who he was—though if not, why would *he* be here?

No, they must know who he was—but it could have been an old acquaintance who saw him and followed him home and saw he was living under a fake name. It didn't mean the whole game was up.

It didn't mean Felix was in danger.

His throat nearly closed as his feet took him up to the second floor.

What if Felix was in danger? Was he still here, with Josef? Was he still trained to hide in his room the moment someone knocked at the door, or had he grown lax? Had Corinne picked him up yet? If not, at least she would be here soon. His boy wouldn't be left alone for more than a few minutes.

Please, God. Please, may they both be safely

away from here. Please, give me your words and wisdom now. Please, make a way for Josef.

Oh, please, God . . . what if Felix reacted to his voice as he had the last time and came running out?

But no. He wouldn't. This time, they hadn't been separated for nearly a year. This time, he was used to hearing his voice again.

But he was *used to hearing his voice* again and used to running to greet him. He wouldn't pause to listen to what was being said, he'd just react like a little boy who loved his *vati. Please God, may he be gone!*

There was no reason to believe the worst.

But every reason to fear it.

All too soon, the door stood before them, its brass letter-number combination mocking him. He shot what he hoped was a challenging grin at the soldier who had mentioned his lack of French. "Perhaps we should work together on the communication. You take point—but I'll give you the words, quietly. Practice will improve your skill."

The soldier made a face but didn't argue. He slid into position in front of the door and raised a hand.

Before his knuckles could rap on the wood, heavy, slow footsteps sounded from the opposite stairwell.

He knew those steps, and welcome they were not. Christian craned past the soldiers, praying his face looked only mildly curious—and perhaps a bit put out—but not as panicked as he felt. "Ackermann. I thought you wanted me to handle this."

The *oberstleutnant* shrugged, his smile lazy and far too pleased. "I decided this would be too fun to miss." He gestured at the door. "Go ahead, *soldat*. Knock." Ackermann kept up his easy pace, skirting the four soldiers to stop beside Christian as the knock rang through the corridor. "Perhaps I should have had you bring your aide—that Kraus is hungry for action, like a soldier ought to be."

The others exchanged confused looks. "There's never any action for these, sir," the same one who had claimed it before said.

Ackermann's low chuckle made a shiver of warning scrape up Christian's spine. "There will be this time. Isn't that right, Bauer?"

Christian had to swallow past the rising bile. "Sir?"

"You know what I realized this morning, sitting in that woman's classroom? You university types, you 'men of letters' as you call yourselves—you all know each other. And you, you're no young thing, like your idiot friend Gustaf. You were professor already when Hitler was elected, weren't you? Already doing your great work in the university library. When swine like *this* were still sullying our lecture halls." He jerked a thumb toward the door.

It was all Christian could do to lift his brows in question as shuffling came from behind the door. "I've never met anyone by the name of Joseph Henriot."

Ackermann leaned close, hatred gleaming in his eyes. "And what about Josef Horowitz? Hmm? Will you claim not to have ever met *him?* Your father's old friend?"

Christian held his gaze. Just one blustering scholar who thought he knew something, staring down another with an opposing view.

He was going to be sick. "I don't know what you're talking about."

"Who is it?" Josef called from within in French, his voice sounding every bit as miserable and weak as it had that morning on the phone.

"You don't know? That's not what Kraus said." Ackermann sneered and turned back to the door, pushing the others aside. "This is Oberstleutnant Ackermann, along with several of my soldiers." He spoke in German, as much bark as words. "Open up." He pounded his fist for emphasis, as if Josef wasn't clearly on his way already.

Kraus? What did Kraus know—what had he *said?* Had Christian slipped up? Had his aide followed him one night when he didn't know? But even if he had, how would he know *that,* that particular tidbit?

His throat closed off. He had a cousin, didn't he? At the University of Berlin. A cousin studying "something with books." A cousin who could have been in Christian's classes—or his father's. A cousin who had perhaps asked questions for Kraus?

"Oberstleutnant?" Josef's voice, muffled by the door, did a remarkably good job of stumbling over the German syllables, as if he had a French tongue which was unused to so many consonants. When he opened the door, bafflement lined his haggard face. "I apologize," he said then, in halting, awkward German. "My German bad. French?"

Christian opened his mouth, ready to volunteer as a translator. To preserve whatever bit of the facade was left.

Before he could breathe a word, Ackermann shoved against the door so quickly, so forcefully that it sent Josef sprawling, his head cracking against the end table. "Ackermann!" Christian meant to push past the soldiers, but they were already spilling inside, sidearms in their hands—because Ackermann had drawn his and was now leveling it at Josef's chest.

"Try again, old man," Ackermann growled. "We know very well that you are no Frenchman. You are Josef Horowitz, a German Jew."

Josef's nostrils flared at the word *Jude*—something he'd have understood these days even if he *were* French, given that all French Jews' citizenship had been revoked, that as of two weeks ago, no Jew in Paris was allowed to work. He pointed to the wall—to the crucifix. "Catholic." Holding that hand up, he reached the other for his neck and pulled out the medal he always wore—St. Michael, the Archangel. "*Katholisch.*"

Christian edged closer, trying to get between Ackermann and Josef. "Ackermann, calm down. You have the wrong man. And even if you didn't, Josef Horowitz is just a professor. You don't need a gun—"

"No." Ackermann moved neither his aim nor his eyes from Josef. "If he's Horowitz—which he *is*—then he's here in Paris under falsified documents in an attempt to defraud the Nazi government, which makes him at best stupid and at worst a spy. And if I find that you *knew* he was here under falsified documents and didn't turn him in immediately, do you know what that makes *you,* Bauer? A coconspirator. Unger—cover the *sonderführer.*"

Cover him? What did that . . . never mind. Before his mind could finish forming the question, one of the four soldiers swung his pistol to point at Christian, an unreadable look in his eyes.

Christian raised his arms. *So much I could teach you, if only you'd listen.*

Josef swallowed, his larynx bobbing around the bright silver chain still held in his fingers. Even now, he didn't so much as glance at Christian. Didn't glance at the closed door that likely led to Felix's room. Didn't crumple into wild begging.

Christian felt about to. "He is an old man, and look at him—he's sick. He's no threat to—"

"You are no better than that ridiculous woman professor, claiming that dissidence is no *threat*. It is the greatest threat! We let one Jew get away with claiming a heritage that isn't his, thinking that he can escape his grandfather's blood, that it doesn't label him as the swine he is, and they will *all* try it. Subhuman chattel, moving among us, mocking us!"

"I am not saying not to question him." *Calm. Stay calm. Defuse the situation.* Easing himself to a place at Josef's feet so as to partially block him from Ackermann, he turned to face his superior, even though it meant the barrel of the gun all but pressed into his chest. *Authority—claim the authority. Don't show him any weakness.* "I am only saying to put away the *gun*. First of all, you're wrong about a lot of things you're assuming. And even if you weren't—do you think one old man is going to put up a fight? Stop drooling at the thought of violence like a dog over a bone and bring him in so I can do my job."

"Your job?" Ackermann pressed the gun to his chest. He could have sworn it burned straight through his uniform, his shirt, his heart. "What is that, exactly? Goebbels's orders never quite made sense to me. You're to deal with the garbage books. All right. And you're to find all the traitor writers and Jews—and then what? You interview them. You put their name on a list—and *what?* They ought to be sent back to Germany! We *know* who they are, we know what they've done, the treason they've written. They ought to be sent straight to a prison camp—"

"And since when does an *oberstleutnant* get to decide that?" He gripped his fear, twisted it, turned it into indignation. "Will you question Berlin? Your own general? Fine. Then send your questions up the channel—but I intend to follow my orders, and nowhere have they told me to threaten old men and wave guns in their faces. We are a *civilized* people, Ackermann—act like it!"

He expected the snap of anger. He expected the push and had already braced for it. What he didn't expect was the low snarl—"Jew-loving traitor!"—or the movement of the other soldiers, who seemed to surge in response to Ackermann's rage.

Guns, so many guns pointed at him. At his godfather. So many bullets that could tear through flesh or through walls.

What if Felix was in the room behind the closed door? The one called Unger was pointing his weapon in that direction. It could pass right through the flimsy barrier. Right into his hiding, quaking, brave little boy.

He had to calm them down, all of them. Say whatever he must. Turn himself in, if it kept their weapons silent and still. *God?*

Behind him, he heard a shift. *No, Josef—no. Stay still!* A faint, "I will come." The pop of knees taking an old man's weight.

Lost, lost in the explosion from Ackermann's lips. "Traitor!"

Did he mean Josef this time? Christian again? His gaze seemed to encompass both and neither.

Christian shifted to keep himself between the Nazis and faithful Josef, hands still out at his sides. "Gentlemen—"

Lost. Lost in the thunder, in the fire. It pierced his eardrums—from the left? Right? Straight ahead? It was everywhere, *everywhere*. Just like the fire that was eating through him. Roaring, all of it. Deafening.

"No!" *Josef.* Josef's voice, shouting over the thunder. "No—I'm coming. Stay back—*stay back!*"

But they didn't. The world was a blur of gray shirts. And then white ceilings. Thunder and then echoes and always the fire, fire, fire, and then . . . the cool blessed kiss of night.

A gunshot! Corinne pressed her hand over Felix's good ear, pulling him down another step, toward the courtyard, even while everything within her screamed to run back up those stairs and into Josef's flat and try to *do* something.

"Vati." He didn't shout it, this trembling little boy with the wide, wide eye. He just dug his fingers into her shoulders and whispered it like a prayer in her ear. "*Vati.*"

"Vati's fine." Her voice shook over the syllables—a prayer in God's ear. "Shh."

"Stay back," Josef screamed. *"Stay back!"*

She knew it was a command for her, not for the Nazis in his flat. And she knew that if Felix weren't clutched in her arms, she'd disobey the command in a heartbeat.

"A warning shot." The words whispered out of their own volition. Her arms tightened around the little boy. "It was probably just a warning shot. Grandpapa is fine. Vati is fine."

Nothing was fine. There was shouting, scuffling, words she couldn't make out. Then, finally, the slamming of a door, punctuating one roared command: "Leave him!"

Leave him. Who were they leaving? Not Josef—he still shouted from the corridor, his words echoing toward the courtyard through some open door or window, that same demand to stay back repeated over and again, louder and louder.

Fainter and fainter.

"Tante?"

"Shh." She bent her knees, put Felix on his feet,

his overnight bag with him. Brushed his curls back from his face, then did it again for her own comfort. She met his one good eye. "Stay here a moment, *mäuschen*. All right? Stay pressed against the wall here, behind this plant. Just for a minute. I'm going to peek inside, but I'll be right back. All right?"

Tears crowded the blue of his iris. But Felix gripped the enormous planter and crouched down beside it.

"Good boy." Though she darted a suspicious look toward the other people who poked their heads out, they all seemed more alarmed at the gunshot than anything. No one had a look about them that said they were responsible for the Nazis coming in.

But then, what would that even look like? How would she know? She was no Oncle Georges, not even a Hugo, able to read people in a glance. She was just a professor playing at spymaster, collecting information that meant nothing from students too willing to put themselves at risk while she stayed safely in Paris. A woman who'd lived most of her life in a classroom. A woman who had spent her life on words but had never had to shed her blood to defend them.

No words could change the picture she saw when she slipped back in through Josef's back door, though, through the kitchen, and peeked into the living room.

Furniture, overturned. A potted plant, spilling earth onto the white floor.

Red seeping, creeping, pooling under the still form. Male legs—male legs clad in a Nazi officer's uniform.

"O God . . . O, Lord God . . ." She could find no other words to pray as she scurried into the room, tripping over her own horror.

Christian. Christian lay on the floor, blood coming from somewhere or everywhere or—there. His chest. His *chest!* "Christian!" Her shout was nearly silent, from lack of breath more than thought. She fell to her knees at his side, reaching clumsy hands for his wrist. His neck, when his wrist slipped from her shaking hands.

Did he have a pulse, or was that hers? Was he breathing? "Christian!"

No flutter of lashes. No lift of his chest. But yes, there, a pulse too slow to be hers. Biting back a keen, she fluttered a hand over his jaw, dropped it to his life-leaking chest, and then pushed herself to her feet.

He needed help, and he needed it now, and who was she supposed to call? A hospital—but then what? He'd been shot by his own men, and they'd *left him* there! Ackermann had *ordered* them to leave him there, to let him bleed out, to let him die. If he showed up in a hospital, his superior would know.

Her hand knocked the phone receiver off its

cradle, then fumbled to grab it, raise it to her ear. She had to try three times to dial her uncle's number and realized only when it rang that she'd used the wrong one. She'd dialed the secondary number first, she'd—

"Hello?"

"Oncle." Her eyelids pressed tight. God must have guided her numb fingers to the right number. "My heel—it's broken. I can't walk. I'm *hurt,* Oncle, please. Please come and get me and *hurry.*"

"Where are you, *mon chouchou*?" He must have heard the very real panic in her voice, because his was rushed, urgent, in a way she hadn't heard it since he came bursting into their house in Pozières, saying Minette was still bleeding, it wouldn't stop, and the baby wasn't breathing . . .

She dragged in a breath. "At cousin Josef's. I was picking up Felix. *Hurry.*"

He had the address already—he'd deliberately shown up last week to meet Felix and become reacquainted with Josef and had demanded all such details.

Perhaps because he'd known. Or at the very least, always wanted to be prepared. Because, he always said, one never knew when everything would go sideways—so one always had to be prepared for anything. For everything.

"Good—I'm only five minutes away. I'll be right there."

She turned, letting the phone cord twist around her, and looked at Christian's too-still legs. "I need a doctor."

A pulse of silence, a low curse, and then the line went dead.

"Tante?"

Felix. She set the phone back in its cradle and rushed to the kitchen door, where he stood hesitantly on the threshold. Tears coursed down his right cheek. "I'm sorry I didn't stay there. I was afraid, I—"

"It's all right." She dropped to her knees in front of him and pulled him in. What was she supposed to do? Keep him from the sight of his bleeding father? Or let him have what could be a last moment with him, a last time touching him?

God!

She pulled back, certain she'd never stop trembling again. Met his unflinching gaze. "Vati is hurt—but he's alive." *For now.* "You can stay here in the kitchen or—"

He wrenched from her light grip and ran through the kitchen, into the living room. He didn't scream, but by the time she turned and followed, he'd already taken the place she'd been in, Christian's big hand clutched in his arms. "It will be all right, Vati," his little voice promised, trembling. "I'm here. I'm here. I'm here."

The same words Christian had said over and

over to him, when they were reunited in another of Josef's living rooms.

Towels. She needed towels. Pressure on the wound. Stop the bleeding . . . or something. She grabbed whatever came to her hands on the kitchen shelves and dashed to Christian's other side.

Ciel, he was white as the towels, and he didn't so much as stir as she unbuttoned his jacket and pressed cloth to the bloodstained mess of his shirt. "Hail Mary," she forced from her lips, needing all the intercession she could get—and who better to understand the horror of watching a beloved man bleed and die? "Full of grace." She pressed harder, eyes burning. *Grace,* she needed grace, and strength, and whatever other virtues God could spare her. "The Lord is with thee."

Lord. Lord, be with him!

Felix sniffed, held his father's hand to his chest. "Blessed art thou among women. Blessed is the fruit of thy womb—"

"Jesus," she said with him, pushing the word out as a cry to heaven, an exhortation, the deepest cry of a still-beating heart. The turning point of every prayer—the hinge of every act of faith. "Holy Mary."

"Mother of God." Felix uncurled Christian's fingers and rested them against his little cheek.

"Pray for us sinners." She couldn't push hard enough—how could anyone ever push hard enough to hold in life that was trying to escape? She was just a woman. Chosen by no one but this man. Not the mother of God the Son, not a chosen vessel of immortal grace, nothing but weakness and doubt and pride and failure. Sinners, both she and Christian, trying to grope their way through a world gone dark, trying to find the Light through a valley of shadows and death. Sinners who could do so little. Who could only try and fight and cling to the nail-pierced hand of a Savior who often felt so far away. When their enemies were so very close.

"Now." Felix tilted his head down, burying it in his father's palm.

Corinne choked on a sob. "And at the hour of our death." *Not yet, Lord. May it not be yet. Not for him. Please—please, Lord, save him. Mother Mary, pray for him. St. Michael, fight for him!*

"Corinne!" Footsteps pounded—two sets.

She couldn't look up, couldn't tear her eyes from Christian's still face. What if he died? What if this was the hour of his death? What would she do without him?

Hands pulled her away, gentle and unfamiliar and masculine. "There now, *mademoiselle*. Let me have a look." A black bag bumped into her leg.

Doctor. Oncle Georges had brought a doctor. She blinked as her uncle crouched down beside Felix. His mouth was a firm, unyielding line as he took in who he was trying to save. "The *sonderführer*?"

"My *vati*." Felix didn't move his gaze from his father. Tears streaked his voice as much as his cheek.

He didn't see the way Georges jerked, how his eyes went wide, the way they flew to hers. "He is Felix's *father*?"

He could be angry with her for not telling him later—right now, they had to save him, if they could. "His superior shot him—or one of the soldiers he brought, I don't know. I couldn't see, we were just listening outside the door to the courtyard. They'd found out who Josef is, somehow. They were trying to arrest him or—I don't know. I couldn't hear it all. I don't know if Christian just got in the way as he tried to talk him down, or if it was on purpose. But he—he told his men to *leave him*."

Georges muttered another curse and scrubbed a hand over his face, through his hair. He stood. "They'll come back though, after they think he should be dead. We can't be here when they do."

"We're not leaving him!" She jumped to her feet too, fingers curling her palm.

They were wet. Hot. Sticky with the blood of her beloved.

Oncle Georges lifted his hands, palms out. "I meant we have to *move* him, Rinny. Doctor?"

Corinne spun, terrified that she'd see he'd

stopped working already, that Christian was *gone* already. But no—the doctor still bent over him, dabbing the wound, a hand probing his back. Searching for an exit wound, perhaps? "I won't know until I can examine him properly what damage has been done. But the bullet exited his body—which *could* be a good thing, if it didn't find his heart or any major vessels on the way through. He's still alive for now, at least. If we can stanch the bleeding, he may have a chance." He looked up, unfamiliar dark eyes gone darker with focus. "My office will do for now—but he can't stay there long. The patrols come through too regularly, to make certain I'm not treating Jews."

"We'll deal with the after, after. For now, let's get him into the car and to your office." Oncle Georges bent down, scooped up Felix, and delivered him to Corinne's arms with a reassuring murmur about getting his papa well again. And then he sent a scathing look into her eyes. "And *after,* Corinne—you're going to tell me everything you haven't. Are we clear?"

She could only hold Felix tight as he wrapped his legs around her waist and nod.

EIGHTEEN

The clock said eight, but Corinne couldn't remember if it was morning or night. The blackout curtains gave her no clue. The lamp had been burning, low and muted, forever. She'd sat in this place for so long that her every muscle ached. Her arms strained under the weight of the sleeping child curled up against her. Her eyes refused to move their focus from the still form on the bed.

If she looked away, he'd stop breathing. If she looked away, that shallow life barely clinging to his body would flee. Soul, wing its way to heaven.

He deserved it. He deserved rest. Peace. All the eternal promises that she knew were waiting for him.

But she wasn't ready to let him go. *Stay with me, Christian.* In her mind, she shouted the words, over and over and over until they were a litany, set in rhythm to match the *tic-a-tac* of the clock. *Rest-ez a-vec moi. Rest-ez a-vec moi.* Or perhaps the German, if he was too far gone to heed French? The words were too short to fit the half-second rhythm, but she could stretch them out. *Bleib ... bei ... mir. Bleib ... bei ... mir.*

A shadow moved, a board creaked. It could

have been Death, swooping down. An angel, ready to usher his soul into heaven.

It was, of course, only Oncle Georges, setting a hand on her shoulder so lightly she barely felt it. Whispering words so softly she barely heard them. "You need to rest, *mon chouchou*. Eat. You'll be no good to anyone like this."

What good was there left to be? *Rest-ez a-vec moi. Bleib . . . bei . . . mir.*

Her uncle sighed. "Rinny—"

"You can go." Her voice sounded so *normal* as it slid up her throat, past her lips.

She'd given him the answers he wanted. Earlier—yesterday?—while the doctor did whatever he could do in his clinic. They'd been enough to convince him that Christian was worth saving. Worth hiding. Worth risking for.

But he was still angry with her. She knew he was, even if it didn't show in his voice or his hands or his words. It glinted still in his eyes. *You should have told me,* he'd accused earlier—yesterday? *Why didn't you tell me?*

Because his world was so much bigger than hers had ever been, and even her efforts to join him in his had been so useless. So insignificant.

Because he would have told her a forbidden romance wasn't worth risking it all, that the work *could* be significant, and demanded her complete concentration.

Because he'd never fallen in love with a

supposed enemy, so how could he understand?

Because if she'd given it, shared it, it wouldn't be *hers* anymore.

Rest-ez a-vec moi. Bleib . . . bei . . . mir.

He crouched down beside the chair—Maman's chair, in Maman's room, pulled close to the bed that Felix had slept in before. Upon their arrival at her flat, Felix had started out there, curled up beside his father. Little hands trying to give the comfort that big hands usually gave *him*. Rubbing circles. Tracing patterns. Holding fingers that didn't hold his back.

It had broken something, she suspected. To hold his *vati*'s hand and feel no pressure in return. He'd retreated with a sob and curled up here in Corinne's lap, and she'd held him and held him and held him and promised she'd never let go.

Oncle Georges passed a featherlight hand over Felix's curls. Then over hers. "If you won't rest for yourself, do it for him. He's going to need you strong . . . whatever comes."

Her left arm was numb under Felix's head. That was all the strength she could give right now. She could hold on. She could love him. She could make sure he knew that she loved his father. "We'll be fine."

Georges hadn't been fool enough to suggest they try to find someone else to take care of Felix, at least. He hadn't suggested for a moment that he and Christian go anywhere but here.

Rest-ez a-vec moi. Bleib . . . bei . . . mir.

Her uncle sighed and levered back to standing. "I need to see what I can find out about Josef. The doctor will come by at eleven—three hours. Do you hear me?"

"Eleven." Morning, then. The doctor whose name she didn't know said he'd come by in the morning, with fresh IV bags and blood, too, if Christian needed more.

Oncle Georges turned but didn't leave. "Is he Catholic? Like Josef?"

Her chest went tight. She could still hear the faint words she'd caught from Josef's back door. *Catholic! Katholisch*! Claiming what he was as a denial of what he also was—part Jew.

When it becomes illegal to be what you are . . .

When were those words from? A century ago. A millennium.

"Corinne?"

She jerked her head in a nod. "He's Catholic."

"Then I'll stop by and find Father Serres too and send him here. For the last rites."

Her arms convulsed around Felix. "He doesn't need *last rites*." He was still alive. He would *stay* alive, because she wouldn't look away. She wouldn't move. Wouldn't give his soul a chance to run away with the angels.

Her uncle didn't sigh this time, didn't argue. He

simply said, "Then perhaps it'll work a miracle, like it did for Bastien. Regardless, I'll see he comes."

She squeezed her eyes shut against the burning. *Rest-ez a-vec moi. Bleib . . . bei . . . mir.*

Oncle moved off, the door opened, closed, a lock slid into place thanks to his copy of her key. When she opened her eyes, she saw Christian still. Breath, shallow and slow, still moving his chest just a bit. Just enough.

But she saw Papa too. A stranger, big and frightening, in the one little bed Maman and she had once shared. Taking up all the space in their cottage. The mud cleaned from his beautiful face. Fever burning through him. She saw the village priest bending over him, saying words too low for Corinne to understand. Forcing a single crumb of the blessed host past his lips. She could hear Maman, praying in a combination of French and Latin for this stranger she'd taken in, whose name she didn't know.

He wasn't Catholic. They hadn't known it then. In later years, when Papa was better, he would joke that he hadn't been much of anything, not before. He'd say that he'd become so in that moment. When the precious Body entered his and began a healing. When the Lord gave him new life and new love and bade him do something worthwhile with it.

Rest-ez a-vec moi. Bleib . . . bei . . . mir.

She would give Christian hers, if she could. He would do more with it than she would. He would save books and raise his son and teach a generation of lost children how to forgive and love and fight for something more than supremacy. He would protect exiles and make friends and reveal wisdom to people who thought they already knew it all. He would love someone, secrets and all, and never ask for what he thought wasn't their best.

He'd refuse to learn what could harm another.

He'd drop to his knees and sob over a lost lamb returned.

He'd step, time after time after time, between the innocent and the bullies trying to hurt them. Even when he knew it would hurt *him* instead.

Felix shifted, stirred, making fire light in her leg and arm and side as he unwittingly dug elbows and tailbone in and let blood flow where it hadn't in too long. His eye patch lay discarded on the too-smooth blanket beside his too-still father, so she saw how the skin around his missing eye pulled and stretched as he blinked his good one, trying to mimic the movement. She felt him tense and then go limp as he saw his precious *vati*, still unmoving, still alive.

He craned his head to look up at her. "Where's Grandpapa?"

Her fingers tingled, sparkles of pain, as she lifted her hand. She watched her fingers touch his hair but couldn't feel them do so. "I don't know, *mon chouchou*. Oncle Georges is going now to find out."

Arrested. Not just brought in for an interview but *arrested*. That much she knew. What it meant? That she didn't. Would they lock him up, here in Paris? Send him to one of their prison camps? Would there be a trial, a chance for justice, or did the Nazis not grant such basic rights to those they deemed enemies?

She didn't know, didn't know, didn't know.

Felix's head sagged. "I'm hungry."

Of course he was—they'd had no dinner last night, no bedtime snack, and it was morning now, and Oncle Georges's words rattled through her head. *Do it for him.*

She didn't want to. Didn't want to move, didn't want to take her eyes off Christian, because what if his soul flew away the moment they were gone? But she *did* want to, too, because this was his precious boy, and the only thing she could really do for Christian right now was love Felix.

She pressed a kiss to his brow, nudged him to slide off her lap, and stood on tingling legs. "Let's get you some breakfast then."

A new ugly truth stared back at her from her sparse kitchen shelves. She had ration coupons only for one. Sharing her meager portions with Felix probably wouldn't be too big a hardship, but as Christian healed and needed food—which *he would*—then how would she feed *him?* Thirteen hundred calories a day was all they were granted, assuming they could find food enough to fill those coupons. Enough for one small woman, perhaps one small woman and one small boy. But a grown man too?

Her stomach cramped, sympathetic to its future self. They'd make do. She'd just have to let Liana slip her some of what the Cartier customers shared. She'd have to let Oncle Georges bring her black-market meat and cheese and *pain au chocolat*.

Liana—*juste ciel*. What was she going to tell her friend? How much?

"Tante?"

Corinne jolted and pulled some bread and cheese out, added a few raisins, and slid the plate in front of Felix, where he sat in his chair at her table. "There you go, little mouse. Sorry I don't have more to offer."

He gave her a wan smile, too old for his years.

She made coffee, more habit than desire, and was still sipping it when a knock came at the door—two raps, a pause, then three. The knock Oncle Georges had said to expect from anyone he sent. She motioned for Felix to keep eating, though he froze at the noise. "It is either the doctor or my priest. Nothing to worry about."

Father Serres stood there when she opened it, serenity on his face but worry in his eyes. "Good morning, Mademoiselle Bastien. Your uncle sent me to . . . ?"

She motioned him inside, locking the door behind him, and led him toward Maman's bedroom. Only barely did she keep herself from leaping into the room, rushing to feel his breath on her fingers, his heartbeat under her palm.

Still there. For now, still there.

Rest-ez a-vec moi. Bleib . . . bei . . . mir.

But oh, how little he looked like her Christian. His eyeglasses were folded on the bedside table beside him, wire frames glinting in the lamplight. No color in his cheeks. His long-fingered hands, usually moving while he talked, were not only still but connected to the IV dangling from its pole via a slithering tube, tape holding it secure on his hand. No hated uniform, the stark white collar of his shirt peeking out. Instead, a white bandage wrapped round and round his chest, not quite covered by the sheet and blanket.

"He doesn't like his shoulders covered," Felix had said yesterday, frantic as he tugged them back down when the doctor had raised them to his chin. "He says it strangles him. Don't strangle him!"

Corinne let the priest take whatever chair he wanted—he chose the wooden folding chair Georges had been making use of—and steadied herself with a hand on the wall. "His name is Christian."

Father Serres nodded, sat—and then sucked in a breath. "I know him."

"You . . . do?"

He reached for Christian's encumbered hand, mindful of the needle and tubing. "He has come to reconciliation. I was leaving, last time, when he came in. He asked if I had time to hear him— the first I saw his face, though I knew his voice by then."

She didn't ask what Christian had told him, because she knew well the priest would never say. But his gaze shot to her, eyes wide. "His little boy? Is he all right? Georges told me only that a friend was shot and possibly dying—"

"Felix is in the kitchen." He knew of him— Christian had told him. Which meant that Father Serres already knew their biggest secrets. "Josef was arrested."

Father Serres sketched the sign of the cross and muttered a prayer, kissing his fingertips on the *amen.* "Will Felix be staying here then, now? With you?"

"Yes." There would be details to sort out. What to do with him during the days, how to perhaps claim him legally, as that cousin's boy she'd been saying he was, so they could get more rations. Enroll him in school.

Problems for another day. A day when Christian wasn't so still. Wasn't so pale.

Little fingers, sticky from raisins, slipped into

her palm. "Good morning, Father," Felix said in his little-mouse voice.

Father Serres gave him the same warm smile he'd always given Corinne. "Hello, Felix. Would you like to come hold your papa's other hand while I pray for him?"

He squeezed hers instead. "Don't do the dying prayers. He isn't going to die. Do the living prayers. The ones to make him better."

The priest's gaze shifted to her.

She squeezed Felix's hand. "Anointing of the sick. That's all he needs." He'd hear it in her voice—the fear that she was lying. The desperation to be telling the truth. The need to stand as one with Felix.

He nodded, smiled. "Of course. The anointing of the sick—I brought my oil. But I will still give him the eucharist, all right? So the Body of Christ can do its work in him. And he has been recently to confession anyway."

She pressed her lips together. Confession and the Eucharist were what differentiated the last rites from the anointing of the sick. But agreeing didn't mean she was agreeing he was dying—look at Papa. The rites had worked healing in his body, not just in his soul. Given him years with them. Years to love and to restore and to make life worth living. She dipped her head once, in a nod too tired to lift upward again.

She took her hand from Felix's and pressed it to his back. "Go on. Hold Vati's hand."

He scrambled onto the bed, sat cross-legged beside Christian, and took his hand into his lap.

Somehow, as Father prayed, she ended up in Maman's chair again. She felt her hand lift in the right places, laying claim to the sign of the cross. The blessing. The protection. The covenant. Forehead—*Lord, rule my thoughts.* Heart—*Lord, rule my heart.* Left arm, right—*Lord, guide my actions. In nomine Patris et Filii et Spiritus Sancti.* In the name of the Father, the Son, and the Holy Spirit.

All other words, however, were a blur. Echoes. Cadences. Rhythms. *Tic-a-tac-a-tic-a-tac.*

Rest-ez a-vec moi. Bleib . . . bei . . . mir. Pa-tris, Fil-i, Spr'tus Sanc-ti.

She jolted when another knock came at the door, sucking in a long breath and blinking gritty eyes. Asleep—she'd fallen asleep! Panic choked her, then abated as her eyes focused.

Felix still sat on the bed but facing the other direction now. Smiling as Father Serres showed him his rosary—he wouldn't be smiling, wouldn't be sitting there so calmly if Christian weren't still breathing.

The priest had moved the folding chair to the opposite side of the bed, had clearly settled in to keep watch while she slept, and to entertain the little one.

His kind eyes were on her now. "It will be the doctor. I can let him in—"

"No, no. I'll get it." She pushed up, head going light as she stood, limbs going heavy. The doctor, already? She had to stare at her watch for a long moment as she stumbled from the room, not quite believing its hands.

It was eleven. She'd slept in that chair for more than two hours while Father Serres kept Felix company.

The doctor bustled in with a simple nod when she opened the door for him, heading straight for Maman's room. He'd come with them yesterday to get him situated. Make him comfortable. Set up the IV on its pole by the bed and instruct them in how to put a new bag on when the first ran out.

Oncle Georges had been the one to do it, so that she wouldn't have to disturb Felix.

She trailed the doctor in, not daring to sink onto Maman's chair again, not given how close sleep still felt. She stood at the foot of the bed instead, arms folded over her stomach to try to hold herself erect. *Tell me he's improving,* she willed the physician's way. *Tell me he'll pull through.*

The doctor said nothing. He checked something on the IV, pulled down the bandages and checked the wound. Took his pulse, eyes tracking the second hand on his watch while his fingers rested on Christian's neck.

She blinked away the rhythm before it could lull her again.

At last, he set down a vial of something, along with a syringe, on the bedside table and stood, gaze cutting straight to her. Through her. "If he gets agitated, seems to be in pain, administer some of the morphine."

Morphine? Morphine was what they gave Papa when he was dying. She forced a swallow. "Is that just pain management or . . . ?"

The doctor sighed. He looked tired, shadows circling his eyes. "I don't have answers for you, *mademoiselle*. If he doesn't wake soon, the chances that he ever will go down dramatically. And yet rest is also the best healer. He is in God's hands now."

He always had been. Always would be. As would they all. She forced herself to step toward the medicine, the syringe. "Show me. Show me how much, and how often."

She saw the doctor out shortly after, and Father Serres not long after that. She sat beside Christian, she held his hand. She read a bit of the storybook Felix pressed into her hands. They nibbled at a lunch that neither of them wanted and then finally, *finally* a key turned in the lock and Oncle Georges stepped inside, and she sprang from her chair.

He had packages in his arms, some of which he deposited in the living room, others he brought with him into the kitchen. He barely glanced at her, just started filling her cupboards and drawers. "Josef is gone."

Her hands gripped the back of her chair like it could right the rocking world. "What do you mean, *gone*?"

"Not in Paris. They sent him . . . somewhere. A prison camp, most likely."

Her knees buckled. "He was still sick. Will they . . . treat him?"

Silence was her uncle's answer. Silence, and the sliding of provisions onto shelves. She frowned when she saw the things he'd brought her. Not the expensive, ration-breaking items he usually tried to slip her. Dried pasta. Flour. A small packet of sugar. A few tins of vegetables and potted meat.

"They'd searched his flat, probably looking for Bauer, but they didn't take anything. So I brought it all here. His books, his clothes—he and Bauer look about the same size, you'll need them."

Tears blurred her vision. Josef—*gone*. And even as it ate at her, as she wanted to scream at the injustice, she wanted to weep, too, at having his things here. His books. His clothes. She knew he'd want that—his things helping Christian. Feeding Felix.

"I have paperwork being drawn up, using a different surname for Felix now but the same general story. Granting you custody as the closest living relative. He's good, the fellow I have working on it. It'll hold up to inspection. You'll be able to get rations for him, enroll him in school."

She sank back onto the chair. Apparently her decision to put it off until another day simply meant "Oncle Georges will take care of it." The tears spilled over when she blinked. "Thank you. Oncle—I don't know what I'd do without you."

"Rinny." He abandoned the kitchen and moved to wrap his arms around her, press her head to his stomach. "You know I'd do anything for you. Move heaven and earth, if I had to. You're . . . you're the closest thing I'll ever have to a daughter. You know that, don't you?"

She nodded against the soft wool of his jacket, wrapped her arms around his waist. Held on, like she was Felix's age again, like when he'd first covered for her when he caught her in mischief that would have made Maman see red. What had it even been? She couldn't remember, not the trouble she'd found—only the friend. The sure knowledge that Oncle Georges would always have her back, and a wink, and a *bonbon* for her in his pocket. "I love you, Oncle."

He leaned down, pressed a kiss to the top of her head. And then reached over to tousle Felix's hair too. "And I love you. We'll get through this, *mon chouchou*. Whatever it takes."

The anger probably still simmered, somewhere

inside him—because it would have hurt him, knowing she'd kept such a secret. She shouldn't have. She could see that now. "I'm sorry. That I didn't tell you. I just . . . it wasn't quite real."

He chucked her playfully under the chin and stepped away. "Matters of the heart have rules of their own. I understand that, Rinny. I was only upset because I'd have had other precautions in place, had I known. To keep you safe. All of you."

She didn't ask what they were, not given the way his face shifted.

"His aide—Kraus, isn't it? He's at the library. Just sitting outside the door like a lost puppy. You should go down. Let him tell you what happened. See what story he gives you." He motioned toward the living room windows. If she peeked out, she could see the library entrance.

She didn't bother. The last thing in the world she wanted to do was leave her flat, go so far from Christian . . . but they needed to know all they could. And Kraus was more likely to talk to her than her stranger of an uncle. She nodded and reached for the cardigan draped over the back of the third chair.

Oncle Georges cleared his throat. "Perhaps first you ought to change out of . . . that." He nodded toward her dress.

Yesterday's dress. Still stiff with dried blood at the hem, where she'd knelt beside him. She'd washed it from her hands but hadn't taken the time to change her clothes.

Part of her wanted to be embarrassed at the doctor and Father Serres seeing her in such a state. The greater part didn't care. But it certainly wouldn't do to go outside like this. To let Kraus know she'd been there.

A quick change, a brushing of her hair, a touch of rouge on her cheeks to distract from her paleness, red on her lips to steal the attention from the hollows beneath her eyes. She didn't look good by any stretch, but "almost normal" was all she was hoping for.

A few minutes later, the biting air inspired her to hug her light jacket closer and wish she'd grabbed her wool peacoat. But she continued down the front steps, along the wrought iron gate that surrounded the library, and paused when she spotted Kraus.

Just as her uncle had said—sitting there on the stoop, back against the door, staring into space.

"Kraus? Are you all right?" She let herself through the gate, praying her voice sounded normal as she spoke to him in German, knowing the conversation would be too complicated for his limited French.

He blinked, gaze meandering her way. "Have you heard?"

"Heard what?" She slid a few steps along the pavement and then halted, still several feet away.

He motioned toward the building at his back, larynx bobbing. "He's dead—the professor. Shot."

"What?" It was easy, so easy to let horror into her voice. To let her hands fall, limp and useless, at her sides. "When? How? He was just sitting in my classroom yesterday morning—"

"Yesterday evening. It was—he . . ." His face crumpled, and he rested his elbows on his raised knees, covering his face with his hands. "It was my fault. It was all my fault."

His fault? She froze, all but the blood pulsing in her ears. "What do you mean?"

"I told Ackermann what my cousin had said. I didn't think—he wasn't supposed to *shoot* him! Just make him take a stand, denounce the Jews. That's all I thought he'd do. That the professor would stop talking about them like they were our *equals,* I didn't think he'd defend one like that—die for him."

Then he didn't know Christian at all. But that wasn't the point. "What cousin? What did he say?"

"He's a student. At the University of Berlin." His voice went echoey, distorted by the tunnel he'd made of his arms. "I only wanted to know more about the professor. Be a better aide. I just asked him to tell me what he knew about him, what people said about him. How his classes were. I thought he'd send a few funny stories, and I could tease him, and he'd laugh and ask how I'd heard that. I thought it would make me sound *clever.*"

Her throat went dry. "And instead?"

He looked up, straight through her, eyes haunted. "He said the professor had been a walking ghost last year, in the class he had him for. His son had just died. He'd lost his wife years before—things he never even *told* me. But Tabb said before the kid's death, he'd given a few inflammatory lectures. Things he shouldn't have said, things they had to report. He was surprised to hear he was *here,* working for the Reich. They all thought he'd finally been arrested, he'd said—arrested! For speaking against Hitler. For defending the Jews."

Her fingers twisted in the too-thin lapel of her jacket. She said nothing.

He didn't wait for her to. Just sagged again. "Apparently his father had a bunch of Jewish friends. Men who used to be professors there too—men who came *here,* to Paris. That was why I gave the letter to Ackermann. He was supposed to *ask* him, to question him, to get him to declare his loyalty. He wasn't supposed to *kill* him."

Acid burned her throat. Kraus—Kraus was the reason all this had happened. *Kraus* was the traitor, the one who had turned on a man who'd been nothing but kind to him, who had gone behind his back to a beast like Ackermann. "Idiot boy." The words came out as acidic as the bile in her throat, and he winced as they landed on him. "You handed a weapon to a bully and expected him to *talk?*"

His face twisted.

She didn't care if her words hurt him. No, she did—she *wanted* them to, because Christian was lying inches from death because of *him*. "You expected him to subscribe to your hatred? To agree that his father's friends were subhuman, just because *you* wanted to feel clever? Superior? You think those men who wrote books and essays and poems and treatises are *your* inferior? Why—because thousands of years ago, their forefathers came from a different country than yours did? A land that gave us our Bible, our morals, our ethics, our very civilization? You think *they* are inferior to *you?* You're nothing but an ignorant farm boy with delusions of power because you put on a uniform!"

He lurched to standing, but she spun around so she didn't have to look at the plea on his face. Stormed the two steps she'd taken from the gate.

Halted with her hand on the cold iron.

Because she blinked, and she saw Christian in her mind's eye. Christian, lying on her mother's bed, the priest praying over him. She felt the cross she'd traced over herself. *Lord, rule my thoughts. Lord, rule my heart. Lord, rule my* actions. *In the name of the Father, the Son, and the Holy Spirit. Amen.*

She squeezed her eyes shut. Saw Christian sitting in her classroom, this boy at his side. Saw him laughing in her living room, Felix in his arms.

Heard his words, the night he'd told her of his wife, their baby, his fight to give Felix the right to live. *I thought I could make a difference there, with them. That if I could just help them see that these ideas are mad, convince them to keep their minds open . . .*

Imagined him now, wincing at her words. Reaching not for her, but for Kraus. She squeezed her eyes shut and prayed the cross would give her the strength she needed to turn around.

Kraus still stood in front of the door, his face a wreck of regret and pain. Her nostrils flared. "Forgive me," she said, hoarse now instead of shouting. "I shouldn't have said those things. It is the shock, but that is no excuse."

Kraus collapsed against the door. "No. You're right. It's my fault."

"It isn't. It's the fault of the man who pulled the trigger." She took a step. Another. A third. Made herself reach out and rest her hand on his shoulder. Made herself offer the forgiveness she always craved but was so slow to give. "Do you know what Professor Bauer saw when he looked at you?"

He winced, mouth twisting. "An ignorant farm boy with delusions of power?"

"No." Her voice cracked on the simple syllable. "He would never have said something so hurtful and cruel. So untrue. When he looked at you, Kraus, he saw a young mind ripe for learning. He saw a young man with all the potential in the world. One with his whole life spread out before him. He spoke of you like one of his favorite pupils—and he prayed for you. Every day. Prayed you would follow the path God had for you. A path of love rather than hatred."

She knew it was true, even if Christian had never said as much. She knew it because she'd seen the way he looked at his aide—the same way she looked at her students. With the same hopes and fears and prayers.

His shoulders shook, though no tears escaped his eyes. "He would hate me now though. If he'd lived. I turned him in. It's my fault."

"He would forgive you. And he would tell you to think, next time, before you blindly chase your ideology. He would ask you to *think,* not just to feel. To ask, always, if you could be wrong. To listen, *always listen,* to the other points of view. Because the moment we stop granting someone the right to disagree, Kraus, this is what happens. Do you understand me? This is what turns men into tyrants. This is what leads to fear and death."

A lecture he clearly hadn't heard yesterday. A

point that hadn't sunk in. A lesson he'd ignored.

But yesterday, he was an angry young man with his cousin's words burning in his pocket, wondering if his mentor had lied to him.

Today he was a different young man. A young man who saw the cost of choosing a policy over a person.

A young man with his whole life spread out before him, who would need to choose, every moment of every day, what path he would follow. What fight he'd make his own.

She squeezed his shoulder and then let go. Stepped away. Turned.

Christian would forgive him. She knew he would. But it was a path she'd have to choose to walk every moment of every day. And she'd be fighting her own fallen nature every step of the way.

NINETEEN

Friday crept into Saturday. Saturday wept into Sunday. Sunday stretched its way toward Monday, all promises of a resurrection on the Lord's Day withering a bit more in Corinne's soul with every mocking *tic-a-tac* of the clock.

How long had her papa lain unconscious when they'd found him? How long had he gone in and out, fighting delirium? How long had he struggled for each breath?

She didn't remember now. And knew it didn't matter, because Christian wasn't Papa. His chances were *better*—he had antibiotics coursing through his veins, along with the fluids. *Magic*, they would have called it in ages past. A man three days without a drink, but not dying of thirst. A man with a hole in his body, but not fighting infection.

A man who still hadn't opened his eyes, even though night had fallen again, even though she'd begged him in every language she knew, whispering her plea whenever Felix was out of the room. *Wake up, Christian. For Felix. Wake up and live for your boy. Wake up so I can tell you again that I love you, without any qualifications. Because I can, I can, I can!*

Felix slept now, beside him, curled around the

stuffed bear Oncle Georges had brought him from somewhere or another, thumb dangling from his lips.

I'll have to break him of that again, Christian had said just last week. But he'd looked at his boy like he didn't really care if he stopped. Didn't mind the reminder of how little he still was, really. Didn't care what it did to his teeth if it brought comfort to his soul.

What if he died? What if Felix was left only with *her*? She didn't know when to urge a child to stop sucking his thumb, or how. She didn't know the right words to croon when he awoke in a nightmare. She didn't know what patterns to trace on his back when he needed comfort or how to soothe him after a bully's taunts or encourage him to open his heart when a pretty girl first caught his eye. She didn't know how to be a mother.

She'd have to sleep tonight, somehow. Because tomorrow, she had to pretend to be normal. Pretend that it didn't matter that much to her if an acquaintance was presumed dead. Pretend relief, even.

One fewer Nazi in the world.

One fewer good man, if he didn't open his eyes.

Oncle Georges would come in the morning. Stay with Christian, with Felix. She would go to the Sorbonne. She would talk about Plato and Aristotle. She would translate *Faust*. She would read the papers that her students ought to have dropped through the slot of her office door on Friday, while she was shouting at Kraus.

She'd say, whenever someone told her how horrible she looked, "You know that flu that's been going around?" and let them assume that's what had kept her home all weekend.

She set down the book she'd been clutching in her lap, just to have something to hold on to. One of the books that Christian had brought to her, that night she'd kissed him. One of the books she'd never sent out because it had been lost to her. Trapped in the library. One of the books filled with encoded instructions on what her students ought to be watching for and how to get word back to her if they saw it.

Hands free again, she picked up Christian's cold hand, positioning her fingers around the tape and the needle and the tube that was keeping him alive. "I'm supposed to tell you," she said in the quietest of whispers, eyes on his face, "that it's all right to let go if you need to. That I'll take care of Felix—and I will. You know I will." She tightened her grip and let herself pretend he was gripping back. "But I'm not ready to lose you, Christian. One kiss isn't enough. One 'I love you' is too few to see me through the rest of my life. I'm selfish. Greedy. I need *more*. More of you. And I am so, so sorry I didn't make use of what days we had. I'm sorry I let fear hold me back.

Sorry I let your uniform stand in our way, even when I *knew* it was a lie."

She closed her eyes, listening to the steady, deep breathing of the sleeping child. Yearning for a hitch in Christian's, but only if it was the kind that accompanied waking up. Not the kind that stretched on and on and on into eternity. She prayed and she pleaded and she lifted his hand to press a kiss to each dry knuckle, chilled from being out of the blanket. Chilled, because the flat was getting cool and there was nothing for heat. Not this year. No coal, no oil. Only blankets and warm trousers instead of stylish skirts.

His finger twitched in hers. She held her breath, watching. Waiting. Praying. He'd twitched before, but then *nothing,* so she'd had little choice but to admit they'd just been small muscle spasms. Not an attempt at communication.

"Christian." She splayed his fingers over hers, letting his long fingers reach to her wrist. "Christian, come back. Please. I know you're tired. I know it hurts. But please, there is so much left for you to do. So many young minds to fill with wisdom. So many debates you still need to have. Don't give up. Please, don't give up."

Another twitch—and a press. *A press* of his finger into her wrist.

Tears stormed her eyes, punched her in the nose, and she had to sniff before she could speak again. "Come back to us, beloved. To me, to

Felix—he's right here. We're here, and we're not letting you go."

The pressure eased, and she nearly sobbed—but then his breath caught. It *caught,* and then he drew in a deep breath, deeper than he had in all these days, and when she looked from his hand to his face, he was blinking.

Who knew that a blink was the most beautiful sight in the world?

"Christian!" She couldn't shout, because their world had to be ruled by whispers now. But every ounce of feeling she'd ever felt was in those few syllables. She leaned closer, into his line of sight, so he wouldn't have to move his head. "I'm here. Felix is here."

He blinked again, and from the confusion on his face, she had the heart-stopping fear that he wouldn't know her. Wouldn't know his *son.* Wouldn't know why they were worth fighting his way back to life for.

He squinted and rasped, "Fuzzy."

"Oh—your glasses are off. They're right here though, when you're ready for them and . . . you need water." She'd been putting balm on his lips, but when they'd tried dribbling water between them, it dripped right back out.

He nodded now, though, and tried to shift.

"No!" She dropped his hand and reached for his shoulders, stilling him. "Don't try to sit up, not without help. You'll hurt yourself."

The tension left him, his head relaxing against the pillow again, confusion still on his face. "What happened?"

She told him as she put the flexible paper straw in the cup of water she'd had ready, just in case, and helped him drink. As he reached a hand toward Felix and settled it on his son's sleeping back. As his eyes slid closed again, but the way his fingers wrapped around hers said he was still listening.

"I can't stay here," he croaked once she was finished. "I'm putting you in danger."

"Don't be an idiot. They think you're dead—they're combing the river and dumps for your corpse, not searching flats for you. And where else would you go, back to your hotel room?"

He winced, letting his head loll in her direction and opening his eyes again. They were so blue. Like Felix's in color—so very different in what shone out of them. Exhaustion in place of innocence. Worry in place of trust. But love. They had that in common.

She brushed his hair from his forehead, trying to quell the quivering of her lips. "You're not leaving this flat. Not until you're well and we can get you somewhere safer. And then, we'll go together. All of us. Somewhere safe, somewhere that the Nazis won't find us. England or America or . . . the North Pole, I don't really care, as long as you're alive and I'm with you."

Because that was all that mattered. Oncle and her students could carry on without her. What good was she really doing anyway? Maybe that had never really been what God intended her to do during this war. Maybe it all had only been to lead her here. To him, to Felix.

Perhaps the movement of his lips was the beginning of a smile. Perhaps it was an abandoned attempt at words. Either way, it relaxed again, and his eyelids drooped.

She kissed his forehead, the tip of his nose, his lips. They pressed against hers—weakly, briefly, but he kissed her back and that was all that mattered. "Rest," she bade, kissing him again. "We'll sort it all out later."

His head moved the slightest bit in acknowledgment. Then his eyes opened again, brows creased. "Rin . . . books."

"Books?"

"With the words in the margin. I know I said . . . but I have to know. Why those? Why not your own?"

Why had she sent her students with borrowed titles from the Library of Burned Books? Stupidity. Brashness. A desire to thumb her nose at the encroaching tyrants and use the very books they'd tried to obliterate to undermine them. She offered a weak smile. "Poetic justice?"

His lips turned up too.

She watched him for a moment, telling herself

that he'd just be *sleeping* now, not whatever that other unconsciousness had been. That he would wake up in the morning. But that made her suck in a breath. "Christian?"

His eyes fluttered open again.

Good. "If I'm not here in the morning when you wake up and a man is instead, don't worry—it's just my uncle. His name is Georges, and he's helping us. All right? He knows everything. He's a friend. He's taking care of Felix while I'm in class."

He held her gaze as he gave a weak nod and then slid shut his eyes again.

She didn't know if he'd actually remember—but it didn't matter. He'd woken up, he'd spoken, he'd drunk . . . he wasn't going to die.

The rational part of her knew that one waking didn't guarantee that. Didn't mean infection wouldn't overrun the antibiotics or that internal damage wouldn't yet take him. But she knew. She knew he'd live, because he wasn't ready to die yet.

The fear hadn't retreated enough that she went to her own room that night for longer than it took to grab her pillow and a blanket. But she slept on the floor beside the bed and only woke up six times to check on him.

Disoriented was too meek a word for the way Christian's senses swam, for the cacophony of sounds and fire and light and agony all trying to elbow their way into his awareness. His back hurt—no, his whole torso, in a cocktail of pains that he hadn't known got along so well. Piercing and throbbing and aching and screeching.

But he bullied his eyes open, because last time he'd managed it, Corinne had been there. Blurry gold and cream in a vague shape, but her voice had pulled him toward consciousness, out of the darkness that weighed him down.

He listened now, but he couldn't hear her. Couldn't see her fuzzy outline or feel her beautiful fingers wrapped around his, squeezing life into him.

He heard laughter though, young and bright, and then a deeper echo. Felix and Josef, playing in the living room.

Only . . . no. Not Josef.

He squeezed his eyes shut, trying to remember what he wanted to forget, wanted to deny. Not Josef. He had an image of Josef burned into his eyes, but not him laughing with Felix. On the floor. On his back. Hands held up, his necklace in his fingers. Panic in his eyes.

His voice rattled in Christian's ears, but not lifted in a silly song like the one coming from outside this room. Screaming. Screaming, *Stay back, stay back, stay back!*

Corinne had told him, whenever that was that she'd held his hand and kissed him so tenderly he'd known he must have been every bit as hurt as he felt. She'd told him Josef had been arrested, sent only God and the Nazis knew where. She'd told him that Ackermann had shot him. Based on something Kraus's cousin had shared in a letter about Christian's behavior at the university.

She'd told him something else, too, about a man who would be watching Felix. A friend. An uncle.

She'd mentioned an uncle before. Georges, that was it. And when he tried to sit up and ended up grunting and collapsing back down again, the agony feasting on him so greedily everything went dark again for a moment, he knew he was about to meet him.

"Easy there, *mon ami*." Strong, large hands steadied him, helped him settle. A masculine blur filled his vision when the darkness retreated again.

Christian blinked, squinted. It was one thing to see only the outline of Corinne, whose every feature he'd long ago memorized, whose mannerisms he knew so well. But if he was going to meet a stranger, he'd like to be able to see him. "Could you . . . glasses?" he managed between the waves of pain.

A moment later they were positioned on his nose. The earpieces didn't settle quite right, but he'd worry with that later. Right now, he could at least see the man.

He wasn't as old as he'd expected when Corinne called him *uncle*. Mid-forties, perhaps, with streaks of silver in his middling-brown hair, smile lines creasing his face, and a decided absence of a smile as he regarded him with brown eyes that pierced to his very soul.

On an ordinary day, he could imagine that look would have made him squirm. Just now, his soul felt stripped down to its essence, no secrets left to hide. He nodded his thanks for the help. "Georges, isn't it?"

"Georges Piers. Most of the time." It took a long few seconds for the words to register as the man sat in the dainty armchair Corinne had been in before. For Christian's muddled mind to realize that he wasn't speaking French, wasn't speaking German, but that they were words he ought to know.

English. They were English.

"Other times," the man continued in an accent that didn't sound like the polished ones the BBC chaps used, "I'm George Pearce."

Christian was too tired, too aching to frown. "You're British."

"I was stationed here in the Great War. Spent four long, arduous years serving and scouting and learning this land inside and out, top to bottom." He shifted back into French. "I fell in love—with the country, but mostly with Minette. My wife, God rest her soul."

Christian nodded. He didn't know why this man was telling him his story—but he had a feeling it was important.

"Corinne—she was five when I met her. Most precocious, bravest, most trouble-seeking child I'd ever met, and that was saying something, because I grew up in a pack of street rats in London's seediest neighborhood. Do you know how she'd found the dying soldier who became her stepfather?" Georges didn't give him time to answer, just leaned forward. "She was searching dead bodies for tins of food. Rations. Hardtack. Four years old at the time, and that mite was scavenging from *corpses* left in the battlefield by her village in Somme."

Christian winced. Wondered briefly if this would turn into an accusation—it was Christian's people who had killed those men, who had helped churn up that mud, who had fought against this man in that war. Not *Christian,* not even his father, but even so. His people, then. His people, now.

Enemies.

But Corinne had said they were friends. That he could be trusted. That he knew everything.

So he waited.

Georges sighed and eased back again. "I'd promised Minette, when we married, that I'd take her back to England with me. Introduce her to my family, who by that point had all made something of themselves. My one sister's married to a novelist—another to a musician. My brother, the one who gave me his last name because I didn't know my own—he works for a division of the government that blokes like you aren't supposed to know exists."

"Germans, you mean?"

Georges's lips twitched. "That too. But mostly I mean ordinary people. People who just live their lives, as long as they're able."

Christian's weary eyes shifted toward the door. He would have lived his life, if they'd let him. Raised his son. Taught his classes. He'd have been content to leave his mark on the world only in words and papers and lectures. Perhaps a book, when he had the time to write one. Thoughts—that was all he'd ever imagined he would offer. Just *thoughts*.

"But you know what I found, when we made it back to London?" His eyes didn't leave Christian's face. "I wasn't fit for it anymore. For *society*. And Minette, she wasn't a city girl. She missed her little French town, where everyone knew her name. So we came back. And I thought, let me see this place, now that it's healing. Now that the war's just a memory. And I went looking for the grave of a friend's brother, thinking to give his family that closure, and instead I found Bastien. Alive, newly married to Yvonne. I found Corinne, trying to steal a stick of gum from my pocket like I wasn't a thief long before she was born. I found a brother in him, and a sister for Minette in Yvonne, and a little girl who wrapped me around her finger in about ten seconds flat."

That part he could imagine easily enough, and he risked a small, aching smile that made his lips strain toward cracking. "I will do anything for her," he said, because that must be what Georges was getting at. "Anything you tell me to do. I'll leave as soon as I'm able, if that's what you want. I won't put her in danger if I can help it."

Georges hooked an ankle over the opposite knee, the picture of ease. "Do you love my little girl, Christian Bauer?"

"More than life. More than anything but my son."

He was going to make him promise to leave—he knew he was. He was going to name all the reasons that this couldn't work, all the risks Christian brought with him, all the pain he'd already caused. He would say, as Christian had tried to when he last awoke, that he was putting Corinne's life in danger by being here.

Instead, he nodded. "Then you have common sense to match your intellect—I'm never willing to assume as much. And I can put you to work, if you want to be useful once you're well."

Had he not learned his lesson just minutes ago, he would have tried to sit up. Because cryptic offers like that weren't meant to be received lying down. "What sort of work do you do?"

The man's grin was disarming. Boyish and full of a mischief that left no doubt as to why he and Corinne got along so well. "This and that. At the moment, I'm working mostly in words. That should appeal to you, shouldn't it?"

"Words." An Englishman, in France, with a brother in a division of the British government that people weren't supposed to know about. Christian suddenly wished for more water.

Georges dropped his smile, his ankle, and the pretense of being nothing but a doting uncle. He leaned forward again, eyes burning now. "From what Corinne tells me, you hate the Nazis more than any of us. Is that true?"

Hate. It was the word he would have used, had someone asked him before. Before his soul had passed so close to the fires of death. Just now, he didn't want to give that word safe harbor in his spirit.

But whatever word he chose, the idea would be the same. "I was against the Nazi Party before the rest of the world even realized they were a threat."

"Your work here—you've been subverting them as much as you could. Correct?"

He half expected Ackermann to leap from the shadows, that gun in his hand again. "As much as I dared." Paltry efforts, and they'd come to nothing. But he probably knew that already.

"Perhaps we can find a way for you to do more. I can connect you with others—with French, with English contacts. We could look into trading what you know of them for safe harbor in England, if you want to take Felix and Corinne there."

Desert? He shifted, uncomfortable against the pillows. "Turncoats have never been respected by either side of a war. You surely know that, Georges. No one trusts a man who turns on his own country. Much as I despise the party in charge, they are not all of Germany."

The older man granted it with a tilt of his head. "True enough. And I'll be honest—England could be the next place to come under Nazi rule. Much as we're fighting against it, they could overcome us. They could win. In which case, England would be no safer than here. Paris may, in fact, be the safest city in Europe just now."

Christian's head sank in half a nod. It was true. Paris might be under Nazi rule, but there were no bombs falling. No attacks. The same couldn't be said of England or any other free country left in Europe, and crossing the Atlantic was a bigger risk still. Strange to think, but this captured territory was quite a safe haven.

Georges leaned closer. "If you want to stay here and work with the Resistance, I could try instead to get you new papers. Claiming you're French—for now, for the duration."

The Resistance? He said it like it was a . . . a

thing. An organization. Something more than a phrase intoned by a defeated general trying to rally his countrymen to fight on in his absence. "You don't think that would be too big a risk? I have not been unseen in Paris. My face will be recognized, by Nazis and Parisians alike."

Georges pursed his lips. "I know. You would have to remain hidden, for the most part. Only daring a few meetings now and then. Largely . . . you'd be in hiding. Here, or wherever else we could find for you. But you could still help. Somehow."

It sounded less like an opportunity than a meager attempt at a handout. Hiding. A life where he could never show his face in daylight, in public. A life where his very existence here would mean danger for Felix, for Corinne, for Georges.

His eyes slid closed. He was so tired. In such agony. And he'd learned such a hard lesson already, struggling against the might of the Party: That those only fighting *against* something never won. It was only when you had something to fight *for* that you stood a chance.

He'd fought for Felix. He would fight for Corinne.

But abstract concepts like freedom, brotherhood, equality? He saw their goodness. He wanted them. Wished he had energy enough, even without a bullet hole in his chest, to pursue them. But those slippery concepts were so hard to keep hold of when your fingers were tired and your chest was aching and every breath burned. When something concrete and living and breathing demanded your whole focus.

Georges's expression softened. "Just things to think about—you don't have to make any decisions now. I just want you to know you're not alone. We'll find the best way forward for all of you." He patted his knees and then stood. "You need rest. Corinne will have my head when she sees how I've exhausted you. But I wanted you to know. We're even now—all our secrets on the table. Equals. Maybe, once you're better, we can be friends."

He was friends with Gestapo and Nazis, with outcasts and exiles, with Jews and Aryans, with atheists and Christians. But he'd never been able to claim an English street rat as a friend. He mustered up all the smile he could. "I'll hold you to it."

TWENTY

15 November 1940

Though her feet itched to run straight from campus after her final class of the week, Corinne knew she couldn't. At least, not if she meant to keep her position. She hadn't kept her office hours as much as she should have been, she was behind on grading essays, she'd failed to attend the faculty meeting a week ago—it had been on Friday, while she was still wearing a blood-soaked dress and counting *tic-a-tac*s with her prayers. Her students deserved better. The university did too.

She knew it—but still, everything in her strained toward Boulevard Arago, toward the three fellows who would be waiting for her. Christian was sitting up now. Eating a bit. The doctor had finally been willing to grant that, barring infection, he should eventually make a full recovery, though it would take months.

Months. Glorious, beautiful, unfettered months when he could just be there. There, in her flat. Playing with Felix. Talking to Oncle Georges. Smiling up at her. Months when his enemies thought him dead so wouldn't be watching him. Months when they wouldn't have to guard their every look and thought and word.

"Careful," Liana said as she swooped to her side, linking their arms together with a laugh. "If you don't wipe that look off your face, everyone will think you've fallen in love." She bumped their shoulders together, winking.

Georges was the one who had brought the entire Moreau family to dine with *them* last night. "It is important not to trust many, *mon chouchou*," he had whispered into her surprise. "And just as important to trust a few implicitly. The Moreaux are good people. Good allies. Good friends to watch after you whenever I'm not in Paris—even now."

She'd think later about when next her uncle would leave. For now, she bumped Liana back, letting her lips mirror the smile. "Me? No one would believe it. They've all given up hope for me, after trying for a decade to set me up with their every nephew and son and brother and cousin and friend from church."

Liana laughed again and reached to hold her beret down against a sudden gust of November wind. "If only Josef had offered to make introductions to his godson ages ago, though, eh?"

"If only." But time was too precious to waste any on could-have-beens. They had *now*. Months, at least, before they'd have to decide what came next. Time to heal and discover and learn what it would be like to be a family.

"Maman's worried, you know. About the propriety." Liana tried, and failed, to tamp down another grin. "She's already doing up Gigi's old room for Felix. And Martin's for Chris."

Corinne nearly stumbled over a seam in the walkway. "She—what?" Babette wanted to steal them from her, when she'd only had them for a week, three days of which Christian had been unconscious and at death's very door?

"Relax—though also be forewarned." Liana winked and reclaimed her arm. "She is only concerned for your eternal souls, after all. It isn't that she doesn't *trust* you. And she knows the poor man can scarcely move right now."

Corinne blew out a breath as her friend hurried off to her next class. Another something to worry over later—because the poor man could indeed scarcely sit up for more than thirty minutes at a time, and her uncle was there more than he wasn't. There was no threat to her virtue.

Even if she *had* snuck a kiss from him this morning that made her toes curl in delight when she remembered it.

A glance from the corner of her eye showed her Gustaf striding along the path toward her, an arm raised, but she pretended not to notice—she wasn't quite ready to face Christian's sole Nazi friend just yet. She couldn't exactly stop him from seeking her out, but she could hope that if she made him work for it, he'd decide he didn't have time quite yet if he meant to observe a class.

Then perhaps, perhaps she'd be gone for the day before he came and found her.

One of her colleagues held the door to their building open for her, giving her a nod and a smile. "Good to see you looking more yourself again, Dr. Bastien. That nasty flu gone for good, finally?"

"So it seems. Thank you, Dr. Guilliams." She fished in her bag for her key, hurrying in before Gustaf could shout loud enough that she couldn't pretend oblivion.

After her office hours, she would go to Maman's office under the guise of tidying up. Really, to soak her in. She hadn't words enough in their encoded language to tell her what had transpired in the last week, even though her soul ached with the need. Maman had been her whole world for so long. Her confidante. Her best friend. She wanted so much to curl up with her on the sofa, steaming coffee in each of their hands, and just *talk* to her. Tell her everything. Confess that finally, finally she understood how Maman had felt for Papa.

How it had torn her apart to watch him lie there, dying. How it had given her heart wings when he beat death back. How the future could both look grim as the dark and sparkling as the stars when you faced it with someone you loved.

They'd spoken yesterday afternoon, as they had each Thursday since Oncle Georges received the wireless. In Father Serres's office, that time. Too briefly, too simply. Too little said. All she'd been able to manage was, "Do you remember our old friend with the horrid plaid chair? I met his godson. I want you to meet him someday."

Enough to let her mother know there was someone special, and even, vaguely, who. Not even close to enough to unburden her heart.

She reached for her knob, scattered thoughts gathering. Focus snapping. Instincts curling. Shoulders hunching.

Her door was ajar. Ajar, when she knew very well she'd closed and locked it before class that morning, because she'd dropped her keys twice in her hurry to get out on time.

Goosebumps prickled on her arms. Someone had been inside, and for what? Why? Who?

Suddenly she wished she hadn't outpaced Gustaf. When another colleague sauntered by, toward his office, she reached out to snag his arm. "Claude—I wanted to ask you something about the meeting I missed. Do you have a minute, after you put down your things next door?"

Claude was six foot four inches of good-natured burl, old enough to be her father and always happy to play that protective role on campus. Better still, he *sounded* every bit as intimidating and huge as he looked. He smiled amiably. "Of course, Corinne. I'll be right over. Five minutes? I need to jot something down before I forget."

"Five minutes is perfect."

If her things were just gone through, that would be time enough to sort out what and right it. But if someone were inside, they'd know better than to jump her. One scream, and this man with his deep, booming voice would come running from his office next door.

And thank you, Lord, for sending him.

She toed her door open, giving it enough force to swing through its full arc and hit the wall.

It didn't. It stopped at forty-five degrees. As if someone were standing behind it.

She could have called for Claude. Would, if she had to. But indignation burned in her veins where fear should have lived, and instead she dropped her bag into her hand, ready to wield it like a club if necessary—and with the five books in there, it would pack a wallop. She stepped inside, to the side, away from the door. Reached for the Greek carved walking stick that a student had given her after they'd studied the *Iliad* three years ago. Used it to catch the door and swing it shut again, then held it before her like a sword.

Oberstleutnant Ackermann stood there, smirking at her. Not so much as flicking a gaze at her improvised weapon. "Good afternoon, *Doctor*," he said in German, making her title sound like a slur.

She eased her bag off her shoulder and onto the ground and got a better grip on the stick. "These *are* my office hours, Oberstleutnant, but they're for students. Not for you."

"Office hours." Smirk still in place, he stepped away from his hiding place, but not toward her. No, toward the framed diplomas on her wall, studying them each with a click of his tongue. "So well *educated* you are. And yet still so, so stupid. Thinking you can demand a position that isn't your right to hold. Thinking you can make a mockery of the proper order, just because you don't *like* it."

He reached for the frame holding her doctorate in philosophy, fingers curling around the wood.

She was there in a heartbeat, using the end of her stick to hold it in place. "Perhaps taking other people's things without asking is acceptable in Germany. But in France, we call it theft, and it's against the law."

He chuckled, turned so that her stick pressed against his chest. But he also dropped his grubby hands from her diploma. "You are a spirited one, aren't you? Good. I like spirit in a woman. Once you learn to direct it into the right place, that is."

He wanted to be casual, mocking? She could play that game too. She rolled her eyes, lowered the stick, and moved backward to perch on the edge of her desk. "Do tell, Oberstleutnant. Because I have certainly never heard this speech before. What, pray tell, is this 'right place'? The home?" She feigned surprise. "Shocking! I have never guessed at such a theory! Had I but known, I would have abandoned my dreams long ago and accepted the proposal of the first misogynist to come along."

From the flicker in his eye, he wasn't familiar with that term, despite being one himself, from all appearances. And he didn't like that. He stepped closer, lowering his chin, broadening his shoulders. Menace and might.

"You should watch how you speak to your betters, Corinne."

It wasn't the threat in his eyes that made her fight back a shudder. It was hearing her name on his lips. He made the *C* too harsh, the *N*s too hard a stop, gave no space to the *E*. He punched it more than he spoke it.

What choice did she have but to lift her brows. "I do, when I'm around them." She made a show of looking at her watch. "Did you need something in particular? Because I have appointments."

"No, no." He showed his teeth, but it would have been an insult to the word to call it a smile. "I just wanted to see you here. To see how you love it. To see the fear in your eyes when you hear that today will be the last day you step foot in this office."

No. No—he was bluffing. And even if he wasn't, she couldn't, *wouldn't* show him that stab of fear. She would give him only what he deserved—disdain. "Are you the rector of the university now? Congratulations—I hadn't heard."

"If you look at that letter behind you on your desk," he drawled, taking another step closer, "you'll see to whom the rector answers."

She wanted to crane around, see if there was a letter, see what it said, if so. But she didn't dare take her eyes off him. "And why exactly am I being let go, then? Because I'm a woman? Or because you misunderstand the nature of education and think it means just teaching people to agree with you?"

Another slow step. Ignoring her words, of course, as if she hadn't even spoken. "But I can make this go away, Corinne. If it's that important to you."

Of course. Of course, that's all this was—a sick little game. His own planned script, which he'd just expected her to play along with. Had he thought she'd panic at the mention of the letter? Be overwhelmed by fear? Did he think she valued this position so highly that she'd do *anything* to keep it?

She loved her job. Her students. She'd always considered it her calling. But she'd known the moment Gustaf showed up from the Ministry of Education that her days here could well be numbered.

So be it, if so. She still had the contact with all her scattered students to keep up that work, and she'd find something else, anything else, to pay the bills—with all the foreign residents and aliens barred from positions, she'd heard the *lycées* were in desperate need of teachers. Perhaps younger children had never been her heart's desire, but she could adapt. Adjust. And then someday, when this madness was over, when they'd shoved the Nazis back out of their borders, she'd take her place here again, if God willed it.

She didn't have to force the scoff of a laugh. "You're pathetic. Will you really try to threaten me—and what are your terms?"

His gaze dropped from her face. Slid down her, slowly enough to make her skin crawl. Back up. "You're such a clever girl. I bet you can guess."

She leaned forward too, because she never did have the sense to back down from a fight. "I would sooner starve than be your whore."

His hand shot out, fast as lightning. Palm? Fist? She didn't know which struck, only knew that it was hard enough to make her see stars, to make pain explode over the whole left side of her face, to make her drop the stick and grope for purchase on her desk to keep from sprawling over it.

She must have screamed, because her throat ached. And then she added another, not from pain or fear, but from rage.

She could hear Father Serres in her head, yes, telling her to turn the other cheek.

But Oncle Georges was louder, and his advice

had been long ingrained. *You know how to stop a bully from hitting you again, Rinny? Hit him back harder—and below the belt whenever necessary.*

When he lunged for her, she brought up her knee, landing it in his groin with every ounce of strength she had. And when he grunted and staggered back that crucial step, she grabbed the first solid object her hands could find—a hefty tome—and swung it flat into his nose.

She had a feeling Father wouldn't call defending her virtue a sin . . . but he'd probably have something to say about the satisfaction that hummed in her blood when she heard the cartilage crack. Blood spurted from his nose, onto his hands, onto her rug, and today it looked like triumph instead of defeat.

Her door, still half-open, flew into the wall. Claude was there, yes—and Gustaf too, with horror on his face. Her friend went straight to Ackermann, hauling him back with one meaty hand.

Gustaf darted for her, hands out and hovering around her face. "Corinne! What happened? Your eye!"

It was swelling shut, now that he mentioned it. But she scarcely cared.

"What *happened?*" Ackermann roared, knocking Claude's arm away. "I'll tell you what happened! That woman attacked me!"

Well, his words were a bit more colorful, and a

bit less flattering to her. But she censored them for herself. A fat, black line over his insults. And she lifted her chin. "I most assuredly did. After he threatened to have me sacked unless I slept with him and then punched me when I refused. If that's how your officers behave, Sonderführer—"

"It is *not*." Gustaf spun to face Ackermann, his neck splotchy and red. "You are a shame to your rank and your people! How dare you treat a lady so?"

Ackermann sneered. "She's no *lady*." But the insult fell flat, given the nasal sound of his voice.

Gustaf's hands curled into fists. "This is unacceptable! Though I suppose I should expect nothing different from a man who would murder a fellow officer for daring to insist upon civility—during an interview where you should not even have been present."

Murder—had Gustaf really just called it a *murder?* What did that mean?

Gustaf lifted a hand, jabbed a finger in the brute's general direction. "You may outrank me, Ackermann, but you have *no* authority on this campus. *I* am the Ministry's authority here. And you have overstepped too many times. I'll have *your* job for this. And if I hear that you so much as look at Dr. Bastien again, I'll have you busted down to *soldat*!"

She could see the thoughts stomping through Ackermann's mind. The bluster. The disbelief.

Then the doubt. The question. "Who exactly do you think you are, you little pencil pusher, to threaten me?"

The heat of adrenaline began to ebb, making Corinne shiver. She'd like to know the same.

Gustaf smiled. "Perhaps you should have asked that before you intruded on my jurisdiction. Because I'm sure my family will be very interested in your behavior. Who do you think I should tell first? Cousin Otto . . . or Onkle Carl-Heinrich?"

Corinne didn't recognize the names, but by the way Ackermann's face blanked into panic, the way he cursed and obeyed the pointing of Gustaf's finger toward the door, the two relatives were important.

Claude stomped out after him. "I'll see him off campus, Sonderführer."

"Thank you, Doctor."

When they were gone, Gustaf spun back to her. "What did you hit him with? I think you broke his nose."

"I hope I did." She raised the book. Smirked when she saw what it was. *The Complete Works of Josef Horowitz.*

Now *that* was poetic justice.

Gustaf insisted on seeing her home, despite her every loud protest—but at least he agreed to go no farther than the front steps of her building.

Otherwise, she would have led him to someone else's flat, knowing well her neighbors would play along.

And truth be told, by the time they reached her boulevard, she was grateful for the supportive arm. He'd found ice for her, and she'd held it to her eye during the Métro ride, but her head was pounding, and she couldn't see through the swelling, ice or no ice.

She still didn't know what it meant, that he'd called Ackermann's shooting of Christian *murder.* And it hadn't seemed like a wise topic of conversation to be held on the train with countless sightseeing Germans and suspicious Frenchmen.

Now, though, she chanced a glance up at him through her good eye. "What did you mean back there—about Ackermann committing murder? If he'd done such a thing, why hasn't he been arrested?"

Wishful thinking? Perhaps. But Papa had taught her to wish on every star that caught her eye, and this one twinkled with hope.

Gustaf's face went tight, limned with sorrow. "My friend, Christian Bauer—the other *sonderführer* who sat in on your class a week ago. He was killed later that day. Had you heard?"

Given that she could see Kraus's uniform here from the corner, positioned as usual outside the Library of Burned Books, she saw no point in feigning ignorance. She nodded, in fact, toward the glum *soldat*. "Kraus told me. I admit, I was distressed and shocked. To learn someone I had just spoken to hours before had been shot . . ."

Even now, even knowing what Gustaf didn't, her breath tangled up in her chest. Because she could still feel his hot, sticky blood on her hands. She could still see his skin, white as parchment as all his color spilled onto the floor.

She cleared her throat. "Kraus made it sound as though he was suspected of disloyalty. That Ackermann was within his rights to shoot him for interfering in an arrest."

"It wasn't even Ackermann's arrest to make!" Gustaf's words sliced, spewed. Soothed. "No. I don't know what information Ackermann thought he'd received, but Bauer's files were sent from Berlin the moment the brass requested them after the incident, as were *his,* and the picture they painted is clear. Bauer was just a good man insisting on civility, even when dealing with a criminal—as he *should* have done. Ackermann is a bully who is constantly overstepping the bounds of his authority. And he's going to pay for it."

Files—files that were squeaky clean, just as Christian had said his was when he was interviewed for this position. Files that must have been tampered with, somehow. By someone. Perhaps that friend he said he had in the Gestapo?

They were drawing near to her building. To the library. To Kraus, sagged against the door as always. She paused, not wanting the young man to hear them. "Then why hasn't he paid for it already? If he's guilty of murdering another officer, why was he still free to break into my office today and threaten me?"

She wasn't about to tell this man who clearly savored the chance to be someone's champion that she'd take a dozen black eyes, if it meant she had the chance to break that monster's nose.

Yes, Father Serres would *definitely* have something to say about her sudden bloodlust, when she confessed it. She could already feel the ache in her knees from all the time she'd have to spend on them, praying that God would change her hatred into his own love.

Gustaf grunted. "The other soldiers who were there are backing him. And Ackermann still has that letter from a student claiming Bauer was a dissident before his son died." He winced and started them forward again. "But regardless of that, he's gone too far by threatening the rector into dismissing you. He has no authority over the workings of the educational institutions in France. None."

Perhaps she should have been irritated that Gustaf's offense was more the affront to his own pride than to her position, but frankly, she didn't care *why* he was on her side. The point remained that he'd secured her position again, at least for now. And that he was trying to get justice for Christian. She appreciated it, even if it wouldn't change anything. Even if he failed, which was likely.

Perhaps in the grand scheme, it didn't matter if Ackermann paid for what he'd done. Perhaps it would have to be enough that God would mete out eternal justice in its proper time.

Perhaps she needed to start praying now that she could see that monster as the man whose salvation God craved. Because at the moment, she couldn't. She could only see the one who'd tried to kill the man she loved.

"Although." Gustaf's voice shifted, as had his face, when she looked over at him. Gone was the fire. In its place, something that looked strangely like apology. "That *is* why I was seeking you out this afternoon. I wanted you to hear it from me before someone else."

Her every muscle went still. "So I *am* being dismissed?"

His hands lifted, his eyes went wide. "No! That is . . . well, everyone is. The Sorbonne is shutting down. Today is the last day. All students will be dismissed back to their provinces. Local ones will have to report every morning to the police."

She could only stare at him, his words scarcely making sense. "But . . . why?"

He sighed, motioning toward Paris at large.

"All the graffiti on the posters and mocking the Reich—we know it's them. The students. We've found pamphlets circulating too, too well written to be from anyone *but* the university crowd. You, Dr. Bastien, are a worthy professor—but your students are dangerous. I have conferred with my superiors in the Ministry, and we decided this was the safest course of action. But you needn't worry!" He smiled, as if he weren't tearing apart everything she'd worked for. "The lower schools will remain open, for the younger children. I happen to know of several positions for which you'll be perfectly suited."

Positions she could find on her own, with no help from him. But she wasn't going to argue. Wasn't going to turn his favor into ire. She forced a smile, knowing that if it didn't look quite sincere, he'd chalk it up to her swollen face. "I do thank you for the courtesy of letting me know."

"It's the least I could do."

He was right about that.

Kraus came to attention as they neared—and then darted toward the gate. "Dr. Bastien! What happened?" He sent an accusing look at Gustaf.

"Ackermann," Gustaf shot back, effectively bringing Kraus to a halt and making him pale.

He sought her eyes, as if hoping she'd deny it.

She didn't. She stepped away from Gustaf's arm though. "Thank you for ensuring I got home safely, Sonderführer. Good afternoon, Kraus. If you'll both excuse me . . ." She hurried into her building before either could detain her and made it all the way into her flat before anyone else saw her.

She needed some aspirin. More ice. To lie down for a few minutes. And more than any of that, she just needed to be among the people she loved.

Christian wasn't just sitting—he was sitting in the *living room*. She had a feeling Oncle Georges had all but carried him there, but even so, joy pounded at the cage of her ribs when she saw him in his chair, a book in his lap, while Felix built a castle on the floor.

Christian, her Christian. Alive and healing and looking at her bruised, swollen eye with the exact same horror as her uncle.

Georges leapt to his feet, horror turning to fury. "What happened?"

She gave them both a smirk. "Don't worry. You should see what I did to the other guy."

TWENTY-ONE

20 December 1940

He was a ghost. The words that Kraus's cousin had written about Christian hovered always in the back of his mind, despite that he'd only heard them thirdhand. He'd never read them. Hadn't seen that stark print upon the page.

If he had, would he have recognized the script? Known the student? Or was he one of just too many hazy images from last year?

Christian sat in his usual chair in Corinne's living room, his ear attuned to the street. It was unseasonably warm today, enough so that Corinne had cracked the window open just a bit. Enough to get fresh air into the flat without sacrificing any precious warmth they'd likely need tonight. Enough to hear the chatter of neighbors and the rhythmic plodding of Kraus's feet next door.

It was the closest thing he could risk to freedom. An inch of breeze through the window. An inch of noise from the street.

He'd never thought himself the restless type, the kind to get irritable if he was cooped up inside too long. But then again, he'd never been faced with a situation where putting foot on pavement could mean disaster for everyone he cared about.

Though a book lay open on his lap, he hadn't read more than a chapter since he groaned his way into his favorite chair an hour ago. According to the doctor, he needed to begin moving as much as possible to restore strength to atrophying muscles.

Corinne's lips had gone tight at that. She'd exchanged a look with her uncle. *We'll find a way. A place,* Georges had sworn.

But where? Christian had been to too many parts of Paris, both in his duties and to weave that image he'd wanted to present to Ackermann. And in his dratted quest to be seen as more than one more Nazi, he'd had too many conversations with too many people.

Every librarian and many library patrons in Paris would recognize him. Many teachers. Professors. That certainly left plenty of the city that *wouldn't* know him if he slunk down their sidewalk, but it would only take one chance encounter to put everything, *everything* at risk.

"Here, Vati." Felix walked on his knees to Christian's chair from his pile of blocks, holding out a paper with a grin.

"Papa," Christian corrected him, even though he hated to do it. He had always been *Vati*. But no French boy would call his father such a thing.

Still, it tore him up every time he had to remind Felix of it, every time he made his little boy frown. "Sorry. Papa. I drew us a Christmas tree!"

It required no effort to smile at the drawing, bright with color and hope and dreams. "And what a marvelous tree you've drawn. I imagine Tante Corinne will hang it right on the wall, where her tree usually goes."

"That's a fine idea," Corinne said from the doorway to the kitchen, drying her hands on a towel. His heart swelled at the sight of her—just a woman, doing normal things. Here. With him. She'd been gone most days during his recuperation, first interviewing for different positions at *lycées* around the city, and then daily once she landed a prime job at a girls' school. It was farther for her to go than the Sorbonne and didn't pay nearly as well, but it was security.

He hated that he couldn't provide any of his own. That he was not only too weak to stand more than ten minutes at a time, but that there was absolutely nothing he could do to contribute to this household. This family that he wanted to be his, and yet was keenly aware he was nothing but a drain on. Worse, that he was a danger to them.

"I have an idea," Corinne said, moving into the room and grinning down at Felix. "Why don't we tape paper all over the wall here and you can color us a *life-size* Christmas tree? We can cut out decorations to paste on it and everything."

Felix's eyes went wide with delight, clearly not pausing to think that the task would take all day.

Perhaps several of them, if his attention lagged. Corinne would know, though, that it would keep him occupied for countless hours.

Small children might never have been her focus, but she was good with them. With Felix, and with her new students too, given the stories she told.

He watched with a smile as they made a plan—to lay the papers out on the floor and sketch out the tree, then color it in. The smile froze when he heard a sound he knew too well coming from the window—the growl of a German engine, not just approaching but cutting out right outside. Then the squeak of the gate from the library next door. Of their own volition, his eyes flew to the clock. Not a time Kraus usually took a break or left his station—and cars rarely came here.

An auto door slammed, and more footsteps sounded. Christian's stomach dropped seconds before Kraus's voice made it plummet even lower. "Good day, Oberstleutnant. Can I help you with something?"

Christian's thoughts barely had time to spin through the denial before the last voice he ever wanted to hear again made its way through that crack in the window. "Back to your post, Kraus. This has nothing to do with you."

"You're not . . . you're not here for the Bastien woman, are you? We both know that Sonderführer Gustaf warned—"

"My business here is no concern of either him or you, *soldat*." He practically snarled the reminder of Kraus's rank.

A thousand words, none of them particularly suited to his son's young ears, vied for a place on Christian's tongue. His gaze snapped to Corinne's. She'd gone still, her pencil clutched in her fingers. He saw no fear on her face, none of the panic that he felt rising in his own chest. Just calculations, dozens of them whirring through her eyes as fast as they were surely whirring through her mind.

She set the pencil down. Stood.

Christian did too, as quickly as he could.

They had a plan for this, for any time someone came to her door unexpectedly. They'd already done it twice when a neighbor knocked on her door.

But a neighbor wasn't Ackermann. A neighbor wouldn't be looking for anything, absolutely *anything* to hold against her. A neighbor didn't already count her an enemy against whom he had a score to settle.

He felt his hands and feet going through the necessary motions—shelving the book he'd been reading, picking up his glasses, removing all evidence of himself from the room. He glanced again at the clock, his mind screaming a plea to heaven. Georges should be back any moment. *Please, Lord, send him quickly.*

Corinne had already proven that she could take care of herself, but he didn't want her to *have* to.

His eyes snagged on Felix. Every paternal instinct he possessed made him want to scoop his son up and take him with him into the corner of the closet he'd be stuffing himself into. It wasn't part of the plan—Felix was officially Corinne's ward, part of her life, expected to be there.

But the panic gnawed. What if Ackermann had somehow gotten his hands on more details of Christian's life? What if he knew he had a son who matched Felix's description? What if he'd somehow seen a photo and recognized him?

No. No, it was unlikely. He knew it was unlikely. More, he knew—hoped, prayed—that Felix's presence could perhaps keep Ackermann in check.

Plus, there was no way to hide evidence of Felix so quickly, and if Georges returned while Ackermann was still here—*Please, God!*—without Felix, then how to explain where he was? Ackermann too much liked knowing every facet of his targets' lives so he would know what to use against them to let something as obvious as a child under Corinne's care go unquestioned. Unexamined.

Unthreatened.

Felix had been as well drilled as the rest of them. After a squeeze to Christian's legs and a silent look up at him that promised he would be a good little mouseling, he went back to his drawing.

Christian moved silently toward the bedroom he'd been staying in, into the corner of the closet he'd already prepared to fit him. Chest aching, that his son had to learn these lessons. Breath fisting, that Ackermann was no doubt even now climbing the steps. Prayers thumping, the same litany over and over again.

Lord, protect them. Lord, send Georges home now. Lord, blind his eyes.

He had barely managed to get the suitcases rearranged in front of his legs, the long winter coats in front of his torso, the closet shut again, when the pounding came on the door.

Even given the complete darkness of his hiding place, still Christian squeezed his eyes shut, as if that would somehow make him vanish, or make his prayers reach heaven the faster.

"Who is it?" Corinne sang out, her voice as cheerful and bright as if she truly expected it to be a neighbor or friend on the other side of that angry fist.

Why? Why was Ackermann here, after all these weeks of silence? They'd hoped he'd decided Corinne wasn't worth retribution, not with Gustaf acting as her champion, not with him apparently having two high-ranking officials as relatives. They'd thought it had been enough to convince Ackermann to cut his losses. To ignore her.

"Oberstleutnant Ackermann. Open the door immediately."

He could all but hear the purse of her lips. "With all due respect, Oberstleutnant, I'm uncomfortable doing that, given our last encounter. But my uncle will return momentarily from his errands, so if you would—"

"Open the door or I kick it down. Your choice."

She heaved a sigh, nearly lost to his ears. "Very well, but please be aware that I have a child here, and I expect you to behave civilly." The slide of her chain, the click of the dead bolt. "I'm certain you don't want France's children to cower in fear of our *liberators*."

"Tante Corinne?" Felix, sounding frightened, just as they'd practiced. He would be moving to her side, wrapping an arm around her leg. His perfect French—any accent long gone, in the way of children—would give credence to their story. "Is everything all right?"

"Everything is fine, Félix." She pronounced his name in the French way, the vowels longer than they were in German. The door squeaked open. "At least I hope so. What brings you to my door, Oberstleutnant? I thought our business quite concluded when the Sorbonne was closed."

Ackermann's heavy steps sounded, striding straight into the center of the living room, from the sounds of it. "I will decide when our business is concluded, *mademoiselle*. What do you know of Christian Bauer?"

Oh, God, please. Please. Please.

A pause. Would she be lifting a brow? Frowning? Pursing her lips in supposed thought? Whichever response she chose, it would look convincing—he should know. He'd already been the recipient of her playacting more times than he could count.

More important would be Felix's response. If they were still doing as they'd practiced, his son would have his face buried in her side, so any involuntary reactions he had would be hidden. *Please, God. Please.* His fingers trembled where he had them resting against his thighs.

"I know he was a professor. I know you and he butted heads. I know you shot and killed him." Her voice went hard, cold as ice on that one.

"Do you?"

"That's what Kraus and Gustaf both said."

Oh, how Christian hated that low chuckle. It had never once preceded anything good. "It's true I shot him. But I'm beginning to wonder if it killed him. His body has still not been recovered."

Blast. Georges had debated whether they should find a corpse of similar size and general description, dress it in his uniform, and hide it somewhere to be found once decomposition had made it nearly unrecognizable . . . but that had seemed every bit as risky as having no body turn up. What if they were unconvinced? Then the Nazis would *know* someone was trying to fool them. They'd decided it was better to just leave the mystery. Let them think the fledgling Resistance had found him, kept the uniform, and hidden his body somewhere—that it was long gone now.

"I hadn't heard that part. I thought there was no question of his death. From what Kraus said, you shot him directly in the heart at point-blank range. And—forgive me. Félix, dear, why don't you go and play in your room for a bit? Go on. That's a good boy. Go ahead and close the door."

Christian breathed a bit easier when Felix came into the room they shared, closing the door behind him. It made it more difficult to make out their voices, but far less likely that Ackermann would search in here, at least in theory.

As he'd been trained to do, Felix dumped a basket of blocks onto the floor—right in the middle of the path between the bedroom door and the small closet.

From the living room, Corinne's muffled voice just reached his ears. "I find that very odd indeed, Oberstleutnant. Is this the prevailing suspicion among the authorities? I would have thought Kraus would have mentioned it."

"The *soldat* is hardly party to the goings-on of

the officers. And *I* will ask the questions now that your—nephew?—is out of the way."

"Cousin, technically speaking." She sounded so casual, as if she had no qualms at all about having Ackermann under her roof. Georges's training? Or her own indomitable nature? "But given the age difference, '*tante*' seemed a reasonable thing for him to call me. I'm afraid he was caught in a collapsing building in—"

"I don't really care about the brat's missing eye," Ackermann spat out. Much as it made Christian wince, it was also good—he was just going to dismiss Felix entirely. Which was better than any other alternative. "I want to know how well you know Christian Bauer."

Any relief sank back into unease. *Know,* he said—not *knew.* He really believed Christian lived. Bad, bad, bad.

"I saw him coming and going from the library. He was always polite."

"And when he visited you here? Was he polite then? Friendly, I imagine? How friendly?"

A pause. Christian could well guess how Corinne's mind spun, because his was doing the same thing. How much did he know and what was he just guessing at?

The same thoughts he'd had at Josef's flat. And that had gone so, so poorly.

"To what visits are you referring, Oberstleutnant? Because I don't much like the tone of your voice nor the implication I hear in it." Leave it to Corinne to sound outraged, angry, instead of defensive.

Was Ackermann stalking closer? Looming over her in that way he liked to do? "I have been checking up on you. I paid a visit to one of your neighbors at his place of employment. He said that Bauer made visits here, to your flat, somewhat regularly. Said you always seemed annoyed by it, but . . . I wonder. Two *bücherwurms*, all alone up here . . . what did you really think of the professor?"

Her laugh might have been muted, but he could still hear loud and clear the disdain she'd first held him in. "Honestly? I thought him a bore. Everything came back to Germany with him— how the German people did this or that. And his lectures on why burning and banning books is a good idea were infuriating. I couldn't have been more relieved when Gustaf finally arrived in Paris and gave him someone else of intelligence to talk to."

Not as inflammatory a response as he'd been afraid she'd make, truth be told.

"And yet he still came. Why?"

He could imagine the lift of her chin. The glint in her eye. "According to my neighbor, he was enamored. If so, he was too bashful to ever admit it to me. He talked a bit about his wife, whom he clearly loved very much. But generally, it was all books. I can detail for you his opinion on each text, if you'd like. I don't much consider them opinions worth sharing—but they will likely tickle your fancy, given your shared ideology."

Ackermann's laugh was a bite, a snarl, low and cruel. "Oh, I promise you, *mademoiselle*, our ideology is quite different where it counts."

"Well. I suppose that's true. He didn't seem to think he had to physically harm anyone who didn't agree with him. How's the nose, by the way? Looks a bit . . . crooked."

Christian squeezed his eyes shut. She just couldn't help but antagonize him, could she? He strained to hear Ackermann's reaction, and the silence made his every tired muscle go taut. What was he doing? Had he made some response too low to reach this corner of the closet?

Or, worse—he could have grabbed her by the throat, silencing *her* reaction. He could have snapped her neck. He could have—

"What exactly are you doing?" Corinne again, but more distant. And back to outraged.

"Just having a look."

"In case, what? I have your dead professor hidden in my kitchen? I admit to enjoying the occasional horror or tragedy in a book, but I am not so macabre as to—" A shriek. "Get your hands off my books! You think he's hiding in a bookshelf?"

A crash that sounded as if an entire bookshelf

was sent to the floor. Christian winced, knowing Corinne wasn't exaggerating her shouts now. "Are you such an idiot you cannot look at the space between this wall and the kitchen and see there's no possible way for anything to be hidden? You monstrous brute! They are only—*books!*"

Another crash.

"I'll be reporting you to your superior! Gustaf will hear about this, along with those relatives of his! You cannot treat a law-abiding citizen like—"

Crash.

"Tante?" Felix shouted, though he didn't move toward the door. Just as they'd taught him.

"Stay in your room, Félix!"

The final shelf in the living room must have given way to Ackermann's rage, given the fourth crash. His heavy steps then moved out of the living room, toward Corinne's room. Her litany of objections continued, providing Christian with a narration of his search through her drawers, under her bed, and into her closet.

Blast. He'd search this one too. Neither Felix nor his blocks would provide enough determent, clearly. *Lord, blind his eyes. Make me invisible. For their sake. If he catches me here, I don't know what he'll do to them.*

Christian's throat went tight as the steps thundered their way and the door crashed open. "Out, boy!" Ackermann barked.

"Well if you would move out of the way enough to *let* him out . . ."

Felix started crying as he rushed from the room, and Christian knew well it wasn't just because of the invader's presence in his space. His boy knew what was at stake. He knew what was coming.

A drawer slid open. "Men's clothes!"

"My uncle's. I *told* you he was just out running errands. He and Félix share that room, and he stays with him while I am teaching."

"A likely story." A squeaking, heaving sound, from the space where the bed sat. Or had. It sounded like he flipped the whole thing over.

The closet door opened. Christian held his breath, not daring to move so much as a millimeter. Not daring even to blink lest he hear it.

And then, praise God, another voice, from the living room. "Corinne? Corinne! What is going on?"

"Oncle Georges!"

Christian had no idea if Georges's appearance would stay Ackermann from any intentions he had, but his arrival at least distracted him for a moment. "Who are you?"

"Georges Piers. Corinne's uncle. Who are *you?* And why have you turned our flat upside down?"

"Because your *niece* is suspected of harboring a fugitive."

"What?" Georges sounded genuinely baffled—and every bit as outraged as Corinne. "This is a tiny flat, not some old house with hidden passages. Where would she hide someone? And who the devil would she try to hide?"

Ackermann must have turned back to the closet. Clothes moved on their hangers—but they couldn't move far. They'd packed them in here for that very purpose—Yvonne's still taking up their usual places, but George's and Josef's packed in too, to fill it out. No empty space.

It wouldn't stop him from pulling it all out. He knew it wouldn't.

But another voice came from the door. "Excuse me, sir. The radio in your car was calling for you. You're needed at headquarters immediately." *Kraus.* Had there really been a message coming in or . . . or was he trying to help? Had he heard the crashes?

He wouldn't be trying to help *him.* But he could be trying to spare Corinne. Perhaps.

Ackermann bit out a low, German curse. "For what?"

"Weren't willing to say when they heard it was me on the line and not you. I apologize if I overstepped by answering, but I was afraid it was something important."

For a moment, it felt as though the entire flat held its breath. Felix's sobs had quieted, Corinne's hushing noises had stilled. Georges said not a word, nor did the two Nazis.

Then the boards creaked under Ackermann's

feet. He kicked blocks into the wall—out of his way. He stomped out of the room, snarled, "You haven't seen the last of me," ordered Kraus out ahead of him, and slammed the front door behind them on the way out.

Christian sagged into his corner, suddenly aware of how hot and close his breath tasted in his mouth. Of the mere inches that had separated them. Of the clear provision of God.

And of the fact that God could well have said *no*. Today, he'd extended his mercy. His grace.

But as too many in Germany had already learned, sometimes he didn't intervene. Sometimes he let the monsters come. Sometimes good people, good Christians, good Jews were dragged off in the night, no matter the prayers they cried. He'd promised to be with his people through persecutions—not to prevent them.

"Vati?" Felix's voice came in a whisper so soft even Christian barely heard it from inches away.

Certainty burned, from his nose all the way to his gut.

Ackermann would not give up. He knew Christian was alive, and he would hunt him until he found him. He would likely kill him, if he didn't decide a camp would be a longer, slower death. But that wasn't what made his limbs so heavy as Georges whispered the all clear and Christian pushed his way through long woolen coats and into his son's arms.

Ackermann would punish Corinne. Felix. Georges. They would all pay.

The flat was a shambles of broken furniture and books, scattered like paper teardrops all over the living room. Another bonfire of books ready for a match, that's what it looked like. Mountains of beautiful tomes, condemned. Not all, this time, because of the author or the words. But because of the woman who owned them.

No. Because of *him*. Because she'd let him in. Because she'd offered a way for him to see his son. Because he'd enraged that brute and hadn't had the good sense to back down.

After a long moment just standing there, Felix in his arms, beholding the damage, he finally lifted his gaze and met hers.

She must have read him in an instant. Her eyes went wide. Her nostrils flared. "No. Don't even consider it."

"He'll be back. You know he will. He isn't going to let this go. He'll turn the city inside out looking for me, a dog with a bone."

"We'll move you." Georges's face was firm, unmoved. His eyes were calculating. "We only need to buy a bit of time. I just got word that he'll go before a tribunal sometime before the new year—that's probably what has him in a rage. If he's punished—"

"If." Christian shook his head, moving to wrap an arm around Corinne. "He has the backing of the soldiers who were there—isn't that what Gustaf said? There will be no witness to testify against him for anything. At worst, he'll get a slap on the wrist. You know it's true. Gustaf might convince his relatives to put something on his record about overstepping his bounds with the Ministry of Education, but that won't be enough to banish him from Paris."

Corinne lifted a hand to his chest and curled her fingers in his shirt. Felix's little ones covered hers. Knitting them, knotting them.

His nose burned. "I have to. It's the only way. I will present myself at the tribunal. Tell them what happened and pray they listen."

She shook her head wildly. "If you turn yourself in, they'll court-martial *you* too—you know that! You'll be tried for desertion if not the treason Ackermann will try to convince them of. You disobeyed his orders, you—they'll *kill* you."

"They won't. The army considers its officers to be its most valuable commodities. They'll . . ." What *would* they do? There had been examples already, of officers refusing to carry out immoral commands. Some were busted down in rank, sent to the front, others reassigned, when it was their "dangerous" influence over their current troops they were denounced for. "They'll reassign me. Maybe . . . maybe send me to the front."

Tears actually filled her eyes—a sight he never thought to see. "You're a pacifist. You don't even know how to *hold* a weapon. How will you fight? No—let Oncle Georges get you away. To England or—"

"And leave that monster free to terrorize you all?" He shook his head. "I never want to take arms, that's true enough. But I *will* protect my family in the only way I can. I will not let him hurt you, Corinne. Or you, Felix."

His son's arm snaked around his neck and squeezed. "Vati . . . you can't leave. Not again."

He didn't want to. Didn't want to give up this oasis of contentment he'd found, against the odds. This family they'd somehow built out of books and ideas and faith . . . and love.

But that last was what sealed it all. He couldn't love them and not do the one thing that could save them.

"We could *all* leave." Her voice, still quiet, sounded frantic. "Go to England."

Georges was the one to sigh. "*Mon chouchou* . . . England is no safer. Hitler will invade it any day now. Nowhere is safer than Paris. You might escape Ackermann, but I . . . I fear there's no outrunning the Nazi army. And if he's caught somewhere else—there won't be a trial then. There will be bullets for you all."

Christian met the older man's gaze and saw within it exactly what he hoped for—an apology, and agreement.

Corinne and Felix first. Their safety above his.

That was all that mattered. "Will you be able to learn when this tribunal is?"

Georges gave a single nod.

Christian mirrored it. "I'll do it then. It's the best hope of protecting you and of me getting out of this alive. And that's what matters, isn't it?" He pressed a kiss to Felix's head. "We may be apart for a while, but it won't last forever. Tante Corinne will take care of you."

She blinked away the tears. Drew in a breath. And, being Corinne, lifted her chin. "Of course I will—but not as Tante Corinne. If you're going to do this fool thing, Christian Bauer, then you're going to marry me first. He's going to be my son. I'm going to be his *maman*. Do you understand me?"

Somehow, Felix vanished from his arms. Somehow, the door to their bedroom closed, and it was only Christian and Corinne in the wreckage of books and shelves. Only Corinne in his arms. Only Corinne before his eyes.

He didn't know what he'd done to deserve her love, to deserve even a minute to claim her as his own.

But he wasn't fool enough to turn down the sweetest gift in the world. "I've never understood anything so perfectly in my life. And I've never agreed with anything more."

TWENTY-TWO

23 December 1940

December was the perfect time for a secret wedding. Even in an occupied city, no one thought anything of families bustling into a church with packages in their arms, or of young women laughing together or a child bouncing along like he had rubber balls in place of feet. Tonight, three days after Ackermann's attack, Corinne didn't have to think about the flat they'd only stayed in long enough to put it to rights before seeking refuge with the Moreaux, or the looming threat of the *oberstleutnant*. Tonight, she could focus solely on the family they would create.

A secret wedding was, by necessity, small. The only guests would be the Moreaux, Abraham and his wife, and Oncle Georges. They all arrived separately at the church, spaced ten minutes apart, with Father Serres letting each party in with a grin and a nod.

As Corinne stood in the little back room, craning to try to see herself fully in the handheld mirror Liana had smuggled in, she was too keenly aware of the people who *weren't* there. Josef. Maman. She'd fought back tears more than once that day already, wishing her mother were the one helping her get ready along with Babette Moreau. Wishing she were there to hug her and whisper how happy she was for them. Wishing she had words of approval for her choice—all her choices. Wishing Josef had been there for Christian, doing the same for him.

"You look beautiful." Babette smoothed one of the seams that had been put in so quickly to make the dress fit right. "Worthy of *Vogue*."

Corinne laughed. That part was strangely true. She'd been all set to wear either her favorite Sunday dress or to remake Maman's wedding dress—which had been simple and outdated even in 1918. But Hugo had burst into the Moreau home with a garment bag and an impish grin. It seemed that some woman with more money than sense had thrown a fit at one of the boutiques and insisted that the wedding gown underway was all wrong and had to be thrown out and started over . . . and so he'd taken the liberty of trading the frazzled dressmaker some black-market chocolate for it.

It wasn't the gown she ever would have dared to choose—because it was made of too fine a silk, covered with too beautiful a lace, drew too much attention to curves and waist. And in any other time, the price tag would have been far, far too steep. But she'd accepted the gift, and she let Babette alter it for her, and now she stood in it with her hair carefully coiffed and her makeup perfectly applied and happy nerves fluttering like tiny acrobats in her stomach.

A knock sounded on the door a second before it opened, and Oncle Georges stepped in. He had a suitcase in his hand, one too familiar now to bring anything but a smile to her face. He motioned for space to be cleared on the table. "I thought the bride might appreciate a special call from her mother."

"Oh." Tears flooded her eyes, and she had to blink them back quickly to avoid smearing her mascara. "Really? Even though it's not our usual time?"

Her uncle grinned. "Exceptions can always be made, *mon chouchou*. You think she wouldn't be here, however she could, on your wedding day?"

"Here." Liana handed her a handkerchief as Georges set up the radio.

Corinne was nearly back in control by the time she took the receiver from him and held it to her ear. The tone of the static told her they were connected. "Hello? This is Blanche for Evergreen. Over."

"Blanche." Even through the miles and the airwaves and the distortion, she could hear the happy tears in Maman's voice. "This is Evergreen. The dragon slayer sent a report. Not too detailed, but we got the gist. I . . . I am so happy for you, Blanche. So sad I'm not there. Over."

"Me too." Her heart twisted and ached—and

then went calm. Because Maman *was* here. Just as Christian still would be, whatever happened. "But I've been thinking of you all day. Remembering yours. You've been here with me, and it is so, so good to hear your voice today. Over."

As always, they could only talk for a few minutes, and what they said was vague and coded. But it didn't matter. Just having her mother's voice here, now, lit peace inside her.

After they ended the call and stashed the radio, Liana handed her a bouquet of dried flowers. Oncle Georges walked her down the aisle as Babette quietly sang for them. Wings of promise and peace fluttered inside her as she met Christian's gaze, where he stood waiting for her. She smiled when he reached out to place a steadying, calming hand on the top of his son's still-bouncing head.

So precious, those two Bauers. And hers, both of them.

The stained glass windows were shrouded, their stories covered by black fabric and cardboard and protective wire. But that only meant that each lit candle kept its light close by, lighting up the otherwise dark church like stars. She heard Liana whisper, "This is *so* romantic!" from her place at Corinne's side, and she had to agree.

A secret wedding in a blacked-out church with a special license and a man who was supposed to be dead. Someday, decades from now, she'd tell stories of this night to their grandchildren, and they wouldn't believe it. Someday, decades from now, she'd look back and remember every impossible detail. She'd remember the way the candlelight gilded her friends, her family, her priest, her groom. She'd remember the lingering scent of incense from the altar. She'd remember the way Hugo's watch went *tic . . . tac* into the silent room, and how her heart pulsed in time, whispering the same claim in every language she knew.

Mien. Mein. Mine.

Nothing frantic. Nothing panicked. Nothing fearful. Just all things good and noble and bright. It didn't matter that Ackermann was still trying to destroy them. It didn't matter that soon Christian would leave. It didn't matter if cupboards were bare.

What mattered was that as Father Serres led them through their vows, she felt the weaving of the miracle. The sacrament. The covenant. Two, becoming one. *Three* becoming one. One family. One unit. One force to weather the storm.

The air was cold again, and it grew colder by the minute. Colder, somehow, the brighter the sky grew. It seeped up through the step he sat on, through the door at his back, cutting straight through the wool of his uniform. Christian felt it in every inch of flesh, down to his very bones by the time morning had banished the last of the stars.

But only to his bones. Only in his skin. It couldn't touch the warm peace he'd been adding fuel to each and every day since he'd made his choice. The smoldering backlog he'd lit when he married Corinne. The log after log they'd built together during that stolen, blissful Christmas in a borrowed flat the Moreaux had arranged for them.

Georges's knock last night hadn't taken it from him. If anything, his "Tomorrow—present yourself tomorrow" had only closed the furnace door, set the damper, and let the warmth flow out through his whole system.

He'd been sitting here since an hour before the end of curfew, so that no one would see him arrive. He had no watch—his had stopped working after being bathed in his blood—but he knew when curfew lifted. A few people had begun to stir, to bustle to whatever shift at whatever job was awaiting them, but none had so much as looked his way—just one more shadow blending in with the night.

His fingers were cold, even through his leather gloves. His toes ached. And he relished each discomfort, because he was alive to feel them.

Next week as 1941 dawned, he could be in a trench somewhere. Or in a prison camp. This would seem warm, then.

Worst-case scenario—worst for Corinne, for Felix, for Georges—he would be dead. Never cold again. Safe in the embrace of the Father. If that were to happen, then he prayed now that he would have the honor of praying still then. Praying for them, every moment of eternity until they joined him. Praying from the very throne room of God.

Christ had said the angels of little ones were always before the Father, interceding for them—he would find Felix's. He would intercede too, if that were his fate.

Dawn went from slate and purple to rosy pink to royal gold, and finally he heard the footsteps he was waiting for. Kraus, shoulders hunched against winter and life, striding to his post. Christian studied him in the morning light. He'd lost weight, even though soldiers were given more than enough food to keep them healthy. His face was chapped from endless days outside in the wind. His eyes were listless. Lightless. Lifeless.

He didn't even spot Christian, there on the doorstep, until he'd come through the gate and drawn the key from his pocket. And when he did, he jumped, dropped the key and his bag and nearly fell over the wrought iron fencing behind him, disbelieving curses streaking the air.

Christian stood. Held out his arms. "I'm not dead, though it was a near thing. A Good

Samaritan found me. I've been healing, these weeks."

It was all he would ever admit to anyone, a truth he'd recited over and over and over until it became the only one his lips would give.

Kraus stared. His chest heaved. One hand gripped the wrought iron.

Christian stepped forward, bent down, and retrieved the keys. He motioned toward the door. "Do you mind? I could use a break from the cold before we go." Not actually waiting for agreement, he unlocked the library and took his first step inside in two months.

It smelled like old paper and stale coffee and . . . hope. He stepped inside and breathed it deeply, waiting to see if Kraus would join him.

He did, latching the door softly behind him, as if afraid too loud a noise would wake him from a dream. "Where are we going?"

"To the tribunal." He looked away from the shelves with their jumble of familiar titles. To the young man he'd always known could be a threat. Whom he'd wanted to make a friend. "You're going to escort me."

Red stained the pale, hollow cheeks. Fire lit the dark, empty eyes. "No! I *won't* turn you in, I—"

"I know about the letter, Kraus—it's all right. You did what you were expected to do, what you were taught to do. I do not blame you for that." It was scarcely warmer in here than outside, but at least there was no wind. Christian pulled his gloves off so he could rub his hands together. "But I am hoping you will help me now. That you will testify to Ackermann's behavior. I have heard that he ransacked our neighbor's flat, and that you saw it. Perhaps if we both testify to his rage, he will answer for it."

"Testify?" Kraus sagged against the door, his foot bumping the return bin that had only ever had one book in it, in all Christian's time here. The one Corinne had slipped him, when Felix was ill. "I will risk his wrath. And *you*—you'll be charged with desertion, for all these weeks, and for all he accused you of to begin with. Why . . . why not just stay disappeared?"

"I considered it," he admitted. He set his gloves on the circulation desk. "But I can't, Gunter. I can't let innocent people's lives be destroyed because Ackermann hates *me*. So . . . I will answer for my part in it all. I will confess that I am not a Nazi—but I'm not a traitor. I'm a German, just like you. A man who loves his country, even as he hates what it's become." He reached for a book—the book Kraus had tried to toss into the rubbish bin their first day here.

Would Kraus remember that? Maybe.

Christian sighed. "A man who knows that true freedom means extending to others the right to hold opinions I don't agree with. The right to be *wrong.* You have every right to believe what you do." He held out the book. "Take it. Read it. Or if not this one, another. Read a page, read a chapter. *Think* about the words, whether you agree with them or not. Think about them and try to understand why someone else *would* agree. Try to understand their perspective and recognize it as *valid,* even if it's not right. Even if you aren't willing to face Ackermann at the tribunal, do this much."

Though he looked as though the book were a snake that might bite him, Kraus stepped away from the door, reaching out until his fingers closed around the book. "But . . . they're *verboten.*"

Christian breathed a laugh. "Do you even know why? It was because a bunch of college students got together and decided they didn't *like* this book or this author or this idea. They decided it would harm their ideology."

He braced a hand against the desk, leaning forward. "Because they knew, they *knew* that if they kept reading them, their own ideas couldn't stand the test."

Kraus flinched, turning his face away. But he held on to the book.

Christian drew in a breath. Let it out. "I can't make you come with me today. But grant me this much, Kraus. One promise. *Read.*"

Kraus's larynx bobbed, the debate raging in his

eyes clearly about more than a banned book. "A page? Every day?"

"A page, at least. A chapter. A whole book. Read novels, because they will put you in someone else's skin. Read poetry, because it will give wings to your soul. Read science, because it will show you what's possible. Read politics, because it will teach you how strongly people care about how their fellow men are treated, wherever they stand on what the best way is." He pulled books off the shelf, books he'd been putting there since June, wondering how he'd ever convince Kraus to read them.

Maybe he wouldn't. But maybe he *would*. "Read things you hate and things you love and things you never thought you'd understand. And never, *never* accept the excuse that you're not strong enough to handle it if you read something that offends you. You *are*. You're strong enough to be offended and then try to understand why. You're strong enough to grant that someone can be different and still be worthy of dignity. And if you aren't?" He slammed one more book onto the stack. "Then read more, until you *are*."

Kraus studied the stack of books. When he looked back to Christian, his eyes were wet with doubt and pain. "Why? Why do you even care if I get stronger? I've already ruined everything for you."

Christian moved forward, clasping his hand

to Kraus's shoulder. "Do you know what my father told me one day, after bullies had beaten me up when I tried to defend my brother? He told me the only way to ever truly defeat your enemies . . . was to make them your friends." He stepped around him, toward the door. "You're my friend, Kraus. In my eyes, at least, you're my friend. Whether you choose to act like it now is up to you."

Gripping the banned book in his hand, Kraus pressed his lips together and marched out the door.

TWENTY-THREE

Corinne had no idea where they were, or how her uncle had known the circuitous maze of rooms and passages to take them there. But she trusted him enough that she wasn't exactly surprised either when he led her up a seemingly forgotten stairwell to a darkened balcony, or when she peeked out into a hotel ballroom that had clearly been converted into some sort of military headquarters. The way it was set up reminded her a bit of...

She sucked in a breath and turned wide eyes on her uncle. "This is where they hold their tribunals?"

Oncle Georges motioned to one of the seats cloaked in the shadows. "I didn't imagine you'd just want to *guess* at what happened to him."

She sat on one of the plush brocade chairs, squinting at the figures hovering behind the chairs at the table at the head of the massive room below. "I should have brought my opera glasses."

Chuckling, he handed her a pair, and then pulled out a second for himself.

She shouldn't have been surprised, she supposed. *He* had known where they were going. And she was far too interested in the gathering below to question his foresight. Most of the movement seemed to be focused around two men who occupied the center two seats. Both had uniforms bedecked with medals and ribbons and had, if she was discerning details well enough from here, general insignias on their epaulettes.

What arrested her attention, however, was how *alike* they looked. Same face shape, same build, same mannerisms as they spoke—though one had that horrid little mustache over his lip that Hitler favored and the other was clean-shaven. Brothers? Cousins? "Who are they?"

Her uncle pointed to the one on the left, the one with the mustache. "General Otto von Stülpnagel, military governor of France." The one on the right. "General Carl-Heinrich von Stülpnagel, commander of the Seventeenth Army."

Otto . . . and Carl-Heinrich. Corinne lowered her opera glasses. "Gustaf's family?"

"And what we were waiting for—Carl-Heinrich's arrival in Paris, to celebrate the New Year with his cousin. The Stülpnagels are one of Germany's leading military families, old aristocrats—and if my sources are right, Carl-Heinrich at least is no fan of Hitler's."

The history rang a distant bell. Though she'd had no idea Gustaf belonged to this family—his mother must have been his link to them, given the different surnames. "But . . . didn't the other one, Otto, write a book defending German war crimes after the World War?"

Her uncle's lips twitched. "Leave it to you to know only the books. He was also forced into retirement two years ago when he fell out of favor with the Reich—only to be called up again when they needed more senior staff to hold Austria."

So two of the generals who made up the tribunal might be inclined to side with Christian.

Gustaf strode in, the ballroom doors swinging behind him. He moved straight toward the two generals, who both hurried around the table to greet him with claps on the back and loud laughter.

Her nerves were jangling by the time Otto clapped his hands and told everyone to get settled. If Christian had arrived with Kraus, they weren't within her view. They hadn't talked about what kind of entrance he planned to make. Subtle? Grand?

The panel of officers dispensed with a few other cases first—she barely even heard what they were about. But then Ackermann was called forward, and he strutted into view to stand before the table, not so much as a hint of uncertainty in his posture.

Her fingers dug into the arms of the chair, and she had to drag in a deep breath to steady the opera glasses.

"Oberstleutnant Peter Ackermann, you are charged with the interference of the business of the Ministry of Education, the interference of the business of the Ministry of Propaganda, and the accidental shooting and death of Sonderführer Christian Bauer. You have been recommended for disciplinary action. How do you plead?"

"One moment, General." Gustaf stepped up beside Ackermann, shoulders back. "I contend that he is guilty of the *purposeful* shooting and murder of Sonderführer Christian Bauer, attacking a French woman with intent to rape, and destruction of her property weeks later when he discovered where she lived and ransacked her flat despite having no cause to suspect her of any questionable behavior."

Corinne had no idea how these proceedings usually went. Was Gustaf out of order to interrupt? Did he get away with it because he was a von Stülpnagel, or was it perfectly acceptable for officers to argue even about the charges?

Otto frowned. "This is the first we've heard of attacking a woman. Have you witnesses of this behavior?"

"Well . . . I myself saw the initial—"

"He did *not,* sirs," Ackermann spat. "He came in afterward and *assumed* he knew what had happened, taking the word of a dissident Parisienne above my own."

The general sighed. "And the second part? About a visit to her home?"

"I had just cause to search her flat."

The generals looked toward Gustaf, and though

453

she couldn't see his face, she saw the way his shoulders stooped. "Without witnesses to these accusations, we have no choice but to dismiss them and focus on the original charges," Carl-Heinrich said.

"Wait!"

Her heart stopped when the new voice rang out, even though she'd heard it just that morning, whispering in her ear. One last round of I-love-yous. *Je t'aime. Ich liebe dich. Te amo.*

Christian didn't exactly *stride* up the aisle, given the weakness he still battled from his wound. But he walked steadily, Kraus at his side.

Gustaf spun. Gasped. Ran forward and pulled Christian into one of those hearty, masculine one-arm embraces that men always seemed to favor. Even from here, she could hear him say, "Bauer! We thought you were *dead!* Where have you been?"

"I nearly was." He cleared his throat and nodded to let Gustaf proceed. They traveled as a trio to the front, where Ackermann glared, slack-jawed. "Would have been, generals, had a Good Samaritan not taken pity on me and doctored me when my commanding officer shot me and left me for dead. I'm afraid I've only just regained my health enough to present myself for your justice."

Carl-Heinrich leaned forward. "To our *justice?* So you grant, then, that the accusations Ackermann has submitted in his report have merit, despite the lack of evidence in your record to corroborate it?"

She could only see the back of his head—but she knew the quirk of his lips that he'd be giving the generals, his judges. The twinkle in his eye. "Good sirs, I won't admit to the merit of anything I haven't read for myself. But I know what he accused me of during the altercation with me, and if those are the same ones he reported to you, then yes."

Gustaf sucked in a breath. Kraus's head lifted.

Christian held out his arms. "My father was friends with any number of professors in the twenties and thirties, some of whom have since exiled themselves to Paris when their politics or ethnicity banned them from Nazi Germany. When that same government tried to force me to euthanize my child, I was disgruntled, to say the least, and gave public lectures in which I stated for all to hear that *all* life is sacred. The young. The old. The disabled. The homeless. The sexually divergent. The dark. The light. I said it because I believed it then, and I still believe it now. I believe God loves my enemy every bit as much as he loves me. I believe he weeps when we harm each other, kill each other. And I believe that love runs so deep that he sent his own son to die to redeem us. All of us."

He turned to Ackermann, whose lips were set

in a permanent snarl. "And I did indeed step between Oberstleutnant Ackermann's gun and the sick old man he was arresting, even though it was supposed to be *my* job to bring him in for questioning, the man he threatened to kill even though he was not resisting that arrest. If believing in the inherent human dignity of a person is as much a crime as having a different political opinion or daring to call a Jew a friend, then yes. I am guilty, and I submit myself to your judgment."

For a moment, she could have heard a butterfly's wing. And then pandemonium, chaos, shouting, the pounding of a gavel she hadn't even seen on the table, in the hand of Otto. Ackermann was the last to stop shouting, shoving a finger toward Christian over and again that would have landed straight in the place he'd shot him if Kraus hadn't stepped between them to take the blow.

"What more do you need to hear?" echoed into the newly forced silence.

Corinne had to blink at the words. She'd read similar ones that morning as she waited for Georges to get her, after Babette had picked up Felix for the day. She'd read them in Matthew 26, when Jesus stood before the Sanhedrin. When he let his own words condemn him, because they were the truth that would set mankind free.

"Thank you, Sonderführer." Otto turned a fierce scowl on Ackermann. "We are all glad to see you well, despite the efforts of your superior officer to let you die alone, heedless of every tenet of the German army. Ackermann, what is your defense?"

Ackermann growled. "I don't *need* a defense. You heard him—he admitted to being a traitor."

"I heard him admit to being an academic who follows his conscience. Whether or not that conscience is right is not what is on trial today. Did you or did you not purposefully shoot the duly appointed *bibliotheksschutz*, who was sent to Paris by Goebbels?"

Ackermann squared his shoulders. "I did."

"Did you or did you not purposefully keep him or his office from conducting an interview with one . . ." He checked his notes. "Josef Horowitz, living under the name of Joseph Henriot, and instead sentence this same Josef Horowitz to a prison camp without any interrogation or interview whatsoever?"

"I did."

Otto lifted his brows and glanced toward Gustaf. "Well, while you're being so forthcoming . . . did you or did you not then threaten the rector of the Sorbonne with physical harm if he didn't agree to dismiss a female professor, despite the fact that you had no jurisdiction in the university system which was in fact, even then, being shut down, rendering your threat moot? Did you or did you not find her at her flat and destroy her property without filing any official cause for suspicion?"

This time he said nothing, and she could imagine the ticking of the muscle in his jaw. Saw the way Gustaf, standing in profile, glared at him.

Kraus cleared his throat. Took a half step forward. "If I may, generals . . . I was not at the university. But the professor in question lives next door to the Library of Burned Books. I heard the crashes as he ransacked her apartment, and when I went up to investigate, I found him there. Alone. He had no soldiers with him, which he ought to have if it were a proper investigation."

"Oberstleutnant?" Otto snapped.

Ackermann's chin lifted. "I am not ashamed of my actions. The woman in question is of questionable ideology, and I had reason to believe she was hiding this coward." He shot a glare at Christian.

"Soldat? You were Bauer's aide. Is Ackermann right to think they have such a connection?"

Kraus shook his head. "Not that I ever witnessed, sirs."

One of the other men on the tribunal had been flipping through papers and leaned forward now, his eyes still upon the page. "Kraus—you are listed by Ackermann as one of his primary sources that led him to doubt Bauer to begin with. Were you reporting your superior's behavior to him?"

"I . . ." Kraus sagged. "Yes, sir."

"Why?"

"Because . . . because Oberstleutnant Ackermann did not trust a nonmilitary man to hold such a position. He asked me to keep him apprised as to how Bauer handled it."

The questioner frowned, leveling it at Ackermann. "You do not trust the decisions of Goebbels?"

Ackermann's shoulders edged back. He made no reply.

The man turned toward the generals. "That, I think, is the key problem here. Peter Ackermann does not trust the chain of command or the authority duly given to our *sonderführers*. He is therefore overly suspicious and too quick to overstep the bounds of his own authority."

"I have overstepped nothing! I have witnesses ready to testify that Bauer deserved—"

"We have already read the reports of the *soldats* present the night Bauer was shot," Otto said. "Nothing in their testimony provided an excuse for shooting a duly appointed agent of the Ministry of Propaganda without an inquest or trial. You are a soldier, not a judge of your fellow Germans. And it is *not* befitting an officer to shoot his own, nor to act as a savage with a woman who has spurned your advances. And as you have admitted to the actions, this hearing will move to the sentencing phase."

Carl-Heinrich leaned forward. "One moment."

Otto lifted his brows. "Yes?"

The younger general's lips played at a smile. "I am curious. It is rare that we have standing side by side two men who admitted to such things as you two have, clear enemies. If you don't mind, Otto, I'd like to pose a question to each of them, before we make our decisions."

Otto waved a hand. "It's the holidays. Have whatever you like, Carl."

Carl-Heinrich rested his elbow on the table. He looked first to Ackermann. "Two months ago, you deemed this man worthy of death and shot him for his dissent. Yet here he stands, despite your actions. What do you think we ought to do with him, sir, given his confessions before us today?"

Ackermann didn't let even a second pass. "Death penalty, General. You cannot let a man with his opinions walk free. He is a menace to our society and will demoralize our soldiers if they hear him say such things. Or if you are feeling merciful, given the holidays, then a prison camp. At least there, he can only lead astray other prisoners and not our men."

"I see." Carl-Heinrich moved his gaze to Christian. "And what of you? What do you think Ackermann's punishment ought to be?"

Christian's shoulders moved as he drew in a long breath. Corinne held hers until his voice rang out, steady and even. "Mercy."

Her breath caught. She'd expected him to demand justice—wasn't that the whole point of turning himself in? To remove Ackermann from Paris? Remove the threat he posed to her and Felix?

The general's lips twitched into a small smile. "Really. You don't want him dead? Sent to a prison camp?"

"No, sir."

"Why not?"

"Because a man cannot change after he is dead. And no man deserves the conditions of those camps."

The cousins exchanged a glance. The younger looked to Christian again. "What, exactly, do you think mercy would look like in this case, where justice must also be served?"

A pause, and she could imagine the contemplation in his eyes. The way the blue would go darker as his brows furrowed, how his glasses would glint in the light, obscuring them. "Reassignment. Perhaps to a division where he would serve under a firm, well-grounded commanding officer. Somewhere away from Paris and the civilian woman he has targeted."

"And demotion? Would that be merciful?"

Ackermann growled.

Christian shrugged. "I don't know, sir. I would leave that to your wisdom. My primary concern would be to remove him from the particular people he has offended and pray that in different environs, he would find the strength of character to build up instead of tear down."

"You are an optimist, aren't you?" Otto leaned forward again. "Well, I don't know where my cousin was going with this, but the path seems clear to me. You are both valuable assets to Germany. Ackermann, before you climbed the ranks, you were an excellent soldier with a pristine record. Power, however, doesn't seem to have settled well on your shoulders, according to your file and the testimony we have heard today. I recommend to the assembly a demotion and immediate relocation to Poland. I have a friend there from whom I think he could learn much."

Ackermann didn't dare to protest. Not when each of the other men at the table said, "Agreed" one after another.

"As for our professor who has returned from the dead . . ." Otto frowned. "I can respect a man who doesn't deny his beliefs, even when he knows well they have fallen out of favor. I respect your bravery, especially, in presenting yourself before us today—and in the presence of the man who tried to kill you, no less. In light of your own pristine record, Professor, and how highly your aide has spoken of you in his deposition, how highly Gustaf has spoken of you in his—I am inclined to extend to you your own mercy. A decrease in pay grade, since demotion is a bit odd for a *sonderführer*, and a reassignment to . . . Greece? I daresay your expertise would be welcome in Athens, and—no offense—it doesn't seem you'd be any help at all in combat. Best to keep you somewhere you can do some good. Gentlemen?"

"Agreed."

"Agreed."

"Agreed."

Corinne had to press a hand to her lips to hold back the gasp, the sob. She'd known that, whatever their decision, he'd be taken from her. But he would *live*. And not be forced to fight.

He would live. He would live. He would live.

And he'd come back to her.

The air was still cold. But the sun felt bright in his eyes, warm on his skin as Christian stepped back out onto the street. He wouldn't have freedom, not as long as he was in Paris—they'd made that very clear. He would be escorted to a hotel room. He would be escorted to a train. Escorted to Greece. Escorted to whatever new quarters they would give him there. He would be on probation, his new superior keeping a close eye on his every word and action.

But he was so much freer than he'd dared to hope. They wouldn't force a gun into his hands. They wouldn't send him to a prison camp.

Kraus strode beside him on one side, Gustaf on

the other. Not exactly the guards he'd expected, but Ackermann had been the only one to object, and he'd been dragged off in a different direction soon enough. Christian breathed in the sunshine and breathed out a prayer.

They would be safe. Corinne, Felix, Georges. They would be *safe.*

"Sir? Sir!"

Liana? They all paused at the familiar voice, turning. Liana jogged forward, a beret in her hands, which she waved above her head. "This just fell out of your pocket, sir. Thought you'd want it." She shoved it toward Christian's chest—and added a dubious look. "Though if you want my advice, if you're looking for a souvenir of Paris, a nice miniature of the Eiffel Tower would suit you better."

He breathed a laugh and folded the felt into his palm. "Indeed."

She sent a wink to Kraus—just daring him to question her—gave a cheeky grin to Gustaf, and flew away again like a leaf on the breeze.

Kraus held his tongue. Gustaf shrugged.

Christian felt the crinkle of paper in the folds of fabric. He knew what it was, because Georges had promised he'd get it to him, somehow, if he lived. An address where he could write to Corinne, and give her an address to write to him, too.

Because he wouldn't be a prisoner, wouldn't be

dead. He'd still be a soldier—and soldiers could get post.

What took him aback was when they turned a corner and Hugo Moreau darted toward them, his hand lifted too. "Ah, Monsieur Bauer! Good, good, I was hoping I would catch you. I have your watch repaired, good as new."

He held out a box—a Cartier box.

Christian blinked at it. At him. And reached to take it. "I . . . thank you."

"And I added the inscription you requested—if you'd like to check it?"

The only watch he'd ever worn—a respectable timepiece on a leather band, a gift from his parents on his graduation—was the one that had died when he was shot. A far cry from the silver watch that glinted up at him from the box, its value gleaming with every nook and cranny. He pulled it out, turned it to examine the back of the face.

There, in tiny script, were the words, *It is always the right time to love you.*

He smiled and slid it onto his wrist. The fit was perfect. "Thank you, *monsieur*." Because he knew well that while the inscription was from Corinne, the watch itself had to have been a gift from the Moreaux. Perhaps it, like Corinne's wedding dress, had been a castoff of a disgruntled aristocrat.

Either way, it was a message he knew would get him through the years to come.

As would the vision that met him at the next corner. Corinne, standing with Georges, as if they were simply going about their business. She walked toward him, all fearlessness and beauty—and with mischief in her eyes.

"Dr. Bastien!" Gustaf waved to her, and then at him. "Look! We've been given a miracle—Bauer lives!"

Perhaps, to their eyes, her smile would look casual. Perhaps, to their eyes, the hand she reached out toward him as they neared would be what any acquaintance would offer another who'd just been returned from the dead.

Perhaps, to their eyes, when she leaned up to kiss his cheeks, she looked like any other Parisienne, offering a warm greeting.

But he saw the love in her smile. Felt it in her fingers. And soaked it in from her lips.

"I can," she whispered into his ear, too quietly for his companions to hear. "I can, I can, I can."

She pressed a book into his palms—a small tome. Innocuous. Innocent. Approved.

But his lips quirked up when he peeked beneath the cover. Something very different rested inside. Poetry, by Josef Horowitz.

With pencil markings in the margins.

EPILOGUE

14 June 1945
Boulevard Arago, Paris, France

Corinne swiped her cloth over the shelf, straining up on her toes to reach farther back than anyone would ever see anyway. She didn't know why she bothered—whoever took over this space would likely dismantle the shelves, turn it back into a house, and obliterate all evidence of what it had once been.

But she cleaned it anyway, because it helped. Helped put all the memories into their places, securing them for the years to come.

The books had all been boxed up over the years, most of them sent off long before the Americans had liberated the city. Several loads had made their way up to her flat. A few had been smuggled to the other board members or friends who would appreciate them. Some had vanished into Germany with the other rare and valuable editions, and who knew what ever became of them.

Some had been destroyed. Burned. Thrown away.

She wiped the last of the dust off the last of the shelves and sighed. Another sigh echoed hers. "Is there anything more forlorn than an empty bookshelf?"

Corinne didn't bother looking over her shoulder as her mother moved into the space beside her, her own dustrag in hand. Corinne nodded. "A whole library of them."

"*Touché.*" Maman bumped their shoulders together. "You saved what you could."

"And what I didn't will live on elsewhere, in other editions. Other copies. I know." Even so, she felt no victory as she walked into the periodicals room, where once upon a time, Germany's exiled writers had created new works, had plotted how to get them back into their homeland, had sat around philosophizing and arguing and brainstorming.

The poster of Goebbels was the only thing left, still tacked to the wall. That fallen Minister, standing in front of a pile of burning books, the flames leaping up the side of the paper and igniting the Reichstag.

Maman strode over to it without hesitation and tore it down. "I suppose I ought to be praying for his immortal soul—and heaven knows I feel sorry for the children he and his wife murdered before they committed suicide. But all I really want to say is *Good riddance.*"

Corinne could only shake her head. She'd never understand how some people could embrace such evil and call it good.

But she could be grateful for the ones who changed. Men like Kraus, who had ended up reading so many of the books in this library before he packed them up. Who had invited her in, once a week, to help him sort the stacks and talk through the concepts he didn't always know what to do with. Who might have worn that Nazi uniform up until the last, but who had become something more beneath it, thanks to the books he'd guarded so long.

Yes, about that she could smile. Because that was the funny thing about books—the more you tried to ban them, the more brightly they burned in the hearts and minds that found them anyway. Books were a lot like her—always determined to do what people said they couldn't.

A pounding came from the front, glass and wood rattling from the force of an exuberant knock.

Maman rolled her eyes. "I guess Georges made it back today after all."

"Felix?" Corinne called. "Can you let your uncle in?" She wasn't sure where, exactly, her son was, but his usual favorite spot was near the front door, in the same old leather chair that Corinne had curled up in as an undergrad, a novel hidden inside her textbook. He'd no doubt have a novel too, despite the fact that he had three weeks left before the end of third term. But he always got the highest marks, so why would she chide him for it?

"Yes, I'll get it, Maman," he called back.

Her own *maman* angled toward the hallway, a smile upon her lips as she craned out for a glimpse of her grandson. She'd only been back in Paris for two weeks—but she and Felix had become instant friends. "Such a good boy," she said again now, as she'd done at least once a day since she finally met him in person. "So much good work you did, Corinne, during the war—so much information you helped the Allies get. But that boy—he is surely your biggest achievement."

Corinne only grinned. And then froze, when she heard the door open and a shout came from her son. She was already moving, brain trying to identify likely threats and solutions, when she realized it was joy in his voice, not alarm. When the word to follow hit her, just as it had the first time she'd heard him scream it.

"*Vati!*"

Vati: Daddy. Papa. The diminutive form of *father*, usually used only by small children . . . or by a growing child who hadn't seen his father in four and a half years.

Vati. Christian. "Christian!" She felt as though she were moving through syrup as she ran down the hallway, toward the open door. She wondered if she was dreaming as she saw them silhouetted there, arms around each other.

Not *exactly* the image that had won her heart. Felix was so much bigger now, reaching to

Christian's shoulder. Her beloved didn't need to fall to his knees to embrace his boy, just to pull him close. He wasn't sobbing, as he'd done at that first, unexpected reunion when he thought he'd never see his little mouse again. He was laughing, they both were, and she was too as she tossed herself their way.

"Corinne. *Meine liebe.*" He caught her with one arm, not letting go of Felix with the other, and pressed a long, hard kiss to her lips.

She didn't know whether to cling to him or slap at him—well, of course she did. She slapped his chest. And then kissed him again. "You said it would be next week before you could get everything in order and help get Erik out of Berlin."

Everything was chaos there, he'd said. So many soldiers, returning in defeat, while the city was divided up between the Soviets, the Americans, the British . . . and the French. His last letter had made it out to be a madhouse of the worst kind—which was why he and Georges had met on the outskirts and worked together to get Christian's old friend out. She'd known he had to do that before he returned to her—save the man who had saved him with his doctoring of Christian's files, saved Felix.

Even so, it was one more delay, when she'd only wanted this. Him. Back in her arms.

He grinned down at her, kissing her again.

"Shall I leave for another week? Come back on Monday?"

Her answer was to wrap her arms around him. "Don't even think about it. Did you have trouble at the border?"

"No. Georges's papers were as good as he promised." He was looking at Felix again, and she couldn't blame him for that. She'd sent photos, whenever she could, but they weren't the same.

Felix grinned up at him. "And did you get Onkle Erik to safety?"

He smiled. Bright and yet tempered. "I did. I met his wife, his two children. And the twelve Jews they had harbored throughout the war. Georges and I helped them all settle in Alsace."

"Twelve!" She knew Parisians had done the same, when "registering" turned into something far more deadly. She would have hidden Abraham and Mathilda, if they hadn't managed to get out of Paris, or any of her other friends, had she been able to find them. But they'd scattered like seed in the wind. Some, she prayed, were safe.

Some she knew were not. Josef had died in that camp not long after Christian was sent to Greece, taken by pneumonia.

Seeing the reports that had been in the news, she knew now that it was a mercy.

"And then there was the work no one saw. Like what he did for me." He kissed Felix's head, and then hers. "It seems books aren't the only words that can have such impact. I doubt we'll ever know the lives he saved, just by altering files here and there."

"I want to meet him someday." Even as she said it, she pulled him farther inside, out of the doorway. Toward Maman, who still needed an introduction.

She did—someday. Someday they would go to Alsace to meet the Reinholdts; someday they would return to Germany, and she would apply at a university there, and she would help Christian teach a new generation how to *be* when the world hated them. How to love despite it. How to thrive and think and grow.

One page at a time. One chapter. One book. Until they were strong enough to change.

But just now, today, *this* someday, they needed this. An old, empty library. Stories of the years apart. A too-small flat with cupboards that were still too empty, and long nights spent with their lights turned on and their curtains thrown wide to the world.

They needed freedom. Paris. Shelves teeming with books.

And all the words written in the margins. *I love you, even when I can't. I love you, as long as I am.*

A NOTE FROM THE AUTHOR

Dear Reader,

When I learned about the existence of the Library of Burned Books in Paris, I was immediately intrigued. I heard about it first in a book called *When Books Went to War* by Molly Guptill Manning, an intriguing look at the role books played in World War II, in censorship, and in how stories impacted a generation.

But Ms. Manning had only a few short paragraphs about this library. She told of its foundation by the exiled writers from Nazi Germany, whose books were burned and then banned in 1933. She mentioned that at its start, it was fueled by the attention of "banned" writers like H. G. Wells. And then she closed by saying that when the Nazis took Paris, this library "was kept under lock and key." Which of course made my brain begin buzzing. Why was it guarded instead of being emptied, destroyed? And what would the soldiers who did that guarding have learned from the books inside?

I needed more information, of course, so I turned to *Burning Books* by Matthew Fishburn, which not only gave me details and photographs about this ill-fated library but also dove deep into the psychology of why people and cultures have burned books throughout history—and how only after these burnings in Germany did it become seen as a tragedy of censorship. Fishburn also shared some intriguing details about the books smuggled back into Germany under benign covers, and how the library became the center of research of "anti-Hitlerism" in France. But he also told the rather sad history of our Deutsche Freiheitsbibliothek—that people quickly lost interest in it, that the once-inviting library became overcrowded, neglected, and all but abandoned by the time France was invaded, and that no one really knows what happened to all the books inside. Only one of them ended up in Paris's National Library. The others have never resurfaced, so far as we know. Even so, one of the very first acts of the new Vichy government was to hand the library's keys to the Nazis as they took Paris. Presenting it on a silver platter, as it were. Alfred Kantorowicz was the actual director of the library; all other patrons mentioned in this book were fictional.

Since so many of my wartime stories focus on espionage and intelligence, I thought it would be fun to use some of the backstory I'd already had brewing in my mind concerning a brother lost to the mud in one of my previous books, *Yesterday's Tides*. What if, my husband had asked, Sebastian had lived? I loved that idea, and decided that another frequent cameo character, George Pearce, would be the one to find him. And Georges then offered me a perfect way to bring a bit of intelligence work into this book too, and a vague link to the world of English intelligence that I've written so much about.

I love having a book-loving heroine playing at spymaster with the help of these books . . . but of course, she wouldn't have had free access to the library once Paris was occupied. To get a view within the stacks, I needed a German hero. More, I needed a hero who was, at least in name, a member of the Nazi Party, to have been sent to Paris for such a role. Christian came to me in bits and pieces, his story unfolding as I pondered what sort of *bibliotheksschutz* (library protector) he would be, and why he would be there. He really clicked into place when I realized he had a son in Paris, in hiding—a son that the Nazi Party wanted to destroy.

It's so easy to look at the German people in the 1930s and '40s and see only the horrors—because there were many. But they were so much more than the horrors. They were more than the Gestapo and the SS. They were also everyday people just trying to survive. They were people who couldn't fathom some of the atrocities being committed—not turning a blind eye purposefully, but simply incapable of thinking that their government was lying to them about what the camps really were. They were people trying to fight for the country they loved, whatever regime was in power, because they believed it was worth fighting for.

They were also a people who had been crushed by the defeat of the Great War, who were desperate to be worthwhile, to be valued, to be great. Many followed Hitler because he gave them something to believe in.

Many didn't, because they saw the lie for what it was. Some spoke out, all through the war; others worked quietly, wherever they could; some fought openly, violently. I was especially fascinated by a few historical records I read. First, the many, many occasions when Nazi officers refused to carry out immoral commands, especially concerning Jews. Sometimes they were court-martialed. Sometimes they were reassigned. Sometimes they were slapped on the wrist. But most of the time, they weren't executed, because officers were too highly valued.

Another story that caught my attention was about a vocally anti-Nazi professor. He knew for a fact some of his more incendiary lectures were reported to the Ministry, but one day, he was called before them not for punishment, but for a special assignment—the Nazi Party was sending him to Rome to create a new German translation of Machiavelli for them. He went, utterly baffled as to why they didn't seem to know that he was against them. He used that time in Italy to actively work with Resistance members. Years later, toward the end of the war, he was finally arrested for other activities, and even then, his files were mysteriously blank about so much of what he'd said and done publicly—even though the Gestapo was renowned for their thorough files. His best guess as to how this happened was that there were other anti-Hitler personnel at the Ministry, people who deliberately "lost" or altered reports. I decided it would be a lovely tribute to those silent, mysterious people for Christian to have had such a guardian angel in his old friend, Erik Reinholdt, whose story I intend to tell in short form too, so visit my website for details on that!

The history that Christian shares about the euthanizing of children with birth defects is sadly true. What began as a secret program in the midthirties became—upon the insistence of the parents of special needs children—mandatory. And that, to my mind, was the true horror. Not that a tyrannical government would make such a policy, but that it was in response to parents who were ashamed of their imperfect children. Who better than a father who adored his child to tell us about it?

Censorship, a key theme in any book like this one, is as old as time. But I maintain that the best cure to any "cancel culture" isn't to argue. It's to read. Read broadly. Read things you don't agree with. Read things you love, and read things you hate. Read fiction, nonfiction, and poetry. Read politics and science and religion. Read not to pick apart but to put together. Read, always ready to ask, "What if it's true?" Read, and grow, and discover. And if you're not strong enough to take it—then read some more until you are. Read until you understand that other perspective . . . and until you can love those who hold it. Because you never win by fighting your enemies—only by making them your friends.

ACKNOWLEDGMENTS

It seems that the writing of each story has its own story—and those who need to be thanked for making it possible. In the case of *The Collector of Burned Books*, when I sat down to write it, I had no idea that the exhaustion I was fighting was because I had cancer . . . but I learned it not long after turning in the first draft to my editors.

You can imagine the uncertainty that filled me as my doctor told me the news and I considered what my next few months were *supposed* to involve, and what they would now involve instead. But the amazing Tyndale team made it clear from the moment I told them that they would work with me and pray for me and prioritize my health. Thank you so much to Elizabeth, Kathy, and the rest of the team for doing just that, every step of the way, and helping me turn this book into what it was meant to be. It's been such an honor and privilege to get to know you all through this process, and I look forward to many more books with you!

Thank you as always to my agent extraordinaire, Steve Laube, who encouraged me to fight for this story. To Stephanie, who was with me on our grand Pensacola Beach writing retreat when I got the news that Tyndale was going to publish it, and who cheered me on from afar while I pounded out the story months later. To David, who would rearrange the very heavens if he could, to give me all the time and support I need to write, and who was, as always, my very first reader. To my mom, sister, and grandmother who always wait so impatiently for their turn, and my awesome kids, who put up with a lot from their wacky novelist mother.

And finally, to my amazing direct-support group, Patrons & Peers, who walked with me virtually through every step of this book, from our retreat where I wrote the first chapters and brainstormed with you all up through the last. You ladies have become such a huge part of my life, and an unending blessing—as are all my readers, every time. You are why the Lord has put these stories in my heart, and I thank and praise him endlessly for the honor. To him be the glory.

DISCUSSION QUESTIONS

1. Christian's father taught him that the only way to ever truly beat an enemy is to make him your friend. Historically, we see this as the way the Christian church has grown and flourished in times of persecution as well—not by overwhelming their oppressors, but by converting them through love. How does this play out in the story? Do you agree with the philosophy? Have you ever found it to be true in your own life?
2. Through Corinne's eyes, we get a peek at what life was like in Paris during those early days of the occupation. Was there anything that surprised you? Do you think you would have fled or remained behind?
3. Christian and his childhood friend Erik debated whether it was better to speak out against a regime they didn't approve of or instead work quietly to counteract them wherever they could—a decision many had to make in Nazi Germany. If you were in their place, what would you have decided? What did you think of Christian's decisions as they came to light throughout the story?
4. Though Corinne and Christian are ostensibly on very different sides, they find common

ground through books, even before she realizes the truth of him. Have books ever helped you understand or connect with someone? What did you think of the progression of their friendship?
5. When Christian is reunited with Felix, we see his determination to love him "now," in whatever moments they had. How would your priorities shift if you had this constant awareness of what you could lose in the next moment? What did you think of this big revelation of what Christian was hiding?
6. When Christian is walking Corinne home at night, she reflects on the beauty of the night and reminds herself to count those small, unexpected blessings. How is this especially helpful when life is challenging? Is it something you've made a point of doing at any point in your life? What blessings do you think Corinne and Christian clung to in the years ahead?
7. Who was your favorite character? Your least favorite? Why?
8. Christian found himself in a position where he believed his staying put those he loved in imminent danger. We, in retrospect, know that England would have been a safe haven, but people in 1940 truly believed it would fall within months. If you were in Christian's position, what would you have done? What

did you think of how that part of the story played out?
9. After de Gaulle challenged every French citizen to resist, many found ways of doing just that, even when they had no idea what good, if any, it would do. But many more ended up embracing the "new normal" of life under Nazi rule and informing on neighbors and friends and even family in order to preserve themselves. Where do we make compromises today?
10. When it comes to topics of censorship, we all tend to bristle at the thought of someone banning *our* books . . . but we are also often quick to wish *other's* books were banned. How do we as a society decide how to handle these questions? Who should get to decide? Do the conversations had in this book help you understand your own views?

ABOUT THE AUTHOR

ROSEANNA M. WHITE is a bestselling, Christy Award–winning author who has long claimed that words are the air she breathes. When not writing fiction, she's homeschooling, editing, designing book covers, and pretending her house will clean itself. Roseanna is the author of a slew of historical novels that span several continents and thousands of years. Spies and war and mayhem always seem to find their way into her books . . . to offset her real life, which is blessedly ordinary. You can learn more about her and her stories at RoseannaMWhite.com.

Center Point Large Print
600 Brooks Road / PO Box 1
Thorndike, ME 04986-0001 USA

(207) 568-3717

US & Canada:
1 800 929-9108
www.centerpointlargeprint.com